Beneath th
By Ellis C

Prologue

Several months had passed since the fall of Kinross. The fires had burned out, the blood had dried, and the dead—at least the ones who could be buried—had been laid to rest. Jennifer walked again, her strength returning more each day, and Callum's leg, though stiff in the cold, no longer slowed him. New Haven had held together. Barely.

But peace, they were learning, was a fragile thing.

Dr. Aria Hensley sat in what had once been the councillor's office, now converted into a makeshift research room. The woman they'd pulled from cold stasis at Ellis's hidden lab was more than a scientist—she was a warning wrapped in flesh and secrets. Bellamy had been watching her closely ever since she had whispered those haunting words:

"You don't know what's coming..."

At first, no one believed her. The community was focused on healing, on rebuilding. But Aria had changed. She stopped eating. She slept in snatches, muttering in the dark. She filled stolen notebooks with frantic scribbles, margins crowded with equations and symbols no one else could understand. And when her voice broke through in the dead of night, it was always the same phrase, repeated like a curse.

"Phase two."

Derek stood atop the perimeter wall just before dawn, the sky bruised with grey, stars fading to ash. Behind him, New Haven breathed quietly—children dreaming, fences humming with new power, hope flickering like candlelight.

But he couldn't shake the feeling.

Something was out there.

Watching.

Waiting.

And whatever came next wasn't going to knock on the gates.

It was going to tear them down.

Chapter 1

The morning sun cast pale streaks over the prison walls, now fortified with scrap metal and salvaged concrete. The north watchtower creaked as a light breeze swept across New Haven, stirring loose dust and the scent of earth newly turned. Derek stood near the edge of the dirt yard, his hands on his hips, surveying the southern section of the wall. The space beyond it, overgrown, unused, forgotten, was where the next expansion would begin. A second gate. A second way in and out.

"We've had one exit for far too long," Callum had said during the latest council meeting. "One road in and out. That's how you get trapped."

Now, the council's decision is becoming reality.

Wooden stakes were marked out, string lines drawn. Lee and Bill had already begun clearing brush. Reggie had assigned half the gardening crew to shift soil, and Bellamy, now reluctantly trusted, had brought over blueprints from an old city depot. The structure was rudimentary, but sturdy. Derek had approved it that morning.

As the hammering echoed faintly behind him, he made his way back to the planning shed. The others would be waiting.

—-

Inside, the room buzzed with quiet debate. Callum was leaning over a map, Daryl resting one foot on a bench. Anne had her notebook open, lines of scribbled teaching schedules running down the page. Jillian, seated off to the side, caught Derek's eye as he entered; the look they exchanged, unreadable to the rest.

"We've agreed on routes for the lumber teams," Callum said as Derek closed the door behind him. "But south gate security will be thin until we can pull some of Bellamy's people from A-block."

"Then we train more guards," Derek said simply.

"And who's training them?" Daryl grunted. "Half the recruits can barely aim a crossbow, let alone hold a perimeter."

Beneath the Silence

© 2025 Ellis Grayson

All rights reserved. No part of this book may be reproduced, distributed, or transmitted in any form or by any means, including photocopying, recording, or other electronic or mechanical methods, without the prior written permission of the publisher, except in the case of brief quotations embodied in critical reviews and certain other noncommercial uses permitted by copyright law.

This is a work of fiction. Names, characters, places, and incidents are products of the author's imagination or are used fictitiously. Any resemblance to actual persons, living or dead, or actual events is purely coincidental.

First Edition: 2025

"We start rotation drills at first light," Derek replied. "Twice a day until they can."

No one argued.

Jillian spoke next, quieter but firm. "We should also use this space to build more homes/shelters. A southern gate means a southern road. If there's anyone left out there worth knowing, we are more than likely to run into them."

Maggie nodded. "It's about time New Haven looked like a community, not a tomb."

Derek listened, his mind balancing the present with the shadows of the past. Months had passed since Kinross fell. Since Ellis fell. Jennifer was back on her feet, though the scar on her shoulder still ached in the cold. Callum had shed his crutch only weeks ago. But their peace was fragile. Survivors trickled in every few days, some lost, some broken, some looking for something to hold on to. And beneath it all, one question still haunted Derek.

What did Dr. Hensley mean when she said this was only the first phase? That answer hadn't come. And as the dust stirred from the first swing of a pickaxe against the southern soil, he wondered if they had truly buried the past... or if something darker was still to come.

—-—

The clang of tools faded into the background as Derek leaned against the fence, his thoughts miles and months away. His eyes weren't on the skeletal frame of the new southern gate anymore. They were on a cold corridor deep beneath shattered concrete, where the truth had clawed its way out of the dark.

It had been months since they pulled Dr. Aria Hensley from that stasis tank in the wreckage of Ellis's last lab, her body limp, mind clouded, lungs barely strong enough to whisper. She'd barely spoken the words, but they'd landed like thunder.

"This... was only the first phase."

When they brought her back to New Haven, they gave her food, warmth, and time, but not freedom. She remained in the medical wing under watch, guarded by Steph and Bill in alternating shifts. Every day she got stronger. And every day, the questions grew sharper.

Derek remembered the council's first sit-down with her. It was Jillian who'd broken the silence.

"Phase one of what, Aria?"

Dr. Hensley hadn't hesitated.

"Population trials. We were measuring societal collapse, infection rates, the psychological breakdown of survivors... and the behavioral patterns of the undead." She paused, eyes rimmed red. "Ellis believed that control could only come after absolute disintegration. He saw the outbreak as the beginning of human evolution."

Callum scoffed. "And killing thousands was just part of the experiment?"

Aria nodded grimly. "Millions, actually. And Ellis wasn't the only one running it."

Those words stayed with them all.

Not long after, a small team had gone back to what was left of the facility. They found the servers, some corrupted, others intact. The data confirmed it all. Phase one had been global in scale. Targeted outbreaks. Engineered chaos. And Ellis, mad as he was, had only been one node in a much larger web. They didn't leave the place standing. Lee and Ortega rigged the structural core with salvaged fuel cells. When the dust settled, the last of Ellis's legacy was buried beneath fifty tons of steel and fire.

"Derek!" Jillian's voice snapped him back. "Council's reconvening." He nodded, pushing off the fence and letting the hum of memory fade behind him. The past wasn't done with them. But for now, the gate was rising, and the south wall was no longer just a dream.

—-

Inside New Haven's infirmary wing, Jennifer awoke to the quiet hum of the lights overhead and not the chaos she once knew, but the steady rhythm of a place healing alongside her. The sheets clung to her legs as she sat up slowly, muscles aching with the kind of dull pain that had become her constant companion these past months. She winced. Not from the wound. That pain had faded. This was something else, something deeper. A hollow she hadn't figured out how to fill yet.

Maggie stepped in with her usual soft tread and a tray in her hands. "You're up early," she said, setting it down on the small table beside the bed. Jennifer gave a tired smile. "Didn't sleep much." "Any pain?"

"No... not the kind you can treat, anyway."

Maggie didn't press. She just nodded and handed over a cup of warm broth. "Vitals are holding. You're walking better every day. Honestly, you're the toughest patient I've had since Callum's stubborn ass."

Jennifer gave a short laugh, then paused.

"It should've been worse," she said quietly. "Ellis shot me, Maggie. I should be dead."

Maggie folded her arms. "You're not. You're here. That counts for something." Jennifer nodded, staring out the window where early morning light crept across the yard.

In the months since the war, she'd come to understand just how much she'd missed. The fights, the rebuilding. Derek had rarely left her side for the first few weeks, reading to her when she couldn't sleep, holding her hand when the pain spiked. But now... he was different. Distant, almost. The lines in his face had deepened. Something weighed heavy on him.

And though he never said it, she felt it too.

Jillian had been there often, caring, helpful, always with a warm smile and a gentle word. But sometimes, Jennifer would catch a glance that lingered too long or a silence that felt heavier than it should have.

Still, she said nothing. She'd survived worse than doubt.

She'd survived Ellis.

Her thoughts drifted back to before the fall. To parties and weddings she once planned, to weekends abroad with Derek, sometimes joined by Jillian. High school sweethearts, she and Derek had married young. They'd dreamed of a life far from this one.

As she snapped back to reality, Jennifer set the broth aside and swung her legs off the bed. Her strength was returning, and she was done being a patient. The community needed her. Derek needed her. She took one step, then another. No pain. Today, she would walk the yard herself. And maybe, just maybe, she'd walk back into who she used to be, or someone stronger.

—-

A few weeks after Kinross fell, the smoke from the burning lab had barely settled before New Haven had changed. With Ellis dead and Kinross no longer a threat, the survivors began to look forward, instead of over their shoulders. But peace, as they quickly discovered, came with its own weight.

—-

Callum sat in the old workshop, carefully disassembling a rusted rifle. His leg, still stiff from the break, throbbed occasionally, a reminder of the day everything nearly fell apart. He never talked about Raven's death or the explosion that threw them from the rooftop. But it was there in the way he worked, meticulous, focused, relentless. He'd taken on more than security. These days, Callum was training others: young adults, once scared and helpless, now learning how to fight, defend, survive. He had no time for mourning. Not yet.

—-

Daryl had taken to the outer perimeter. Patrols. Recon. He was rarely inside the walls for long, preferring the forests and roads beyond the fences. He said it was about staying ahead of the threats, but the truth was simpler: he didn't know how to slow down. Since Raven's death, he hadn't let anyone close. Not even Bill, who'd started watching him from a distance, like an old friend unsure whether to reach out or give space. They all grieved differently.

—-

Bill had moved into the watchtower permanently. The cameras hummed now, solar-powered and sweeping every angle of New Haven. He'd started keeping a log — not just of movement or intrusions, but of people: who came and went, who smiled, who didn't. It made him feel like he was keeping them safe, even when he couldn't protect everyone. When he'd heard about the lab, the few test subjects who'd somehow broken free before the collapse, he'd doubled the night shifts. Quiet didn't mean safety anymore.

—-

Anne had converted the old rec room into a proper classroom. The children, those too young to carry weapons, were being taught how to read, write, plant crops and when needed, shoot. Education was survival now. Anne knew that better than anyone. At night, when the building fell silent, she'd sit at the back of the room and trace names in the ledger. Names of those who didn't come home. She never cried in front of the kids.

—-

Munroe still struggled to feel like he belonged. He and Bellamy had earned their place in New Haven, but ghosts clung to them. Former enemies turned allies didn't find peace overnight. He worked maintenance now, repairing fences, hauling supplies. Sometimes, he spoke to Father Luke. Sometimes, he sat alone with a bottle and said nothing at all.

—-

Bellamy had changed the most.

Where once he stood with orders barked and fists clenched, now he led with caution. His own people, what remained of Kinross — had integrated slowly into New Haven's rhythms. He didn't push. He didn't demand. He worked. He listened. He showed up. And for the first time in a long while, people followed him not out of fear, but trust.

Still, the guilt lingered.

He visited Jennifer in the infirmary often. Said little. Just sat, head bowed. Maybe it was penance. Maybe something else.

—-

And then there was Jillian.

She had thrown herself into the morale committee, organizing community dinners, music nights, whatever helped people feel human again. Smiles were easier now, but her eyes always drifted to the watchtower... or the infirmary... or Derek. Her secret was still hers alone. But sometimes, in the dead of night, she'd sit outside her cell and watch the stars, whispering to no one, "I'm still here. Still waiting."

As the survivors moved on, healing became the new battle.

—-—

That evening, as shadows stretched long, Derek walked alone. His hands buried in his jacket pockets, jaw tight. He wasn't avoiding Jennifer—at least, not deliberately. But between the gate, the council, Aria's warning... maybe he hadn't wanted to face her.

"Derek."

He turned. Jennifer stood near the edge of the garden, arms folded across her chest, her expression unreadable. She looked healthier than she had in weeks, colour back in her cheeks, hair tied back, eyes sharp. "We need to talk."

He nodded slowly. "Yeah... we do."

They moved toward the bench beneath the old twisted birch tree, a place untouched by blood, war, or infection. A rare quiet spot. For a moment, neither of them spoke. The silence stretched. Jennifer finally broke it. "You've been distant since we got back."

"I know," Derek said. "I've had—"

"I'm not blaming you," she interrupted gently. "You've had the weight of everything on your back. And I get it. I do."

He looked down, fingers laced, knuckles white. "I almost lost you."

Jennifer's eyes softened. "But you didn't."

"That doesn't make the fear go away." His voice cracked slightly. "Every time I close my eyes, I see you lying there. Burning up. Barely breathing. I couldn't fix it. I couldn't do anything."

She reached out, took his hand. "You did everything, Derek. You saved me." He looked up, meeting her eyes for the first time in what felt like days. There was still something between them, a thread pulled tight, but not broken.

"I'm sorry I pulled away," he said quietly. "It wasn't fair."

"No, it wasn't," she said. "But I'm here. And I'm not going anywhere." A pause. Her thumb brushed over the back of his hand. "I know this world doesn't give us easy moments. But I don't want to lose this, whatever we've built. Even if it's complicated. Even if we're both a little broken."

Derek let out a long breath. "I still love you, Jen. I never stopped." She leaned forward and pressed her forehead to his.

"Then let's fight for it. Together." The night settled around them. Beyond the walls, darkness moved. But inside, in that small space between two people, there was something steady again.

Hope

Chapter 2

It had been nearly three months since the fall of Kinross and the uprising that ended Ellis's reign. In that time, New Haven had transformed from a repurposed prison into something resembling a true settlement. Crops flourished in the yard. Guard rotations were consistent. Children had laughter in their voices again.

And now, the next phase was beginning, expansion.

The old south wall had all been marked out for where it was being pulled down, making way for the construction of a new gate and staging area. The goal was to build a second access point: not just a safety measure, but a path for future development. A new farming plot. Maybe even housing.

Callum stood at the edge of the site, surveying the posts that were placed into the earth. Plans were sketched on a piece of plywood resting atop an old toolbox. Sweat clung to his brow, and he wiped it with a gloved hand. "Tell me again how I got roped into leading this?" he muttered.

"Because you don't complain as loudly as Daryl," said a voice beside him. Corwin Tate, one of the newest residents, leaned against the rusted frame of a wheelbarrow. Tall and broad-shouldered, with ash-blond hair and a surprisingly dry sense of humor, Corwin had arrived with a small group of survivors rescued near the river two months ago. He'd earned a reputation fast, reliable, calm, and skilled in both carpentry and fortification. "Besides," Corwin added, "you drew the shortest straw."

"Damn rigged draw," Callum said with a smirk.

—-

A few meters behind them, a woman in dark cargo gear paced out measurements beside the wall's foundation. Lana Mire, ex-engineer, or so she claimed, had shown up alone a month back, asking for shelter. Her story was hazy, but she'd proven invaluable with the technical side of the expansion.

If anyone asked her about the past, she'd say, "Before the fall, I built bridges. Now I just build fences to keep the dead out."

Across the work zone, Taye and Renna, two teens from Kinross who had chosen to stay and contribute, were helping Daryl unload steel reinforcements from the back of the truck. Taye, wiry and fast with a slingshot, had a knack for spotting weak points in structures. Renna rarely spoke, but she worked tirelessly.

The group was a strange mix, veterans of battle and newcomers alike, but together, they were building something that might outlast the horror.

—-

As the sun climbed, Lana called out, "We need to be careful here, the foundation looks weak; we will need to reinforce it"

"I'll flag it," Corwin said, grabbing red spray paint from his belt.

Callum stepped back, rubbing his chin. "You think it's really possible?" he asked quietly. "Turning this place into more than just a refuge?"

Corwin didn't look up as he marked the earth. "I think anything's possible if we keep the right people alive long enough." Callum chuckled, but the weight of it lingered.

In the distance, New Haven bustled behind the walls, laughter, hammers, patrols, children. Beyond the south gate, the world still waited. Unknown. Dangerous. Changing. But here, for the first time in a long time, something was being built. Not out of desperation, but out of hope.

—-

The frame was built within the day. It was hard going, the new fencing and support beams were all in place too. As the sun began to dip low, casting orange streaks across the yard, that's when the digging crew hit something strange. It wasn't the usual twisted rebar or concrete slab, this was something older, and deeper.

"Callum!" Taye called out, half-buried in the trench with dirt up to his knees. "You better come look at this." Callum jogged over, Daryl not far behind. Taye stepped aside, revealing a section of rusted steel embedded horizontally in the soil, several feet below ground level. At first glance, it looked like an old pipe or utility duct. But as Lana arrived and brushed more dirt away with a gloved hand, a strange outline emerged, rectangular. Reinforced.

"This isn't part of the prison's structure," Lana said, voice tight with sudden unease. "It's too old. Too deep."

Daryl narrowed his eyes. "What is it then?"

"A hatch," Corwin said. "Or... a vault door."

The word dropped like a stone.

—-

Everyone went quiet.

Lana knelt beside it, brushing away more earth. Faint lettering was embossed into the metal, though corrosion had rendered much of it unreadable. Only one word remained legible:

"TALOS."

Callum frowned. "Does that mean anything to anyone?"

"No," Lana said. "But this thing wasn't meant to be found. That much I can tell you."

Corwin shook his head and stood back, arms crossed. "You want to open it?"

Callum hesitated. "No! Not until we speak with Derek. I'm not repeating another Ellis situation because we got curious."

Daryl nodded. "We secure the area tonight. No one comes near this thing. We'll tell Derek in the morning."

As they marked off the site and rolled a tarp over the exposed hatch, the sky dimmed fully into twilight. Whatever lay beneath New Haven's south wall had been buried long before the outbreak. Forgotten. Hidden. Now, as survivors dared to build a future, the past was stirring beneath their feet.

And it might not be done with them yet.

—-

The next morning, Derek was already outside near the perimeter when Callum and Daryl approached. Their faces were grave, boots still caked in dried soil from the trench. "Morning," Derek said, wiping sweat from his brow. "Everything alright with the southern wall?"

"Not exactly," Daryl said. "You need to see something."

Within minutes, Derek stood over the newly uncovered hatch, the tarp peeled back to expose its oxidized face. He crouched, running his hand across the embossed metal. His eyes narrowed on the single word: TALOS. "Any idea what it is?" he asked.

Callum shook his head. "Buried deep. Solid. Definitely not prison infrastructure. We didn't open it."

Derek stood, his jaw tight. "I want to see Hensley."

—-

Inside the old councillors room-turned-lab, Dr. Aria Hensley sat by a window, a medical book open in her lap. She looked up as Jillian escorted Derek in. "I was told you wanted to see me urgently," Hensley said, setting the book aside.

Derek didn't waste time. "We found a hatch beneath the southern trench. Rusted, sealed. Labeled with the name 'TALOS.' Ring any bells?"

For a moment, the name didn't register. Then something flickered in her eyes, almost imperceptible, but it was there. "No," she said calmly. "Never heard of it."

Derek stared at her. "You're sure? You were Ellis's lead scientist for years."

"I was one of many. But Ellis was just a cog in a much larger engine." she replied

Daryl, who had followed Derek inside, crossed his arms. "So this could be something even Ellis didn't know about?"

"Possibly," Hensley replied. "Or something older. The military had research contracts all over the region. Before the outbreak."

Derek nodded slowly, frustrated by the dead end. "We're not taking chances. We're opening it."

—-

Later that day, Derek gathered the council. A crude map of the southern trench sat on the table. "We open the hatch tomorrow," Derek said. "Small team only, Daryl, Callum, Lana for technical support, and myself."

Bill raised a brow. "Could be another lab. Another nightmare."

"That's why we do it smart," Daryl said. "Tethered descent. Masks. If it smells wrong, we come back up."

Maggie exhaled. "Let's just hope it's nothing."

But no one believed that. Because in their world, nothing buried ever stayed quiet for long.

As the evening approached the moon hung low and pale over New Haven, casting long shadows along the walls and rusted fences. Derek walked alone along the southern perimeter, hands in his jacket pockets, boots crunching gravel. Sleep had evaded him. Again. His mind churned, not just with thoughts of the hatch buried beneath them, but something else. A truth Dr. Hensley had quietly revealed to him months ago in the privacy of the old med-lab.

"You need to understand something," Hensley had said, eyes grave. "It's not just the bite that turns someone. If the brain is intact... they come back. No matter how they die."

"Are you saying anyone?" Derek had asked, stunned.

She nodded. "Anyone. That's what Ellis learned during Phase One. That was the foundation of his experiments controlling the inevitable." Now, every person he saw walking the yard... laughing in the mess hall... resting beside family... they were all just one fatal accident away from turning. It changed everything.

A soft voice behind him pulled him out of his thoughts. "You really don't sleep anymore, do you?" He turned. Jillian stood a few feet behind, arms crossed against the breeze, her hair tied back loosely. There was something in her tone, familiar, careful, but still warm.

"Could ask you the same," Derek said, managing a tired smile.

She stepped beside him, leaning against the cold metal of the perimeter rail. "I saw you heading out. Thought maybe you'd want company... even if you didn't know it." Derek looked ahead, silent for a few moments. "Something on your mind?" she asked gently.

"Too much," he admitted. "This hatch. What it could mean. And..." He paused. "There's something Hensley told me. That's weighing heavy."

Jillian turned to him fully, concerned. "What?"

Derek hesitated, then lowered his voice. "If you die, bitten or not, as long as your brain's intact... you turn."

Jillian's breath caught, the words hitting harder than she expected. "God..."

"Yeah," Derek muttered. "Just... imagine what that means. We've been walking among potential threats. Sleeping beside them. Every accident, every fall, every fight..." He shook his head and looked down.

Jillian reached out and gently took his hand, grounding him. "You don't have to carry all of this alone," she said softly. "You've always tried to, but you don't have to. You have people. You have me." Derek looked up at her, their eyes meeting. "I've missed you," she whispered. "Not just your friendship, you. You've been distant since..." She paused, letting the memory of their last kiss hang unspoken. "But I'm still here, Derek. Still the same. Still someone who wants to help you forget the crazy. Just like I said before."

He didn't pull away. He didn't move closer. Just stood still, caught between guilt and comfort, between duty and longing.

"I know," he said finally. "I haven't forgotten."

Jillian squeezed his hand once more, then slowly stepped back. "I'm here when you need me," she said with a half-smile. "Even if it's just to walk the wall and say nothing." And with that, she walked back toward the central yard, leaving Derek under the watch of the cold, quiet moon... and a weight he wasn't sure how to set down.

—-

The weak morning light filtered through the cracks in the old guard tower where Derek had finally collapsed into sleep just before dawn. It wasn't much, maybe two, three hours at best, but it was enough to dull the sharp edges of exhaustion.

He dreamt of life before the fall. He was a manager of a major construction firm in Edinburgh. It was a job he was hesitant to take as he didn't like ordering people around. He preferred to be working on the tools rather than sitting at a desk, but it was thrust upon him by the retiring manager. They were working on a massive site of new housing and a retail park. He dreamt of dinner parties with Anne and Callum. The long walks around Loch Lomond that normally included Jillian, The three of them were very close.

"Derek," a voice whispered, followed by a gentle shake to his shoulder. He blinked and looked up to see Jennifer crouched beside him, her warm eyes laced with concern. "Council's gathering. You okay?"

He sat up slowly, rubbing his face. "Yeah. Just needed to shut down for a bit."

Jennifer smiled faintly. "Come on. Everyone's waiting."

—-

The meeting room was already abuzz by the time Derek arrived. The familiar faces were all present, Daryl, Callum, Bill, Anne, Jillian, and Lana, who had been growing more vital to the group in recent months with her quiet efficiency and sharp mind.

A dusty map of the prison's lower levels and tunnels was spread out across the table. A clipboard of sketches and notes sat beside it, observations Daryl and Callum had compiled after discovering the hatch during the expansion dig.

"Best guess," Callum was saying, pointing to a shaded section of the blueprint, "is that this thing leads into some kind of auxiliary substructure. Could be storage. Could be older security tunnels."

"Or another lab," Lana added bluntly. "We don't know what Ellis was up to when he was alive"

Derek stayed silent, listening to the speculation bounce around. Finally, he raised his hand slightly to quiet the room.

"There's something I need to tell you all before anyone sets foot down there," he said. The tone in his voice drew the attention of every eye in the room. "A few months back, after the lab... Dr. Hensley told me something. Something that Ellis found out during Phase One. It wasn't about a cure. It wasn't about immunity. It was about what happens after you die." He paused, his hand resting on the edge of the table. "If someone dies, even without being bitten, if their brain is intact, they turn."

Murmurs erupted across the table. Anne looked horrified. Lana clenched her jaw. Daryl and Bill exchanged a stunned glance.

"You're saying any death?" Lana asked, her voice low. "Even natural?"

Derek nodded. "Unless the brain's destroyed. Hensley told me Ellis learned this early on, once the fall happened. That's why he took people as test subjects, to try and control them after they turned."

Silence held the room for a long moment before Callum finally broke it.

"So what's the plan then?" he asked. Derek leaned over the map.

"The four of us, myself, Daryl, Callum, and Lana, will go down. We'll be armed. Tethered if needed. The moment anything feels off, we fall back."

"We're not just looking for answers anymore," Daryl added. "We're looking for confirmation. If there's anything under there that connects to Ellis's work, we end it. Permanently."

Jennifer stood quietly at the back of the room, arms crossed, worry written across her face. She didn't speak. She didn't have to.

Derek looked around the table, into the eyes of the people who had fought beside him for nearly a year. "This world has changed. Again. And we're running out of time to get ahead of it. So we start now." No one objected.

Outside the meeting room, the hatch waited. Cold. Unmoving.

But not for long.

Chapter 3

As morning approached, the team were already assembled, getting ready to go down the hatch. Derek asked Bill and Steph to stand guard at the entrance while the rest of New Haven got on with day to day chores. The metal hatch groaned as they opened it. Down the ladder they went. As Derek and the others stepped onto the final rung of the rusted ladder their boots landed with a dull thud on the concrete floor. A sterile coldness met them, the kind found only in places untouched by time.

Daryl swept his torch across the dark hallway. "No smell," he muttered. "Not like the last lab." Callum kept his rifle high, scanning ahead.

Lana walked near Derek, flashlight tight in her grip. "This place hasn't been disturbed for years," she said.

The corridor led them past dusty filing cabinets and shattered glass doors. They bypassed a pair of sealed quarantine rooms, one with a long-dried smear of blood on the inside of the window. But there were no bodies. No zombies. Just echoes and silence. Finally, they came to a heavy metal door. Derek tried the handle. Locked. Lana stepped forward, held up a small crowbar, and wedged it between the frame and latch. With a few sharp jerks, the lock snapped.

—-

Inside, the room was dry, airtight, and packed. Walls were lined with filing cabinets and paper-stuffed shelves. A terminal with a blank monitor sat in one corner beneath a dusty security camera. The air smelled of paper and metal. Derek stepped in first. On the wall behind the desk was a chalkboard, still faintly legible.

Scrawled in block letters:

> CHIMERA STRAIN – PROJECT GENESIS

Callum looked at it, eyes narrowing. "This was no medical station," he muttered. "This was part of the outbreak." Daryl opened a cabinet. Inside were dozens of handwritten notebooks. Most were lab records, chemical formulas, or patient logs.

Lana grabbed a thick binder marked "Phase Zero – Origin Trials." She began flipping through it, brow furrowing.

Derek leaned over her shoulder. "What is it?" She paused and read aloud:

'Initial exposure from bioprospecting samples gathered in Eastern Siberia. Frozen pathogens recovered from a melting permafrost pocket in 2011. The chimera strain exhibited unprecedented latency...'

She looked up. "It didn't come from a lab. Not originally. They found it in the ice."

Callum let out a low whistle. "And instead of destroying it, they studied it."

Daryl flipped through another folder. "They engineered it. Look, notes about genetic splicing, viral load variations... They were weaponizing it." Another note slipped out of the folder and fell to the ground.

Derek picked it up.

It was a final log entry. 'We lost control of Subject 41. It showed signs of cognitive preservation... it remembered faces. It followed light. We shut down further trials. We sealed the site. If anyone finds this, do not replicate our work. Do not attempt control. The virus learns.'

A chill passed through the group. Lana whispered, "It remembers..."

Derek stood still, the folder still in his hands. His voice came out low. "They didn't start this on purpose. But once they realized what they had... they tried to make it theirs."

Daryl stepped closer to the terminal and flicked a few buttons. The screen remained black. "Power's dead. We'll have to bring the logs topside."

Callum moved toward the exit. "Let's take what we can. But we tell no one until we understand it."

Derek agreed.

He turned back toward the chalkboard. Beneath the "CHIMERA STRAIN" title was one final phrase, scrawled in red marker:

Phase One was survival. Phase Two is evolution.

—-

Derek didn't like the sound of that. Back in the council meeting room it was silent, except for the soft hum of the overhead lights. The binder sat in the middle of the table, bound with a cracked leather spine and stained with age. Derek had dropped it there like it might burn through the metal surface. Callum stood nearby, arms crossed, eyes sharp. Dr. Aria Hensley looked down at the binder. Her face remained unreadable, but her hands trembled slightly as she opened the cover. She didn't speak right away. Her fingers turned the pages slowly, like she was seeing ghosts stitched between the lines.

Finally, she whispered, "Chimera..."

Derek leaned forward. "You recognize it?"

Hensley nodded once, almost reluctantly. "I do. The Chimera strain was discovered nearly fifteen years ago, long before the outbreak, a long time before the world fell."

Callum frowned. "Where?"

"A frozen site in Siberia. A team was doing deep-core drilling into the permafrost. They were looking for dormant microbial life samples for biotech companies. They found something else instead. Something old."

"Old how?" Callum asked.

"Prehistoric. Not a virus we'd ever seen. It didn't behave like anything in our databases. It latched onto whatever genetic material it could find, rewrote it like code. The labs labeled it a chimera, a hybrid, unstable and unpredictable. But it was adaptable... terrifyingly so."

Derek narrowed his eyes. "And someone thought that was worth keeping?"

"Worse," she said. "They tried to harness it. First as a rapid-adaptation gene therapy platform. Then for military applications, programmable mutation. But the trials spiraled out of control."

"And so this is what caused the outbreak?" Callum asked.

"I think so. The strain was supposedly destroyed. The facility that handled the research was shut down. All samples, data, and personnel reassigned or removed."

"But you worked there," Derek said.

"I was at a supporting site. My team never handled the strain directly, but we were briefed. When the orders came to purge everything we did, we thought it was over."

She looked up at Derek, her eyes dark.

"They lied. Someone must have smuggled it out. Someone kept the research going."

Derek stepped back, jaw tight. "And Ellis found out about it, could he have started researching it again."

She closed the binder. "Looks that way."

Callum sat down slowly. "How dangerous is it now?"

"That depends," Hensley said. "If the strain is still active, even in residue, it could mutate again. But the bigger risk is the data. With enough time, someone could replicate what Ellis was trying to do. Or worse."

Derek nodded grimly. "Then it stays locked."

Callum stood again. "We've moved the notes to a cell in Segregation. Only Derek and I have keys."

Hensley gave a slow nod. "You made the right call."

Derek turned to leave, then paused. "One more thing. Is it possible the zombies... are changing? Getting smarter?"

She hesitated. "Chimera doesn't just reanimate. It evolves."

Outside the security room, the wind picked up, howling through New Haven like a whisper of the past they had tried to bury. But the truth had clawed its way back, and now it sat under lock and key.

Waiting.

—-

Derek called for the rest of the council members to join them. The meeting room had never felt so still. Every seat around the table was taken. Derek stood at the head, arms folded, his jaw tense. To his right sat Callum, stone-faced, and to his left, Dr. Aria Hensley, visibly uneasy under the weight of so many eyes. Jillian, Anne, Daryl, Bill, Maggie, and Munroe all leaned forward slightly, the room heavy with expectation. Derek took a breath, then laid it out.

"We found research in the hatch, binders filled with notes, diagrams, and test results. We've locked it down in Segregation. Only Callum and I have keys." He turned to Hensley, giving her a small nod.

She straightened and looked around. "The strain... the virus... It's called Chimera. It wasn't engineered before the fall. It was discovered in Siberia, a frozen microbe found deep in the ice, more than a decade before the outbreak. The military took interest. Research began. But it was volatile. Unstable. Dangerous."

"Why was it kept?" Maggie asked.

"They saw potential," Hensley said quietly. "A bio-adaptive system. Perfect for weaponization, even if it couldn't be controlled. When the trials failed, we were told it had been destroyed."

"But it wasn't," Daryl said grimly.

"No," she said. "Someone must have snuck it out of the lab. Maybe people at Rosebank lab. Maybe the people who tried to weaponize it. I don't know."

"What kind of danger are we talking about?" Munroe asked.

"Mutation," she answered, "faster turn times. Possible intelligence. I've only seen fragments of the data, but if they had time to run trials"

"They did," Derek interrupted. "ZF-13s. Then 16s. Obedient zombies. Fighters." That drew silence. Derek scanned the room. "That research, and this conversation, stays in this room."

Jillian looked hesitant. "You're saying we don't tell anyone else, that keep it secret?"

"I'm saying we protect people," Derek said firmly. "Panic spreads faster than plague. If anyone found out what this virus is capable of, it could shatter everything we've built here."

Callum leaned forward. "For now, the plan is containment. The notes stay sealed. Only Dr. Hensley works on them, and only under supervision."

"And if someone asks?" Anne said.

Daryl replied, "Then we say the hatch was empty."

A long pause followed.

One by one, they nodded.

Maggie spoke last. "Alright. It stays between us. But if any of this surfaces again..."

"We act," Derek said. He stood tall, hands braced on the edge of the table. "This is our home. Our people. And I won't let the past rise from the dirt and destroy it."

No one argued.

The council had seen war. They had seen death. But this was something older. Something buried. And it was knocking. A silence hung in the air after Derek's firm declaration. The council members were still digesting the weight of what they'd just agreed to, secrets, science, and shadows long buried.

—-

Jennifer, who had entered quietly during the latter half of the meeting and stood near the back wall, finally stepped forward. Though still healing, her presence carried weight. "So the hatch, the secret base..." she began, her voice steady, "could we use it?" Derek looked at her, brow furrowed. "As a fallback shelter," she clarified. "If New Haven is ever breached, could we reinforce it? Make it a safe zone. Somewhere to fall back to if everything else fails?"

The room stirred with interest. Anne and Bill exchanged glances. Jillian nodded slowly. Callum stood and rubbed his temple. "It's... possible. The infrastructure is strong, steel-reinforced walls, powered ventilation, isolated systems. If we ran lighting and water lines down, maybe even created additional exits—"

"Is there another way in or out?" Jennifer pressed. Derek turned to Hensley.

She hesitated, then nodded. "From what I've read in the files so far there was an access tunnel, used by the scientists in the lab. If it hasn't caved in, it would lead out a few miles to the south."

Derek paced slowly, processing. Then he looked up. "We've been thinking of it like a tomb. But maybe it's a bunker. A vault. Something we can turn to our advantage."

Callum added, "It could be an edge. A place to train. Store emergency rations. Even house newcomers if we need to expand."

Jillian looked at Derek. "You want the information kept quiet, that's fine. But if this place can save lives... we should use it and let everyone know." Derek considered the faces around the table, his council, his people.

Then he nodded. "Alright. We move forward carefully. Quietly. We'll draw up plans. Assess the second exit. And if it's safe... we fortify." Jennifer gave a small smile, then leaned against the wall, her strength not yet fully returned but her voice unwavering.

"One secret might just save us all."

The meeting ended with purpose. And beneath New Haven, something that once threatened to destroy them... was now beginning to serve as their greatest defense.

Later that evening around New Haven. The council meeting had ended hours ago, but the weight of what they had learned still clung to the air like smoke after a fire.

—-

Anne and Callum were outside the chapel, Anne sat on the low stone wall, kicking her boots against the crumbling brick as Callum leaned beside her. "You think we're doing the right thing?" she asked.

Callum didn't answer right away. "Depends what you mean by 'right.' Keeping it quiet? Yeah. People panic too easily. Using the bunker? That's harder to say."

Anne looked at the stars. "Feels like we're playing god with something we barely understand."

Callum nodded. "Yeah... but we've been doing that since day one. When we choose who gets a bed, who goes on runs. We're already in the fire, Anne. At least now we've got a fireproof door."

She cracked a smile. "Dark. But fair." She paused for a moment and then asked Callum "do you remember the good old days before the world went to shit! Dinner parties, weekends in the garage with Derek and Jennifer, falling out the doors at 3 trying to get a taxi home, arguing with the driver cause he took less the week before".

Callum cracked a smile, "yeah those were the best days ever, no worries, no zombies to dodge, apart from a Sunday morning when people didn't know when to stop drinking". They both had a slight chuckle.

—-

Bill and Maggie were at the perimeter wall in one of the guard towers. Maggie adjusted the scope on her rifle, keeping one eye on the treeline.

"You buy any of that?" Bill asked, leaning against the rail. "The virus backstory or the whole 'turn no matter what' twist?"

"Both." She sighed. "I don't know, Bill. But I've seen enough bodies get up after a 'clean death' to know there's truth in it."

He nodded slowly. "Still feels like we're sitting on a bomb."

Maggie tightened her grip. "Maybe. But at least we know where it is now. Better than it going off in our faces."

Bill grunted in agreement, his eyes scanning the horizon. "Still... I'll be sleeping with one eye open for a while."

—-

Munroe, Bellamy, and Daryl were sitting outside the barracks courtyard. A small fire crackled between them, its orange glow casting long shadows on the prison wall.

"Wish I could say I was surprised," Munroe muttered, tossing a stick into the flames. Bellamy rubbed the back of his neck. "I spent years under Ellis, watching men toy with death like it was a pet. Of course there was more to it."

Daryl stirred the fire with a long branch. "Yeah, but this is bigger. A strain that infects everyone, no matter how they die?"

Munroe looked up. "How do we even fight that?".

"We don't," Daryl said. "We survive it. And now... we use that lab to help us do it."

Bellamy grunted. "Just hope it doesn't bite us in the ass later."

"Everything eventually does," Daryl muttered. "So, what did you guys do before the world went to shit?"

"I was an army sergeant" Munroe replied "Bellamy was the major, we must have done over what, 9 tours together?"

"Yeah and I saved your arse on all of them" Bellamy added. "How about you Daryl?"

"I used to run a hunting and convenience store, my wife Ellie helped me loads, she set it up. Basically ran it. I was just the face of it all." he replied.

"What happened to her?" Bellamy queries.

"We lost her in the fight at the school, zombies got her as she tried to flee"

Bellamy and Munroe sat flabbergasted, they both apologize profoundly for everything that's happened.

"It's ok" Daryl replies "we all lost people, I don't blame you two, you were following orders. It was all down to Ellis, glad he's dead! Although I would have liked to have been the one punching his face in."

The 3 men sit there, reflecting on what's happened.

—-

Jennifer and Jillian were by the infirmary. Jennifer leaned against the wall, arms crossed. Jillian stood beside her, hands in her pockets. "How are you holding up?" Jennifer asked.

Jillian nodded. "aye ok, how about you?"

Jennifer didn't answer right away. "Learning you can turn even if you're not bitten... it's been messing with my head."

"Same." They stood in silence for a moment. "You think we're doing the right thing?" Jillian asked.

Jennifer turned to her. "What other option do we have? We can't scare everyone. But we can prepare."

Jillian's gaze fell to the floor. "I just wish it didn't feel like we were walking through fog. Like we're heading into something we can't even see."

Jennifer placed a hand on her sister's arm. "Then we hold onto each other. Walk carefully. And hope we're not already too deep."

Jillian nodded. "Do you remember that weekend we all went away on holiday, you and I, mum, dad and Derek, the one when our car broke down so we all squeezed into Derek's little Corsa."

"Yeah I mind that one, we got to the lodge, walked in and there was someone at it on the couch." Both girls snigger. "I don't think I've ever seen anyone so embarrassed. Then Derek walked in. Bold as brass, saying this wasn't the time for a fivesome, the in-laws are here." Jennifer replies. "He always knew when to say the most inappropriate things"

Both girls are now chuckling away. Watching the night sky. Hoping that what comes next is something that helps them.

Chapter 4

The next morning, the sun hung high overhead, casting long shadows across the main yard of New Haven. The entire community—every able-bodied man, woman, and child—stood gathered beneath the open sky, forming a loose circle around the old flagpole in the centre. Tension hummed through the air, curiosity etched across tired faces. For once, the usual routines of patrols, repairs, and gardening had halted.

Derek stood at the front, hands behind his back, eyes scanning his people—his people. Jennifer stood off to the side, still pale but recovering well, while Jillian lingered just behind him, arms folded and silent.

Derek cleared his throat, his voice steady as it echoed across the yard. "I want to talk to you all about something we discovered beneath the prison—just a few days ago." He paused as a few heads tilted, the crowd leaning in. "During the recent expansion near the south wall, a team uncovered a sealed hatch. What we found beneath it wasn't just an old supply room—it was a fallout shelter. Built long before the world fell apart. Forgotten, sealed, and buried by time." The silence deepened. Even the kids stood still, sensing the weight of his words. "It's sturdy. Defensible. With rooms, filtration, and space. It may not be modern or perfect—but it's a chance. A second line of defence if we're ever overrun or attacked again. Somewhere to hide. Somewhere to survive."

Bill, arms crossed near the front, gave a slow, approving nod. Reggie and Anne exchanged glances. Even Callum, leaning on a crutch, looked determined.

Derek continued. "We're calling it The Shelter. And it won't be a secret. Every single one of you will know where it is. How to get there. What to do if the alarms sound. No more chaos. No more confusion."

Jennifer stepped forward beside him. "We're preparing it now," she added. "Cleaning it, stocking it. Making it safe. But we also believe there's a main entrance—one that's been lost. Buried. Maybe it's collapsed. We need to find it before we ever need to use it."

There were murmurs—this time more hopeful than fearful.

"Starting today, a small team will begin scouting for that entrance. If you're willing to help with prep or scouting, see Callum or Daryl. If you've got skills that could help reinforce the structure or store supplies, speak to Maggie. And if you have ideas, real ones, my door's open."

Derek let his eyes scan the crowd one last time, lingering for a moment on Jennifer, then Jillian, then the tired but unbroken faces staring back at him. "We've come too far to let our guard down now. The world out there hasn't changed. But here, we're building something that can last."

And with that, the work began.

Back inside the meeting room, Derek stood with Lana, Callum, and Daryl, pouring over the aged, brittle blueprint that had been uncovered in a forgotten filing cabinet, buried beneath decades of neglect. The shelter's full schematic was mapped in faded ink, its corridors, chambers, filtration systems, and, most notably, four potential exits.

Only one of them, according to a scribbled note in the margin, had actually been constructed. But which one? There were no records. No confirmation. Just guesses, and the need to be sure. Derek circled the four exit points in red marker, then tapped the blueprint. "We split into four teams. One exit was built, but we don't know which. We'll check them all!

Team One was Daryl and Lee. They take the northern path, a slow hike into overgrown thicket where deer trails cut through the underbrush. According to the blueprint, the exit should be just beyond a rocky outcrop near an old ranger station. They found remnants of old fencing, rusted metal and vines thick as ropes. After nearly an hour of searching, they finally found something, Daryl knelt beside a small hill, brushing away moss and dirt to reveal something beneath, concrete. A hatch, maybe? But the hinges were completely rusted through and sealed tight.

"Might be a decoy," Lee muttered, running his hand over the surface.

"Maybe," Daryl said. "But maybe not. We mark it and head back. We'll need tools to open it if it's real."

—-

"Team Two was Bellamy and Munroe, heading to the riverside area marked on the map. As they walked in silence along the overgrown trail that once ran parallel to a small stream south of the prison. The blueprint showed a possible drainage tunnel hidden by an old maintenance shack. They found the shack, collapsed, overgrown, but behind it was a concrete culvert partially hidden beneath roots and debris. Bellamy climbed inside, flashlight sweeping over cracked tiles and a rusted ladder that descended into blackness.

"Could be it," Munroe said, voice echoing. Bellamy nodded. "Or just sewage." Either way, we need to check. As they climbed down the ladder and stepped onto the floor, they only made it 50 feet before they saw the cave in, "if this was it, then we have hell of a lot of digging to do," Bellamy says, they made a note and headed home.

—-

Team Three was Anne and David; they were tasked with the abandoned storage compound two miles east. According to the blueprint, it may have once been connected via underground tunnel for supply drop-offs. Most of the buildings collapsed or were looted, but one storage unit had been boarded up from the inside. Anne and David pried it open and stepped inside. Cold. Empty. But in the far corner, a metal grate on the ground. Too small to climb through, but it had airflow. Anne crouched, holding a hand to the draft.

"Something's down there," she whispered. They marked it. And headed home.

—-

Team Four was Derek and Jillian, they took the most unsettling location, a small, old cemetery once maintained for prison guards and staff families. It sat on the outskirts of the nearby town. Moss and overgrown grass covered most of the cemetery. Headstones tilted with age. According to the blueprint, an access tunnel may have been hidden beneath the old caretaker's shed, now nothing more than rotted beams. As they carefully searched,

Jillian froze. "Derek... here." Half-buried in moss was a thick steel door embedded into the ground, no handle, just a keyhole and two circular indentations on either side.

Derek crouched, brushing off the dirt. "This isn't part of the shed," he muttered. "It's reinforced... camouflaged." They exchanged a look. "I think this might be it."

All the teams had returned by nightfall, each with findings, theories, photos. Daryl's might have been an old service access. Bellamy's culvert could be usable with work. Anne's airflow was promising. But Derek's site, the one beneath the graveyard, felt different. Purposeful. Secretive. As they pinned photos to the map wall,

Derek circled the cemetery site. "This is where we focus next. We're going to need tools, and a locksmith, or someone who can pick locks."

The council silently agreed. Whatever this hidden exit was, it wasn't just a way out. It was a secret someone wanted buried. While the scouting teams searched outside for the rumored exits, Callum, Lana, Steph, and Ross were tasked with searching the interior of the old shelter. The air was stale, heavy with decades of dust and mold, but the deeper they went, the more they uncovered. The corridors were narrow and rust-streaked, illuminated only by portable lanterns strapped to their belts. They followed the faded markings on the walls, strange, cryptic identifiers: E1, E2, E3, and E4, presumed designations for the four tunnel exits noted on the blueprints.

—-

Ross and Steph were the first to split off. They followed the path marked E1, their boots echoing on metal grates. As they walked the two men spoke about life before the fall, Ross used to coach an amateur football team, between that and his dogs he didn't have much time for anything else. Steph told him he was a house husband, his wife worked for a pharmaceutical company and worked long hours. He looked after the kids, done day to day house admin, and the weekend for family time. Eventually, they reached a sloped shaft partially filled with rubble. The tunnel was impassable, completely caved in.

"No way anyone's getting through that," Steph muttered. Ross agreed, marking the wall in chalk: E1 – Collapsed.

—-

Lana, curious and methodical, moved alone down the E2 corridor. She passed through what looked like an old equipment storage bay, most of it rusted beyond use. The tunnel beyond was sealed with a heavy steel door... bent inward from the pressure of a collapsed ceiling beyond it. She tried to move the debris but it was no use.

"Dead end," she radioed. "E2's a loss."

—-

Callum, alone with a map and a stubborn streak, pressed toward E3. This one was better hidden, down a narrow staircase and through an old surveillance room. Beyond the door, the tunnel seemed intact, until fifty feet in, it sloped downward into a wall of waterlogged stone and twisted steel. He shook his head. Another one gone. "Mark E3 as collapsed," he said into his radio.

As he headed back his mind wandered back to when he was first introduced to Anne. She was one of Jennifer's childhood friends, it was an instant attraction for both of them. They spent most of their free time together, at the cinema, out for dinner often doubling up with Derek and Jennifer. The two of them were inseparable, what he wouldn't give to have that back again.

—-

Ross regrouped with Lana and Steph at the junction leading to the final tunnel, E4.

This one... was different.

The passage was still intact, no visible structural damage. The walls were lined with rusting conduits and crumbling emergency lights. After fifty feet, they found a heavy steel door, intact and closed but unsealed. Ross spun the wheel, and with effort, the door groaned open. Beyond it: a tight tunnel stretching into darkness. The air here was stale but breathable. No signs of collapse. No signs of water. Just silence.

"This one's holding," Lana whispered.

They marked it carefully: E4 – Intact.

—-

Later that afternoon, Derek stood before the council and a few trusted residents, both maps laid out on the table, the surface search and internal tunnel routes. "Three are unusable," he said plainly. "One might still be our way in... or out."

Callum tapped the shelter schematic. "E4. South route. It lines up with the cemetery exit."

The room went still.

"That can't be coincidence," Jillian said. "They built it to be hidden... and they made damn sure the others couldn't be used."

Derek nodded. "Next step—we open that door. Topside or from the tunnel. If this is our backup plan... we make sure it works." Derek stood with arms folded, staring at the map spread across the meeting room table. His jaw clenched in quiet thought as Callum briefed him and the others on the tunnel's condition.

"E4's intact, but it's old. We need to reinforce it so it doesn't become our grave," Callum said.

Bellamy leaned over the blueprint. "I can help with the reinforcement, Kinross used similar supports in the early days. I'll get a team together."

"Start with metal sheeting, piping, anything we can scavenge," Derek instructed. "No one goes further until we know it's stable, and find out if anyone is a locksmith, or knows how to pick locks."

—-

Later that day, the work began immediately. Under flickering lantern light, Callum, Bellamy, Lana, Ross, and Steph hauled steel beams and scavenged wood into the tunnel. Tools clanged against concrete. Sparks lit up the dark as welding torches sealed brackets into the walls. They reinforced the key weak points first, junctions where the ceiling had minor cracks, and narrow choke points where collapse risk was highest.

"This isn't going to stop a bomb," Bellamy muttered, tightening a bolt, "but it'll hold against time. We are going to need generators and lights so we can see down here," he added.

Top side, Munroe and Daryl worked to rig a generator line into the tunnel. A mess of cables was run from the prison's secondary power supply, extended underground and carefully protected from the elements. As night fell, the first light bulbs flickered on inside the tunnel E4, revealing the damp, dust-laden walls, and what lay further ahead. About 150 feet in, the passage widened into a small underground maintenance station. Dust-covered benches, sealed metal crates, and yellowing signs on the wall labeled things like Evac Protocol, Ration Logs, and Triage Station.

"This place just gets weirder and weirder," Lana said.

They cleared the area, taking inventory. Some crates still held aged emergency supplies, plastic water containers, empty med kits, and broken tools, but most of it was salvageable. They found a floor plan of the tunnel which showed there were still three more sealed rooms to check before the tunnel ended beneath the old cemetery.

—-

Back top side, Derek paced the catwalk above the yard, watching the teams haul back crates from the tunnel. Jillian joined him, brushing dust off her jacket.

"Looks like we've got a viable shelter," she said.

"For now," Derek replied. "Until we open that cemetery door, we're still boxed in."

"Better to be boxed in than dead," Jillian said with a half-smile. He gave her a nod.

"Once the reinforcements are done, we move to breach the far end."

"And if it doesn't open?" Jillian asked

"Then we make it open." Derek replies.

With the tunnel reinforced and lights flickering steadily overhead, Derek approved the next stage: opening the three sealed side rooms in the widened section of Tunnel E4.

"No surprises," he said firmly. "If it sounds like anything's moving behind those doors, you don't open it. Blockade it and we deal with it later."

Lana, Callum, Bellamy, and Ross took the lead. Each door was numbered: R1, R2, and R3. Heavy steel, secured with industrial bolts and rust-covered handles.

—-

Bellamy and Ross tackled R1, the door was marked storage. A few creaks, a lot of sweat, and the door finally groaned open. The stale smell of dust and chemical preservatives rolled out. Inside, rows of metal shelves lined the walls. Some had collapsed from moisture damage, but others still held: Vacuum-sealed rations, well past expiration but still edible. Crates of emergency blankets and water purifiers.

Dozens of sealed tins labeled "SURGICAL DISPOSABLES."

"This is a goldmine," Ross said, holding up a roll of gauze. "Maggie's gonna lose her mind."

Bellamy nodded. "Tag and log everything. We'll send a crew to collect."

—-

Callum and Lana hesitated outside R2. The door had a warning stenciled in faded red:

BIOHAZARD – ENTRY REQUIRES AUTHORISATION

"Could be nothing," Lana said.

"Could be a grave," Callum replied grimly. He tapped on the door. Silence. After a shared glance, they opened it, just a crack. Flashlights cut through the darkness. A single medical gurney sat in the centre, empty. Cabinets filled with IV bags, syringes, and old diagnostic equipment lined the wall.

What caught their attention, though, was the bullet hole-riddled wall and the faint trace of blood long dried on the floor.

"Someone didn't make it," Lana muttered.

"Someone made sure they didn't come back," Callum added. They locked it back up after logging the contents. Derek would want to know.

—-

Room R3 was the last one to open. This door took longer. The hinges were warped, as if the door had been forcibly closed under stress. Derek had joined them by now, overseeing the effort.

"Push on three," he said. "One... two... three." The door snapped open. Inside, the walls were lined with dusty communications equipment, shortwave radios, transmitters, a flickering ancient computer in sleep mode, and... a solar-powered backup battery, somehow still working.

Lana stepped forward and tapped a button.

The screen blinked awake.

New Message – Received 34 days ago.

Everyone froze.

"Play it," Derek said.

Lana hit the key.

A distorted voice came through the speakers, barely audible:

"To any survivors... This is Outpost 9. We received your last signal. We had a breach! Evacuation protocol was initiated. We're holding. Supplies low. If anyone hears this, do not come north. Repeat... do not come north. It's not just the normal zombies... it's something else..."

The message cuts off.

Silence.

"Outpost 9?" Callum said quietly.

"That message is only 34 days old," Derek said, stunned. "Someone's out there."

Back in the meeting room, the council gathered once more. Derek placed a printed copy of the message transcript on the table.

"Outpost 9," Jillian repeated. "Whatever's up there, scared them more than the infected."

Bellamy exhaled. "Then maybe we're not done fighting."

"We're never done," Derek replied. "But now... we're not alone."

Chapter 5

The council room was quieter than usual. The message from Outpost 9 still echoed in everyone's mind: "Do not come north... It's not just the infected..." Derek stood at the head of the table, the transcript of the broadcast clutched in his hand. The air was heavy with tension. "We can't ignore this," he said. "Someone out there sent a warning 34 days ago. That's recent. They may still be alive."

Callum leaned forward, elbows on the table. "If we go, we go prepared. We don't know what Outpost 9 is, where it is, or what we're walking into."

"Agreed," said Bellamy. "But we can't go yet. Not until the second gate is complete. And that tunnel exit, we need to get it open, it means the shelter is safe, and we can also use it as a secret way into New Haven."

Maggie tapped a pencil against her notepad. "So we split tasks. One team finalizes the tunnel and one team does the gate. Some can work on trying to find out where Outpost 9 actually is."

"Lana's working on that already," said Jillian. "The comms room had logs, partial coordinates. She's cleaning it up."

Derek nodded. "Then it's settled. We secure the shelter. Get the second gate up. And in the meantime, we find Outpost 9."

—-

The lights buzzed overhead as Derek, Callum, Daryl, and Lee walked through the now-reinforced passage of Tunnel E4. Braced timber, steel plating, and fresh wiring now made the once-collapsing corridor feel like a bunker. At the very end, a thick concrete blast door stood at the top of a short staircase, streaked with years of moss and grime. Behind it, they knew, was the old cemetery, quiet and overgrown.

"If we can open it without blowing it," Daryl said, tapping the surface, "this gives us a hidden second way out of New Haven."

Lee ran a hand along the rusted locking mechanism. "It's old, but it's mechanical. We might be able to disengage the locking bolts without too much force."

"Did we have any joy with a locksmith?" Derek asks, Lee shook his head and told him no one admitted to being able to pick locks.

Callum knelt beside it, checking the hinges. "hinges look ok but rusted, but the locks are engaged. We'll need to cut through the latches to get it open."

Derek turned to Lee. "Tell Lana to get more lights down here, we want to be sure where and what we are cutting through."

Within the hour, sparks danced silently along the concrete, as a slow, methodical cut began. Not explosive, just time, patience, and care. They wouldn't risk this door. If it failed, they'd lose their best fallback plan.

—-

Back top side in New Haven, plans are taking shape. Jillian and Lana worked in the comms room, logs and maps spread across the table.

"There," Lana said, pointing to a faint line of an old map. "These coordinates might be Outpost 9. It's a region near an old dam north of Stirling. Mountainous terrain. High up, hard to reach."

"And hard to leave," Jillian murmured."

"Which might mean they're trapped," Lana replied. "You better go get Derek, he will want to see this." Jillian nods and heads for the shelter, in search of Derek.

—-

As night approached, the final sparks ceased in the tunnel. The hinges of the old blast door groaned but held. With a combined heave, the group pulled it open. Beyond it, the shed, moonlight filtering through the windows. Fresh air. And the cemetery beyond.

Derek exhaled. "We've got our escape hatch." They reinforced the doorway with additional support from the shelter side, then set up a manual locking system, steel bars across the frame, secured with custom-welded brackets.

It wasn't perfect. But it was theirs.

The final clicks of the reinforced blast door echoed down the tunnel as the team stepped back, their hands and clothes streaked with grime, soot, and rust. Derek gave the locking bar one last test pull, solid. "Call it in," he told Daryl. "Let them know the tunnel exit is secured. We've got our exit."

Callum wiped his forehead with a rag. "Never thought I'd be happy about a tunnel ending in a graveyard."

Lee smirked. "Nothing like a bit of symbolism, huh?"

As the 4 men heading back topside they were chatting about how life used to be.

"Mind when the only worry was what the plans were for the weekend?" Lee asked. The other 3 nodded, Lee continued, "Couldn't wait for a Friday afternoon at 2, home from work shower, shave, straight to boozer, nice cold pint."

"Next run we do, we need to search a pub or off license" Daryl says, "could you imagine everyone's face if we strolled through those gates, back of the truck filled with supplies but also a cargo."

The 4 men chuckled

"Ok then, if it's safe enough and not going out our way let's do it" Derek replies "everyone could use a little distraction."

About halfway back, the silhouette of someone appeared ahead, walking quickly toward them, Jillian. She slowed as she saw Derek, her face serious, but her eyes lit with urgency.

"We might've found it," Jillian said, breath slightly short.

"Outpost 9." Derek stepped forward. "Where?" She handed him a map, partially annotated with marker lines and handwritten coordinates.

"Lana cleaned up the static in the recording. There were fragments, data pings, timestamp trails. She triangulated them with our old archives. It led us here." She pointed to a stretch of rugged terrain near the Loch Voil Forest, far north of New Haven. "It's isolated. Steep. But there's a dam and what looks like an old ranger station or facility built into the mountainside."

Daryl leaned in, scanning the map. "That's damn far. That region's been dead on the grid since the fall."

"And that's what makes it perfect," Jillian said. "High ground, natural defenses. If I wanted a last-stand bunker? I'd pick there."

Derek nodded slowly, taking in the information. "We'll need to confirm this. Boots on the ground. Quiet."

"Already ahead of you," Jillian said. "I've put together three possible routes in. One through the glen, the other up along the old rail line. The third? A longer, more forested path that avoids open roads altogether."

Lee let out a low whistle. "That's not a scouting mission. That's a full-on expedition."

"We don't need to go now," Derek said. "Not tonight. But soon." He folded the map, slipping it into his jacket. "We finish securing the shelter. Get the second gate up. Then we go north."

Jillian nodded. "I'll let Lana know to prep a file for the council." She lingered just a moment before turning to walk back toward the main compound. Derek watched her go, the faint light ahead throwing long shadows across the tunnel floor.

Callum clapped him on the shoulder. "Bedtime boss."

"Ok but we need to let the other know what's happening first, once we get back topside we will get the council together," he replies

Derek turned, the sound of boots echoing as the team continued topside. Behind them, the graveyard door stood firm, and in the distance, a hidden outpost in the mountains waited in silence. The second gate is nearly complete. But now, a new problem demanded the council's full attention. Outpost 9.

—-

The meeting room glowed with muted lamplight, shadows dancing on the walls as everyone leaned in around the table. Old maps, hand-drawn schematics, and scraps of scavenged files covered every surface. Lana tapped her finger against a weathered forestry survey. "This symbol here," she said, circling a point northeast of New Haven. "It's marked as a communications relay, but cross-referencing the layout and location... I think it's Outpost 9."

Murmurs passed through the council.

Lana continued, "Best guess? It was a remote site, maybe for early-stage viral mapping. Built into the hillside. Minimal footprint. If it's still there, it could have data, or worse, leftovers."

"So we send a recon team," Callum said. "No deeper than the entrance. Masks, weapons, fallback protocols. If it looks compromised, we walk."

Bellamy pointed to an old ranger tower nearby. "There could be cover up here, could be our fallback point." They worked through the rest in practiced rhythm, supplies, radio checks, exit routes, fallback signals. The tension in the room was quiet but taut. As Derek took final notes, a flicker of movement caught his attention. Across the table, Jillian sat leaned back in her chair, one leg crossed over the other, lightly twirling a pen in her fingers. Her eyes were locked on him, the corners of her mouth playing with the hint of a smile.

She didn't look away.

She wanted him to know she was watching.

Her mind wandered back to the early days when she first met Derek, he was cocky, but in a funny way, always knew what to say and when. The first time he met their parents when Jennifer introduced them was a catastrophe. He shook her dad's hand and introduced himself, but when he went over to her mum, he tripped over her dads feet and landed right on top of her, and Derek being Derek said "I was warned your mum had a magnetic personality". A smile and small laugh crossed her face as she snapped back into the meeting

—-

One by one, the room emptied. Jennifer gave Derek a tired kiss on the cheek and whispered, "Come to bed soon." He nodded absently. "I won't be long."

Moments later, it was just Derek and Jillian. He was finishing the last of his notes when she spoke. "You know," she said lightly, "you get this little crease between your eyebrows when you're concentrating. It's very serious. Very... commander-y." He glanced up, brow still furrowed.

"Is that your professional opinion?"

She smirked. "Totally. I have a master's degree in Derekology, remember?"

He chuckled despite himself, leaning back in his chair. "I forgot how sarcastic you get when things calm down."

She stood slowly, walking to his side of the table and resting a hand on the back of his chair. "That's because we haven't had a minute to breathe in months." He looked up at her, and for a moment the air between them shifted. There was something playful in her voice, but her eyes were sincere.

"I've missed this," she said softly. "You and me. Talking. Laughing. You letting your guard down."

"Can't afford to let it down too often," he muttered.

"Maybe not." Her voice dropped slightly. "But sometimes, even just a little... helps." He didn't answer. The weight of everything, Jennifer's recovery, the shelter, the virus, hung over him like a storm cloud.

Jillian's tone shifted, more teasing now. "Well, if you ever need help forgetting how heavy the world is, you know where to find me." Derek raised an eyebrow. She gave him a wink and started toward the door, pausing just long enough to say over her shoulder, "Remember I'm here to help you forget the crazy." With that, she was gone, leaving Derek alone in the silence.

He stared at the doorway for a long time... unsure whether he felt steadier, or more off-balance than ever.

Derek leaned forward, elbows on the table, running his hands down his face. The room was silent now, but his thoughts were anything but. He should have said something more. Something clearer. Put up a wall. Instead, he'd let it hang there, her smile, her teasing tone, the softness in her eyes.

And it wasn't the first time.

He stood slowly, pacing once, then again. The maps on the table blurred into the grain of the wood.

All the plans in the world couldn't solve what he was feeling. Jennifer was recovering. He loved her. Didn't he? She'd stood by him through everything. The fall of their old world. The rise of this one. The war at Kinross. Nearly dying. But when things got quiet, when the noise fell away, he sometimes thought of Jillian's arms, Jillian's lips, Jillian's voice whispering "I'm here when you need to forget." It hadn't been fair. To anyone. Least of all her.

He moved to the window, gazing out over New Haven's courtyard. The solar lights buzzed faintly in the night. Guards moved along the wall in quiet patrol. Somewhere, a child laughed, brief and innocent.

He wanted to protect that. All of it.

He didn't know if he could do that and be who everyone needed him to be. The leader. The partner. The man holding the line. The weight never left. It just shifted.

A soft knock pulled him from his thoughts.

Jennifer stood in the doorway, wrapped in a blanket, her face pale but peaceful. "You not coming to bed?"

He turned, forcing a smile. "Just needed to clear my head." She stepped in, leaned her head against his chest. He held her without thinking. Familiar. Warm. Heavy with memory.

"Everything okay?" she asked softly. He hesitated, then kissed the top of her head.

"Yeah. Just tired." And in that lie, he found some strange sense of truth. Because being tired was easier than being uncertain. Tired didn't have to choose. As she took his hand and led him back to their quarters, Derek cast one last glance at the empty meeting room behind him. It was going to be a long road.

But tomorrow... they'd head for Outpost 9.

And that, at least, gave him something to hold on to.

Chapter 6

The following morning, the air in the council room was heavy with tension. Flickering lanterns cast wavering shadows across the large meeting table where Derek, Callum, Daryl, Jillian, Bellamy, Lana, and the rest of the council gathered. On the table lay the worn documents recovered from Tunnel E4, the most recent find inside the shelter's sealed archive room. Most of it was water-damaged and faded, but some pages had survived intact: detailed schematics, scattered logs, and a handwritten note repeating one phrase:

"Outpost 9 is key. Remote. Hidden. Fail-safe."

Lana pointed to a spread of yellowed paper, a map of the surrounding region drawn by hand, likely from before the fall. She'd been poring over the paperwork since it was discovered. "This mark here—" she circled a faint X near the base of a wooded ridge to the northeast of New Haven, "—matches grid notes from a maintenance log cross-referenced with some of the old supply route manifests. I think this is it. Outpost 9."

"There's nothing marked on any modern map," Daryl said. "Could've been buried, or just forgotten."

"Or intentionally hidden," Bellamy added.

"Do we know what it was for?" Anne asked.

Lana shook her head. "No. Just that it was classified higher than the shelter. Whatever it held — supplies, data, maybe early research — someone went to great lengths to erase it from records."

Derek folded his arms, brow furrowed. "We send three teams. One to verify the structure. One to sweep the perimeter. One to secure a fallback location."

He turned to the chalkboard, outlining the plan.

—-

"Team One will be the entry team. We head to the front door. It consists of myself, Jillian, Daryl and Lana.

Team Two will be the perimeter team, checking to make sure there's no one; — living or dead — that could flank us. This team consists of Callum, Anne, Ross, Abby and David.

Team Three will secure the fallback location. We reckon the forest ranger hut should be the fall back location, if things go south we meet back there. The team will consist of Bellamy, Steph, Ortega, Vicki and Maggie.

"What if there's nothing there?" Lee asked.

"Then we come home empty-handed but happy that there's nothing there," Derek replied. "But if Outpost 9 is real — and it's intact — it could be the missing piece of what started all this."

Jennifer nodded quietly from her seat, worry etched into her face. "Just promise you'll all be careful."

"We always are," Daryl replied, then muttered, "until we're not."

The room quieted.

They all understood what was at stake.

The sound of boots crunching gravel echoed through the cool air of early morning. New Haven stirred slowly in the pale light of dawn, but at the main gate, everything moved with purpose.

The council chamber meeting had stretched past midnight, and sleep had been scarce. Now, with the sun only just beginning to climb the horizon, the recon bus sat ready — engine rumbling low, modified for the terrain ahead. Armor plating, reinforced windows, mesh screening over the tires. It wasn't pretty, but it was tough. Reliable.

Derek stood at the head of the group, clipboard in one hand, crossbow slung over his shoulder. A deep fatigue lined his face, but his eyes were focused. Behind him, the three teams loaded gear with quiet efficiency.

No one spoke much. They all knew what was at stake.

"All teams on board," Derek called out, raising his voice slightly over the low growl of the engine. "It's a long ride — 4 hours minimum to the fallback site. We won't be splitting until we get there, so settle in. Rest while you can."

Jillian climbed into the bus first, taking a seat near the middle beside Lana, who was already unfolding a large map between her knees. Callum, carrying a satchel full of motion detectors and tripwire alarms, gave Derek a nod before climbing aboard. Daryl and Lee moved to the back, checking rifles and supplies, whispering quietly between themselves.

Bellamy was next to step into the bus, flanked by Ross. Ortega followed, tossing a canvas bag full of flares and emergency lights into an overhead rack before slumping into a seat near the front.

Ortega was a quiet man, never spoke much, explosives expert in a previous life, never really felt like he fit in anywhere. He met Bellamy in their army days, part of a team that was in Afghanistan. He never really got over seeing his lieutenant blown up only feet from him. He kept himself to himself, helping when asked, he preferred just to follow orders.

Jennifer stood a few feet away, arms crossed, her expression unreadable as she watched Derek and the others prepare to leave. She moved toward him, didn't speak. Just hugged him. He hugged her back and kissed her.

"We will be careful" he tells her and she looks and just nods. "Final check," Derek muttered to himself as he stepped into the driver's seat and looked in the rearview mirror. His voice rose again. "If anyone's got doubts or nerves, this is your last chance to change your mind."

No one replied.

He started the engine with a heavy foot, and the reinforced gates of New Haven creaked open, sunlight spilling through the breach like a silent blessing. The bus rumbled out onto the broken road, carrying its full weight of hope, firepower, and unanswered questions. The forest swallowed them soon after, branches scraping the sides like reaching fingers.

Hours passed.

The terrain changed gradually — thicker trees, twisting dirt roads barely wide enough for the bus, and stretches of silence so deep it swallowed the growl of the engine. Inside, most of the group rested where they could. Heads leaned against windows. Fingers drummed quietly against thigh straps and rifle barrels. Derek drove, eyes narrowed, muscles tense. Jillian occasionally glanced at him in the mirror. Sometimes, he met her gaze.

After four hours, the bus crested a ridge. Bellamy tapped Derek's shoulder. "That's the spot, the ranger station should be down there ."

Nestled in a clearing surrounded by thick trees and natural rock walls, stood the fallback site. Its wooden observation tower still stood, though weathered, and the old service cabin had been patched and reinforced over the years. It was defensible. Remote. Perfect.

Derek brought the bus to a halt and cut the engine.

"Alright," he said, standing to address everyone. "This is where we split. You all know what we have to do, radio check every 20 minutes. You see anything strange — smoke, flare, silence — fall back"

Bellamy get your team ready and secure the ranger station. Bellamy nodded firmly. "Copy."

Derek turned to Callum. "Your team runs the perimeter sweep. Scout the hill. Look for signs of movement." Callum adjusted his pack. "Got it."

Daryl and Lee secured weapons, while Lana checked the last of the notes from the files recovered in Tunnel E4.

"We go for the front entrance," Derek said. "Direct approach. We're not going inside unless it's stable. You all know the drill."

With that, the three teams stepped into position. Final nods were exchanged. Radios checked one last time.

Then the teams split — Bellamy's group securing the fallback location while Derek and Callum's teams disappeared into the woods. And somewhere ahead, buried under a forest lost to time, Outpost 9 waited.

As Derek's team vanished into the dense treeline and Callum's unit cut a path around the rocky perimeter, Bellamy stood for a moment in the clearing beside the now-silent bus, watching the forest slowly swallow his allies.

"Alright," he muttered, rubbing the back of his neck. "Let's make this place a fortress."

The fallback site—an old ranger station—rough but promising. The wooden ranger tower, weather-beaten and sun-bleached, still stood tall at the northern edge of the clearing. Near the base, a squat stone-and-log cabin leaned slightly under its own age but remained largely intact.

"Maggie, get eyes on that tower," Bellamy ordered. "If it's safe to climb, I want someone up there watching the treeline within the hour." Maggie nodded and jogged toward it, rifle slung tight against his back. "Steph, check the interior of the cabin. I want to know what we're dealing with. Ortega, you and vicki start unloading gear. Priority is fortification—barricade windows, reinforce the door, and set tripwires on the trails leading in."

"You got it," Ortega replied, cracking his knuckles.

Bellamy made his way around the clearing, noting natural choke points and exposed lines of sight. There were remnants of an old wooden fence and broken posts — probably the original barrier — now long decayed. He flagged it mentally as a secondary perimeter line. If they had time, they'd rebuild it.

Inside the cabin, Steph was sweeping dust from the corners and pulling back rotted curtains. "No bodies," he reported. "Signs of long abandonment, but there's a cast iron stove, an old cot, and some shelves. Could be a decent fallback point if things go sideways."

"Then we make it liveable," Bellamy said. "Fast."

An hour passed in purposeful silence.

Maggie and Vicki climbed the tower and gave a quick thumbs-up from the top — clear line of sight on both ingress trails and part of the forest slope. Ortega had already strung two motion traps using cans, wire, and an old hunting bell from the supply pack. Munroe was stacking crates by the doorway for fast cover, and inside, a solar lamp from New Haven lit the cabin with a dim, reliable glow. Bellamy took a long breath and stepped back to assess the work.

It wasn't perfect.

But it would do.

He keyed the radio.

"Fallback post secure. Visibility's good. Defenses in place. This is Bellamy. We're green."

Static crackled for a beat before Daryl's voice came through.

"Copy that. Stay sharp."

Bellamy clipped the radio to his vest and walked slowly to the edge of the clearing. His eyes followed the fading footprints down the forest path toward Outpost 9. He didn't know what they were going to find. But whatever it was... they were ready.

—-

Callum's boots crunched softly over pine needles and brittle soil as his team advanced in a loose formation beneath the looming canopy. The air was still, the forest heavy with a silence that felt watched — like the trees themselves were waiting.

Behind him, Anne, Ross, Abby, and David moved cautiously, weapons drawn, eyes sharp. Each of them knew the stakes. This wasn't a raid — it was a recon mission. But that didn't mean it was safe.

"Up this ridge," Callum whispered, pointing toward the moss-covered incline ahead. "The structure should be buried somewhere near the crest. We spread out, but stay within sight."

They moved in, flanking the hill from different angles. The forest was reclaiming everything — fallen branches, twisted metal remnants, vines snaking over collapsed fencing. It was hard to tell what had once been natural and what had been man-made.

Ross let out a low whistle. "This place feels ancient."

"Old-world infrastructure," Callum replied. "Built to be forgotten."

Just ahead, Anne called softly, "Eyes on something."

The group converged on her position. Tucked between two trees and hidden beneath years of foliage was a rusted ventilation shaft — dented, but mostly intact. Ross knelt beside it, brushing away debris with his glove.

"Steel. Welded seams. Definitely not logging equipment."

Callum tapped the shaft. It let out a hollow thud. "Ventilation. Possibly for a bunker. Could be connected to the outpost."

"Usable entry?" David asked.

"No. Too narrow. But if it's moving air, it means something's below."

Abby marked the site with orange cloth and jotted coordinates in a notebook. They continued sweeping clockwise around the hill. The silence pressed in thicker the closer they got to the far edge. And then David stopped, raising a hand.

"Something there," he whispered, pointing through a tangle of underbrush. Callum pushed forward, hands brushing away vines and rot until his glove hit cold metal.

A reinforced steel hatch—low to the ground and half-buried. No rust on the hinges. No labels. Just matte-gray steel and a sealed locking wheel in the centre.

"Holy shit," Ross breathed.

Anne crouched beside it, inspecting the welds. "This wasn't made to be found."

"No markings," Abby noted. "Nothing on the exterior. It's not decorative. This is military-grade."

Callum tapped his radio.

"Derek, this is Callum. We've got something. Possible entry point — hatch on the east slope. Matches the shape from the blueprints Lana found. It's sealed tight."

A brief pause, then Derek's voice responded.

"Copy that. Mark it. When you're done, fall back to Bellamy's position."

"Understood," Callum replied.

He looked around once more — this forest had teeth. Whatever had happened here before the fall, it had been buried for a reason. But now the ground was shifting. And Outpost 9 was almost awake.

The forest thinned near the eastern base of the hill, giving way to rocky terrain and jagged outcroppings. Moss-covered stone walls jutted from the ground at awkward angles — remnants of a time when this land was molded by machines instead of decay.

Derek led the group in silence, weaving through the trees, crossbow in hand. Behind him moved Jillian, Daryl, Lana, and Lee, their steps quiet, eyes alert. Birds had long since abandoned this part of the world. Even the wind seemed hesitant to pass through.

Lana consulted the yellowing map in her hand. "This is the spot. It was buried under hillside development, but..." She looked up, frowning. "That rock face. Something's wrong with it."

Derek motioned them forward. As they approached, the stone gave way to something artificial — a concrete facade carved directly into the side of the mountain. Time and nature had done their best to hide it. Ivy clung to every edge. Dirt and moss blanketed what must once have been a clean entrance.

Then, there it was: steel doors, wide enough to allow trucks through, reinforced with bolts the size of fists. The surface bore no signs of damage, no scorch marks, no claw marks or frantic escape attempts.

Just silence. Heavy and patient.

Daryl stepped closer, crouching near the side panel. "Derek. You might want to see this."

Derek moved to his side. There, beside the sealed doors, was a keypad — mostly intact, its casing cracked in places, but the small LED screen at the top still glowed a faint green. A blinking red light pulsed every five seconds.

"That means they have power," Lee muttered. "Somewhere in there, something is still alive."

Derek stared at the keypad, his expression unreadable. "No guards. No bodies. No sign of struggle."

Lana knelt and ran her fingers along the bottom edge of the panel. "These locks... this is high-grade. Military. You don't just break into this."

"No signs of forced entry," Daryl added. "And no scavengers made it in either."

Derek straightened. The weight of what they'd found was starting to settle in. "So... this is it. Outpost 9."

"It's awake," Jillian whispered, eyes locked on the blinking keypad.

Derek looked over the team, then toward the trees where the fallback point sat somewhere in the distance. "No one touches the panel," he said firmly. "We regroup with the other teams, tell them what we found and we open it together."

The others nodded. They didn't know what waited on the other side of those steel doors. But after everything they'd seen — every ruin, every lie, every secret unearthed — Derek had learned one thing:

The worst truths were always the ones buried deepest.

—-

The air near the fallback site was still and tense. Low clouds clung to the hills, filtering the mid afternoon light into a dull gray. From their elevated vantage point, the teams had a clear, direct view of the tree-covered slope and the location of where outpost 9 sits.

No one spoke much. The recon teams had returned to the fallback location just after noon. Derek, Callum, and Bellamy regrouped and laid out the full picture: one working keypad, no visible threats, no damage to the entry. And no sign of life.

Now, they watched — all of them — eyes fixed on that still, silent structure.

Bellamy stood near the ridge edge with binoculars, scanning for movement. "Nothing," he muttered for the fifth time. "Not even a bird."

Daryl adjusted his crossbow sling and sat down against the stone wall of the old ranger tower. "Either it's abandoned... or they're watching us already."

Derek sat by the radio, fingers drumming on the casing. Jillian had brought him a thermos of water, but it remained untouched. His focus was fixed. They had a plan—the next morning they would descend together: Derek's team first would approach the main doors, try and hack the keypad and assess for traps or surveillance. Callum's team would circle behind, sweep the rear again and see if they could open any of the hatches that they found. Bellamy's group would remain posted at the fallback tower, coordinating from above and providing support if anything went wrong.

But for now, they waited.

—-

The main gates of New Haven stood quiet under the midmorning sun. A soft breeze rustled the tattered banner above the archway — the symbol of New Haven. Strong. Worn. Still flying. Jennifer sat in the old warden's office, now the council chamber, across from Bill, who looked more tired than usual. A mug of lukewarm tea sat between them, untouched.

"They said four hours," Jennifer muttered, glancing at the old wall clock. "That was yesterday morning and we still haven't heard from them."

Bill grunted. "Long trip. And if they're being careful, that means they move slower. Maybe took them five or six hours to get there. Radios might be out of range."

"It's been over thirty," she said quietly.

Bill didn't answer.

The room was too quiet without the others. Without Derek's clipped commands, Jillian's sly sarcasm, Lana's methodical logic. The walls seemed to echo with silence.

"They're good people," Bill said finally. "Smart. Prepared. If anyone can make it back, it's them."

Jennifer stood and walked to the window. Below, a few residents were tending to crops, sorting food, teaching children. New Haven ticked on — but slower, more cautiously, missing its backbone.

"How long do we wait?" she asked.

Bill looked up. "You're the acting head. What does your gut say?"

Jennifer closed her eyes. Her heart screamed to leave now. To find Derek. To bring them all home. But her head said otherwise.

"Four days," she said at last. "If no word by then... we form a search and recovery team."

"And if something happens before that?" Bill asked.

Jennifer turned. Her voice was steel. "Then we go sooner."

The first rays of dawn crept over the ridgeline, casting long shadows across the moss-covered rocks near the ranger station. The teams were moving with quiet efficiency, final checks underway. Backpacks were zipped, radios tested, weapons cleaned and holstered.

Derek stood by the reinforced table they'd fashioned as a tactical map station, studying the terrain one last time. Jillian approached with a canteen and gave him a subtle nod.

"Everyone's ready."

"Good," he replied, eyes still locked on the map. "We move in ten."

Suddenly, the still morning air was shattered by the sharp snap of a wire — followed by the hollow ping of a tin can clattering against stone.

"Tripwire!" Daryl barked, already moving toward the perimeter.

Within seconds, everyone was in motion, guns raised and spread in a semicircle around the treeline beyond the ranger tower. The air was tense. Guns raised. Fingers on triggers. The tripwire lay slack where it had been triggered, a tin can still rolling in the dirt. Four figures stepped from the shadows of the treeline, hands raised — not in surrender, but caution. , the men stepped forward.

"Marcus..." he muttered.

Marcus gave a tired smirk. "Nice to see you too, Bellamy. Though I have to say — you've upgraded your company."

Derek raised his crossbow and stepped forward. "Who are they?"

Bellamy exhaled. "There scientists. From the old network. They warned me about Ellis... and what he was doing."

"You've got thirty seconds to explain why you're here," Derek snapped.

Marcus's tone turned cold. "You're heading to Outpost 9, right?"

"We are," Callum said, rifle not quite lowered. "How do you know about that?"

"Because we were part of it," said George, stepping up beside Marcus. "We helped build it. Staffed it. Watched it spiral out of control."

A tense silence followed.

"Outpost 9..." Marcus began, "...was the start of it all."

Lana's eyes narrowed. "The outbreak?"

"yes," Marcus said grimly. "The outbreak. The entire collapse. The virus... the mutations... It all started here. Because one test subject — Patient Zero — got out."

"Escaped?" Derek asked, stunned.

"Yes," Samuel cut in. "The subject was meant to be terminated, the early strain — unstable, volatile. But there was a breach. Containment protocols failed. Patient Zero made it out of the compound and disappeared into the surrounding forest."

Marcus continued, his voice flat. "He infected a lumber crew five miles from here. Then a small village. Then it was everywhere."

Bellamy muttered under his breath. "Jesus Christ..."

"It was classified," George added. "Covered up. We were told it was a remote incident — localized. That it had been cleaned up."

"But it wasn't," Marcus said. "You know the rest."

Daryl stepped forward. "Is there still something alive in there?"

We don't know," Marcus admitted. "But if a fragment of the original strain is present, it's dangerous. That facility wasn't just research. It was a vault. For the worst biological prototypes the military dreamed up."

Derek looked at his team, then back at the scientists. "We're not turning back. But if you've got information that can help keep my people alive in there — you're coming with us."

Marcus didn't argue. "Then we better talk. Because if you thought the end of the world started with a bang..." He looked toward the hidden steel doors in the hillside. "...you should've heard it whisper first."

—·—

Derek crossed his arms, his expression hard. "Then it's time to stop holding back. You said this is where it started — Outpost 9. Patient Zero. What happened?"

Marcus let out a slow breath. "It began with Subject 001. The Chimera strain was meant to be the key to extreme regeneration — rebuilding organs, slowing aging. But what we created... it changed him."

"Changed how?" Daryl asked, eyes narrowing.

"He became something else," George replied. "It didn't make him superhuman. It made him unstable. Violent. He attacked the staff without warning — savage, animalistic. And then..."

Samuel picked up the thread. "Those he bit died. Then came back."

There was a ripple of reaction — quiet murmurs. But the survivors already knew this part.

"Here's what you don't know," Marcus said, his tone darkening. "We tried to contain it. We developed an antidote — something to stop it before it spread. But someone higher up... changed the plan."

Derek tilted his head. "Changed it how?"

Harold stepped forward, voice low. "They aerosolized it. Turned the antidote into a gas. Told the public it was for immunity boosting — to protect the population from rising viral threats."

"And they spread it through chemtrails," Marcus finished. "Planes. Global distribution. It was in the skies before anyone realized what they were breathing."

Jillian blinked. "Wait... you said they released the antidote into the air?"

"That's what they thought," George said. "But someone switched it, it was the virus they released, everyone who inhaled it — everyone — was infected. Silently. No symptoms. Not until death."

"And when they die...they turn" Lana muttered.

Harold confirmed this. "Whether they were ever bitten or not. That's how it became global in weeks. Not through bites. Through the air."

Derek looked down the ridge, where the treetops concealed the overgrown structure of Outpost 9. "So this... is the place where the world died." Derek folded his arms, his expression unreadable as the revelation about the chemtrail-borne virus hung in the air like a fog no one could breathe through.

But he wasn't done.

"We received a transmission," Derek said flatly. "Thirty four days ago. It came from Outpost 9. Just a single voice… male. Said: 'It's not just infected here. Don't come.' Then the signal cut off."

The silence that followed was heavy.

Marcus's brow furrowed. "Thirty four days?"

Derek nodded. "You're telling me no one's been in there since the outbreak. But someone… something sent that message. We thought maybe survivors."

The scientists exchanged uncertain glances. Harold was the first to speak, hesitantly. "If that's true… the only possibility is Dr. Vincent Keller."

George looked down at his feet. "He was head of security for the facility and a senior virologist. He refused to evacuate when the breach happened. He thought he could contain it from the inside."

"He sealed the main lab manually," Samuel added, "so we could escape through the external tunnels."

"You left him in there?" Jillian asked, stunned.

"He made the call," Marcus said, his voice tinged with regret. "We didn't abandon him. He locked himself in. Thought he could finish the failsafe—"

"Failsafe?" Derek cut in sharply.

But Marcus shook his head. "It never worked. He was trying to corrupt the Chimera strain's neurological pathing, shut it down through its own protein decay. We never heard from him again."

"But if he's still alive…" Daryl said, letting the sentence hang.

"It means he's been sealed in that bunker for months," Lana finished. "Alone."

Derek's jaw tightened. "Then what the hell did he mean by 'It's not just infected here'?"

That was the question no one answered. The scientists went quiet. Eyes turned to one another. Shrugs. Nervous silence.

"We don't know," Marcus finally admitted. "We never got back in. And we haven't heard from Keller since that day."

"Well," Derek said grimly, "we're going to find out."

Chapter 7

The forest was quiet, the trees — heavy with creeping moss and decay — stood like silent sentinels as Derek's boots crunched on gravel and dead pine needles.

Before him loomed the steel front doors of Outpost 9, recessed into the earth and framed by the moss-covered mountain wall. The massive blast doors bore deep rust scars, but the small, still-blinking keypad beside them said one thing loud and clear:

Power was still running.

Derek glanced over his shoulder. Behind him, the rest of his team — Jillian, Daryl, Lana, Lee — waited in silence. Callum's team — Anne, Abby, Ross, and David — stood further back, guarding the path in and watching the treeline for movement.

The scientists, Marcus and George, adjusted their glasses nervously. They had barely spoken on the walk here — not since Derek had made one thing very clear before leaving the fallback point:

> "You two are opening the door. No one else touches that keypad."

Now they stood in front of it, facing their past... and the ghosts of what had been locked inside. Marcus inhaled slowly, then stepped forward and wiped the grime off the keypad with his sleeve. The others raised their weapons instinctively, just in case.

George leaned toward Derek. "We had to change the code just before the breach. Security protocol."

"Don't care," Derek muttered. "Just open it."

Beads of sweat rolled down George's temple as he tapped in the sequence: 7-4-9-2-1-9-0.

A pause. Then—

CLUNK. HISSSSSSS. VRMMMM.

The massive steel doors shuddered, a mechanical groan echoing from deep inside the mountain. Gears turned. Locks disengaged. A thin line of stale air spilled from the widening crack in the centre, the scent of dust, metal, and rot escaping into the morning light. The doors slid open just wide enough for one person at a time. A red emergency light flickered weakly from within. Beyond it, a descending concrete corridor stretched down into darkness.

No alarms. No movement. No welcome.

Only silence.

—-—

Derek raised his crossbow, eyes scanning the corridor. "Lana, Daryl — on me. Callum, hold the entrance with your team. If you see anything move behind us... kill it."

Callum nodded. "Got it."

Marcus adjusted the strap of his pack. "There's a secondary blast door about thirty meters in. If the systems are intact, I might be able to override it from the access panel inside."

Derek gestured toward the corridor. "Then let's get to it. Quietly."

The first steps inside echoed like thunder. They didn't know what they were walking into — only that they had just stepped into the birthplace of the end of the world. And the door had just reopened.

The deeper they went, the colder it became. Moisture clung to the walls like sweat on skin, and every few steps Derek's boots sloshed faintly through stagnant puddles pooled in hairline cracks along the concrete floor.

Jillian walked just behind him, flashlight raised and trembling slightly in her grip. The beam passed over cracked wall panels, scorched ceiling tiles, and collapsed wiring that sparked intermittently. Daryl, more calm than most, scanned each corridor junction with his crossbow, tight to his shoulder, moving like a man used to darkness.

Lana and Lee took the rear with Marcus and George between them — neither scientist looking particularly eager to reclaim their old workplace.

After maybe thirty meters — just as Marcus had said — the corridor opened into a small square chamber. At its centre stood another steel blast door, this one embossed with a large black number: 0-9. To the side, a busted security desk lay overturned, monitors shattered, old blood dried into the grout of the tiles. One set of fingernail scratches raked down the wall near the corner.

"Cheery place," Daryl muttered.

Marcus stepped toward a half-shattered control panel beside the door. His fingers danced across the buttons, then stopped. "It's locked down," he said. "Code won't work here — too much structural damage. But if power's still flowing, I can reroute the circuit and force a bypass... assuming the generator room's still online."

"How long?" Derek asked.

"Fifteen minutes. Maybe twenty."

Derek glanced around the room, mind already cycling through contingency plans. "Alright. Jillian, Lee — set up a perimeter. Daryl, you're with me — we sweep this hall, make sure it's clear. Lana, stay here with them. Anything looks off, shout."

Marcus sat cross-legged and began removing the scorched access plate. George stood behind him, arms crossed tight to his chest, flinching at every creak and pop of the old building groaning under its own age.

Derek and Daryl moved into the left corridor, weapons raised, flashlights cutting through the dark. Posters still clung to the walls. Faded motivational garbage. "Pride in Protocol. Safety First." A child's drawing was taped beside one — some kind of makeshift morale booster, long since warped by moisture. At the end of the corridor, a room sat open. Inside, a security terminal flickered weakly — backup power humming just enough to keep one dusty screen alive. Faint green lines of code scrolled across it.

"Looks like some kind of log system," Daryl muttered.

Derek stepped in, brushing away cobwebs as he leaned over the keyboard. A name blinked on the screen.

Dr. Emory Voss – Last User Logged In

Derek tapped a few keys. The logs were old. Fragmented. But one sentence stood out, half corrupted but legible:

"...locked himself in... refused evacuation... subject containment failed... this place is death..."

Derek's jaw tightened. "I think we just found the guy who sent that message," he said.

Back in the main room, sparks flickered again — then a low hum started as the second blast door's locks began to whir. Marcus stepped back as the machinery rattled to life. "Got it," he said. The door split open down the middle — slower than the one before — and a gust of stale, icy air rushed out.

Beyond it? Darkness.

Long halls. Rusted steel. And secrets.

Derek stepped back into the room with Daryl, meeting the eyes of the others. "No turning back now," he said.

—-

As they crossed the threshold, the door shut behind them with a metallic thunk that echoed down the corridor like a warning. Ahead, thick industrial lights hung from the ceiling, coated in dust and grime. Only a few still flickered with life, casting ghostly, intermittent shadows that stretched and shrank with every step they took.

Derek moved point, weapon raised. Jillian and Daryl flanked him, while Lana, Lee, and the scientists followed closely behind. Every breath felt loud in the silence, the kind that pressed on your ears like deep water.

The hallway curved slightly and descended by a shallow ramp. The walls here were different—reinforced, thick concrete lined with steel support beams. More secure than anything they'd seen above.

They passed shattered glass partitions, overturned desks, and bulletin boards full of yellowed memos. Then they reached a large room — once some kind of operations hub. A circular terminal sat in the centre, surrounded by inactive screens. Beds and supplies were scattered — signs someone had lived here, but not recently. Derek stepped forward. On the desk lay a digital recorder. He pressed play.

"This is Dr. Emory Voss. Day... 142. Still no extraction. Communications are down. I've sealed myself in. Everyone else is gone. Or turned. I failed to stop it. Failed to contain it. If anyone finds this—burn it all. Don't let it out again." The message cuts to static.

Daryl turned to Marcus, who looked visibly shaken. "This was your guy?"

Marcus nodded grimly. "He was one of the original virologists on Project Chimera. Brilliant. Obsessive. But he had a conscience."

Jillian moved toward a steel door at the far end of the operations room. A faded sign above it read: LAB LEVEL 3 – BIOHAZARD CONTAINMENT. "We need to know what's in there," she said quietly.

Marcus hesitated. "This is where the first infected were held. Where Subject 001 was taken after initial mutation. The virus evolved in that room."

Derek turned toward the others. "Gear up. No one goes in alone. No physical contact with anything. We document and pull out."

With a heavy breath, they breached the door. The lab beyond was sealed and cold. Frost coated the glass of broken containment pods. One lay smashed, claw marks gouged into its sides from the inside. Scorch marks blackened the far wall. Bones littered the floor — human and otherwise. A data drive blinked on a side console.

Lana moved to it carefully and detached the core. "It's intact. We can take it back."

Jillian's voice cut in sharply. "Derek... over here." She was staring at the last pod. Still sealed. Inside, a body sat slumped forward. Dried blood clung to its hospital gown. A name tag was taped to the pod window.

SUBJECT 001 – NICHOLAS WARD

Derek didn't blink. "Someone is still alive in here."

Marcus stepped forward, face pale. "He shouldn't be in there, subject 001 was destroyed."

The body moved.

Everyone froze.

Just a twitch — the faintest shift of a shoulder, the slow rotation of a neck.

Then its eyes opened. Black. Hungry. And alive. It smiled.

"Back. Back now!" Derek barked.

The pod hissed. Warning lights began flashing. A vent in the corner roared to life.

Containment breach protocols.

"Run!" Lana shouted.

They sprinted back the way they came, Marcus screaming into the radio to prep the fallback team. Alarms howled through the facility.

Outpost 9 had woken up.

And it was not empty.

BENEATH THE SILENCE

—-—

The alarms blared like sirens from hell, red strobes flashing violently against the steel walls. Warning klaxons echoed through the corridors. > "Containment breach detected. Lockdown initiated."

The doors leading into LAB LEVEL 3 hissed shut — but not before Subject 001 rose to his feet, his blackened eyes watching them with unnatural calm.

Derek was already dragging Jillian back. "Move! Now!"

Lana sprinted beside Lee, clutching the recovered data drive. Lee fired a few panicked rounds down the hall as the first containment door slammed behind them.

Daryl skidded to a halt, pulling out a flare and tossing it behind them to mark their retreat. "Doesn't matter. It's up. We're getting out."

They backtracked through the corridor, their boots pounding against concrete. A second alarm triggered — this one deeper, almost subterranean in its tone.

"Secondary security protocol activated."

Suddenly, another door behind them slammed closed — this one from the direction of their entrance.

Lee cursed. "We're boxed in!"

"No," Marcus said quickly. "There's an emergency evac lift. This way!"

He pointed toward an old cargo elevator to the left of the ops room — one they'd barely noticed on entry.

Derek kicked it open. It groaned but didn't resist. "Get in!"

They piled inside — all except Derek, who held his ground.

Jillian grabbed his arm. "What are you doing?!"

"I'm buying us time."

"Don't be an idiot, Derek—"

Daryl stepped out of the lift too. "If you stay, I stay."

Derek nodded. "Two minutes. Then we all run."

They turned and aimed their weapons down the corridor as the sounds began — not footsteps... but scraping. Inhuman groans. Something else was moving. Not just Subject 001.

Marcus yelled from the lift. "You don't understand — there were more! Others like him. Failed prototypes—some dormant. But if containment failed—"

"We got the message, Doc!" Daryl shouted. "Shut the hell up and prep the lift!"

The sounds got closer — claws, dragging limbs, echoes of low rattling growls. Derek fired the first shot. It tore through something pale and fast. Then the horde came. Half-human things with pulsing veins and collapsed eyes. Some slow, others impossibly fast. A dozen at least, and more behind them.

"NOW!" Derek screamed, grabbing Daryl by the collar.

They dove into the lift. Lana hit the emergency lever. The doors screeched closed just as a clawed hand slapped against the seam. Thud. Silence. Then ascent. The team collapsed to the floor in a heap of adrenaline and disbelief.

Marcus, barely breathing, muttered, "I told you not to open it..."

Derek, his chest heaving, looked at the drive Lana clutched.

"What the hell did we just wake up?"

—-

The cargo lift groaned and shuddered as it climbed through the steel shaft, sparks raining down from damaged circuits. The alarms hadn't stopped, but now, a deeper, colder voice echoed through the station's failing speakers:

"Third Security Protocol Activated. Self-Destruct Sequence Initiated. Destruction in 30 seconds."

Everyone froze.

"What?!" Lana gasped, gripping the railing.

Marcus's face went pale. "It's a full burn protocol — thermite charges. They're going to incinerate the entire structure."

"Why would they—" Jillian started.

"To contain whatever we woke up!" Marcus snapped. "They didn't plan for survivors!"

The lift slammed against the upper lock with a mechanical jolt. The doors opened.

"20 seconds."

"Move!" Derek barked.

Boots pounded the corridor floors. They tore through the long tunnel back toward the main doors, the air already warming unnaturally, dust shaking from the ceiling above.

"Lana, get that damn door open!" Derek shouted.

"I'm trying!" she said, racing ahead to the keypad — already pre-entered from before. She hit the release. The massive steel doors groaned open like the mouth of a beast.

"10 seconds."

"Go!" Daryl shouted, grabbing Lee by the arm as they all shoved into daylight, lungs gasping cold, fresh air.

Derek was the last out. He dove, shoulder-first, through the narrowing door just as—

"3... 2... 1..."

BOOM.

The mountain behind them erupted. Fire, stone, and steel exploded outward as the earth trembled violently. The shockwave knocked them all to the ground. Heat rushed over their backs, and a wall of smoke billowed skyward, black and furious. Chunks of metal and charred concrete rained across the forest line. Trees near the outpost caught fire instantly. A low roar filled the air, like the world itself was screaming.

For a long moment, no one moved.

Derek slowly pushed himself up, ears ringing, coated in dust. "Roll call!" he rasped.

"Here," Jillian coughed, blood trickling from her lip.

"Daryl," came the reply. "I'm good."

"Lee—ugh—also here... barely."

"Lana!" Derek shouted.

A groan to his left. She was half-buried under a snapped tree branch. He rushed over, pulling it off with Daryl's help.

"I'm okay," she whispered, dazed. "I think."

Derek looked around at his team, huddled and battered — but alive. Then he turned and stared at what used to be Outpost 9 — now nothing but a flaming crater.

"What the hell were they hiding down there?" Jillian asked quietly.

Derek didn't answer. He didn't know.

But he knew one thing for certain.

> Someone had triggered that last protocol. And whoever sent the message 34 days ago…hadn't made it out.

Chapter 8

Smoke still rose from the smouldering mountain behind them as the teams limped back through the treeline, bruised, scraped, and haunted by what they had seen—and what they hadn't. The forest had gone eerily quiet.

The fallback site came into view through the thinning trees—an old ranger tower and a ring of cleared brush surrounding makeshift tents and perimeter posts. Bellamy stood first, his rifle half-raised until he saw their faces.

"They're back!" someone called.

Callum, Ross, and Anne rushed over as the rest of the New Haven team emerged from camp. Their expressions shifted quickly from relief to concern.

"What happened?" Bellamy asked, eyes jumping from the dust-caked figures to the distant smoke. "We saw the blast."

Derek didn't stop walking. He just shook his head. "Outpost 9 is gone," he said. "It's a hole in the side of a mountain now."

The silence that followed was immediate, crushing.

"What do you mean, gone?" Bellamy asked, catching up beside him.

"I mean whatever was left in there triggered a self-destruct protocol. Thermite. Security layers. Someone—or something—made sure the place didn't survive." He didn't mention the whispering. Or the glass cage. Or the final moments in that lift.

"Did anything... escape?" Bellamy asked low.

Derek's jaw tightened. "We didn't see anything make it out. But if something did... we'd know by now."

That wasn't confidence. That was hope.

—-

Later that afternoon, most of the group were recovering—patching wounds, downing water, loading up what remained of the supplies for the trip back to New Haven. Lana sat quietly with Lee and Daryl, comparing notes and mapping where Outpost 9 used to be. Callum was making plans to scout the blast site again in a few hours—just to be sure. But Derek wasn't with them. He'd walked back toward the bus and climbed aboard without a word, finding it mostly empty—except for Jillian, sitting in the back row with her legs tucked under her and her head resting against the window.

She didn't turn when he entered, but he knew she'd heard him. Derek moved slowly, his limbs aching. He took the seat across from her and leaned forward, arms resting on his knees.

"Too loud out there?" he asked softly.

"Too crowded," she replied, eyes still on the woods. "I just needed... a second."

He nodded. "Same."

The silence between them was comfortable this time, not loaded or awkward. Just quiet. A space to breathe. Jillian finally looked at him, her eyes softer than he remembered seeing in days. "That place... it felt wrong. Like something underneath it all was still alive. Did you feel it too?"

Derek nodded once. "Yeah. Whatever Outpost 9 was... it wasn't just a lab. It was something else."

They sat in that silence for a little longer. "You did good," she said after a moment. "You got us all out."

He looked down at his hands. "Barely."

"But you did," she repeated, firmer this time. "You always do."

He glanced up, their eyes locking. She gave him the faintest, tired smile. The kind of smile that said she understood—what it meant to carry everyone on your back. She stood and stretched slowly, muscles tight. "I'll leave you be." But as she reached the aisle, she paused—turning back slightly. Her voice softer now, more intimate.

"If you need company before we go," she said, stepping closer to him, "I'll be around." She leaned down and kissed him gently on the cheek—warm, lingering just long enough to mean something more than simple comfort.

Derek opened his mouth to say something, but for a second, nothing came out. He looked up at her, startled, searching her face for an explanation. But she just smiled—that same quiet, steady smile—and straightened again.

"Thanks," he finally said, voice low. "I might take you up on that."

Jillian gave a small nod, then stepped off the bus, leaving Derek alone with a thousand thoughts and the lingering warmth of her touch. He leaned back against the seat and exhaled.

Outpost 9 was gone. But not everything buried stays buried. He moved to the back and lay across the seats, eyes heavy after what had happened. He tried to sleep but every time he closed his eyes, all he could see was subject 001, staring and then running straight for them, ready to rip them all to shreds…he stood up and walked off the bus.

—-

Outside, the midday sun burned through a slate-grey sky. Wind pushed ash and dirt across the flattened ridgeline where the outpost had once stood. Bellamy zipped his jacket up to the neck, the scent of smoke and scorched metal still heavy in the air.

"Lock and load," Callum said, checking the magazine in his rifle before slinging it over his shoulder. "No chances."

The team assembled quickly—Callum, Bellamy, Ortega, Steph, Ross, Maggie, and Daryl. Their weapons were loaded, extra ammo packed tight. The path back to the blast zone wasn't far, but Derek had made one thing clear: assume something survived until proven otherwise. Derek met them at the perimeter. "Scout the edges. If you see movement, anything unusual, don't engage—radio first. If it's clean, document everything. Then get back."

Bellamy nodded. "We'll make sure there's nothing left to crawl out of that crater."

The seven of them disappeared into the trees, boots crunching dry leaves and soot. The rest of the crew prepared for departure. Vicki and Abby loaded canisters into the rear storage hold while Anne and Lee checked the side compartments and reinforced windows. Lana sat near the front of the bus with a notepad, cross-referencing supply inventories.

—-

Inside the old ranger shack, Jillian stood with Derek at a dusty table. A faded topographical map of the region was spread out between them, held flat by old ammo cans.

"Forest to the west's already been picked through," Derek muttered, tracing a line with his finger. "But here—" he pointed, "—abandoned fuel depot. Might still have fuel or tools."

Jillian watched him quietly for a second before replying, "You really don't stop, do you?"

He smirked. "Try not to. Stopping gets people killed."

She stepped around the table, shoulder brushing his. "Thank you," she said softly, "for getting me out of there. For always pulling me out when everything goes to hell."

"It's becoming a habit," Derek replied, his voice low, almost teasing.

Jillian smirked and gave him a playful slap. "Next time I'll be the one to pull you out."

"Believe it when I see it," Derek replied.

Outside, the wind howled against the shack's windows. Inside, for just a minute, they let the world disappear.

—-

The forest gave way to a sloped clearing, blackened trees framing a jagged scar in the side of the mountain. Smoke still curled from deep within the rubble, and the scent of scorched earth and synthetic compounds hung in the air like a warning.

Callum held up a clenched fist. The team halted a few paces behind him. Weapons at the ready, eyes scanning the massive crater ahead.

"What the hell," Ross muttered. "It's like something tore this place from the inside out."

"It did," Bellamy said grimly. "That was the facility's own self-destruct protocol."

Daryl took a few cautious steps forward, kicking aside a blackened panel. "Third security protocol, remember? Destruction in thirty seconds. This is what it looks like when a ghost burns its own house down."

"Whatever was still inside... didn't walk out," Maggie said, staring into the ruined remains of what had once been the entrance tunnel. "They blew it to stop something from getting out."

Callum knelt at the crater's edge, examining the twisted metal embedded in the slope. "Steel reinforced concrete, two meters thick. That blast came from deep inside. This place was meant to be buried."

Bellamy let out a low breath. "If something did make it out, we'd be seeing the aftermath by now. The town to the east. Burned. But it seemed quiet."

Daryl looked up the mountainside toward the treeline. "For now."

They spent the next half-hour searching near the site to see if there were any tracks or signs of something that had escaped. Maggie took photos with the solar camera. Finally, as the wind shifted and the last of the smoke began to fade, Callum keyed the radio on his shoulder. "Derek. Blast site secure. Nothing left to salvage or study. If something escaped, it's long gone. We're heading back."

"Copy. We'll have the bus ready. Good work."

As they turned away from the crater, Bellamy glanced back one last time. "Whatever happened in there... they wanted it erased. Let's hope they got what they wanted."

—-

Callum's team returned with confirmation: Outpost 9 was gone, reduced to scorched rock and ash. Whatever had lived beneath the mountain was now gone. The blast had left a crater where the entrance once stood, nothing remained but charred debris and a lingering smell of ozone and ash. They'd all stood in silence for a time, considering what had nearly escaped — and what it would have meant.

Derek spread a map across a weathered table. Everyone gathered around as he pointed out several marked zones they hadn't yet explored. "There's an old supply depot here," he said, tapping a road just east of the blast zone. "Maybe looted, maybe not. And here—" he traced his finger further along "—a small health centre. That's the priority."

They nodded. A quiet agreement.

Everyone walked toward the bus, rechecking gear and fuel supplies. As they loaded up, Derek lingered, eyes scanning the map one last time. He folded it neatly and turned — only to find Jillian waiting near the door. "Got a second?" he asked. She stepped aside with him, out of earshot of the others. His voice dropped low. "I've been thinking," Derek began, "about us—about everything that's happened between—"

But Jillian cut him off gently, a calm smile on her lips. "Listen," she said, "I'm not wanting to take you away from Jennifer, I'm here to help you forget the crazy... even if it's messy, even if it's just a moment of madness." She leaned closer, her voice barely above a whisper. "It's our secret."

For a moment, Derek said nothing. The tension, the weight of everything they'd lost and the things they'd nearly done, sat between them like smoke in the air. He opened his mouth, then closed it again. Words failed him. Instead, he just gave a subtle nod and climbed aboard the bus.

Steph was already in the driver's seat, engine rumbling steady beneath them. As soon as Derek stepped on, he slid the bus into gear and pulled away from the ranger station. They drove in silence for a while, watching the overgrowth blur by through the cracked windows. Tension gave way to a quiet focus.

Two hours passed.

When the silhouette of the small rural health centre rose from the treeline — intact, untouched — Steph slowed to a crawl. The bus came to a halt just outside. It was time to see what they could find.

—-

The moment the group stepped through the health centre's front doors, everything felt... wrong. The main reception area was still. Too still. Dust coated every surface like a thin grey film, undisturbed for months — maybe years. Magazines lay on waiting room chairs. A child's stuffed toy had fallen near the reception desk, long abandoned. The air was dry, stale, with the faintest trace of rot.

"Looks untouched," Maggie whispered, her voice barely audible.

"It's too clean," Daryl muttered, his crossbow already in his hands. "Places like this... they don't just stay untouched."

The team pushed past the double interior doors, their boots creaking against old linoleum as they stepped into the corridor beyond. And that's when everything changed.

The first room was an exam room — blood smeared across the bed. No body, but clear signs of a struggle.

The second room was worse. Blood pooled under the door, dried to a thick, rust-coloured smear. Inside, overturned medical trays, cracked glass, and a wheelchair on its side.

By the time they reached the third room, Derek raised a clenched fist. Everyone stopped. The room was painted with blood. Splatter up the walls. Drag marks across the floor. Scratch marks on the door.

"What the hell happened here?" Lee breathed.

Jillian was quiet, her hand resting on the grip of her pistol, eyes darting from shadow to shadow. They kept moving. Each room is more grotesque than the last. It was clear — something terrible had happened here, and recently.

Ortega, moving ahead near the nurse's station, held up his hand. "Something moved," he whispered.

Everyone froze.

The hallway was quiet again. A tension hung in the air, like the entire building was holding its breath. Then — a thump. In the darkened hallway beyond, something shifted. A shape darted across the corridor at the far end, too fast to catch a clear glimpse.

"Contact!" Daryl hissed, raising his crossbow.

"Hold!" Derek barked. "Could be a survivor!"

They fanned out, weapons raised, footsteps slow and deliberate. Another sound. Scuffling. Breathing. A weak cough. Then, a voice — barely a whisper.

"...help..."

It came from behind a door marked Storage – Authorized Personnel Only. Derek motioned to Jillian and Lana to flank the door, while Callum and Daryl aimed weapons. He reached for the handle slowly.

"Get ready," he muttered. Then he gave a sharp nod to Ortega, who kicked the door in with a loud crack. The door flew open—inside, hunched in the corner, pale, shivering, and barely conscious — was a woman in tattered scrubs. Her eyes were sunken. Her lips cracked. But she was alive.

"Please," she rasped. "Don't let them get me."

Behind her, in the dim room... more movement. And this time, the sound that followed wasn't a whisper. It was a snarl. They'd barely registered the woman's trembling form when a sudden crash at the window stole their attention. Six pale shapes—twisted, angular—pressed their gaunt faces against the cracked glass. Their eyes were empty voids, but the recognition in Derek's gut was instant: the same inhuman creatures they'd glimpsed in Outpost 9.

"Open fire!" Derek bellowed.

Maggie took the lead—her rifle barking twice in quick succession. Callum followed suit, shotgun booming through the corridor. Daryl and Ortega laid down supporting fire, rounds spitting sparks across the peeling wallpaper. The creatures recoiled—scrabbling at the bloody window frame as bullets tore into their shifting forms. One slammed back against the glass, blood blossoming across its chest. It crumpled in a heap, limbs splayed. The others, frantic, vanished down the corridor, silhouettes slipping into darkness as they scattered like smoke before a gale.

Silence crashed in behind the echo of gunfire.

Derek pressed his back against the wall, breathing hard. "Is everyone—"

"Alive," Jillian confirmed, checking beside her.

The injured woman on the floor let out a rattled sob. "They're... they're coming."

Derek dropped to one knee beside her, voice calm but urgent. "We've got you. You're safe now."

Behind them, the corridor lay dark and empty—save for the trail of blood and the echo of distant footsteps fading into the darkness. They'd held the line. But the hunt was far from over.

—-

"We need to leave!" the woman gasped, clutching Derek's arm. "They'll come back—with more."

Derek didn't wait. "Everyone, move! Now!"

The group fell into motion, urgent but controlled—until the howls began. The sound was like nothing human, echoing off the walls in a rising tide of fury and hunger. From the shadowy depths of the health centre, the creatures returned—more of them. Dozens.

"Back! BACK!" Daryl shouted, bolts and bullets flying as the team laid down covering fire. They sprinted for the main lobby, the hallway behind them narrowing with each second. Shapes poured from open doorways—too fast, too fluid. Each one is worse than the last. Near the entrance, the glass doors shattered as one creature burst through with horrifying speed. It pounced on Ross before anyone could react—its claws shredding his chest like wet paper. With a sickening lurch, it buried its face into the gaping wound, gnashing and tearing.

"ROSS!" Abby screamed.

Maggie and Steph fired at once—bullet after bullet slamming into the creature until its head exploded in a spray of black gore. Ross lay limp, his body a ruin.

"We have to go!" Lana shouted, pulling Abby by the arm.

Outside, the bus roared to life—Ortega already behind the wheel. The group stumbled out, gunfire still ringing behind them. Just as they reached the steps, a second creature darted from the side—snatching David and dragging him to the ground. Vicki shrieked as the monster slashed at him with razor-like claws.

"No!" she cried, lunging toward him. "Leave him alone, you bastard"

Callum grabbed Vicki before she got too close. Steph grabbed his shotgun, aimed point-blank at the creature's skull, and fired. The head snapped back in a mist of blood and bone—but it was too late. David was already gone, his body twitching.

"David's lost," Steph said grimly as Callum pulled Vicki toward the door. "We have to move!"

One by one, the survivors clambered into the bus—Daryl dragging Lana, Jillian covering the rear with Derek, and Bellamy at his side. The doors to the centre slammed open again—more of them. A flood of twisted limbs and screeching mouths. Bellamy didn't hesitate. He yanked a grenade from his vest, pulled the pin, and hurled it toward the swarm.

"Go! GO! GO!"

Jillian jumped on first then Derek and finally Bellamy. As he leapt into the bus the grenade detonated, a thunderous BOOM that shook the ground. Flames roared down the hallway, swallowing the creatures in a burning inferno. The few that remained turned and scattered like insects. The bus tore away from the ruined health centre, tires screeching, smoke curling behind them.

Inside, silence. Grief. Shock.

Ross and David were gone.

And whatever those creatures were—they were evolving. As the bus sped along the road, the weight of the mission bore heavily on the survivors. The crash of the explosion, the screams of their fallen comrades—it was all too much. Derek sat near the front, his eyes scanning the road but his mind far from the destination. Two of them had died—Ross, David—taken by the monsters they'd barely managed to escape from.

—-

The others sat in silence, some staring out the windows, others lost in their own grief. Bellamy sat across from Derek, his face hard, unreadable. The loss of life, the loss of time—it seemed to hit everyone differently.

Then there was the woman.

She had been quiet ever since they'd grabbed her on their way out of the health centre. But now, as Derek approached her, she looked up from her seat, her eyes dark, haunted.

Derek's voice was low, but his tone was direct. "We need answers. Who are you? What are you doing here? What the hell are those things?"

The woman met his gaze, her face still pale from the ordeal. Her voice came in a raspy whisper, "I'm no one important. I've been hiding—keeping low."

Derek tilted his head, skeptical. "Hiding from what?"

"From them." She glanced over her shoulder nervously, as if expecting the creatures to burst from the shadows any second. "I've seen them before. I've been running ever since the outbreak hit. After the world fell apart, I stayed out of sight—kept to the outskirts."

Derek's eyes narrowed. "You know what they are, don't you?"

She nodded slowly. "I was a researcher. Before... before everything went to hell. My team was working on the outbreak... trying to understand it, track it. We thought we had a solution. But we were wrong."

Derek frowned. "What do you mean? What happened?"

The woman swallowed hard, her gaze dropping to the floor as she seemed to wrestle with the words. "There was no solution. We thought we could cure it, reverse it... but it was too far gone. The virus—it mutates, adapts. We thought the antidote would work, but it was a lie. They told us it was tested, refined... but it wasn't. The moment we injected it, things... changed." Her voice broke slightly. "We unleashed something we couldn't control."

Derek stayed silent, waiting for her to continue. The weight of the world had been on his shoulders for far too long, but this—this felt like it could be something more. Something dangerous.

"After the initial outbreak," she continued, her voice steadying, "they called it a 'project,' a 'protocol.' They used us—used people to test theories, the virus, its progression. We watched it spread, and we couldn't stop it. The government sealed off everything, tried to clean up their mess. But it was too late. I don't know what happened to my team, to the others. I've been hiding ever since, running."

—-

Derek took a step forward, the weight of her words sinking in. "And the creatures?" he asked. "Are they part of this... project?"

She nodded grimly. "Yes. Those things... They were part of the testing. I think... they were failures—some were just experiments gone wrong. But others..." She hesitated, eyes clouded with fear. "Others are something else. The mutation, the aggression—it's evolving. Worse than the zombies you've seen."

Derek's blood ran cold. His hand instinctively went to his weapon at his side, though it wasn't out of fear of her—it was fear of what she might say next. "The real danger," she said, her voice now trembling, "is not just what you've seen. It's what's coming."

—-

Derek stood still, absorbing her words, then nodded slowly. He couldn't let his guard down—not with this new information. "Is that why you came with us?" he asked, suspicion thick in his voice.

She looked up, meeting his eyes, her gaze steady and direct. "I had no choice. I'm not looking to put anyone in harm's way. But if I stayed hidden much longer, they would have found me, and potentially killed all of you as well."

Derek didn't know what to say. There was too much happening—too much to process. But one thing was clear: they couldn't afford to leave her behind. "We'll keep you safe for now," Derek said, his voice low but firm. "But you need to be straight with us from now on. We don't have room for secrets."

The woman nodded, her expression softening for the first time. "I understand."

—-

As Derek turned to walk back to the others, his mind raced with what she'd said. The mission, the casualties, the fallout from what happened—it was all connected. And now, with this new information, the world seemed even darker than before. He didn't know what would come next, but he knew one thing for certain: the fight wasn't over. And it was only going to get worse.

As the bus drove home the survivors all sat in near silence, Jillian and Maggie were up the back, trying to console Vicki, Lee Daryl and Steph were quietly talking about how those creatures just tore Ross and David to bits with ease. Ortega and Bellamy switched out driving duties when they needed to. And Derek sat right at the front. Head in his hands, wondering what was coming next, and if this was ever going to end.

Chapter 9

The wind carried a stillness over New Haven, broken only by the rhythmic thuds of hammers and the occasional bark of orders from the guards on patrol. The second gate had been finished days earlier, and with it came a renewed sense of security—one they desperately clung to as time passed without word from the outpost teams.

Jennifer stood at the map table inside the meeting room, arms folded, brow furrowed. Her eyes drifted over the pins marking known locations, lingering on one that had been circled in red: Outpost 9. It had been over a week since Derek and the others had left. Every morning she expected a message. Every night, she stayed up wondering if something had gone wrong.

Bill sat across from her, flipping through radio logs. "Nothing. Not since three days ago," he muttered.

Jennifer sighed. "Maybe it's time we consider sending a search party."

"We don't even know what we'd be walking into," Bill replied. "They said they'd be gone a while. Derek's smart. Daryl too. If something had happened, I think we'd have known by now."

"I know," she said, rubbing her temple. "But it's the not knowing that kills me."

Just then, the knock came at the door. It was Ashley, followed by Mary and Father Luke. Behind them trailed Jonas, their newest volunteer helping with construction.

"We wanted to run some ideas past you," Jonas said as they entered. "About the new defensive sections."

Jennifer welcomed the distraction. "Go ahead."

Jonas unrolled a hand-drawn layout of the expanded perimeter. "I was thinking we could turn this section here into a second-tier wall, like a buffer. That way, if the main line is ever breached, we fall back and still hold strong."

Ashley chimed in. "And we've been talking about adding a watchtower to the south treeline. Visibility's weak in that sector, and it wouldn't take much to build something tall enough."

Mary added, "And I've got an idea for a raised garden plot behind the south wing. Elevated beds, well-protected, good for rotation crops."

Jennifer nodded, clearly impressed. "You've all been busy."

"We've had time," Father Luke said gently. "And we figured you could use the help while most of the council's away."

"Thank you," Jennifer said sincerely, exchanging a glance with Bill. "We'll go over these in detail this afternoon."

Before another word could be spoken, a shout rang out from above.

"Bus! It's the bus!"

It was Lexi—sharp-eyed as always. The young girl leaned over the wall near the new gate, pointing down the road.

Jennifer and Bill rushed outside, pushing through the gathering crowd. Others followed quickly—faces filled with a mix of hope and uncertainty.

And then, there it was.

The bus, armoured and dust-covered, rumbling down the path from the horizon. Its engine groaned under strain, but it moved steadily toward home.

Jennifer's breath caught in her throat.

"They're back," she whispered.

Bill squinted. "But how many of them?"

As the bus approached, slowing to a crawl, no one said a word.

Not until it stopped, and the door creaked open.

—-

The armoured bus hissed to a stop, its engine sputtering in protest. Dirt and dried blood streaked the windows. Its once-white paint now looked more rust than steel. Silence blanketed New Haven's main yard as the residents gathered, waiting.

The door swung open.

Derek was the first to step off.

His face, normally composed even in chaos, was hard. Weathered. Grief weighed in his eyes. Behind him came Jillian, followed by Callum—his limp heavier than before. Maggie, Steph, Vicki, Bellamy, Abby, and the others followed in grim succession.

Jennifer stepped forward instinctively, but Derek raised a hand—not to push her away, but to signal: wait.

He turned to the gathered crowd. Everyone was here now — Bill, Father Luke, Jonas, Mary, Ashley, even some of the older kids, wide-eyed and quiet.

Derek took a breath, steadying himself.

"We made it back," he began. "But not all of us did."

He looked toward the ground, then raised his eyes again. "We lost David and Ross. At a medical centre we thought it was untouched. Something was waiting for us. Something... like the things we saw at Outpost 9."

Gasps rippled through the crowd. Jillian shifted beside him, her arms folded tightly.

"I won't lie to you," Derek continued. "Whatever was in that place—it's not natural. It's worse than anything we've faced. Faster, smarter. It killed two good men before we even knew what hit us."

He glanced toward Jennifer, who was frozen in place, tears gathering in her eyes.

"But we got out," Derek added. "We brought back what we could. Supplies. Information. And now, we've got decisions to make. New ones." He looked around, meeting as many eyes as he could. "Rest today. Hug your families. But tomorrow morning, we meet. Council and civilians alike. Everyone deserves to know what we're facing."

A silence followed.

Then Bellamy stepped forward, voice low. "We burn the bus. It's contaminated. Don't want those things tracing it back."

Derek gave a single nod. "Do it."

The survivors slowly began to disperse. Some hugged those returning. Others wept quietly, learning of Ross or David's fate. A few stood in silent vigil. Jennifer walked up to Derek and wrapped her arms around him, tightly, wordlessly. He didn't say anything. Just let himself breathe her in. Behind them, the hiss of the bus's fuel line signaled its end. And with a single spark, the fire burned high into the afternoon sky.

—-

As the evening light fell over New Haven, the fire from the bus still crackled outside the walls, but the crowd had mostly dispersed. Grief lingered in the air like smoke. Inside one of the rec room cells, Vicki sat on the edge of a bunk, her hands trembling. The room was dimly lit, shadows dancing on the walls. Her eyes were red and swollen, her breathing uneven. David's name had barely left her lips since they'd returned. Jillian knelt beside her, gently rubbing her back. Jennifer stood near the doorway, arms crossed, her eyes brimming as she watched Vicki crumble.

"I should've... I should've done something," Vicki sobbed, her voice breaking. "I saw it take him, I—he screamed, and I froze. I didn't even move."

"You couldn't have saved him," Jillian said softly. "None of us could. We tried. You tried."

"I let him die."

"No," Jennifer said firmly, stepping into the room. "You loved him. And he knew that. That's what matters now. Not the moment... but the life you shared."

Vicki shook her head, burying her face in her hands. "He was all I had left."

Behind them, Mary and Ashley slipped into the room, each carrying a blanket and a mug of hot tea. Father Luke lingered outside the door, head bowed in silent prayer. Mary handed the tea to Jillian and sat on the opposite side of the bunk.

"He was one of the kindest men here," she whispered. "He helped Jonas build the west fence. Do you remember? He got sunburned so badly, and still refused to stop until it was finished."

That memory, faint and distant, made Vicki let out a choked laugh between sobs.

"He gave my daughter that wooden charm she wears," Ashley added quietly. "Said it was from an old keychain he found, but she treasures it."

The women sat together in silence after that — a quiet circle of shared sorrow and strength. They didn't try to fix what couldn't be fixed. They didn't rush her grief. They simply stayed. And in a world that had fallen apart, that was something.

—-

As the evening was drawing in, the sound of conversation had dwindled across the courtyard. What was once relief at the return of the expedition had turned to a quiet, somber mood. Loss always had a way of reminding the community how fragile their safety truly was.

Inside the canteen, Callum sat alone at a table, staring at the bottle of home-brewed liquor Ross had helped him ferment just weeks earlier. The cap was still sealed, dust clinging to the glass. He hadn't opened it — couldn't. Anne approached slowly, a tin of food in one hand, her face pale and drawn.

"You alright?" she asked, pulling out the chair beside him.

"No," Callum admitted, not bothering to look up. "He was standing right next to me. One second we're watching the hallway... next, he's gone."

Anne placed the food down and leaned forward, elbows on the table. "Ross didn't have family here. Just us. Just New Haven. We were it."

Callum nodded slowly. "He told me once that he never felt like he belonged anywhere. Said this place was the first time he'd actually unpacked a bag."

A long silence followed. Finally, Callum exhaled. "He deserved better."

"We all do," Anne murmured. "But Ross... he was part of the glue that kept people steady. He listened. He didn't talk much, but when he did—he made it count."

—-

Elsewhere in the yard, Jonas and Father Luke were setting up a pair of small wooden markers along the north wall, where they'd created a makeshift memorial garden for the fallen. Ross and David's names were carefully etched into salvaged metal plates.

Behind them, Lee and Lana worked silently, digging a small trench to plant flowers from the old greenhouse. Flowers Ross had once cared for during the spring.

"This was his thing," Lana said, breaking the quiet. "He used to joke that if the apocalypse didn't kill him, his allergies would."

Lee chuckled under his breath. "He said that to me too. Every time he watered those plants, he sneezed like it was the end of days."

They fell quiet again, the weight of memory settling in. At the far end of the training yard, Maggie leaned against the fence with Steph, arms crossed. She looked toward the lights of the shelter entrance, her voice low.

"We're losing too many good ones."

Steph nodded. "And too damn fast."

"You saw what they were. The ones that killed David and Ross. That wasn't normal."

"No," he said. "It wasn't."

They stood in silence, knowing deep down that more loss was inevitable — but hoping for just one peaceful night.

Back in the canteen, Callum finally opened the bottle. He didn't drink it. Instead, he poured two small cups and set them across from each other, one for him... and one for Ross.

"To the quiet ones," he said under his breath. "To the ones who kept us sane."

He raised his cup and drank alone.

—-

As night approached, Derek was in the meeting room with Bill and Jennifer, explaining what had happened. Derek sat across from Jennifer and Bill, the exhaustion lining his face matched only by the grimness in his voice. The flickering oil lamp between them cast deep shadows as he recounted everything: Outpost 9, the lift, the creatures, and the explosion that destroyed it all.

"They weren't zombies," Derek said firmly. "They moved fast—too fast. Smarter too. One of them set off a containment breach countdown. That wasn't a feral reaction... that was instinct. Or memory. Or something worse."

Jennifer leaned back in her chair, hand on her forehead. "And these things were created? Engineered?"

"From what the scientists said, yeah," Derek confirmed. "And that woman we brought back... she knows something. She was already in the medical centre when the creatures showed up."

Bill crossed his arms. "You think she brought them?"

Derek shook his head. "She ran. Warned us. Saved us, in a way. But she still won't say who she is."

Jennifer exhaled slowly, then nodded to the guards outside. "Bring her in."

Moments later, the woman was escorted into the room by Daryl and Father Thomas. Her expression was cold, unreadable. Dirt and dried blood smudged her lab coat, her posture rigid and silent. She remained standing, her eyes watching the trio of leaders but offering no answers.

"Who are you?" Bill asked bluntly.

Silence.

Jennifer leaned forward. "You saw what happened back there. We buried people because of those things. If you know something—anything—you need to talk."

Still, the woman remained silent.

Just then, the sound of footsteps in the hall drew their attention. Dr. Aria Hensley passed by the room but stopped when she caught a glimpse of the woman.

Her eyes widened.

She stepped into the doorway slowly, voice cautious and tinged with disbelief. "...Is that...?" Her voice trailed off as memories surged forward. The silent woman shifted slightly. Her expression faltered.

"I thought you were dead," Dr. Hensley murmured. "We all did."

Derek stood. "You know her?"

Hensley nodded, stepping into the room. "Dr. Linnea Carr. She was one of the original virologists working on the Chimera strain. Pre-outbreak. We collaborated—once."

Finally, the woman—Linnea—spoke, her voice low and tired.

"Collaborated," she repeated. "Is that what we're calling it now?"

—-

Inside the infirmary's back office, Dr. Aria Hensley sat alone with Dr. Linnea Carr. For the first time in years, two women once united by scientific pursuit and later separated by catastrophe faced one another not as colleagues, not even as survivors—but as remnants of something far more broken.

Aria set a cup of tea down in front of Linnea. "You were always the one who vanished without warning. But when the outbreak happened... I assumed you'd died in the first wave."

Linnea allowed herself a faint, bitter smile. "I almost did. Three times. But death isn't what scares me anymore."

There was a moment of quiet. The sound of wind brushing the infirmary windows. The world outside moving on, oblivious to the storm rekindling inside this room.

"So," Aria said, leaning forward, her voice hushed. "What were they?"

"The creatures?" Linnea asked.

Aria nodded. "The ones Derek's team saw. You know what they are."

Linnea's eyes darkened. "They were never part of the original Chimera sequence. They were... additions. Forced evolutions." She took a shaky breath.

"All our early work was meant to be controlled. Chimera wasn't supposed to spread—it was designed for isolation. Specific to neural degradation and reanimation. But someone up the chain—government, military, I never knew who—started demanding escalation. Adaptation. They wanted something more than a reanimated corpse."

"Why?" Aria asked. "What purpose could that serve?"

"They wanted a weapon," Linnea replied flatly. "Something smarter than a bullet. More obedient than a drone. Creatures that could survive any terrain, any war zone, and take out specific targets without leaving a trace. Something that couldn't be reasoned with."

"And that's what those things are?"

Linnea nodded slowly. "They're Alpha variants. We called them 'Reapers.' Designed to learn. To stalk. To hunt."

Aria's breath caught. "And they escaped."

"No," Linnea said. "They were released."

—-—

A knock came at the door. Derek stepped inside, quiet and unreadable.

"Well?" he asked, looking between them.

Aria rose slowly. "She's telling the truth," she said. "And if what she says is accurate... then we are in major trouble."

Derek nodded grimly. "Then maybe it's time we start taking the fight outside of these walls."

—-—

As the heavy silence from Linnea's revelation still hung in the room, Dr. Aria Hensley stood up, her eyes calm but resolute. She reached into her coat pocket and pulled out a small black recording device — an old handheld tape recorder, patched together with cracked plastic and worn buttons.

She handed it to Derek.

"What's this?" he asked, eyeing it with caution.

"The entire conversation," she said. "Every word."

Linnea's head snapped up. "You recorded me?"

Aria didn't flinch. "Yes."

"You had no right—" Linnea stood abruptly, her chair scraping loudly against the floor.

"I had every right," Aria said, her voice sharp but steady. "You came into this place carrying the weight of something everyone here deserves to know. If you had kept your mouth shut, we'd still be in the dark."

Linnea's jaw clenched. "That information could cause mass panic."

"And silence could cause mass extinction," Aria snapped. "You said it yourself — they wanted the world to fall. Well, it didn't. We're still here. That means we fight, and fighting means facing the truth. All of it."

—-—

Linnea's furious gaze darted to Derek, but he was already looking toward the door.

"Daryl. Steph."

The door opened, and the two stepped inside, both armed, eyes already trained on Dr. Carr. "Escort her to a holding cell. She's not a prisoner — but she's not walking free until we figure out what else she's hiding."

"You can't—" Linnea started, but Daryl was already moving behind her.

"Let's go, doc," he said firmly. "Don't make this harder than it needs to be."

Steph took position on the other side, and together they guided the still-protesting Linnea out of the room. Once the door shut, a long exhale left Derek's lungs. He looked down at the recorder in his hand.

"Thank you, Dr. Hensley," he said quietly.

—-

Aria gave him a faint smile. "Please," she said, softening slightly, "just call me Aria."

Derek gave a single, appreciative nod. "Aria."

They stood in silence for a moment. Then Derek turned toward the door. "Council meeting's in the morning," he said. "I'd like you to be there. They'll need to hear it from you directly."

"I'll be there," Aria replied, composed but tired. "We all will."

—-

As Derek stepped out of the office and into the night air, he tucked the recorder into his jacket.

The truth was now out.

And nothing would be the same again.

Chapter 10

The morning sun filtered weakly through the reinforced windows of the council chamber. A thick tension hung in the air — not of hostility, but anticipation. The long table at the centre of the room was fully occupied for the first time in weeks.

Derek sat at the head, his expression unreadable. To his left sat Jennifer, Jillian, Callum, and Daryl. On his right — Bill, Maggie, Anne, Bellamy, and Munroe. At the far end of the table were Lee and Aria, silent but alert.

In the corner, guarded by Steph and Father Luke, sat Dr. Linnea Carr — her expression guarded, her hands bound in front of her more for show than necessity.

Derek set the small black recorder down in the centre of the table and pressed play.

Linnea's voice crackled through the static:

> "This was planned... long before the outbreak. Everything — the Chimera strain, the suppression, the 'cure'... they didn't want to save the world. They wanted to reset it."

"And the creatures? They weren't accidents. They were test subjects, spliced with whatever DNA we had access to. We were meant to push evolution — to control it."

"But we lost control. And they let us."

Silence followed as the tape clicked to an end. Derek leaned forward, eyes fixed on Linnea.

"This is your only chance," he said. "Answer our questions — truthfully — or that cell is your new home. Permanently."

Linnea nodded, her voice calm but resigned. "Ask."

—-

Callum was first. "The ones we saw at Outpost 9 — what the hell were they?"

"Hybrids," Linnea said. "Technically Chimera-Class IV. We engineered them to be faster, stronger, more resilient. We used human DNA combined with select animal traits — mostly for muscle density and sensory enhancement. We thought they could be controlled."

"You thought?" Maggie snapped. "They tore through our people like paper."

"They were never meant to be released," Linnea said quickly. "They were stored. Contained. But when the base failed... everything failed."

Daryl leaned forward. "So why weren't they feral like regular infected? They acted in coordination. They set traps."

Linnea hesitated. "The Class IVs had rudimentary neural links — basically they can share signals, instincts. Not quite telepathy, but close. Think of them like a wolf pack... or worse."

Jennifer's voice was quiet. "You said they were meant to evolve. Is that... still happening?"

Linnea nodded grimly. "Yes. They learn. Fast. They adapt to environments. If they've been loose since Outpost 9 fell, they're not the same creatures anymore."

Bellamy spoke up. "Could they... spread? Infect others?"

"No," Linnea said. "They don't carry the Chimera virus in the same way. But... they can reproduce. That's the true danger. If even a few survived... they could build numbers. Breed unpredictably."

The room fell still.

Anne's voice wavered. "And how many of these things were in Outpost 9?"

Linnea closed her eyes briefly. "Twelve. We lost two during containment. That left ten. You killed some... but if even two survived..."

"...It's enough," Aria finished grimly.

Derek stood, running a hand down his face.

"This changes everything." He looked around at the others. "They're not just mindless infected anymore. They're... something else. And if they're still out there..." He didn't need to finish the sentence. Everyone in the room understood. A new enemy had emerged.

And it was no longer just the dead they had to fear.

—-

The council chamber was heavy with silence. Derek remained standing, arms crossed, the room filled with hushed murmurs and wide, anxious eyes.

Bellamy finally broke the quiet. "Look — it took thirteen of us with full gear to take down a few of those creatures. If they swarm? If even half of them are still alive and breeding? We're talking about an existential threat."

"Then we kill the rest," Daryl said flatly. "Hunt them down before they come back stronger."

"Where?" Callum asked. "We torched the medical centre. Outpost 9's gone. Any survivors scattered. We don't even know where to start."

Maggie shifted in her seat. "We start by protecting this place. We make New Haven a fortress. Traps. Barricades. Fallback lines."

Bill nodded. "We've still got the inner trench, the outer fence, and the lookout towers. But we need more. Tripwires. Pressure sensors. Noise traps. Something that'll slow them down."

"We can dig angled pits," Munroe added. "Wooden spikes at the base. Primitive, but effective. If they move like predators, we treat 'em like animals."

Jillian leaned forward. "We also need contingency plans. If they get inside the walls, what then? Where do the civilians go?"

Jennifer replied quietly, "We move them to the shelter. Lock the inner hatch from inside. It's our last line of defense."

Lee sighed. "All well and good... but we've only got what? Fifteen? Twenty people trained with guns or bows?"

"Seventeen," Bellamy corrected. "And even that's stretching it."

"Then we train more," Derek said. "No more 'civilians' — not when there threat's like this. Anyone who can stand, hold, and aim gets a weapon. We make time for drills. Pair up. Rotate watches. Learn fast."

"And we need more weapons," Bellamy added. "We're low on ammo, low on bows, and even lower on quality blades. We can't hold a wall with scrap metal and good intentions."

Anne leaned forward, worry etched across her face. "But where do we find more weapons?"

Bellamy looked up from his folded hands. "Kinross."

A hush fell over the room.

"There was a weapons storage facility I had kept sealed," he explained. "Tucked beneath the barracks. Only I had the key. We never used it during the fighting — it was meant to be a last resort."

Daryl scoffed, arms crossed. "That place could be crawling with the dead. Or worse — claimed by drifters by now."

"Still," Bill interjected, "worth a shot."

Aria looked up from her quiet contemplation. "And if there are more labs... more outposts like 9... we need to know. I suggest combing Lana's files again, and start building a map of suspected locations. If we're going to survive, we need to know everything."

"I'll help with that," Lana said from the corner.

Callum glanced at Derek. "So what's the move?"

Derek took a breath, staring out the window as if he could see the dangers approaching even now.

"We do both," he said. "We lock down New Haven — reinforce every wall, train everyone who can fight. Meanwhile, we send out scavenging runs — weapons, supplies, clues. We don't sit around waiting for monsters to knock on our gate." He stood, scanning the room with firm eyes. "I want plans. We're organizing now. Scavenging teams for weapons — Daryl, Bellamy, you'll take point. Recon teams — Callum, Munroe, your het. Supplies — Maggie, Anne, that's on you."

He looked to the rest. "Groups of three or four. I want team rosters and route suggestions by sundown. No lone wolves. No half-assed ideas. Tomorrow morning, we move."

Everyone gave a solemn nod, understanding the gravity of what was ahead.

—-

Derek's voice dropped slightly. "Steph," he called toward the door, "take Dr. Carr back to her cell. I'll be along shortly."

Steph approached the woman silently, motioning toward the exit. Dr. Carr said nothing, only met Derek's eyes one last time before turning to leave under quiet escort. Chairs scraped. Council members murmured as they filed out, some heading straight to gather their assigned teams. As always, Derek lingered behind, finishing notes, staring at the map marked with fresh red pins and circled dangers.

Jennifer hadn't left either. She moved toward the door, then paused — and turned back. Quietly, she closed it behind her with a soft click of the lock.

He looked up as she stepped toward him, her expression unreadable. In the space between heartbeats, she wrapped her arms around him, leaned in, and kissed him — deeply, silently, with the weight of everything they hadn't said in weeks. When they finally broke apart, her voice was a whisper.

"It's been too long."

Derek didn't answer right away. Instead, he kissed her again, slower this time. The maps and missions could wait — for a moment, at least. This was their anchor in a world spinning mad. In that quiet, candlelit room, they finally let themselves be close again.

Together — if only for tonight.

—-

The corridor to the holding cells was cold and quiet, the walls damp with the weight of history and secrecy. Derek walked alone, his boots echoing with every step. Steph stood just outside the door, giving a short nod. "She's waiting."

Derek entered. The door closed behind him with a sharp clack.

Dr. Carr was seated on the bench, her posture calm, but her eyes carried something unreadable — guilt, or calculation, he wasn't sure.

"You said the creatures could reproduce," Derek began, arms crossed. "That was enough to scare half the council. But I've got a feeling you're still holding back."

A long silence.

Then: "Yes," she said softly. "There's more."

—

Later that evening in the council meeting room, everyone was seated. The full council had gathered: Derek, Jennifer, Jillian, Callum, Daryl, Bill,

Maggie, Anne, Bellamy, Munroe, Lee, and Aria. The air was heavy with tension as Derek stepped forward, a tape recorder in his hand. "This is the last of it," he said. "Her final confession. Listen."

He clicked play.

Carr's voice filled the room — calm, clinical, horrifying. By the end, no one spoke. Aria looked devastated. Maggie's jaw was clenched. Daryl's eyes burned with fury.

"She knew all this," Callum said bitterly. "And waited until now?"

"She's lucky we didn't leave her in that lab," Bill muttered.

Bellamy exhaled through his nose. "Reproduction every twelve days. That's not an infection. That's a damn plague."

"What do we do with her?" Lee asked.

"She stays locked up for now," Derek said. "She talks when we need her. No more lies."

—-

Derek remained standing at the head of the council table, the room still tense from the recording they'd just heard and the horrors it had confirmed. The weight of the world — what was left of it — pressed heavily on his shoulders. He glanced across the table, his voice steady but urgent. "Have you picked your teams yet?"

One by one, the group leaders nodded.

—-

The meeting room slowly emptied, council members filing out one by one, murmuring plans and whispered worries under their breath. Jennifer was the last to leave — or so Derek thought. She paused beside him, leaning close to his ear. "Don't be long," she whispered, her hand briefly brushing his arm in affection before she slipped into the corridor and was gone.

Derek remained at the head of the table, hunched over his notes. A list of team names. Routes. Contingency plans. The kind of things leaders wrote when the world outside kept finding new ways to fall apart.

He didn't hear the door quietly close again behind him. Arms slid around his shoulders, soft but firm, and before he could even register the presence, warm lips pressed against the side of his neck, then his jaw, and then his mouth. He turned instinctively — and saw her.

"Jillian—" he breathed, startled. "This is too risky. Someone could walk in."

She tilted her head, her voice smooth and teasing. "It's only a kiss. For now."

Then, she kissed him again — longer, slower — and this time, he didn't stop her.

When she finally pulled away, her lips hovered near his ear.

"I'll be in the old guard house tonight," she whispered. "In case someone needs to... forget the world for a little while." She gave him a small wink, then turned and walked away, the soft click of the door behind her the only sound left in the room.

Derek stood motionless.

His heart was thudding.

His thoughts tangled.

The weight of what was coming pressed on his shoulders again, heavier than before.

Now wasn't the time for this. But the temptation lingered like the echo of her kiss.

Chapter 11

Morning had barely touched the sky when the yard of New Haven stirred with motion.

The adults gathered — bleary-eyed, tense — as Derek stood atop the central platform beside the watchtower. His voice was steady but urgent, his expression unreadable.

"Most of you know we've been away investigating Outpost 9," he began. "What we found... was worse than we imagined."

Murmurs rippled through the crowd.

He continued. "There are creatures out there — not just the infected we're used to. Smarter, faster, deadlier. We believe they're tied to the Chimera strain — experiments done on the dead after the fall."

Gasps. Quiet curses. Someone whispered "mutants" beneath their breath.

"We don't know how many are out there, or how close they've gotten. But we're preparing. Teams are already out gathering supplies, weapons, and intel. New Haven will not be caught off guard." He paused, letting the weight of his words settle. "We've discovered they're highly sensitive to human sweat. It draws them. So, starting today, we'll be collecting it — for study, and if needed, for luring them into traps. Jennifer is organising this."

Jennifer, already dressed in athletic gear, stepped forward with a nod. "We're setting up a gym space on the roof of A-block. Anyone fit to exercise, come see me. Bring spare clothes, towels — anything that'll absorb."

With nods of agreement, the crowd dispersed — some toward their duties, others already anxious to be part of the plan.

As bodies moved and the yard began to empty, Derek caught sight of Jillian slipping away toward the northern fence line. He moved to intercept her.

"Jillian," he called quietly. She turned, eyes searching his face. "We need to talk," he said. She stepped closer. There was no one else within earshot. "This can't keep happening," Derek said. "Jennifer... I can't do that to her."

Jillian nodded slowly. "I don't want to hurt her either. But I also don't want to lose this," she said, cutting him off gently. "This thing between us, whatever it is... it's not about love. It's about escape. About forgetting how close we are to the edge every single day." Derek looked away, jaw tight. "I know I can't have all of you," she continued, voice softer now. "But if I can have a part of you... even just in the shadows, when it's safe... I'll take that. I'm not asking for more." He said nothing. She stepped even closer, eyes locked on his. "It's our secret, Derek. I'll protect it with everything I have."

A long silence stretched between them before he finally gave a faint nod. She touched his hand, then slipped away, disappearing back into the crowd as the day's work began. But the weight in Derek's chest only grew heavier.

New Haven was preparing for war.

And he was still battling one inside.

—-

The road back to the ruins of the health centre was quiet — eerily so. Callum sat behind the wheel of the small scout jeep, flanked by Munroe and Lee. The tires crunched softly over gravel, the occasional rustle of birds or wind the only sounds breaking the silence. Each man kept their eyes on the surroundings, nerves stretched tight. The last time anyone stood here, two men had died. Ross. David. Now, they returned not for vengeance, but clarity.

"We get in, follow the trail, get out," Callum said. "No heroics. No detours."

"Understood," Munroe nodded, tightening his rifle strap.

Lee gave a quiet "Yep," and adjusted his crossbow.

They parked a short distance from the health centre and approached on foot. The building was still charred from the grenade blast. Its windows shattered. The front doors hung ajar, scorched and broken. Inside, the hallway remained littered with bullet casings and scorched debris. They moved cautiously from room to room, flashlights sweeping through the darkened corridors.

"No sign of them," Munroe muttered. "No bodies either."

Lee knelt by the floor, pointing at blackened smear trails. "They came back after we left. Dragged the remains. Or fed."

Callum's jaw clenched as he traced the dried fluid. "Let's follow it."

Outside, the trail led through broken brush and torn-up earth. As they moved further into the forest, the ground grew softer, damp with moss. Lee held up a hand. "There."

A dark burrow. Roughly dug. Almost like a den. They approached slowly, weapons raised. Inside was something worse than they could've imagined. Bones — some animal, others unmistakably human — littered the base of the den. Shredded clothes, bits of torn gear... all piled around a strange egg-like structure nestled deep in the centre.

It pulsed faintly. Veined. About the size of a beach ball. Its surface shimmered slightly, as though it were moist. A low hum — so faint it was almost imagined — filled the air around it.

"What the hell is that?" Lee whispered.

Munroe took a step back. "I don't want to find out."

"Nope," Callum said, voice firm. "We're done here."

The three of them turned, weapons still raised, backing away from the unnatural nest.

"We say nothing until we talk to Derek," Callum said. "No one. Not until the council hears it first."

Munroe and Lee nodded in grim agreement. Moments later, the jeep tore away from the forest trail, the trees behind them swallowing the den — and the single egg left growing inside it.

—-

The early morning light crept across the shattered parking lot of Silverburn. From a distance, the shopping centre looked almost untouched — a relic from the world before. But as the women drew closer, the illusion fell apart. Cars were scattered everywhere, some flipped, others burned out. Shopping carts rusted in place. Debris littered the asphalt like the aftermath of a forgotten riot.

"We keep this tight," Maggie ordered, her voice low. "No unnecessary risks. In and out."

Anne took point beside her, while Sarah and Mary flanked. They moved silently through the main entrance — its glass doors smashed open long ago.

Inside, the place smelled of mold and dust. The air was stale, but not decayed. Nothing rotted here — just settled.

"Stay sharp," Anne murmured.

They advanced through the first corridor. Some shops were completely ransacked — empty racks, shattered displays, graffiti scrawled across broken storefronts. But others seemed untouched. A few clothing stores had racks full of clothes, some sealed behind locked gates. In one corner shop, they found a half-looted pharmacy. Sarah and Mary swept it carefully, gathering what remained — a few basic supplies, bandages, even some outdated but sealed antibiotic creams.

"Better than nothing," Mary muttered, stuffing the goods into her pack.

In the food court, the chaos was worse. Tables were overturned, chairs scattered. Food wrappers and cans crunched underfoot. Most of the stalls were either burned out or stripped bare. But among the ruins, they found several packets of powdered soup and instant mash in the corner of a crumpled dry goods outlet.

"Still sealed," Anne said, surprised. "Take it."

Suddenly—movement.

Maggie's fist shot up. All four froze, weapons raised.

"Who's there?" Maggie barked. "Step into the light!"

No reply.

They crept toward the sound, through a service hallway behind the food stalls. Room by room they cleared offices — a dusty candle store office, a perfume shop's break room, even an old maintenance closet. Nothing.

Then Sarah found a map — an old emergency exit plan. She tapped the faded marker with her glove.

"Look — says there's a rest shelter behind the cold storage."

"Employee-only," Anne said, eyes narrowing. "Let's check it."

Behind a shattered counter of a noodle bar, they found it — a hatch camouflaged beneath fallen signage and broken tile. With some effort, they pried it open and descended a narrow stairwell lit only by flickering sunlight from above.

Flashlights on, the women stepped into a dim, cold room lined with old cots. Dust floated in the still air. Someone had been here recently — empty water bottles, food wrappers, a ragged blanket tucked into a corner.

"There's been someone here," Mary said.

A sound.

Soft. Shuffling.

Weapons raised again.

Then — from the shadows — a small voice: "Don't shoot!"

A teenage girl stepped forward, thin, pale, hands raised. Behind her, a younger boy peeked out — no more than seven years old, wide-eyed and terrified.

"I'm Emily," the girl said quickly. "This is my brother, Tommy."

"We're not infected," she added, her voice shaking.

Maggie lowered her shotgun just slightly. "How long?"

Emily's eyes brimmed. "I don't know. Weeks. We stayed here. Dad... he was with us. But he got sick."

"You locked the door?" Anne asked gently.

Emily nodded.

Mary exhaled slowly, her expression softening.

"You're safe now," Sarah said. "We've got people. Food. A place."

Emily looked to her brother. Tommy didn't say anything, but clung tightly to her hand.

"We move now," Maggie said. "Fast. If they've been here this long, there's no telling what might be tracking them."

They emerged from the dark, escorting the children out through the cracked husk of the food court. Outside, the sunlight felt sharp — too bright after the shadowy shelter below.

As they crossed the car park, Maggie glanced back once — at the shattered building, at the emptiness behind it.

"Let's get them home," she said.

Sarah gave a firm nod. "Yeah. Before the world remembers they were forgotten."

And together, the four women — and two new survivors — made their way back to the bus.

—-

The SUV rumbled quietly down the winding road as the morning sun crested the horizon, casting a pale light across the battered countryside. In the distance, the crumbling outline of Kinross began to appear—but it didn't look like the ghost town they expected.

Bellamy leaned forward in the passenger seat, brow furrowed. "Something's wrong," he muttered.

Daryl slowed the vehicle to a crawl. "Place looks... patched up."

And it did. The scorched gates of Kinross were no longer blown wide open. They'd been partially rebuilt, reinforced with salvaged steel sheets and timber. One of the towers had been restored—crudely but effectively—and from its height, a man stood watch, rifle in hand. The SUV rolled closer until the guard raised his weapon and shouted.

"Hold! You're entering Kinross territory. Trespassers will be executed by order of Ellis."

Bellamy's blood ran cold.

Daryl snapped his eyes to him. "Did he just say—?"

"Ellis is dead," Bellamy said, heart pounding.

Steph and Ortega looked equally stunned in the backseat.

Bellamy rolled the window down and leaned out. "We're traders!" he called up. "Food. Ammo. Looking to barter."

The man narrowed his eyes, scanning them from his vantage point. "You're a long way from anywhere safe," he said. "Wait there."

He turned and spoke into a hand radio.

Daryl muttered, "We're not gonna like this, are we?"

"Be cool," Bellamy whispered. "We need to know what the hell's going on here."

A few tense minutes passed before the radio crackled and the guard waved them forward. The gates opened slowly, revealing a town that shouldn't exist like this anymore. It was functioning—sort of. People moved around in the distance. Some were hauling scrap. Others stood watch with makeshift weapons. There were children, too. And the buildings... many were still ruins, but a few had been repaired. Kinross wasn't a ghost town—it was rebuilding.

"This doesn't make sense," Steph whispered. "We watched it fall."

Bellamy nodded grimly. "This isn't what I left behind."

The SUV rolled through the gate and came to a stop inside. Two more guards approached, hands on weapons but not drawn.

"Park there," one ordered. "Don't make any sudden moves."

Bellamy stepped out first, raising both hands calmly. "We come in peace."

The second guard—an older man with a weathered face—looked them over carefully. "What kind of traders?"

"Ammo," Bellamy said quickly. "And food rations."

The man stared. "You got papers?"

"Papers?" Ortega said, confused.

The man grunted. "Everyone clears through the central quarter. You'll meet the Prefect."

"Prefect?" Daryl repeated. "What is this, ancient Rome?"

Bellamy shot him a warning glance. "Lead the way," he said to the guards.

They were escorted down the main street. Bellamy's heart thudded with each step. Ellis was dead—he'd seen it with his own eyes. But if someone here was using his name, pretending to continue his rule... or worse, trying to rebuild what Ellis started...

Then New Haven wasn't safe.

Not by a long shot.

—-—

They walked in tense silence, boots crunching gravel and broken concrete. Around them, the remnants of Kinross were both familiar and foreign. The walls were scorched black, buildings reinforced with sheets of scavenged metal and plywood. And yet, there was structure—order. People swept debris, reinforced fencing, and stood watch with purpose.

Ortega scanned the buildings and muttered under his breath, "Place looks fire-damaged..."

The older man escorting them heard him. "Yeah," he said with a faint nod. "Had a fire a couple years ago. Burned through half the block when someone got careless with a bonfire. Scorched mostly everything. Left the black marks as a reminder."

Bellamy slowed, exchanging a glance with Daryl.

"Two years ago?" he asked, careful with his tone.

"That's right."

But Bellamy knew something the man didn't: the fires that tore through Kinross, the destruction of its towers, and the collapse of its walls—those were just eight months ago. When Ellis fell, Kinross burned. He saw it with his own eyes.

Daryl leaned in closer. "They're not part of the old group," he whispered. "They rebuilt—on the ashes."

Which meant these people weren't loyalists. They weren't holding onto Ellis's madness. They were just survivors—rebuilding a shell they didn't know the full history of.

"Here we are," the older man said, gesturing to a converted civic building at the centre of town. A faded government sign still clung crookedly to its face.

"This is the Central Quarter. The Prefect will meet you shortly. Don't wander."

The guards stationed them in a waiting area made from salvaged pews and folding chairs. Bullet holes riddled the walls. A nearby counter had been turned into a crude administrative station. A young woman with a notepad and a wary stare looked them over from behind it but said nothing.

Bellamy folded his arms and kept his voice low. "We play it cool. Ask our questions. Trade if we can. Then we get out."

"You think they really don't know what this place used to be?" Steph asked.

Bellamy gave a slow shake of his head. "Maybe they do... maybe they don't. But if they're using Ellis's name, even accidentally, we need to tread carefully. No panic. No accusations."

"I don't care what they call themselves," Daryl said, eyes scanning the perimeter. "As long as they've got that weapon stash they can call themselves anything."

"They should," Bellamy muttered. "I kept it sealed in the basement of the municipal records building. Only I had the key."

A door creaked open ahead of them, and a man entered. He wore a patchy military jacket and had a clipboard in his hand. Middle-aged, sharp-eyed, and alert.

"I'm Prefect Joren," he said flatly. "You said you're traders?"

Bellamy stood. "We are. Food, ammo. We're looking to barter."

Joren studied him for a long moment. "Come with me," he said at last. "Let's see what you've got."

As they followed him down the hall, past blackened walls and faint remnants of the war Bellamy remembered too well, one truth pulsed through his mind: This wasn't Ellis's Kinross anymore. But something told him—Ellis's ghost might still be walking the halls.

—-

Joren led them deeper into the Central Quarter, along smoke-stained corridors where cracked tiles and scorched metal told stories of fire and chaos. The walls bore the remnants of war—but it had clearly been rebuilt, just not by anyone Bellamy recognized.

"This way," Joren gestured, stopping at a heavy door reinforced with salvaged steel and crooked hinges. "He's waiting."

The group entered a low-lit office that looked like it had been patched together with whatever scraps were left behind. A desk sat awkwardly in the centre, cluttered with mismatched papers, half-burnt books, and a broken radio that was more decoration than function. A musty scent of damp and ash lingered in the air.

From behind the desk, a young man swiveled his chair around. Late teens—maybe early twenties. Skinny frame. Military coat that looked like it was borrowed from an older brother. He wore it like armor, clearly wanting it to impress.

A cocky grin split his face.

"Well, well. Visitors. Name's Ellis."

Bellamy didn't flinch. Neither did Daryl, Ortega, or Steph. But behind their neutral expressions, the tension was razor-sharp.

This wasn't Ellis. This was some kid playing pretend. But none of them said a word.

"Appreciate the hospitality," Bellamy said evenly, stepping forward. "Didn't expect anyone still holding ground here."

The young man's grin widened. "Kinross never fell. I made sure of that. Took over after the old regime... collapsed. You know how it goes."

He was clearly enjoying the role.

Daryl crossed his arms. "Quite a setup."

"It was worse," the boy said. "Fire tore through the place. We rebuilt. Left some of the scars. Reminder to the others what happens if we get careless."

Bellamy glanced at the charred walls, the still-scorched beams overhead. He nodded like he believed it.

The impostor leaned forward. "You said you had supplies?"

"Yeah," Bellamy replied, keeping his tone friendly. "Tins. Tools. Not a haul, but enough to start a trade conversation."

"Maybe we'll talk," Ellis said, waving a hand. "But no funny business. My men are loyal. You step out of line, they step on you."

"Understood," Steph said, jaw tight.

They played the part. Traders. Passersby. Nothing more. The kid was arrogant, clearly intoxicated by the little empire he'd carved out in the ruins. But Bellamy saw the cracks—saw the fear behind the act. Kinross hadn't been rebuilt out of strength. It had been patched back together out of desperation.

As they were led out of the office, Daryl leaned in and whispered, "That's not Ellis."

Bellamy didn't smile. "No. But he's sitting in his grave."

Steph's eyes scanned the courtyard as they passed. "He doesn't know what's buried here. That's good for us."

"Let's keep it that way," Bellamy murmured.

—-

Night had fallen fast over Kinross. The false "Ellis" and his followers retreated to their inner chambers while Bellamy, Daryl, Ortega, and Steph were left to rest in the east wing of the main compound — close enough to observe, but far enough to talk in private.

Bellamy drew a rough map in the dust on the floor using a bit of broken chalk.

"No more than fifteen guards total," he muttered, nodding to Daryl. "And maybe a third of them can actually shoot."

"They're undisciplined," Daryl agreed. "Weapons sloppy, no formations. Most of these people probably came from whatever's left of the fringe gangs or survivors with nowhere else to go."

"Means they'll break quick if pushed hard," Ortega added, cleaning his sidearm. "They follow that boy because he talks big. But there's no spine there."

Steph pointed to the burned-out structure near the centre of Kinross — the one Bellamy had marked earlier. "Weapons cache?"

Bellamy nodded. "Sealed before the real Ellis turned Kinross into a fortress. Steel hatch, biometric lock keyed to me. If it hasn't been found, everything's still there."

"Then we get it," Daryl said. "Quietly. No alarms."

"Exactly," Bellamy agreed. "We keep our cover for now. Move in pairs. We find the vault, crack it, get the gear. When the time is right, then head home."

But just as the last word left his mouth, a siren wailed through the still night air — harsh, grinding, and broken. An old-world sound forced through scavenged speakers. Then came the shouting.

"The dead! South wall!"

—-

The four of them scrambled to their feet, weapons in hand as guards ran past their quarters in disarray. Shouts echoed up and down the walls — erratic gunfire, screaming.

From the window, Daryl squinted toward the breach. "Small horde. Thirty, maybe forty. Could be worse. But they're panicking."

The Kinross guards were doing just what they feared — firing blindly into the oncoming wave, wasting ammo and doing little to actually stop the slow, shambling mass.

"Idiots," Steph growled. "They'll have a corpse pile six deep before they land a clean shot."

"Come on," Bellamy barked, already moving. "Time to show them how it's done."

They sprinted up the rusted stairwell to the nearest tower. A terrified young guard nearly dropped his rifle at the sight of them.

"Move!" Daryl shouted, grabbing the weapon and pushing the boy aside.

Bellamy and Ortega took position on either side of the tower window, rifles steady. Steph dropped to a knee, picking targets with a cold, practiced calm. The first shot cracked through the air — one walker down. Then another. Then another.

Bellamy's team moved with the precision of hardened fighters. Where the Kinross guards flailed, they struck. Each shot was clean, decisive. No panic. No hesitation. Within minutes, the horde had thinned significantly. By the time the last walker fell, Bellamy's group had taken out more than half of them.

From below, the so-called Ellis watched in stunned silence.

When the all-clear was given, a few of the Kinross guards approached the tower, staring at the group with new respect — or fear.

"You four..." one guard muttered. "You ain't traders."

Bellamy gave a tight smile. "Just survivors. Like you."

—-

The four of them descended the tower stairs in tight formation — rifles still hot, boots heavy on the steel rungs.

As they reached the courtyard, the crowd of Kinross survivors parted like a tide, whispering and watching. All eyes now fell on them — no longer as traders, but something more dangerous. Something organized. Standing at the centre of the yard, flanked by two of his supposed "elite" guards, was the self-proclaimed Ellis.

He didn't smile.

"Alright," the young man barked, his voice shrill in the cold air. "Enough games. You're not traders. Who the hell are you?"

Bellamy didn't answer.

Instead, without hesitation, he raised his rifle and leveled it at the boy's head. "Move a finger and I paint the ground with your skull."

Gasps rippled through the crowd. Daryl and Steph flanked immediately — swift and practiced. They dropped the two guards before they even had time to react, rifles kicked from their hands and bodies slammed to the dirt.

Ortega swept to the left, rifle raised and circling, scanning the rest of the courtyard. His finger hovered near the trigger. "Anyone else feel like playing hero?"

Silence. Tension coiled in the air like a snake ready to strike.

Bellamy's voice was low, firm. "Weapons down, or your little king here dies."

—-

But the reaction they expected never came. A few of the guards... laughed. A short, sharp chuckle at first, then a full burst of laughter from a bearded man near the steps of the guard tower. He stepped forward, hands up but relaxed.

"His name's not Ellis," the man said. "It's Grant. Grant Holloway. He's barely twenty."

Bellamy blinked.

Another voice chimed in from the far side. "We let him play boss 'cause no one else wanted the job. Been calling him 'Ellis' like a joke. Honestly? He started to believe it."

The first man stepped closer now, nodding to the others. "I'm Ian. I was part of the first crew to find this place. The place was abandoned — bodies everywhere, rotting. It looked like a warzone. We cleared it out, patched what we could. Made it home. Never knew who Ellis really was."

Daryl lowered his rifle slightly. "You're telling me you just... moved in?"

Ian nodded. "Figured it was safe enough. Scavenged what we needed. Grant had the loudest mouth and no fear, so we let him wear the fake crown. That's all this is — smoke and ash."

Bellamy looked over at the so-called Ellis—no, Grant—whose face had gone from fury to flushed embarrassment in under ten seconds. The kid's bravado was gone, deflated in front of everyone.

"Stand down," Bellamy growled.

Daryl and Steph backed off. Ortega relaxed his posture, keeping his rifle in-hand but lowered.

"Apologies," Ian said, glancing around at his people. "You had every right to question. You saved our asses tonight. That counts for something."

Bellamy kept his voice even. "We're here for something buried in the old structure beneath Central — before the real Ellis, before all this. Weapons cache. It's sealed. Only I can open it."

Ian raised a brow. "Weapons? You're not the only ones who could use more of those."

"We'll share," Bellamy replied. "If you play straight with us."

Ian glanced around. His people were nodding. Even Grant, still stunned, said nothing.

"Deal," Ian said.

Bellamy extended a hand. And just like that — Kinross changed hands.

—-

The afternoon sun burned low over New Haven, casting long shadows across the yard. The gates groaned open and two dust-covered convoys rolled through — Callum and Maggie's teams had returned. The atmosphere shifted immediately. People flooded into the yard — not just out of curiosity, but hope. A week had passed since the teams departed. Only silence had answered the radios.

Derek was already on the walkway overlooking the entrance. As soon as the first truck pulled in, he descended with urgency in his stride.

Callum climbed out of the lead truck, his face drawn and dirt-streaked. Munroe followed closely behind, his jaw tight. Both wore the look of men who had seen something they couldn't quite shake.

"We need to talk," Callum said without preamble.

Derek nodded. "Infirmary office. Five minutes."

—-

While Callum headed inside, Maggie was already at the second truck, helping two unfamiliar faces down — a young woman in her early twenties and a boy no older than twelve. The woman's arms were protective around the boy, but her eyes scanned everything with sharp instinct.

"Everyone," Maggie called to the yard, "this is Emily and Tommy. Survivors from the shopping centre. They're with us now."

Jennifer stepped forward, a warm smile on her face despite the exhaustion. "Let's get you food and a place to clean up."

Emily gave a grateful nod, but she didn't loosen her grip on Tommy's hand. As the others gathered supplies from the trucks, Derek, Callum and Munroe met in the back room of the infirmary.

Callum was the first to speak.

"We found it. The medical centre." His voice was low. "And we found... what they left behind."

Derek leaned forward. "The creatures?"

Munroe exhaled slowly. "What's left of them. Blood. Carnage. We didn't go in far — but the place felt... wrong."

Callum nodded grimly. "And worse — in a clearing not far from the centre, a nest with an egg. Not broken. Intact. Just one, but..."

"You came back right after," Derek said.

"We didn't waste a second," Callum confirmed. "Whatever made that thing — it's still out there. Or it's making more."

Derek rubbed his forehead, his mind spiraling through possibilities. "We'll call a council meeting tonight. Everyone needs to hear this."

Callum's face darkened. "Still no word from Bellamy?"

Derek shook his head. "Nearly a week. Not a peep from them. I don't like it."

"Should we prep a second team?" Munroe asked.

"Let's give it one more day," Derek said, though the weight in his gut told him otherwise. "If we hear nothing by then... we go."

He glanced to the window, where the golden light of day had already begun to fade.

And somewhere out there — the last team, Derek's mind raced, are they ok? Should we send another team out? Are they dead?

—-

Jennifer walked slowly across the yard, flanked by Emily and Tommy. Both were now in clean clothes—donated from the storage bins. Emily's long hair was pulled back in a tight braid, and Tommy wore a jumper three sizes too big, sleeves dangling past his hands. But they looked alive, less haunted than when they'd arrived.

"This is the mess hall," Jennifer said kindly, gesturing to the old cafeteria building. "Meals are served twice a day, snacks when we can manage. Food's rationed but fair."

Emily nodded, absorbing every word, protective eyes still scanning.

"And this," Jennifer added, leading them along the inner corridor toward the former B-Block, "will be your space. You'll have privacy, clean bedding, and heat when the generators are running."

Tommy poked his head into the open cell and turned back to Jennifer. "This used to be a real prison?"

"It did," she smiled gently. "But not anymore. This place is called New Haven for a reason. We rebuilt it into something better."

Emily placed a hand on Tommy's shoulder, then looked at Jennifer. "Thank you. For everything."

Jennifer nodded. "You're welcome here. But we all pull our weight. Everyone has a job. Maybe security, maybe helping in the garden, teaching, or cleaning. We'll find what you're good at — when you're ready."

Tommy looked up. "I can help now."

Jennifer chuckled. "That's good to hear. Settle in first. Then we'll see what fits."

—-

In the former warden's office — now New Haven's planning and operations room — Derek sat hunched over a large map, red pencil in hand. Defensive zones were marked, supply lines highlighted, and future expansion corridors roughed in beside coded notes. The door creaked open behind him.

"Hey," Jillian's voice was soft but clear.

Derek looked up. "Hey... you heard?"

She nodded, walking in and closing the door. "Emily and Tommy seem like good people. Jennifer's got them sorted."

Derek leaned back with a sigh. "They got lucky. Real lucky."

"Callum's team?" Jillian asked, perching on the edge of the nearby desk.

"Found blood, signs of those creatures... and something worse. One of those things — an egg. Still whole."

Jillian went quiet.

"I overheard some of it earlier," she admitted. "I know it's supposed to be confidential... but that's bad, isn't it?"

Derek pinched the bridge of his nose. "If there's more out there, or worse — if they're growing — we've got a problem much bigger than just survival."

Jillian nodded, voice quieter now. "Do you think they'll come here?"

"I don't know," he admitted. "But I'm planning like they will."

She stood and moved closer, lowering her voice. "You're not alone in this, Derek. You never have been."

He glanced up at her, eyes tired but appreciative.

"Thanks, Jill."

A long pause followed. The tension between them was there — unspoken, but undeniable — like a chord pulled tight.

"I should get back," she said eventually, stepping away, her tone lighter again. "Emily and Tommy are in good hands."

—-

Jillian stepped toward the door, her hand resting on the handle, ready to leave him to his thoughts. But just before she opened it, she paused. Her voice was soft, a whisper in the dimly lit room. "Things are starting to feel crazy again," she said without turning. "Just like before."

Derek looked up slowly. He nodded. "Let's just hope we can stop those things before they grow in numbers, or crazy will be the least of our worries."

Jillian opened the door and left without saying another word.

Chapter 12

It had been over a week since Bellamy and his team had left New Haven. In that time, they'd deposed a pretender Ellis, uncovered a forgotten weapons cache, and made peace with the group of survivors who'd unknowingly taken up residence in the shadow of Kinross' dark past. Though the scars of the old Kinross still lingered in Bellamy's memory, the place had changed. The walls were cleaner, the gates half-mended, and the fear that once ruled it had been replaced by a quiet determination.

Ortega heaved the last crate of rifles onto the back of their transport truck, sweat lining his brow. "That's the last of it," he grunted, giving the tailgate a slap.

Bellamy nodded, wiping his hands. "Let's strap it in, check the supplies, then roll. We're late getting back."

True to his word, Bellamy had shared out some of the weapons — enough to give the new occupants a fighting chance, but not enough to arm a militia. These people were scared, scattered, and disorganized, not dangerous. They'd done what any group would do in the chaos — found shelter, found someone to lead, even if it was just a kid who talked big and knew how to bark orders.

Just as they were strapping the final crate down, a handful of Kinross guards approached them, faces drawn with fatigue and worry. The one at the front looked barely twenty, hair matted with dirt, hands twitching nervously over the strap of a worn rifle.

"Wait!" he called out.

Bellamy turned slowly, eyes narrowing. "Something wrong?"

The young man stepped forward, voice cracking with desperation. "Please... take us with you."

Behind him stood four others, equally ragged, equally hopeful.

"That last breach," he said, gesturing toward the scorched gate in the distance. "That was the fourth in a month. If you hadn't been here... we wouldn't be talking right now."

Bellamy glanced at Ortega, then back at the kid. "You're Finn, right?"

He nodded quickly. "We'll work. Fight. Whatever it takes. But this place... it's falling apart."

Before Bellamy could answer, Ian, the de facto leader of the guards, jogged over, clearly catching the end of the exchange.

"What's going on?" he asked, eyes flicking from Bellamy to Finn.

"They want to come with us," Bellamy said evenly.

Ian let out a long breath, then looked at Bellamy with reluctant respect. "Just keep 'em safe."

"We will," Bellamy said.

The five defectors loaded their gear quickly, little more than small packs and personal weapons. One of them, a wiry girl with a bandaged arm, offered Bellamy a quiet thanks as she passed.

As the truck roared to life and rolled out of Kinross, Ortega leaned on the open window, glancing at the shrinking silhouette of the old stronghold behind them.

"Funny," he said. "You ever think we'd be hauling new blood out of that place instead of bodies?"

Bellamy didn't answer right away. His eyes stayed on the horizon ahead.

"No," he said quietly. "But maybe this is how we start changing things."

The truck sped up, a cloud of dust kicking up behind them, New Haven waiting in the distance — and a future none of them were sure they could fully prepare for.

—-

The mood in the truck had been hopeful —silent, but hopeful. The kind of silence that meant everyone was still alive and heading home, battered but victorious. Bellamy sat in the passenger seat, watching the trees blur past. Ortega was driving, focused and calm. Daryl rode in the back, quietly cleaning his sidearm, while Steph sat across from the five new passengers they'd picked up from Kinross, keeping a careful but non-threatening eye on them.

Then the sky shifted.

A dense column of grey haze spiraled upward in the distance, almost like smoke... but thicker, darker.

The truck groaned to a stop atop the grassy ridge, its tires crunching against loose gravel as Bellamy leaned forward in his seat, eyes fixed on the haze crawling across the valley below.

Ortega cut the engine. Silence swallowed the road.

Daryl had already climbed out and raised the binoculars. "Shit," he muttered under his breath. "Bellamy. Take a look."

Bellamy stepped down, took the binoculars, and steadied himself against the hood.

What he saw twisted his gut.

Thousands of them.

A slow-moving wave of rotted flesh — a horde of zombies flooding down through the forest line toward the flatlands.

Toward Kinross.

"That's... no stray group," Bellamy muttered. "That's a goddamn swarm."

Steph clambered down from the back. "Heading for Kinross?" he asked, though he already knew the answer.

"They'll be on top of them by nightfall," Bellamy said. "If not sooner."

"We've got the weapons," Ortega added. "Maybe we turn around? Give 'em a fighting chance?"

Bellamy shook his head. "With what? A handful of half-trained guards and a kid pretending to be Ellis? They don't stand a chance."

Steph frowned. "We still left people there."

"Yeah," Bellamy nodded. "And that's the only reason we consider going back."

Then—

BOOM.

The sound hit them like a punch to the chest. A shockwave rolled through the valley. Everyone spun to see a fireball rising above Kinross in the far distance. A plume of thick black smoke curled into the sky.

Daryl's voice cut the silence like a blade. "What the hell was that?"

From the back of the truck, Ali – a wiry man with sharp eyes and a haunted expression—spoke up, his voice tight with panic. "We found dynamite... rigged up in the main tower. On nearly every floor. We were gonna disarm it, use it for perimeter traps. Someone must've triggered it."

Bellamy turned on him. "You never mentioned that."

"I didn't think anyone was dumb enough to light the damn fuse!" Ali snapped.

The others didn't have time to argue. The roar of the horde grew louder in the distance—low and deep, like thunder rolling over the hills. The explosion had done more than damage Kinross.

It had drawn the entire swarm.

The undead were now fully fixed on the smoke and flame rising from what used to be the central tower. Kinross was a beacon—and the end of the line.

"We have to go back," Bellamy said quickly, his tone sharp with urgency. "If anyone makes it out, they won't last long."

"We'll have to swing wide," Daryl added. "The ridge south of the river. Avoid the horde's path."

"We're wasting time!" Steph barked.

Ortega didn't wait for another word. He threw the truck into a tight 180, gravel flying as the tires shrieked against the bend. The truck roared back toward Kinross, every eye fixed on the smoke in the sky.

They didn't speak.

Each man inside gripped his weapon just a little tighter. They had no idea what—or who—they'd find when they got there.

But one thing was certain: Kinross was dying. And time was running out.

—-

Smoke choked the air. Fire licked the edges of collapsed stone. The tower—the heart of Kinross—was gone. Reduced to twisted rebar and flaming debris.

Where once stood homes, sleeping quarters, a meeting hall… now there was only rubble. Of the forty or so people who had remained in Kinross, more than half had lived in the tower.

Now they were dust.

Near the southern wall, a hidden steel hatch screeched open. Ian stumbled out, coughing hard. Behind him, John, Mel, and Scott emerged from the tunnel, eyes squinting against the swirling ash.

"W-What the…?" Ian gasped, staggering a few steps into the courtyard.

He froze.

Flames danced across the remains of the tower. A collapsed roof beam groaned before snapping free and falling with a deafening crack.

"Twenty-five people..." Mel said, stunned. "Gone. Just like that."

"It's not just that," John muttered, pointing to the darkening horizon. "That blast... probably heard for miles."

Mel's eyes widened. "Every dead thing out there's gonna come running."

Scott was about to speak when the distinct rumble of a truck engine echoed through the air. Tires screeched. A cloud of dust swept through the outer yard. Bellamy's truck came into view, already skidding to a stop.

"GO, GO!" Bellamy shouted from the passenger side, swinging the door wide.

"MOVE IT!" Daryl barked, climbing halfway out of the cab.

Ian hesitated. "We were in the tunnels... trying to open the lab doors... they didn't move. We didn't know what happened."

"Forget it!" Bellamy snapped. "We'll talk later. Get in, now!"

The four survivors clambered into the bed of the truck. As Mel pulled herself up, a chilling moan echoed from behind the rubble.

The dead.

Rising from the ashes.

Burned, half-charred figures dragged themselves from under collapsed beams. Others were drawn by the noise, the fire... the smell of blood. Ortega punched the accelerator just as one groaning corpse lurched toward the truck. Steph took it down with a clean headshot from the side rail.

Inside the cab, Daryl glanced back. "Is that all of you?"

Ian gave a slow, grim nod. "Yeah," he muttered, eyes fixed on the blazing tower. "That's it. The rest... they were inside."

The truck tore away from the ruins of Kinross, the moans of the dead growing quieter in the distance—replaced only by silence and the heavy grief of what had just been lost. They skidded to a halt a few hundred metres from Kinross, the smoldering wreckage still faint in the rearview mirror. Ortega killed the engine and climbed out, dust swirling around his boots.

"What the hell are you doing?" Daryl snapped, stepping down after him. "We need to get moving. We don't have time to park and reminisce."

Ortega didn't answer at first. He stood with hands on hips, staring back toward the faint silhouette of flames curling into the sky.

"We have a chance here," he finally said. "A real chance to wipe out a horde."

Bellamy, sitting near the tailgate, slowly raised his head. "The Overkill Directive."

Ortega nodded.

Daryl looked between the two of them. "What the hell is that?"

Bellamy stepped down from the truck, face grim. "Back in the early days of Kinross, when Ellis still had sway, there was a plan in place… a last resort. It was called the Overkill Directive."

He pointed a finger back toward Kinross. "About four feet under the surface — running the full length of the perimeter — Ellis had C4 buried. Enough to level the place. Every thirty yards, rigged with redundancy lines."

"Jesus," Steph muttered.

"It wasn't just on the surface," Bellamy continued. "The lab… the place you couldn't get into… that whole thing is lined with explosives too. The directive was simple: if Kinross ever became unsalvageable—overrun, lost, or compromised—you activate the Overkill and erase the threat."

Daryl paced in frustration. "Even if that's true, how? You just said the lab is underground and sealed tight."

"Yeah," Bellamy said, voice quieting. "But the controls are still down there."

Steph's brows furrowed. "How the hell do we get in?"

"There's a secondary access," Bellamy said. "About a mile south of Kinross. It was kept hidden even from most of the command. I've only been down it once — years ago." "It's a one-way mission," Bellamy said. "Once you're in, and you trigger the Overkill, there's no coming out."

Silence fell over the group.

Scott, one of the new Kinross survivors, spoke up shakily. "You're saying… blow up everything? The lab? The walls? All of Kinross?"

Bellamy nodded. "If we don't… those thousands of infected will overrun the region. They'll reach settlements. New Haven. Everything."

Ian looked pale. "This is insane."

"No," Daryl said, rubbing a hand over his jaw. "This... might be our only play."

Steph looked toward Bellamy. "You really gonna do it?"

Bellamy stared out toward Kinross, his jaw set like iron. "I'll go. I knew the risks when we built that lab. I knew what Ellis had planned. This was always going to end this way."

"No chance we can rig it remotely?" Ortega asked, though he already knew the answer.

Bellamy shook his head. "Failsafes. Ellis was paranoid. You have to be physically there, on-site, once the codes are entered the doors slam shut, so the full force of the explosion goes upwards."

Daryl looked at the others, then at Bellamy. "If you're going... you're not going alone."

Bellamy offered a grim smile. "Didn't expect I would."

—-

The narrow path behind Kinross was quiet—too quiet, save for the distant groans echoing through the hills. Daryl, Bellamy, and Ian moved with purpose, dispatching the handful of zombies on the trail with practiced efficiency. Every minute counted now.

The brush opened up into a concealed concrete hatch half-buried in overgrowth. Moss clung to its rusted metal frame. Bellamy wiped it clean and knelt beside the panel.

"This is it," he said.

Ian glanced toward the treeline, nervous. "So how does this Overkill Directive work?"

Bellamy keyed in a sequence. "There's a primary control panel deep in the lab. You enter two codes—one for the surface line charges, the second for the lab's internal explosives. Then you pull the fuse. Once it's live, there's no turning back."

The keypad chirped. A hiss escaped the hydraulics as the door creaked open.

But before Bellamy could react, Ian shoved him and Daryl backwards.

"What the hell!?" Daryl barked, landing hard on the dirt.

Ian slipped inside the threshold, slamming the release lever. "I'm doing it," he shouted. "I've got nothing left. My people are gone. I'm not letting those things reach another soul."

The metal slammed shut with a mechanical groan.

Inside, Ian took a breath and looked at the flickering monitors. One showed the exterior—hundreds, maybe thousands of the undead, swarming through the crumbled remains of Kinross.

He smiled grimly. "Now that's timing."

From outside, Bellamy and Daryl pounded the sealed entrance. "Ian!" Bellamy shouted. "You don't have to do this!"

Ian's voice crackled through the static of the intercom. "Watch the monitor. You'll know when."

Bellamy froze. "...I understand."

Daryl grabbed Bellamy's shoulder. "Come on. We gotta move."

The two men turned and ran. The horde was almost fully inside Kinross now—groans loud, gnashing teeth barely a hundred yards away. Bellamy and Daryl sprinted for the lake near the base of the valley, hearts pounding in rhythm with the thunder of undead feet behind them. They leapt—water crashing over them just as the world exploded.

BOOM!

A violent roar shook the earth. Fire and stone erupted into the sky. Kinross vanished in a pillar of smoke, a shockwave flattening trees and tossing corpses into the air like rag dolls. The mountain roared with fury, as if the earth itself rejected what had once stood there.

It was done. Kinross was gone. And so was the horde.

—-

An hour later, the truck still sat at the same overlook where they'd parked before. Smoke billowed in the distance. No one spoke. No one moved. Then—movement. Two shapes on the horizon.

Ortega's breath caught. "...No way."

Bellamy and Daryl limped into view, soaked, bloodied, but alive.

"Bellamy!" Ortega shouted, jumping out of the truck. "I thought you were—!"

He stopped mid-sentence. Mel stepped forward.

"Where's Ian?"

Neither man answered. Bellamy's jaw tightened. He shook his head once. The silence said more than words ever could. Tears welled in Mel's eyes. The other Kinross survivors bowed their heads.

"He saved us all," Daryl finally said.

Bellamy placed a hand on Mel's shoulder. "He saved more than us. He saved everyone."

Ortega nodded solemnly and climbed back into the truck, starting the engine. As the convoy turned south and the wreckage of Kinross faded behind them, hope returned to their eyes. Not because the road was easy, but because the threat had been stopped. For now.

New Haven awaited—stronger, wiser, and ready to rebuild.

Chapter 13

The gates of New Haven groaned open under the weight of tension and anticipation. Dust kicked up from the tires of the approaching truck, now crawling toward the main yard. Derek stood at the front line, flanked by Jennifer, Jillian, Callum, and the rest of the council. Behind them, much of the community had gathered, whispers buzzing through the crowd.

As the truck rolled to a halt, the engine sighed and cut out.

Bellamy was the first to step out, his clothes stained with soot and dried blood, but his posture strong. Beside him emerged Daryl, Ortega, and Steph, each of them visibly exhausted but alive. Relief swept through the group.

Then came the unfamiliar faces.

"This is John, Mel, Scott, Ali, Erin, Michone, Finn, and Roary," Bellamy called out, gesturing toward the worn and wary survivors climbing out of the vehicle one by one. "We'll explain everything soon, Derek. For now... they've just lost someone dear to them. Can we set them up somewhere quiet?"

Derek nodded. "Callum, Munroe — take them to D Block. Get them settled. We'll meet at the council room shortly."

The new housing wing — D Block — had been completed only days before, built specifically for expanding the community. It wasn't much, but it was clean, warm, and safe. For now, that was enough.

—-

The council room filled quickly. Derek sat at the head of the table, fingers steepled beneath his chin, flanked by Jennifer and Callum. The rest of the council followed: Jillian, Bill, Anne, Maggie, Lee, Bellamy, Munroe, Daryl, and Aria. The weight of recent days clung to the air like humidity before a storm.

Bellamy stood and began to speak.

He told them everything.

About Kinross — or what had become of it. About the boy who pretended to be Ellis. About the fire-scorched walls, the desperate survivors, the hidden weapons cache. And about Ian — how he'd sacrificed himself to detonate the Overkill Directive and annihilate the horde that had descended.

No one spoke for a long moment.

Until Derek broke the silence. "Thank you... for getting them out. And for bringing back what you did." Then he shared their own news. About the egg found at the medical centre. About the signs that the creatures — now dubbed Reapers thanks to Bill's suggestion — were multiplying in ways they didn't yet understand.

Maggie rubbed her forehead. "So we've got Reapers breeding now. Perfect."

"And," Bill added, "we've got new people rolling in like we're a bed-and-breakfast."

Jennifer's voice cut through next. Calm, but firm. "That needs to change. We need to stop taking in everyone who shows up. No more blind trust."

"We need a system," Munroe added. "Vetting. Quarantine. Maybe a safehouse before they get anywhere near the walls."

Jillian leaned forward. "What about the shelter? We could guide them in through the cemetery tunnel entrance. It's far enough from the main compound. We keep them there for a few days — get a read on who they are, what they bring, what risks they pose. Then we bring them through the hatch and into New Haven only if they're cleared."

The room was silent, then slowly filled with nods.

"Clever," Aria said. "They'd never know how to get back even if they wanted to."

Derek looked around the table. "Then it's settled. New standard protocol for new arrivals — vetted, quarantined, cleared. No exceptions." Now, they had a plan for new arrivals.

"All right. Let's talk about the Reapers."

The word hit like a weight. Everyone in the room felt it — the cold edge of something worse than the undead. Faster. Smarter. Born of human cruelty and scientific arrogance.

Callum sat forward, jaw tight. "We already found a nest. Near the medical centre."

That got everyone's attention.

"It was buried deep," Munroe added. "We didn't go in, but what we saw… It was enough. Egg-like structures. One fully formed, probably hatched. We weren't sticking around for more."

Aria's face darkened. "Then they're reproducing close. It won't be long before that nest becomes a swarm."

"And we still don't know what Carr meant by 'evolution,'" Jillian said.

Derek nodded slowly, then glanced toward the sweat collection plan Jennifer had started. "We can use that to our advantage. If sweat draws them, then we have bait."

"You're talking about a trap," Bill said.

"A trap big enough to wipe out the nest before it expands," Derek confirmed. "But we need to be smart. We need numbers. Intel. Backup."

Bellamy spoke next. "Kinross taught us something — small groups can still do big things. If we hit hard, hit fast, and don't get cocky, we can wipe out that nest."

"And if we don't?" Anne asked.

"Then we fortify," said Daryl. "More spikes. Reinforce the second gate. Trenches, kill zones, fallback positions."

"And people," Bellamy added. "We've got what — 80 now? But only 15 or 20 who know how to fight. That's gotta change."

"I'll start training rotations," he continued. "Anyone over sixteen. Firearms, blades, hand-to-hand if we need it. If they want to live here, they fight."

He looked around the room. "We already know where it is. We prepare tonight. Recon, ammo checks, rig the bait. We hit it tomorrow at first light."

"Small team," he added. "Silent approach. Blow it before it grows."

Callum, Munroe, and Lee nodded. They knew the terrain already. They'd lead the assault.

Aria cleared her throat. "And if there's another nest?"

"Then we find it," said Derek. "And we burn it to the ground."

Silence fell again, but this time it wasn't dread. It was focus.

Jennifer exhaled and leaned back in her chair. "So we're at war again."

Derek looked around the table, eyes locked on each of them. "No," he said. "This time, we will finish it. Alright, everyone knows the plan. Go to bed early tonight. Tomorrow we have a big day ahead, and everyone needs to be sharp."

—-

And with that the council room emptied. They all went about finishing off their tasks. Maggie and Jennifer trained some of the survivors with knives and hand-to-hand combat, while Daryl was teaching others how to shoot with a crossbow. Bellamy and Ortega were showing others how to load magazines and shoot with firearms. As ordered, everyone was bed-bound by the time evening approached.

—-

The morning sun had barely risen above the prison walls when the yard began to stir. The air was cool, but the mood was tense — decisive.

Derek stood at the centre of the yard, the council gathered around, along with the best fighters New Haven had to offer. A large canvas sheet was laid out in front of them, loaded with jars of collected sweat and piles of sweat-soaked shirts, gym rags, and towels — Jennifer's roof-top workout plan had worked better than expected.

"This is the plan," Derek began, his voice steady but intense. "We bait them. Sweat-drenched clothes laid in a tight perimeter. Once they move in, we hit them with everything we've got. Bullets. Blades. Fire. Then we burn the nest."

He pointed toward the edge of a rough map pinned to the table. "It's close to the medical centre. That helps us — gives us structure. But it also means there could be more lurking around. If we wipe out the main Reapers, we deal with any nests after — quickly."

Derek turned to Bellamy. "Pick ten of the best. Including me. Munroe knows the terrain, he's going. That leaves seven spots."

Bellamy didn't hesitate. "Daryl. Ortega. Steph. Maggie. Anne. Callum. Lee."

Derek gave a tight nod. "Gear up. Full loadouts. We leave in fifteen. Truck's being prepped. No mistakes."

The council began to move, murmuring quietly among themselves. Just as the group turned to disperse, the door to the main hall creaked open. Steph stepped through, flanking someone Derek wasn't expecting to see again so soon.

"Sorry," Steph said under his breath. "She insisted."

Dr. Carr entered, restrained but calm. Her eyes, however, burned with urgency. "You need to listen to me," she said, looking directly at Derek.

He crossed his arms, wary. "Make it quick."

"You'll get one shot at this. One. If even one of those Reapers escapes that kill zone, it will learn. Adapt. The next time... you won't have this advantage. They'll avoid the traps. Predict your movements. Change how they hunt."

The council exchanged concerned looks. Carr continued, voice unwavering.

"Finish this today. Or you'll be facing something that's not just strong — but strategic."

With that, she stepped back as Steph motioned for her to return to her quarters. Derek exhaled, then turned back to the others. "You heard her. No mistakes."

Bellamy called out names again, confirming the strike team as they geared up: Derek. Bellamy. Munroe. Daryl. Ortega. Steph. Maggie. Anne. Callum. Lee.

Ten.

The best they had.

—-

They mounted the truck, weapons checked, packs strapped, nerves silent. This wasn't just another supply run. This was war. And it started today.

The truck rumbled steadily down the cracked and silent road, its engine the only sound cutting through the thick morning haze. The countryside stretched barren and unmoving on either side — trees stripped bare, old signs tilting with rust, and the distant silhouettes of ruined buildings against a pale blue sky.

Inside the truck, the mood was heavy — surgical. No one was speaking. Derek sat at the front, crossbow resting across his legs, eyes locked on the windshield as if watching for the enemy to appear at any second. Beside him, Bellamy stared at the floor, his mind replaying the weight of Ian's sacrifice.

Munroe drove, hands tight on the wheel, his mouth a hard line of focus. In the back, Daryl and Callum occasionally exchanged nods, Maggie checked over the extra clips of ammunition, and Anne quietly sharpened a blade. Steph sat still, watching the passing scenery with deadpan precision, while Lee and Ortega double-checked the satchels containing their burn packs and sweat-drenched bait.

The plan was set.

And the silence said everything that words couldn't. It was a two-hour drive from New Haven — two hours that felt like forever. The roads were mostly clear, but every bump, every shadow across the cracked tarmac, had someone flinch or grip their weapon tighter.

As they neared the edge of the town, Munroe slowed the truck to a crawl. The trees thinned, the air thickened. The ruins of once-busy buildings now stood like hollow skeletons around them. He finally spoke, voice low but firm. "We're here." The truck hissed to a stop just outside the town's perimeter — one block from the medical centre, the very one where they had lost Ross and David. The place still held ghosts.

—-

Derek stood and turned, addressing the team. "Lock and load. We do this tight and fast. Watch the rooftops. Keep low. We bait them in, hit them hard, and burn whatever's left."

Everyone nodded in silence, each checking their gear one last time. Blades were strapped down. Bolts loaded. Triggers checked. The smell of gun oil and sweat filled the enclosed space.

"Take us in, Munroe," Derek ordered.

The truck rolled forward, slow and deliberate, past shattered glass and silent windows. The buildings looked like they hadn't changed at all — still soaked in the dried blood and horror they'd seen weeks ago. Every shadow could be a threat. Every sound could be death.

But they didn't flinch.

They were ready.

Today was the day the Reapers would fall — or they would.

And as the truck crept toward the kill zone…

The war was about to truly begin.

—-

The truck halted just outside the medical centre, a familiar building now soaked in blood-soaked memories. Derek stood first, boots hitting the pavement, scanning the street. "This is it." He turned back to the group. "Munroe—take the truck around the next block. Keep the engine running. You know the drill—we may need a fast way out."

"Copy that," Munroe replied, hopping into the cab and steering the vehicle quietly down the side road.

Derek turned to the others. "Let's move. Fast and clean."

The remaining nine — Bellamy, Daryl, Ortega, Steph, Maggie, Anne, Callum, and Lee — sprang into action. The trap had been rehearsed back at New Haven, and now it was time to execute.

Sweat-soaked rags, shirts, and armbands — pungent and stashed in airtight bags — were pulled out and scattered around the front of the centre. Jars containing condensed sweat were cracked open and thrown onto the scene, coating the bait pile in a thick, musky stench.

The team split quickly. Half — Derek, Daryl, Maggie, Lee, and Callum — took the ridge overlooking the street. The other half — Bellamy, Steph, Ortega, and Anne — secured elevated positions across from the centre in the shell of an abandoned building.

Seconds passed.

Then came the snarling. Distant, guttural. A shape darted out of the woods. Another from the broken glass of the medical centre. Then more—dozens, crawling out from cracks, alleyways, smashed windows.

At least seventeen.

Some towering and broad-shouldered, others smaller but just as feral. Their skin was tight and greyed, jaws twitching, spines arched unnaturally. They moved in short, twisted bursts, sniffing and growling around the clothes like animals. Drawn to the scent. Entranced.

Derek raised his rifle and whispered into the radio, "On my mark."

The group tensed.

Three heartbeats passed.

"Mark."

Gunfire erupted.

Rounds zipped from both sides of the street, bursting into the exposed backs of the creatures. Bolts flew, accurately piercing eye sockets and soft tissue. Two of the Reapers fell instantly, twitching before going still. The others shrieked and spun in confusion—but were boxed in.

Molotovs rained down next—Ortega and Maggie each lighting a bottle and hurling it into the swarm.

WHUMP—CRASH—FWOOSH.

Flames rolled across the pavement. Screams, unearthly and inhuman, echoed between the buildings. Some of the Reapers tried to leap for the buildings. One scrambled halfway up the wall before Bellamy drilled it through the temple with a single shot. Daryl fired off a pipe bomb—it landed in the centre of the group and—

BOOM!

Concrete cracked. Limbs flew.

By now, only five remained—darting, lunging, almost coordinated. Anne and Steph let off suppressing fire as Callum and Lee picked targets cleanly. The last Reaper charged the ridge, a deep roar in its throat—until Derek calmly raised his rifle and dropped it cold.

Silence.

The smell of blood, sweat, and smoke hung heavy in the air.

"That's it," Derek said quietly. "Hold fire."

The others rose from cover, eyes peeled. The street was littered with burning, bullet-ridden Reaper corpses. Ash from the Molotovs drifted gently like snow.

Bellamy lowered his weapon. "That's... all of them?"

They had done it.

But no one smiled.

—

The smoke still lingered in the air, rising from the charred remains of the Reapers and the Molotov-blackened pavement. The silence that followed the firefight was heavy, but it didn't last long.

Derek reloaded his rifle with precision, his eyes sweeping over the bodies. "That was the attack. Now we look for the roots."

He turned to the group, voice sharp and clear. "They came from three directions — the medical centre, the forest edge, and those apartments across the street. That means one of three things: multiple nests, or one large one with tunnels."

"We're not leaving until we find them," Bellamy added, cocking his sidearm. "Burn the rot out by its roots."

"Three teams of three," Derek said. "Fan out, cover each zone. If you find a nest — don't wait. Burn it. No chances."

He looked around the group and quickly divided them:

Team One — Myself, Daryl, Lee: we will head into the medical centre, to search the lower levels and back halls where some Reapers had emerged.

Team Two — Bellamy, Maggie, Callum: head into the apartments across the street, where some of the creatures had dropped from balconies.

Team Three — Steph, Anne, Ortega: search the forest edge and treeline, where the snarling first began.

"Keep radios open," Derek reminded them. "No one plays hero. If it's more than you can handle—fall back and call it in."

The teams gave tense nods, adrenaline still pumping, boots crunching through broken glass and scorched pavement as they split up and disappeared into the silence once more.

—-

Derek led the way with a flashlight and rifle ready. The halls smelled like rot and antiseptic, a terrible mix of what once was and what had become.

Daryl stepped carefully through the blood-slick floor. "How deep is this place?"

"Too deep," Lee muttered, peering down a stairwell into darkness.

As they reached the basement, they found what they were looking for — black webbing across the walls. Not silk. Not mould. Something else. Pulsing, moist. Almost alive.

Derek exhaled slowly. "Nest."

He lit a ragged Molotov while Daryl opened a can of fuel and splashed it over the nest-like webbing. A single flick of the lighter, and the flames exploded across the room. The webbing curled and shrieked as if in agony. Whatever was left here — eggs, residue, tissue — all burned.

"Clear!" Derek called. "Pulling out!"

—-

Bellamy moved with practiced quiet, pistol raised. Maggie had her bow ready, Callum covered the rear.

Each apartment was abandoned, vandalized, or burned out—until they reached one sealed with a metal sheet across the door. Bellamy kicked it in.

Inside — a twisted nest. Eggs. Three of them. Soft-shelled, the size of soccer balls, covered in glistening grey mucus.

"Christ," Maggie whispered.

Callum dropped his pack. "Time to torch them."

No hesitation. The fire raged out the window as they descended back to the street.

"Second nest down," Bellamy radioed. "Apartments are clear."

—-

Steph was the first to spot the pit — a hollow, camouflaged in dead leaves and branches. Inside were bones, slick mud... and twitching tendrils.

"Burn it," Anne said, already unhooking her lighter.

Ortega threw the last of the fuel. "Say goodnight, freaks."

The flames erupted in a spiral, licking up the trees and through the pit.

"Forest edge clear," Ortega reported. "One more for the pyres."

—-

As each team regrouped near the burnt-out shell of the medical centre, Derek looked each of them in the eye. "No casualties. Three nests confirmed. Three nests gone." He glanced back toward the centre. "Let's hope that was all of them."

But no one spoke.

Because they all knew — it probably wasn't.

—-

One last sweep. One final nest.

Hidden beneath a half-collapsed stairwell near the west wing, Derek, Callum, and Lee found it — dark, damp, and more developed than any of the others. Eight veined, pulsing eggs, slick with fluid, each one twitching as if alive.

No hesitation.

They burned it. Molotovs. Fuel. Fire. They watched until nothing moved.

Outside, Ortega stood near the truck, staring back at the medical centre, smoke rising in thick plumes. "Pity we can't just nuke this place and be done with it."

Daryl scoffed. "Yeah. Pity."

"...Unless," Ortega started.

Everyone looked at him.

"What if we pull fuel from the cars, use the rest of our Molotov's and pipe bombs, and rig a burn line? Something to wipe out everything — the building, the nests, whatever's left crawling in there."

Bellamy's brow furrowed. "Could work. We've got the materials. And time."

Lee added, "Still got that C4 from Kinross. We never unloaded it."

Derek gave a hard nod. "Do it. Strip everything useful. Every drop of fuel. We make this place disappear."

The group split into pairs. Molotovs were tied off, fuses checked. Car tanks were drained, metal drums packed with flammables, and the C4 was buried under the medical centre's foundation. They worked with urgency, nobody speaking unless they had to.

By the time the sun began to dip behind the trees, the entire perimeter had been rigged.

Ortega checked the last charge, then turned. "Ready."

Derek gave a long look at the building. "Everyone in. We're done here."

One by one, they climbed into the truck, sweat-soaked and drained. As Derek reached the cab, he turned to Munroe. "You remember the fallback point?"

Munroe nodded. "North ridge. Five miles."

Derek gave a tight nod. "Take us there. Let the fire have this place."

They drove a mile out. Derek held the detonator. He looked once more toward the silent, shadowed husk of the medical centre. Then he pressed it.

The earth roared. A plume of fire and smoke swallowed the sky. The ground trembled, glass cracked in the truck.

Flames raced down the rigged lines, consuming everything in its path — buildings, nests, blood-stained floors, and every corner the Reapers might've touched.

The place was erased.

Derek leaned back in his seat as the fire died down in the rearview mirror. "Let's move."

The truck rolled north, toward the fallback point. No one spoke for miles. No one had to. They'd won — but they all knew this war was far from over.

—-

The truck bounced along the narrow dirt trail, the scorched sky still glowing faintly behind them. Inside, the group sat in heavy silence — not because there was nothing to say, but because they were simply too tired to speak. Ash clung to their clothes. Smoke hung in the air behind them like a ghost.

Derek sat up front, beside Munroe, who was steering carefully around tree stumps and cratered earth. The rest of the team sat shoulder-to-shoulder in the back of the truck: Bellamy, Daryl, Steph, Callum, Maggie, Anne, Ortega, and Lee — each lost in their own thoughts, the roar of the engine a welcome distraction from the chaos they'd just survived.

After a while, as the adrenaline wore thin and the silence grew heavier, Derek spoke.

"We're heading to the fallback point," he said over his shoulder. "It's an old scout cabin a few miles north — barely on any map. Has a water source, some cover. We'll hold there till the dust settles."

"How long are we staying?" Callum asked, voice hoarse.

"A week, maybe less," Derek replied. "Just long enough to make sure nothing followed us. If any Reapers survived that blast... they'll be looking. We can't lead them back to New Haven."

Bellamy gave a quiet grunt. "Smart. Burn their nest, then vanish. Give them nothing to chase."

Daryl nodded. "And if we see anything?"

Derek's answer was blunt. "We kill it."

No one argued.

The sense of tension slowly began to fade from their faces, replaced with the weary recognition of temporary peace. They'd won this round. They'd destroyed the nest, erased the medical centre, and escaped with every member of the strike team alive — a rare victory in these dark times.

They just needed to make sure it stayed that way.

—-—

As the truck crested a rise, the trees parted ahead, revealing a clearing wrapped in mist. A small, weathered cabin stood nestled in the trees, half-covered in ivy, roof still intact. The fallback point.

"Home for now," Munroe said, slowing the truck to a crawl.

Derek stepped down first, boots hitting the soft earth. He scanned the treeline, then the cabin. It looked untouched.

"Unload, set up watches, rotate shifts," he ordered. "Rest when you can. We hold here until we're sure it's safe."

One by one, the others climbed down. They didn't smile. They didn't cheer. But there was something quieter in their eyes.

Relief.

And just the faintest flicker of hope.

The cabin at the fallback point offered exactly what the group needed — isolation, elevation, and quiet. Surrounded by dense forest and set back from any roads, it became their watchtower, their shelter, their holding pattern while the dust of the Reaper ambush settled.

They stayed for nearly a week.

Each day brought the same routine: clear perimeter, monitor the woods, dispatch any wandering undead. But it wasn't the threat of Reapers that hung over them now — it was the heavy calm that followed chaos. The eerie stillness after a storm.

—-

Callum and Anne had been together since the early days of the fall. Their bond had only deepened through every battle, every loss. At New Haven, they were inseparable — a force on the battlefield and an anchor for each other off it.

Now, holed up in the cabin's loft space, they found stolen hours to simply be. Together, wrapped in old blankets, whispering jokes and memories. There were no guards up between them — no fear of what others might think. Everyone knew they were a couple, and no one questioned it.

Their love was steady. Earned. Quietly fierce.

Chapter 14

The truck's engine growled steadily as it crested the ridge overlooking New Haven. The sight of the settlement — its reinforced gates, the solar arrays glinting in the sun, and faint smoke trails rising from cooking fires — filled the team with something they hadn't truly felt in days.

Relief.

Inside the truck, the atmosphere was a quiet hum of exhaustion and silent reflection. Callum sat with Anne, her head resting on his shoulder. They hadn't said much since the fallback point — they didn't need to. Their bond had deepened in the quiet spaces between violence and survival.

Ortega and Maggie sat near the back, not touching now, but sharing the kind of glance that spoke volumes. Steph was half asleep, head bobbing with each bump in the road. Bellamy leaned against the window, staring out in silence, the toll of what they had done at Kinross and the medical centre etched deep into his face.

Daryl sat beside Derek, both men silent, both thinking the same thing: Did we get them all?

As they neared the gate, the lookout spotted them. The siren didn't wail this time — just a whistle and a waving flag. The gate creaked open slowly as a dozen familiar faces came into view.

Jennifer stood front and centre beside Bill, Jillian just behind them. Abby, Vicki, Father Luke — all waiting with wary, anxious eyes.

The truck rolled to a stop. Derek was the first to hop down.

Jennifer rushed to him, pulling him into a tight hug, whispering, "You're back." He held her close but didn't speak, his mind still replaying the screams of the Reapers. The smell of burnt nests. The silence that followed.

Bellamy helped unload what little gear remained, nodding at Bill who gave him a grateful pat on the shoulder.

"You bring hell back with you?" Bill asked.

"Left hell in a crater, hopefully," Bellamy said quietly.

Callum and Anne moved together toward the medical shed — to report, to decompress, to simply get away. Maggie and Ortega lingered near the front gate, both seeming unsure if they should part ways or stay in the open a while longer.

Inside New Haven, whispers spread fast.

They were back.

The Reapers were dead.

But the cost was visible in every pair of tired eyes and blood-stained clothes.

—-

Later that evening, in the council room, Derek gathered those still able to sit upright. Jillian handed out water while Jennifer brought in updates from the community.

Derek stood at the head of the table. "The nest is gone. The medical centre and surrounding blocks are destroyed. We found and eliminated at least twenty Reapers. Burned three nests. Everything… razed."

Callum added quietly, "There were eggs. But they're ash now."

"No casualties," Daryl said. "A few close calls, but we all made it."

Jennifer exhaled slowly. "And you think they're all gone?"

Derek looked up, eyes hard. "I hope so. But we stay ready. We don't assume anything anymore."

The council nodded, each one weighed down by exhaustion but also steeled with new resolve.

—-

As night fell over New Haven. The fires burned low. Guards rotated along the walls. Children slept soundly. But for those who had stared down the Reapers — who had seen what humanity's worst mistake had birthed — sleep would not come easy. And though the gates were closed and the lights dimmed, deep inside every survivor was the same question echoing:

What comes next?

Inside the walls, it was quiet, too quiet for those who had returned from fire and blood. They tried to fall back into routine, meals, patrols, quick updates, but it was all surface-level. Beneath the calm veneer, each one carried something heavier, something scorched into the soul.

Callum sat on the edge of the bunk inside the medical hut, elbows on his knees, fingers running through blood-matted hair. He hadn't even changed yet. Anne knelt beside him, carefully wiping dried blood from his arm, not his own, but Reaper gore. She winced as she got a whiff of it, that awful mixture of rotting meat, char, and something distinctly wrong, something inhuman.

"Still can't get the screaming out of my head," Callum muttered.

Anne looked up at him. "I hear it too. Every time I blink."

He let out a shaky breath. "They didn't just attack. They watched. It was like they understood what was coming — and didn't care. Like they wanted it."

Anne climbed into his lap and wrapped her arms around him, her cheek pressed to his. "It's over," she whispered. "They're gone."

Callum didn't respond at first.

Then he leaned in, pressing a kiss to her collarbone. "Then let's stay here, just like this, for as long as we can."

Anne didn't answer. She just held him tighter.

—-

Over in the small supply room near the barracks, Maggie sat with her legs pulled up to her chest, back against the wall, Ortega pacing a slow line in front of her.

"The smell," she said quietly, "it's still in my nose. Like it's soaked into my skin."

Ortega paused. "I've seen a lot of death. Fought in wars, seen what humans do to each other... but this?" He looked down at her. "They weren't human. Not anymore."

"No," Maggie said. "But I keep wondering... what if they used to be? What if we were just killing victims?"

Ortega walked over and sat beside her. "We didn't kill people. We killed predators. Monsters. You saw them, Maggie. You saw what they were ready to do."

Maggie nodded slowly. "I know. I do."

Ortega reached out and touched her hand, fingers lacing through hers. "You're not alone in this. And I'm not going anywhere."

She looked at him, her expression unreadable for a moment, then she leaned in and kissed him. Soft, hesitant, but filled with emotion.

When they broke apart, Maggie whispered, "Don't let me go crazy."

Ortega squeezed her hand. "Not a chance."

—-

Bellamy stood at the wall, one boot propped on the railing as he looked out over the treeline. A cigarette burned between his fingers, its glow tiny in the dark. The image of Ian still flashed in his mind, slamming the door shut, yelling for them to run, the flames consuming Kinross behind them. And then the Reaper screams, primal, guttural, feral, echoing in that cursed medical centre. He could still feel the recoil of his rifle, still hear the wet crunch of a headshot. He flicked the cigarette over the wall and muttered to no one, "We've started something. And I'm not sure it's done yet."

Steph and Daryl were in the garage, wiping down weapons in silence.

"You think they're all dead?" Steph finally asked.

Daryl didn't look up. "Don't know. Don't care. We did what had to be done."

"But if even one got out..."

Daryl stopped, looked at her. "Then we kill it too."

Steph nodded slowly. "We always come back."

Daryl smirked just a little. "So far."

—-

Derek stood alone on the wall, watching the horizon. The wind was cool tonight. Clean. But he still heard them. He still saw their eyes, still saw that nest. He clenched his jaw, fingers resting on the railing.

"You came back," Jennifer's voice said softly behind him.

He turned. She joined him at the wall. For a long moment, they just stood there.

Then Derek spoke: "We killed them all. Burned it to the ground."

"And?"

"They screamed," he said. "Like they knew."

Jennifer slipped her hand into his. "And we remember. So we can stop it from ever happening again."

Derek nodded — but deep down, he wasn't so sure.

—-

The sun had barely lifted over the horizon, its light filtering weakly through the meeting room windows as the council took their seats. Some looked refreshed after the night's rest; others carried the weight of lingering dreams filled with gunfire, screams, and fire. Derek stood at the head of the table, arms crossed, his tone direct but weary.

"This Reaper business..." he began, letting the silence fall across the table before continuing. "For now, it's being put to one side. We dealt with what we found. We burned every nest we saw. But" — he paused, his jaw tightening — "part of me thinks we missed something."

Eyes shifted across the room, no one daring to speak first.

Bellamy cleared his throat. "We could take a team. Go back. Sweep the area and see what's left. If anything's moving, we'll find it. But we need to know how thorough our solution really was."

Derek looked at him, considering. "Agreed. But we do it smart. We don't go back the same way we came. The risk of a trail leading straight to New Haven is too high."

"I can chart a long route around," Munroe added, pulling out a map. "Swing from the west forest line, loop south. Takes a few hours more, but it keeps them guessing."

Derek nodded. "Make it happen. Quiet, fast. If we find nothing, we confirm the win. If we find something... we do what needs to be done."

Jennifer leaned forward, her brow furrowed. "And if we're followed?"

"That's why we start using the bunker again," Derek replied. "Not for bringing in new survivors — not yet — but for our own entry and exit. If we're being tracked, they'll end up in a graveyard. And even if they stumble across the shack, they won't find the tunnel door."

Bill nodded slowly. "Makes sense. Keeps New Haven clean. Hidden."

"Exactly," Derek said. "But there's more. I want plans drawn up to reinforce the tunnel. Steel doors, fallback points, even traps if we can rig them. If something gets in, I want to know we can contain it, fast."

Maggie scribbled notes furiously while Aria Hensley listened, arms folded. Jillian watched Derek closely from the far end, her expression unreadable.

"Who's on the sweep team?" Callum asked.

"Bellamy, Munroe, Daryl. Ortega too, if he's game. Take two others, your choice," Derek replied. "But you leave by nightfall. And you come back through the bunker only."

Bellamy nodded. "We'll be ghosts."

Derek looked around the room, eyes firm. "Everything we've built, everything we've done — we protect it now. Whatever's still out there... it doesn't get in."

No one argued. Because they all knew — it wasn't over. Not yet.

—-

As the sweep team prepared to move out by nightfall, life in New Haven carried on.

The blast of hellfire that had consumed the Reapers still haunted the edges of conversation, but there was a silent, collective understanding among the survivors: survival didn't wait for closure.

Derek had spent most of the morning between the perimeter and the central tower, coordinating the next wave of expansions with Jillian, Callum, and Lee.

"More lookout points on the northeast wall," Derek instructed. "And we reinforce the fencing by the old water tanks."

Callum nodded. "We can pull teams off morning chores. I'll get Munroe and Ortega to handle the security layout."

Jillian glanced at Derek. "Morale patrol starts in an hour. I'll talk to the new arrivals, see how they're settling. Might set up a movie night in C-Block."

"Good," Derek said. "Feels like people are finally breathing again."

Down in the mess hall, Lily sat in her wheelchair, cracking open tins and portioning dried goods with her usual quiet discipline. Her hands were slower now, but still skilled.

"George, make sure the root veg is used today," she called.

George, sleeves rolled up, nodded. "Already on it. Abby and Emily are prepping the stew. We'll stretch it for two nights."

Emily, new but fast adapting, carried baskets of herbs toward the back.

Abby nudged her with a smile. "You'll be running this place in no time."

—-

Out in the gardens, Vicki worked in silence, hands buried in soil. Her grief over David lingered like a fog, but she'd found purpose in the earth.

Reggie, beside her, offered a gentle smile. "The soil's good here," he said, softly. "Things grow fast."

Vicki nodded. "That's the hope."

Across the plots, Ali, their herbalist, sorted drying leaves and bark under the greenhouse canopy. "I'll have tinctures for muscle pain and sleep by tomorrow," she called to no one in particular.

—-

In the west block, Ashley, Sarah, and Mary added colour to walls with old paints salvaged from town. Sunbursts, trees, even cartoon animals for the kids' wing.

"This isn't just survival anymore," Mary said, standing back from a tree mural. "It's about living."

On the tower, Stephen and John rotated guard shifts, while Bill ran drills for new recruits, barking orders with the urgency of a man who'd seen too many close calls.

Inside D-Block, Mel and Scott had turned two rooms into makeshift classrooms.

"Math in the morning. Reading after lunch," Mel told Michone and Finn, who were now trusted enough to help with younger survivors like Roary and Erin.

Father Luke and Father Thomas held quiet prayer circles twice daily. Attendance varied, but there was always someone — seeking peace, or just silence.

—-

As sunset painted the sky in bruised gold and grey, Derek returned to the planning room where Jennifer was updating the food ledgers. Jillian followed soon after, placing a few notes from the morale walk.

"We're holding together," Jennifer said without looking up. "Barely, but it's something."

"We'll need more," Derek muttered. "Always more."

Jillian touched his shoulder briefly. "We'll find it."

—-

With the Reapers wiped from existence — or so everyone hoped — New Haven found a rare moment to exhale. Between patrols, farming, and repair work, something softer stirred within the walls. For the first time in a long while, people weren't just surviving — they were allowing themselves to feel again.

In the makeshift classroom of D-Block, Mel and Scott had fallen into an easy rhythm. Mornings were filled with lessons, but it was in the quieter hours, when the kids had gone to chores or naps, that something more began to grow.

"You always draw the sun too big," Mel teased, nudging Scott's sketch of a solar system.

Scott shrugged, grinning. "I think the world could use a bigger sun."

She laughed, and for a second, forgot everything outside the painted walls. When their hands brushed over shared chalk, neither of them moved away.

—-

Ali, New Haven's quiet herbalist, spent much of her time between the greenhouse and her drying shed. It was there that Jonas, the always-curious scavenger and repairman, started dropping by more and more often.

"Got any more of that balm?" he asked one morning, rubbing his sore elbow.

"Still haven't learned to stretch before swinging that axe, huh?" she smirked, handing him a fresh tin.

He stayed a little longer that time. And the next. Eventually, their conversations turned to the past — families lost, friends remembered — and in between the silences, something unspoken settled between them.

—-

Vicki still wore mourning like a second skin. David's death had changed her, hardened her — but hadn't broken her. She spent her days with Reggie, side by side in the gardens, the silence between them easy, unforced.

One afternoon, as they finished planting late-season beans, Reggie offered her his water flask.

"Do you ever think we get a second chance?" he asked.

She looked at him for a long time, then said, "I think we get a thousand chances. We just don't always see them."

They didn't kiss. Not yet. But for the first time since the funeral, Vicki smiled — not for David, not for anyone else, but for herself.

—-

While others leaned into new beginnings, Jillian remained caught between silence and desire.

Derek had committed himself to Jennifer more clearly since returning from the fallback site — the two were seen laughing together more, touching without hesitation. But Jillian's presence was never far. She still held Derek's gaze a second too long, still found reasons to linger near the planning room.

—-

As dusk painted the skies in faded copper and grey, Bellamy stood near the gates of New Haven, pulling the strap of his pack a little tighter over his shoulder. The cool bite of evening air hinted at rain, but that wasn't what weighed on him. Derek approached quietly, nodding toward the waiting jeep.

"Don't take any risks," Derek said. "I want eyes on the damage. If anything feels off, you come straight back."

Bellamy gave a half-smile. "Since when do I take risks?"

Derek raised an eyebrow, and they both chuckled, though it was hollow. Bellamy turned toward the jeep where Daryl, Ortega, and Munroe were already loading up. Joining them were Erin and John, two newer residents who had proven themselves reliable in recent patrols and calm under pressure.

"Let's move," Bellamy called out. "Long road ahead."

The jeep engine rumbled as the gates of New Haven slowly opened. Derek stood at the edge, watching until their taillights were swallowed by the dark horizon. Then, with a heavy heart, he turned back inside.

—-

They took the northern bypass, a winding trail that carved through old logging roads and back highways long overgrown. The detour added nearly three hours, but it kept them off main routes that could risk being watched — or worse, followed.

The group rotated shifts, Bellamy, Ortega, and Daryl alternating between driving and scanning the road ahead. Munroe, typically silent, sat with his rifle across his lap, eyes rarely blinking. Erin and John, newer to runs this far out, stayed mostly quiet, absorbing everything like sponges.

They passed rusting wrecks and collapsed overpasses. Whole stretches of road gave way to twisted trees and earth, forcing them off-road more than once. It was a cold reminder: the world beyond their walls was still broken.

But when the sun began to rise, casting gold across the skeleton of the land, they reached the outskirts of Hardford.

—-

As they approached Ground Zero.

The destruction was staggering.

From the top of the ridge, they saw it: a scorched wound in the earth where the centre of Hardford used to be. Buildings were reduced to fragmented walls and charred beams. The improvised bomb had done its job, and then some. As they crept the jeep closer through the outer ruins, the devastation came into focus.

The car blockade, where the Reapers were trapped, still stood like a burnt ribcage. But now the bodies were there, just as they'd left them. Charred. Dismembered. Hollow-eyed and unmoving. No signs of tampering, no trails of dragged remains. No scavengers had come. No Reapers had returned.

Ortega leaned out the window. "They're still here," he muttered, nodding toward the ruined corpses. "Which means nothing else has been back since."

Bellamy climbed out, stepping carefully across broken asphalt and glass. "Last time, bodies disappeared. We weren't sure if they were dragged off, eaten, or... collected."

"But now they're still here," Daryl said, swinging his rifle off his back. "Whatever made the last ones vanish, if it even was something, didn't come this time."

Munroe stood still beside the blockade. "Means one of two things," he said flatly. "They're all dead... or they're watching and waiting."

Bellamy crouched next to a scorched Reaper, its teeth still bared in a death snarl, jaw fused by fire.

"No signs of movement. No recent prints. No nesting residue," he observed. "If this was a nest point, we hit it hard enough to scatter them — or wipe it clean."

"Still," John added quietly, "feels too quiet."

Bellamy agreed.

"Let's move in on foot. Small teams. Sweep the area, gather intel. We'll circle back to the centre and make our call."

As they fanned out across the wreckage of Hardford, the scent of ash clung to everything.

This had been a victory.

But whether it was the end of a war... or just the calm before another storm, none of them could say.

The group split into two teams, Bellamy, Daryl, and Erin heading west through the gutted main square, while Ortega, Munroe, and John moved east toward the remnants of what used to be municipal buildings and the old schoolhouse.

The town's core was obliterated. Charcoal walls leaned at broken angles, street signs twisted like dying branches, windows blasted out into glassy dust. But further out, on the fringes of the fire's reach, some buildings had partially survived.

They moved through the remnants of what had once been Hardford's café district. Tables and chairs were little more than melted metal. Bellamy crouched and ran his hand through the soot. Beneath the top layer, something slick and black clung to the pavement.

"Oil?" Erin asked.

Daryl shook his head, kneeling beside Bellamy. "No. Blood. Mixed with ash."

Bellamy stood, wiping his gloves. "Too much of it to be just a stray scavenger. But it's dry. Days old."

They pressed further, reaching the shell of a post office. Inside, it was almost untouched, half-collapsed shelves of envelopes, burned sacks of mail, a few broken filing cabinets.

Erin poked through a desk. "They left fast," she said, showing a clipboard still attached to the wall, half-scrawled.

Daryl pulled a boot from the rubble. Inside it, bone. He tossed it aside.

"I don't like this," he muttered. "Too many half-burned. The blast didn't get them all. Some ran."

Munroe led them silently through the gutted city hall. It had taken the brunt of the blast, and still smoldered at its foundation.

"Smell that?" Ortega whispered.

John nodded. "Rot."

Inside what remained of the building, they found an eerie scene, half a dozen bodies in what looked like a barricaded stairwell. Some human. Some... not.

Munroe prodded one with his knife. The head was crushed, ribs shattered. "Someone finished them. After the fire."

"Scavengers?" John asked.

"Maybe," Ortega said, pulling a burned piece of cloth from one corpse's hand. "Or one of us missed something."

They made their way to the school. The gymnasium roof had collapsed, but the basement door remained mostly intact. A thick trail of soot-blackened handprints led down the stairwell.

"Bellamy needs to see this," Munroe said grimly.

The two teams regrouped near the blockade.

"Basement's sealed," Ortega explained. Munroe grunted as he wedged a crowbar into the crack of the rusted basement door. The soot-caked hinges shrieked in protest as Ortega shoved from the other side. With a final metallic pop, the lock snapped, and the door gave way, releasing a wave of stale air that reeked of mold, sweat, and rot.

Flashlights clicked on.

They descended the narrow staircase slowly, boots creaking on the warped wood. The air was thick — not with smoke anymore, but with the sickly scent of people who had survived too long in too little space. The beam of Ortega's torch hit the far wall first.

A bunk. No... several. Haphazard stacks of wood and metal frames. Torn sheets, piles of threadbare clothes shoved into corners. Everywhere they looked, the signs of desperation: scrawled notes pinned to walls, shattered jars, ration cans licked clean and discarded.

"Someone lived here," Erin said softly, stepping into the centre of the room.

Bellamy crouched near a pile of papers, lifting one gently. A map. Roughly drawn. Points circled in red ink. He flipped through the rest: lists of names, numbers, some crossed out, others underlined. A final note read only:

"Still hear them at night. I still smell the blood."

Munroe ran a hand over the dusty wall. "It's a bunker. Makeshift. Maybe pre-apocalypse, then modified. No ventilation system. They wouldn't have lasted long."

Ortega knelt beside a box of jars. "Nothing but water. All empty." He opened another. "Spoiled meat. They were down here for weeks... maybe months."

Bellamy stood. "No sign of bodies."

"No sign of them leaving either," Daryl said from the stairs. "No blood trail. No bones. Just... gone."

"Or taken," Bellamy muttered.

John's voice was grave. "Could they be Reapers now?"

No one answered.

In one corner, under a collapsed shelf, Erin pulled a box free. Inside, a recorder, battered, cracked, but intact. She handed it to Bellamy. He clicked it on. The voice that emerged was raspy, terrified, and male.

"Day... thirty-one. I think. We hear them now. Scratching. Whispering. They learn. One of us went out last week. Didn't come back. Doors are still locked. But they're in the walls now. They're in the goddamn walls."

Static. Then silence. Bellamy turned it off.

"This place needs to be sealed," he said. "If those things were here once, they'll come back. Or worse, whatever was here... might still be out there."

Ortega nodded grimly. "Let's torch it."

They gathered anything of value — papers, the recorder, a few supplies — and made their way back upstairs. The basement lit up behind them as flames bloomed from a final molotov tossed down the stairs. Smoke billowed upward, carrying the remnants of some long, dark horror into the morning sky.

As they packed up to leave, Bellamy dropped one final molotov into the post office and watched it burn. No one said a word as they turned back toward the truck.

Bellamy turned to the others.

"Let's get home."

Chapter 15

The sky over New Haven was a dull grey, clouds heavy with the weight of summer rain that hadn't quite broken yet. Life inside the walls pulsed on, but the tension from the latest missions still lingered like smoke after a fire.

In the yard, Jillian led a small group of teenagers through self-defence drills, her voice calm but firm. She'd taken her role as morale officer seriously lately — the people needed purpose, and purpose started with preparation. Behind her, Lexi, one of the younger kids, mimicked every move with focused precision.

"You've got it," Jillian said, ruffling the girl's hair. "Just don't try that on Callum unless you want a trip to the infirmary."

Nearby, Vicki and Reggie worked the garden beds in silence, the soil wet and fragrant from last night's storm. Vicki hadn't spoken much since David's death. Reggie did most of the talking — idle chatter about growing tomatoes, which herbs fended off flies best, and how he used to hate gardening until it meant survival.

"I think he'd be proud of you," he said gently.

Vicki didn't respond, but her hands didn't stop working.

—-

Inside the mess hall in A-block, Jennifer and Maggie sat with Sarah and Mary, going over inventory logs and distribution plans. Supplies were holding steady, but barely. The new additions from Kinross had been helpful, eager even, but mouths were mouths, and food didn't fall from trees.

"We'll need another scavenging run west," Maggie said, tapping her pencil. "Another week, two max, and we'll be dipping into emergency rations."

"Let's put together a team tomorrow," Jennifer replied. "Right now, we focus on what's in front of us."

She looked out the window toward the security tower.

"Still no word from Bellamy?" she asked quietly.

Bill radioed in from above. "Nothing. Radio's been quiet for days."

Jennifer's jaw tightened. "They're out there. I know it."

—-

In the newly built D-Block, Erin sat in a corner room, now sparsely furnished with a cot and a small table. She turned a worn photo of a child over in her hand — a memory, or a regret — no one was sure which. Across the hall, Finn, Roary, and Michone practiced cleaning rifles under Scott's watchful eye, the three slowly integrating into life at New Haven.

John, now assigned to the outer wall patrols, stood by the south fence as rain began to spit. He glanced toward the horizon, as if expecting a shape to appear in the mist — a truck, a signal flare, anything.

He muttered, "Come on, Bellamy..."

—-

At the chapel, Father Luke lit a candle as Father Thomas knelt in silent prayer. The flames flickered as if in response to something neither man could name.

"God willing, they'll return," Luke whispered.

—-

And in the guard room, Derek sat alone at the planning desk, eyes drifting over maps, lists, and contingency plans. His fingers tapped rhythmically against the table — not out of impatience, but fear.

Not fear of what was out there... but of what they might bring back.

Outside, thunder cracked in the distance. The wind shifted. And with it came the feeling that something — or someone — was on their way.

Inside B-Block, Lee was going over the new tunnel security measures with Bill, who had just finished checking in with the security teams.

"We've got four reinforced checkpoints built between the shelter exit and New Haven," Bill said, pointing to the schematic laid out on a folding table. "Steel doors, coded locks. We're halfway through setting up the last fallback shutter at checkpoint three."

"Good," Lee nodded. "If we ever have to funnel survivors in through the cemetery entrance again, we'll be able to segregate them and stop them going too far."

"Let's just hope we never need it," Bill replied grimly.

—-

Mel, one of the newly integrated Kinross survivors, had started classes in the old staff lounge turned classroom. Scott assisted her as a co-teacher and watchful eye, keeping younger survivors like Lexi, Tommy, and Emily distracted with reading and basic medical knowledge.

"I still think we should teach them how to shoot," Scott muttered.

"Let them be kids a little longer," Mel replied. "There'll be time for the dark stuff."

—-

Atop the wall, Steph paced while Stephen leaned on the ledge with his binoculars glued to the east.

"They're late," Steph said.

"They were meant to take the long way," Stephen replied. "Give it until sundown."

Steph turned and glanced toward the motor pool. "If they're not back by tomorrow morning..."

"I'll come with you," Stephen offered before she could finish.

Steph gave him a nod and turned back to the horizon. "Let's just hope it doesn't come to that."

—-

Down in the cookhouse, Abby, George, and Emily had just started preparing the evening meal. With tomatoes from the greenhouse and some scavenged pasta, they were putting together a hot meal for the first time in days.

"Did you hear the thumpers last night?" Emily asked, chopping onions.

"Just thunder," George replied.

"Didn't sound like thunder," Abby murmured. "Sounded like something else."

They didn't finish that line of thought.

—-

Back at the gym on the rooftop, Jennifer had set up another sweat-harvesting session, this time including Ashley, Sarah, and a few of the younger adults. Everyone was tired, but Jennifer pushed them with calm authority. They weren't just training anymore — they were collecting what they needed for war.

Jillian appeared at the edge of the rooftop, arms crossed, watching the session below with a quiet smile.

"Bit intense, don't you think?" she asked.

Jennifer chuckled, sweat on her brow. "Better intense than dead."

—-

As the sun dipped behind the hills, casting long golden shadows across New Haven, Derek climbed the north tower alone. He often did this when no one was looking — not to check defenses, but just to breathe.

He looked out across the quiet land.

Still no truck.

Still no word.

He closed his eyes and whispered, "Come home."

Jennifer found Derek in the north tower, where he often escaped to think. She climbed the last few steps and called softly, "You got a minute?"

Derek turned. One look at her face told him this wasn't a social visit. "What's wrong?"

"It's the food," she said. "We're not keeping up. With all the new arrivals, we're going to run out inside a month."

Derek's stomach turned. "You sure?"

"I've been running the numbers with Maggie, Anne, Sarah, and Ashley," Jennifer said. "We've already tightened rations, but it won't be enough."

"Let's go," Derek said without hesitation.

In the map room, the others were already gathered around the table — a faded topographical map of the region spread across it, old notes and hand-drawn marks covering the surface.

"We've marked every location we've heard about from other survivors," Maggie explained. "Word of mouth, old scavenger logs, even scraps from the Kinross archive."

"We've got a few viable leads," Anne added, tapping a spot near the southern outskirts of Blantyre. "There's a food distribution warehouse here — if it hasn't been stripped, it could keep us going for months."

Ashley pointed to another mark farther west. "A co-op farm. Someone at Kinross mentioned it before the fall — supposed to have stored seed, soil treatments, maybe even canned produce. Could be overgrown, could be gone. Still worth a look."

"And here," Sarah chimed in, pointing at an old shopping centre marked in faded red ink. "We already scavenged parts of it. But we didn't sweep the whole second floor — might be worth sending someone back through with fresh eyes."

Derek nodded, absorbing it all.

Jennifer leaned against the edge of the table. "We're not asking for miracles. Just the green light and the bodies to make it happen."

"You'll have both," Derek said. "Tomorrow, we prep teams. No one goes out without backup. You all did good work."

Maggie offered a firm nod. "We'll handle the scouting and lead the runs. You just make sure the gate's open when we get back."

"Done," Derek said. "This is priority now. Reapers or not — we don't survive without food."

He looked down at the worn map — a world that had fallen, yet still offered chances... if they had the strength to find them.

Derek tapped his finger on the marked location of Silverburn Shopping Centre.

"We go in three teams," he said, voice firm. "Four per team. Same rules as before—clear goals, clear fallback plans, no unnecessary risks. But I'm taking the lead on Silverburn. From the last recon report we got, it's not a place I'm sending anyone into blind. I'll handle it."

Jennifer gave him a sharp look but nodded. "Fine. Then I want to lead the team headed west. I'm done watching from behind the walls."

Derek looked at her a long moment before nodding. "Callum stays behind to manage things while we're gone."

She smirked. "Glad we agree."

He looked up at the others gathered, Maggie, Anne, Sarah, Ashley, Lee, and quickly made the teams and wrote them on the board behind him.

Team One – Shopping Centre my team
Derek (Lead)
Michone
Sarah
Lee

Mission: Return to Silverburn. Focus on the east wing and upper floors. Clear it fully. Expect trouble.

Team Two – Industrial Park (Maggie's Team)
Maggie (Lead)
Anne
Ashley
Reggie

Mission: Head east to the industrial warehouses near the old rail station. Look for bulk food storage, tools, and fuel.

Team Three – Town Outskirts (Jennifer's Team)
Jennifer (Lead)
Abby
Ali
Scott

Mission: Small towns to the west. Focus on scavenging homes, clinics, and abandoned roadside stops.

Derek looked around at them all, the last rays of sunlight casting long shadows across the planning room.

"We leave at dawn," he said. "Pack light, move fast, and stay sharp."

Beside him, Michone gave a small nod, gripping her belt knife with one hand. "Let's go take back what's ours."

—-

The sun had barely crested the hills as three vehicles rumbled into place just outside New Haven's main gates. Gear was loaded. Weapons checked. The teams gathered—steady hands and quiet resolve before the road ahead.

Everyone was ready.

Everyone except Michone.

Suddenly, the infirmary doors burst open.

"Jennifer! Derek!" Jillian called, sprinting across the yard. "It's Michone—she's in the infirmary. She won't stop throwing up. Lexi and Erin are with her, but they said she can't go. She's burning up."

Jennifer stepped forward, concern flashing across her face just as Dr. Aria Hensley appeared from the shadows of the building, her expression confirming the news.

"She's not fit for a run," Aria said calmly. "Could be food poisoning. Could be something else. We're monitoring her."

Jennifer exhaled, her focus shifting immediately to Jillian. "Well then—gear up. You're taking her place."

Jillian blinked, caught off guard. "Me?"

"You've been training with Daryl and Maggie. You're ready," Jennifer replied. Then she turned toward Derek, her tone shifting to something half-serious, half-playful. "And you—you better take care of her, or you'll have me to answer to."

Derek smirked and gave a nod. "Yes, ma'am."

Moments later, the cars were lined up, engines humming. The gates of New Haven creaked open as the sun spilled over them.

Jennifer approached Derek one last time. They shared a moment—eyes searching, lingering.

Without a word, they leaned in and kissed, slow and intense. Not goodbye. Just until next time.

As they pulled away, they both spoke at once—"Watch your back. See you soon."

Smiles. Soft, weighted with everything unspoken.

Derek climbed into the front passenger seat of the first vehicle. Jillian took her spot behind him, locking eyes with Jennifer through the open window and giving a small nod.

The engines roared.

The three cars rolled out, splitting paths at the forest fork—each heading toward their own piece of the unknown.

Chapter 16

The three vehicles rolled out of New Haven at first light, each one carrying a team handpicked for the job ahead. The roads were quiet, the kind of quiet that made your skin crawl, as if even the dead were holding their breath.

Derek sat in the front seat of the lead vehicle, Jillian beside him, Sarah and Lee in the back. No one spoke much — there wasn't anything to say that hadn't already been said. Their destination: the shopping centre where Emily and Tommy had been found. The place had seemed quiet then, but Derek had read the report. Something had felt off. He didn't want to risk it again, not without backup.

In the second car, Maggie drove with Anne riding shotgun, while Ashley and Reggie checked weapons in the back seat. Maggie had been quiet the entire morning, her jaw tight with purpose. They were heading for a warehouse district west of town — known supply depots once patrolled by early relief convoys.

The third vehicle, led by Jennifer, moved with similar tension. Abby sat beside her, while Ali and Scott were nestled in back, double-checking their gear. Jennifer hadn't wanted to sit behind the walls any longer. She'd made that clear the night before — and no one had challenged her. They were making for an old food processing plant north of the town, hoping it hadn't been picked clean.

Each group had a route, fallback plan, and rendezvous point — but they were on their own out here. No radios, only signal flares and the hope that they'd all return.

Derek glanced in the rearview mirror at the convoy briefly, then to Jillian beside him. She looked calm, focused, but he could see it in her eyes — the fear, the pressure. He gave her a nod.

She returned it without a word.

And with that, the teams separated at the crossroads, each vanishing into the morning haze — heading toward the unknown.

—-

The cracked road leading to the old food processing plant stretched out like a scar through the hills. Overgrown with weeds and littered with the husks of forgotten vehicles, the path felt more like a warning than a welcome. Jennifer sat behind the wheel, eyes fixed ahead, jaw set. Beside her, Abby checked her pistol. In the back seat, Ali quietly flipped through a notebook of herb lists while Scott, calm and focused, scanned the roadside with his rifle resting across his lap.

"We're close," Jennifer said, pointing ahead where the silhouette of the plant emerged through the trees.

They rolled to a stop outside the crumbling gates of Miller's Agricultural Processing – Est. 1971. The once-proud sign now hung askew, one side snapped from its hinges. Rusted silos stood like giant tombstones, and the factory itself looked half-consumed by time — vines crawling up the concrete walls, doors hanging open like mouths mid-scream.

Jennifer stepped out, her boots crunching glass. "Let's go slow. Check everything. We stay together unless absolutely necessary."

The others nodded and followed her inside.

The factory was a graveyard of industry. Conveyor belts still sat in place, coated in dust. Faded signs pointed to offices, breakrooms, and supply storage. The air was stale and heavy with mildew and old chemicals.

They fanned out.

Scott and Abby headed to the food storage wing. Most shelves were bare, toppled, or picked clean, but in a side storage room, they found old barrels — tightly sealed — likely grain or flour. The seals were intact. A good find. Ali wandered into what looked like an old employee breakroom that had been turned into a temporary first-aid post during the early days of the collapse. It had clearly been looted, but she spotted a loose panel behind a filing cabinet. Inside was a dusty crate containing expired but sealed saline packs, antibiotics, and old IV kits. She smiled faintly. "Still kicking," she muttered, carefully packing it up.

Jennifer moved with precision through the central corridor and the loading bays, eyes sharp, weapon raised. She checked offices, cleared stairwells. All quiet. But twice now — once by the broken coffee machine and again near the freight elevator — she caught movement in the corner of her eye. A flicker. A shape.

She spun around.

Nothing.

She kept it to herself.

The team regrouped after an hour.

"Storage had something," Scott said. "Old grain, sealed. Maybe usable."

"Medical supplies too," Ali added, holding up her find.

Jennifer nodded. "Good. We're not done yet though. We search the west wing and the sublevels. If we're here, we're thorough."

They moved deeper into the facility — rooms with forgotten vending machines, rusted-out office chairs, more signs of life long gone. Jennifer checked each space twice, her unease growing. It wasn't just nerves. She felt it. Again — something at the edge of her vision. A blur.

She froze at the foot of a stairwell. "Did you see that?" she asked quietly.

Abby turned. "What?"

Jennifer stared into the dark. "Never mind."

In the basement, they found what must've been the plant manager's office — caved in from water damage but holding a metal locker in one corner. Inside were maps, safety manuals, and surprisingly, two unopened crates of long-life rations. A windfall. As they loaded everything back into the vehicle, Jennifer glanced once more toward the factory entrance.

There — just for a second — a figure.

Still. Watching.

Then gone.

She climbed into the truck. The others were already talking about what to cook with the rations and what to use the grain for. But Jennifer didn't speak. Not until they were half a mile down the road and the plant had disappeared from view.

Then she whispered to herself:

"I know I saw you."

—-

The sun was already beginning to dip by the time Maggie, Anne, Ashley, and Reggie reached the edge of the suburban retail complex.

Northside Plaza, the sign read in large, rusted letters — most of which were either missing or pockmarked with bullet holes. A once-bustling strip mall, now a husk of glassless windows, crumbled storefronts, and silence.

Maggie killed the engine. "Eyes sharp, weapons loaded."

They all nodded. Ashley checked her rifle's chamber, Anne pulled her hood up tight, and Reggie — with a quiet grimace — secured a crowbar in his belt loop and slung his bow over his shoulder. The parking lot was littered with debris: rusted trolleys, abandoned luggage, broken car doors still swinging in the wind. It had been hit before — probably multiple times — but Maggie had a feeling there was still something here. It just smelled like opportunity... and danger.

They approached the entrance of the plaza on foot, sweeping their weapons across the dark doorways.

"Go quiet," Maggie whispered. "We check the big shops first. Grocery, pharmacy, hardware. Reggie, stay back and mark our exits."

The team split into formation and entered the grocery store first.

Inside, the air was thick — the scent of rot, damp cardboard, and mildew filling every breath. Most shelves had been stripped bare long ago, but as they crept down the aisles, Anne's flashlight revealed sealed jars wedged behind broken display cases. A few unopened tins remained, rolled under collapsed shelving units.

Ashley found a bin of dog food that still had weight to it. "Might not be ideal... but we've seen worse meals."

Maggie smirked. "Pack it."

Near the back, they found the pharmacy cage — its gate twisted and mangled. Most of the meds had been looted, but Reggie managed to find two sealed bottles of antiseptic and a small stash of gauze.

They moved quickly to the hardware store next door.

"Something's off," Anne said quietly.

"What do you mean?" Reggie asked, frowning.

"Too clean. Not ransacked, not burned. Just... like someone swept through and stopped halfway."

Ashley tapped the floor — footprints. Not theirs. Too recent.

Maggie's expression tightened. "Be ready."

They moved slower now, clearing aisle by aisle. Nails, batteries, some tools — all carefully packed into her bag. They took only what they could carry.

Then — a sound.

A clatter from deep within the back corridor.

Everyone froze.

Maggie signaled silently, and they crept toward the rear of the building.

They turned a corner — and saw the source of the noise.

A cat. Thin, half-starved, knocking over a mop bucket.

Reggie exhaled. "Almost pissed myself."

But Maggie wasn't smiling. "Something scared it," she said softly. "Something else might be here."

They did one final sweep — in pairs this time — before heading back to the truck. The sun was setting fully now, sky bleeding orange and purple through broken skylights.

As they loaded up, Ashley muttered, "I don't like it. Felt watched the whole time."

Anne nodded. "Yeah... let's not come back here again."

Maggie looked back once, eyes narrowing at the rooftops. Then she climbed into the driver's seat.

"Let's get home."

—

The sun was already beginning its slow descent when Derek's team reached the outskirts of the shopping centre — a massive, once-bustling complex now overtaken by silence and the creeping vines of decay. It had been nearly a three-hour drive from New Haven, and the tension inside the vehicle had grown heavier the closer they got.

"Eyes sharp," Derek ordered as they pulled into the mostly empty parking lot. "We've had no contact from here in months. Just because it looks quiet doesn't mean it is."

The four of them stepped out: Derek, Jillian, Sarah, and Lee. Their boots crunched on broken glass and gravel as they made their way inside through a shattered side door. The interior was dusty, stale, a faint must of rot hanging in the air — but not overwhelming.

"Pair up," Derek said. "Me and Jillian will sweep the eastern wing. Lee, you and Sarah take the west. Stay sharp, radios on. We're looking for anything sealed, preferably locked down."

The pairs split and fanned out cautiously.

As Derek and Jillian moved deeper into the skeletal remains of what was once a bustling food court, their flashlights cut through long shadows. Dust clung to every surface. Posters hung in tatters. A child's toy lay abandoned in a corner, untouched for years.

As they moved through a defunct staff hallway, Derek broke the silence. "You know... Michone ate the same food we did. So how did she end up in the infirmary, vomiting non-stop?"

Jillian gave a small shrug, her voice low. "Lexi thinks it might have been something she touched. Maybe something from her last scavenging run. Could've been bacteria, not the food. Erin's still not sure."

Derek nodded slowly, clearly still troubled by it. The two continued their search in silence for a while, checking store rooms, old café storage, and what looked like former walk-in coolers — all empty or long since spoiled. Then, just as they were about to head back, Jillian spotted something unusual behind a fallen steel shelf.

"Derek, over here."

They pushed aside the rusted shelf to reveal a reinforced storage freezer with thick padlocks, still intact. Dust covered it, but the locking mechanism looked unbroken. Derek leaned closer, inspecting it.

"This might be it."

He radioed Lee and Sarah. "Get over here. Northeast quadrant. Bring bolt cutters."

Within minutes, the team regrouped. Lee clipped the locks, and with a grunt, they hauled the heavy door open. Cold air rushed out — faint but present. Inside were racks stacked with sealed containers, boxes of frozen meats, preserved vegetables, even prepacked meals. It wasn't pristine, but it had clearly remained frozen long enough to preserve a substantial amount.

They stared in stunned silence.

"This could feed New Haven for months," Sarah whispered.

Derek stepped back, arms crossed. "We can't move it yet. We need a cold storage rig back home. If we transport it without refrigeration, we lose everything."

"Do we even have the power for that?" Lee asked.

"Not yet," Derek admitted. "But I'll talk to Jennifer and Bellamy. Maybe we can get a unit running on one of the backup generators or solar routes. Until then, we seal this up and mark it."

They closed the freezer and re-secured it as best they could.

As they prepped for the return, Derek looked at the building around them. "We'll be back for it," he said. "But next time, we come with a truck and a plan."

As they continued searching, a crashing sound ripped through the eerie silence like thunder. Derek and Jillian skidded to a stop just as Lee and Sarah came running from a side corridor, eyes wide.

"What the hell was that?" Sarah panted.

They didn't need to wait long for an answer. A low groaning sound echoed from below, followed by the clatter of broken glass and dragging footsteps.Derek moved fast, leading the others toward the edge of the second-floor balcony that overlooked the shattered main concourse. Dozens of bodies shuffled and twitched below.

Zombies.

Not Reapers — not fast or clever — but at least fifty of them, stumbling through the large window that had somehow held up all this time... until now.

"Shit," Lee muttered. "We're trapped up here."

"No, we're not," Derek said, already thinking through it. He pointed across the upper level to the old service corridor. "There's a stairwell over there. It leads straight down to the carpark. We split."

He looked directly at Jillian. "I'll draw them up here. You and the others move for the car."

"No," Jillian said immediately, shaking her head. "I'm not leaving you alone, Derek."

"You're not helping if we all get cornered." Derek replied.

"Then we draw them together. You're not doing this solo." Her voice was firm, unwavering.

Derek cursed under his breath, but deep down, he knew arguing with Jillian was pointless — especially when her mind was made up.

"Fine," he relented. "Lee, Sarah — you make for the service stairs. Stay low, be quiet. Get to the car. Once we pull them up here, we'll loop back around and meet you there."

Lee gave a sharp nod. "You better not get bit."

"Would ruin my day," Derek muttered.

The group split — Lee and Sarah disappearing down the hallway toward the service stairwell while Derek and Jillian moved along the second floor, knocking over mannequins, throwing debris, and yelling loudly enough to draw the undead's attention. And it worked. Slowly but surely, groans grew louder, and the first of the undead began dragging their way toward the stairs, lured by sound and motion.

Derek turned to Jillian, nodding once. "Let's go. Stay close."

Together, they prepared to run, hoping to slip down another access stair once the herd had cleared enough from the bottom floor. But with that many zombies, even the best plans could crumble in an instant.

As the undead started climbing the last set of stairs to the second floor, Derek's heart thudded in his chest. He could see Lee and Sarah already climbing into the car. Just as he reached for Jillian's hand to move toward the second stairwell, he caught sight of something that stopped him cold — more of the undead, a massive horde, at least a hundred strong, flooding out from the treeline behind the car park.

"Shit," he muttered, grabbing his radio. "Lee! Sarah! There's more of them, a full horde heading your way. You need to move now!"

Lee's voice crackled back. "Copy that! We see them... we're gone. Hold tight and don't get bit. We'll be back!"

The car peeled away with a screech, dodging through debris, the groaning horde now in full pursuit. That left Derek and Jillian with a problem of their own — fifty zombies, slow but steady, were nearly on them. The moans were louder now, echoing off the concrete walls like a death march.

Derek yanked Jillian back from the rail. "We need cover. Now."

They bolted through the upper level, ducking between storefronts, shuttered kiosks, and overturned benches. Jillian's breathing was heavy but controlled; she was in it, focused, adrenaline-fueled.

"There!" she pointed. An old service corridor door was half-open near the food court.

They sprinted toward it, Derek kicking the door fully open and ushering Jillian inside. He slammed it shut and immediately began dragging a metal trolley in front of it.

The moans grew closer.

Jillian flicked on her flashlight. The hallway stretched ahead in eerie silence — cracked linoleum, grime-stained walls, broken lights. An old maintenance sign hung crookedly: Cold Storage - Staff Only.

"Back route?" she asked.

Derek nodded. "Maybe. If we're lucky."

They moved deeper into the corridor, weaving past stacked crates and old cleaning equipment. The sounds of the dead faded slightly, muffled by the door and distance, but they weren't far.

"We need to find a spot to hunker down," Derek whispered.

Another door appeared — this one rusted but intact, the sign above it worn but still legible: Electrical/Utility Room. Derek tested the knob. It opened. Inside, it was cramped and dark, but defensible. No windows, just a few shelves, old wiring gear, and a bench along the back wall. They slipped inside and shut the door. Derek wedged a broken mop handle under the doorknob to jam it closed.

For now, they were safe.

Both sank to the floor, chests heaving.

Jillian leaned her head back against the cool metal wall. "That was too close."

Derek nodded, trying to slow his breathing. "Yeah... but we're alive."

Outside, the distant groans rose again, muffled but persistent. The dead were still hunting.

"We need to stay quiet," he said, lowering his voice. "And wait for Lee and Sarah. If they can loop back..."

Jillian looked at him — truly looked — in the dim light. "And if they can't?"

Derek didn't answer. He didn't have to. They both knew what that meant. But for now, they were still breathing. Still together. And still fighting.

—-

A few hours have passed, Jillian whispered, "Maybe they left", hoping that zombies weren't there.

Derek didn't answer at first. He couldn't let his guard down just yet. He slowly moved toward the door, peering through a small crack in the wood. The corridor was empty. He gave a sigh of relief. "Let's move," he muttered, reaching for Jillian's hand. They slipped quietly out of the maintenance room, moving quickly down the corridor, past staff-only areas, and toward the other end of the service corridor. Derek stayed close to the walls, eyes darting at every corner, every darkened doorway. He slowly opened the next door and froze. There they were — the zombies. A group of them stood motionless, as if waiting, blocking the exit to the door they had first entered.

"What are they doing?" Jillian whispered, her voice barely audible.

Derek leaned in closer, his eyes narrowing. "I don't know... I've never seen them do this before." His voice trailed off in confusion. Why were they just standing there? Why weren't they moving? He stayed still, watching them, waiting for any sign of movement.

—

The car sped through the outskirts of the city, weaving around rusted wreckage and long-abandoned traffic. Lee's hands gripped the wheel tightly, jaw clenched, eyes flicking between the cracked road and the rearview mirror. Sarah sat in the passenger seat, arms folded across her chest, staring silently ahead.

There was no sign of the horde. No sound but the growl of the engine and the occasional rattle of loose supplies in the back. Lee finally snatched up the radio and keyed it in.

"This is Lee. We're three miles east of Silverburn. Derek and Jillian... they're still inside. We had to leave. There was a second horde, bigger than the first—maybe over a hundred. They cut us off."

A brief pause.

Static.

Then Callum's voice cracked through the radio, calm but sharp. "Copy that. You did the right thing. Find shelter. Stay low and stay put. I'll pull together a backup team and come get you. Hang tight."

Lee exhaled and looked over at Sarah. "You hear that?"

She nodded slowly. "Yeah... but I hate it."

"I know." Lee replied.

They drove in silence for another few minutes, both scanning the road ahead and the treeline for any sign of movement. Every rustle, every flicker of shadow sent their nerves jumping.

"Over there," Sarah pointed. "That farmhouse. Roof's still intact."

Lee nodded and turned off the main road, bumping over uneven gravel toward the small farmhouse tucked behind a patch of overgrown trees. It looked weathered but intact — solid enough for one night. They parked the car behind it, out of view, and quickly swept the place. Empty. Safe. For now.

Lee grabbed the radio again. "Callum, this is Lee. Found shelter. Old farmhouse off M77. We'll hold here until you come. Please hurry."

"We will," came the reply.

As dusk settled over the countryside, Lee and Sarah fortified the doors, boarded a broken window, and sat with their backs to the wall in the living room. Neither spoke for a long time. Only one thought ran through both their minds.

Please let Derek and Jillian be alive.

Back at New Haven, the sun had just reached its peak, Bellamy's team had just rolled in through the gates as Callum came running from the main building shouting at them to get ready to go back out.

"What's going on?" Bellamy asked immediately.

Callum didn't waste a second. "Lee and Sarah just radioed in. Derek and Jillian are pinned down at Silverburn. A horde hit them hard. Lee managed to get himself and Sarah out but had to leave Derek and Jillian behind. They're five miles west, just inside radio range."

Ortega clenched his jaw. "Damn it."

Daryl was already checking his rifle. "Does Jennifer know?"

Callum shook his head. "Not yet. She's still out with her team. I've asked Bill to brief her when she gets back."

Munroe nodded sharply. "What's the plan?"

Callum looked them all over, already stepping toward the motor pool. "We head to Lee and Sarah first. If the horde's moved on or scattered, we go in for Derek and Jillian. If not, we find a way to make it happen."

Bellamy was already moving to the truck. "Let's go."

The rest fell in line. They didn't need a rousing speech. They just needed to get there in time. As the gate rolled open, the engine roared, and the truck pulled out, leaving New Haven in its dust. Time was against them. But they were going anyway.

—-

An hour had passed at New Haven, Bill was in the watch tower waiting. The midday sun cast long shadows as Jennifer's car rolled up the dirt path toward New Haven's gates. Dust trailed behind the wheels, swirling in the warm air as the vehicle came to a halt. The gates creaked open, and Bill was already descending the watchtower ladder in a hurry.

Jennifer stepped out of the car, brushing a hand through her windblown hair. "Where's Derek?" she asked immediately, her instincts prickling.

Bill's face was pale and tight. "We need to talk."

Jennifer froze. "What happened?"

Bill led her aside, away from the others who had gathered to help unload supplies. "Lee and Sarah radioed from Silverburn. Derek and Jillian are trapped inside."

Her eyes widened. "What?"

"There was a horde. Over a hundred, maybe more. Lee said Derek told them to drive off — to save themselves".

Jennifer's face went blank with shock. Her lips moved but no words came out.

"They're alive — or they were," Bill added quickly. "Callum already took a team — Bellamy, Daryl, Ortega, John, Erin, and Munroe. They've gone to find them."

Just then, the second vehicle came into view — Maggie's team, returning with their own share of supplies. The truck rolled into the main carpark and Anne jumped out first, waving casually until she saw Jennifer on the ground and the look on Bill's face.

"What's going on?" Anne asked, jogging over. "Jen?!"

Jennifer turned, eyes brimming with tears. "It's Derek and Jillian... they're trapped in Silverburn. They're surrounded by zombies."

Anne didn't hesitate. She turned to Maggie and Ashley, who had just climbed down from the truck. "We need to leave, Jennifer get in the truck, we head for the farmhouse and the rescue team".

The truck sped away into the distance as New Haven's gates shut. Bill was left to unload the supplies from Jennifer's car and hope that they all came back from Silverburn.

Alive!

Chapter 17

The floorboards creaked under Lee's boots as he approached the narrow window of the abandoned farmhouse. Dust hung thick in the air, filtering through beams of sunlight that pierced the cracked slats. He pulled aside a corner of the curtain. A black SUV rolled slowly down the overgrown driveway, crunching gravel under its tires. The engine cut off. The doors opened — one by one, familiar faces stepped out.

Lee turned toward Sarah, lowering his weapon. "Stand down, it's Callum."

She exhaled in relief but kept her pistol close as the front door creaked open. Callum entered first, followed by Daryl, Bellamy, Ortega, Erin, Munroe, and John — each one of them already looking around, assessing the structural integrity of their temporary shelter.

"Nice spot," Bellamy said, giving a small nod of approval. "Defensible. Quiet."

Callum moved straight toward Lee. "You okay?"

"We're fine," Lee replied. "Got out just before the second wave hit. Derek and Jillian... didn't."

A heavy silence fell.

"They're holed up somewhere inside?" Daryl asked.

Lee nodded. "Last I saw, they were still on the second floor. Derek radioed and told us to go — the horde was coming fast. We didn't have a choice."

"You did the right thing," Callum assured him. "Derek would've done the same."

Sarah crossed her arms. "So what's the plan?"

Callum took a breath, turned to the others. "First, we get eyes on Silverburn. See how bad it is. Then we find a way to get them out. Quiet if possible. Loud if we have to."

Bellamy leaned against the frame. "You're thinking a distraction?"

"Something like that." Callum says

"I've got enough ammo to start a war," Daryl added with a small grin. "Just say the word."

Lee looked around the group — nine of them, trained, prepared. "Let's not make noise unless we have to. These aren't normal zombies anymore — they're lingering. Watching. They waited in the treeline. That's not right."

Everyone nodded grimly.

"We move in an hour," Callum said. "Rest up. Eat. Then we go get our people back."

Outside, the wind rustled through the grass as the sun crept higher in the sky. In the distance, the wreckage of Silverburn waited — and inside it, Derek and Jillian, holding their breath in the silence.

Just as Callum and the group were loading up to head out toward Silverburn, the thunder of a car barreling down the dirt track caught everyone's attention. The vehicle fishtailed slightly as it came to a screeching halt outside the front gate of New Haven. Dust plumed in the air, and the gate guards raised their weapons instinctively — until the doors flew open. Out stepped Jennifer, Anne, Maggie, and Ashley — all armed, all geared up.

"We're coming with you," Jennifer declared before Callum could speak, Jennifer locked eyes with Callum. We're bringing them home. No matter what."

Callum gave a single nod. "Then let's move."

With that, the two vehicles loaded up fast. The engine rumbled as both cars — now a combined strike-and-rescue team — rolled out of the farmhouse, their mission clear:

Get to Silverburn. Then bring Derek and Jillian back alive. No matter what.

The convoy rumbled down the broken tarmac, the early morning light bleeding over the horizon in a dull smear of grey. Cracked road signs bent under the weight of rust and weather. Silverburn lay just a few miles ahead, but the silence pressing down on them made it feel like they were driving toward the end of the world. In the lead vehicle, Lee gripped the radio handset tightly, his knuckles white as he turned the dial, scanning for any response.

"Derek, it's Lee. Come in. You copy?"

Nothing. A beat of static. Then silence.

He tried again. "Derek? Jillian? Anyone?"

Still nothing.

Jennifer sat in the back seat, eyes fixed on the radio with a clenched jaw. Her fingers tapped against her leg, an anxious rhythm growing faster with every unanswered call. "Ten bloody hours," she muttered. "They could be—"

"They're not," Callum cut in from the passenger side. "They're smart. Derek especially. If anyone can survive down there... it's him."

Jennifer didn't respond, her eyes now on the road ahead. In her gut, a quiet storm had been brewing since they lost contact. Something wasn't right.

Around 20 minutes later, the convoy slowed as they approached the rise that overlooked Silverburn's massive carpark. Everyone piled out, moving to the crumbling motorway barrier. From here, they had a full view of the shopping centre below.

A carpet of zombies filled the carpark — hundreds of them, maybe more. But they weren't moving. They just stood there, crammed against broken cars and shattered glass, shoulder to shoulder, packed tight. Their heads drooped or tilted at unnatural angles, and not a single one twitched or groaned. The stillness was unnerving.

Not a growl. Not a hiss. Not even a shuffling footstep.

Nothing.

Lee raised his binoculars slowly. "Jesus..."

Bellamy stood beside him, arms crossed, eyes narrowed. "Never seen them behave like that before."

"They're... waiting," Anne said quietly from behind them.

Jennifer's stomach turned. "No," she whispered. "They're watching."

Ashley stepped forward. "You think they know we're up here?"

"if they don't, then they will soon," Maggie said, her voice low.

Ortega, kneeling by the edge, peered through a cracked pair of field glasses. "Derek's last transmission said he and Jillian were in the service corridor. If they're still in there... they've been trapped all night."

"Then we go," Jennifer said, turning to Bellamy. "Now. We figure out a plan on the move."

Bellamy glanced at her, then nodded. "Gear up. Keep it quiet. We'll sweep around the back entrance — see if we can draw them away without causing a stampede."

A gust of wind blew through the trees behind them. Still the horde didn't move. It was like looking at statues — only statues that could tear your throat out the second you blinked.

The group huddled behind the broken motorway barrier, crouched low among the weeds and fractured concrete. The tension was thick — the kind that made your breath feel loud, even when it wasn't.

"We need to get them moving," Ortega said, checking the string tension on his crossbow. "Test them."

He raised the weapon and took a knee, steadying his breath. Across the road, beyond the cracked embankment and into the nearby housing estate, a rusted blue Vauxhall sat half-buried under debris. Ortega loosed the bolt. Crack. The bolt shattered the front passenger window clean through. Glass sprayed the pavement. The sound echoed off the nearby buildings.

But the horde didn't react. Not a single head turned.

Jennifer leaned forward, eyes narrowing. "What the hell..."

Daryl, perched partway up a skeletal tree, raised his own crossbow. "Alright. Let's see if they feel pain." He sighted a tall, balding figure near the back of the group — one eye hanging loose from its socket, jaw twisted open in a permanent scream. He pulled the trigger. The bolt fired straight and true, sinking into the skull with a dull thunk. The corpse dropped like a sack of meat. Still, the others didn't move. No groans. No turn of heads. Just... stillness.

Munroe stepped back, his voice low, rattled. "What the hell is going on..."

No one had an answer. Bellamy stood, his face unreadable. He reached into his rucksack and pulled out a half-full bottle, already stuffed with a rag. "Time to skip the quiet approach."

"Bellamy—" Lee started, but it was too late.

He lit the rag and threw.

The Molotov arced in the air, trailing flame before smashing against the edge of the carpark near the front line of the zombies.

WHOOSH.

Flames licked up their legs and torsos, igniting dry skin and rotted clothes. Three of them toppled over, fire crackling across their backs. Still — nothing. No screams. No rage. Just eerie, deliberate silence. One by one, the burning infected collapsed, curling into ashen heaps. The fire burned, the wind howled — but the horde didn't move.

Jennifer's voice cracked in the stillness. "They're not reacting. Not to sound, pain, fire—"

"They're waiting," Bellamy murmured, more to himself than the group. "For something. Or someone."

Erin looked over at the others, eyes wide. "What if... this isn't a horde? What if it's a signal?"

Silence. The kind that presses on your chest and makes the sky feel lower than it is.

"We need to move," Daryl said, climbing down from the tree. "Whatever this is... it's wrong. We've all seen zombies. Hell, we've seen Reapers. But this? This is something else."

Jennifer's eyes were locked on the unmoving mass below. "If Derek and Jillian are still alive in there..."

Bellamy cut her and nodded sharply. "Then we don't have time. Flank wide, back entrance. No more noise. No more testing." He looked out at the sea of the dead. "They're already watching."

They moved like ghosts. From the treeline down to the rear perimeter wall of Silverburn's vast complex, the group stayed low, weapons drawn, nerves razor-sharp. Bellamy took point, Ortega and Daryl just behind, flanking with crossbows while Jennifer, Anne, and Munroe brought up the rear with the rest of the group between them. The service car park stretched out before them — half flooded, half collapsed — with a row of rust-stained delivery shutters lining the back of the mall. A flickering light buzzed above one loading bay door, barely hanging by its frame.

They stepped over fallen trolleys and shattered crates, the air thick with mildew and dried blood. It smelled like rot... but older. Like death had gone stale. Then they saw them. Three — no, four — infected near the shuttered entrance. Standing. Staring. Not at the team... but at the wall.

Silent. Motionless.

Bellamy raised a hand, signaling halt. He gestured forward to Ortega and pointed. Ortega moved like a wraith, crossbow raised. One by one, they took down the silent infected with clean shots to the head. No reaction. No sound. Just thuds as they hit the damp concrete and collapsed into heaps.

"What the hell is this?" whispered Sarah.

Lee shook his head. "They're not guarding... they're waiting."

Jennifer stepped closer to one of the fallen. The eyes were wide open, glassy. No hint of decay there. These things weren't just shambling monsters — they'd stopped doing what undead things do. Like they were in some kind of trance. Bellamy crouched near the shuttered door and quietly began to crank it open. The rusted metal groaned slightly before he halted. Everyone held their breath.

Nothing.

The horde in the front car park still hadn't moved. Inside, they stepped into darkness.

The hallway reeked of blood and old oil. Jennifer moved near the front now, her flashlight was clipped to her jacket. The beam danced across stained walls. And then the corridor opened into the rear of the shopping centre. The interior was chaos frozen in time. Display stands overturned. Broken glass everywhere. Bloody handprints smeared across walls. A child's toy lay abandoned in a pool of dried black blood.

And then they saw the first floor.

From the broken mezzanine above, they had a clear view of the concourse — wide open, lined with shops, and stretching into darkness at both ends. Fifty of them. Fifty undead. All standing in place. Some near storefronts, others in the middle of the floor. A few were inches from walls, hands hanging slack. One was even kneeling, head tilted toward the skylight above, like it was praying.

But none of them moved. None growled. None even twitched.

The team fanned out into cover behind what was left of a Pret a Manger counter. The silence was suffocating.

"What in the actual fuck," Ashley whispered. "Are they... sleepwalking?"

"No," Jennifer said, eyes locked on one of the infected nearest to them. "They're focused."

Anne turned to her. "On what?"

Jennifer didn't answer. Because now she saw it. In the centre of the concourse floor — barely visible in the dim light — was something... strange. Something that hadn't been there before. A pattern. Drawn in dried blood, crudely etched into the tiles. Circles. Lines. Almost like...

"A symbol," she muttered. "That's what they're staring at."

Bellamy raised his rifle. "Eyes up. This isn't over. We find Derek and Jillian and get the hell out."

Above them, the distant sound of something metal falling echoed across the upper floor. Then silence again. Only now... it felt like something was listening. Bellamy signaled a slow advance. The team moved cautiously through the debris-strewn floor, hugging cover — counters, broken furniture, overturned benches. They stepped over shattered glass and the occasional corpse long since decayed. But the fifty infected that stood among them... they didn't so much as twitch. Each one is as still as a statue. Eyes wide. Shoulders slack. Faces twisted in expressions of nothingness. It was like walking through a minefield where every step could blow — but nothing did.

Lee crouched near a broken sign from a now-defunct tech store, breathing hard. "This is wrong. They're not dormant. They're... aware. They're doing this on purpose."

"You think they're worshipping it?" Ashley asked, nodding toward the symbol smeared in blood.

"Maybe," Ortega whispered, scanning upward toward the upper floor. "Or maybe it's some kind of... command."

Jennifer, eyes locked on the symbol, felt a chill crawl up her spine. The shapes weren't random. Crude, yes. Hastily drawn. But deliberate. Five intersecting circles with a jagged line through the centre. Like a compass, only cracked.

She turned to Bellamy. "We need to take a sample. A picture at least."

"We're not here to study cult art," he said, glancing around. "We're here to get Derek and Jillian."

"And if this is connected to why those things are acting like this?" she pressed.

Bellamy hesitated.

Munroe interrupted. "We're wasting time."

They moved past the symbol, giving it a wide berth. Still, the infected remained unmoving — like actors frozen in the middle of a scene. As they neared the centre court escalators, Erin stepped slightly out of formation to glance into a side corridor.

"Shit—" Her breath caught in her throat.

Jennifer and Bellamy moved to her side instantly. There, in the hallway leading toward a staff-only stairwell, lay the body of a man — early 40s, neck torn open, slumped against the wall.

Not Derek.

But next to him... A half-finished message scrawled in blood, barely legible, "They're—" Just that. Nothing more. Cut off mid-sentence. The blood had dried long ago.

Bellamy crouched down, studying the man's face. "Not one of ours."

"Then who?" Anne asked.

Jennifer turned back toward the silent infected still standing in the concourse. Her skin prickled with unease. "Scavenger? Or someone who saw what this place turned into."

From above, the metal clatter echoed again — louder this time. Then... A footstep. Clear. Deliberate. Not undead. Above them. The group froze, weapons raised toward the upper walkway.

Then, out of the shadows of the top level, a silhouette moved. Fast. Too fast to see clearly. It ducked behind the shattered remains of a clothing store window and vanished.

"Not a zombie," Daryl said.

"Could be a Reaper," Ortega muttered.

Jennifer felt her stomach drop. "Or worse..."

Bellamy pulled his rifle tighter to his shoulder. "We split into two. Group A clears the lower floor, checks the west corridor. Group B with me — we go upstairs."

Jennifer stepped forward. "I'm going with you."

"No argument," Bellamy said.

Anne, Ortega, Erin, and John flanked them. The rest — Daryl, Lee, Ashley, Maggie, Sarah — moved cautiously into the west concourse.

The team split, moving in practiced silence, the eerie quiet broken only by the soft shuffle of their boots. But even as they moved, those fifty infected never turned. Never followed. Never flinched. They just stood. Watching nothing. Or maybe, just maybe... waiting for something only they could feel.

—-

The upper floor of the centre was colder. Jennifer felt it immediately as they crept up the side stairwell — not just the temperature, but the air. It was dense. Still. Like something had been holding its breath for too long. Bellamy led the way, rifle raised, boots silent against the concrete steps. Jennifer followed close, flanked by Ortega, Anne, Erin, and John. Each had their weapon raised, eyes scanning every shadow. As they emerged from the stairwell onto the second floor, the shattered storefronts loomed like jagged teeth. Entire shopfronts had been gutted — glass shattered, mannequins toppled and cracked, merchandise long since looted or rotted. But it wasn't the destruction that made Jennifer stop. It was the blood. Smears. Handprints. Drag marks. All recent. Some of it was still wet.

Ortega crouched near a blood trail that disappeared into a store on the right. "Whatever happened up here... it was recent."

"Someone ran," Erin said, pointing to the scuff marks in the dried mess. "But not fast enough."

Jennifer looked up. The light from the windows outside wasn't the best. The shadows in this place seemed too deep, too thick. Something felt off — like the walls were listening. Then they heard it. A soft click. A footstep. Bellamy raised a clenched fist — the group stopped instantly. From one of the far stores — an old JD Sports — a figure stepped out.

Not infected. Not undead. But wrong.

Tall, dressed in torn black cargo gear, patches of tactical armor. A pale, emaciated face half-hidden beneath a mop of damp, matted hair. His eyes... blank. Like he wasn't really there. But he looked at them. Or through them.

And smiled. A long, slow, unnatural grin.

Jennifer felt the hair rise on the back of her neck.

"Reaper?" Anne whispered.

"No," Bellamy muttered. "That's not like any reaper I've seen."

The figure tilted his head. Then — he started to hum. A slow, tuneless sound.

Bellamy stepped forward. "Don't move!"

The humming stopped. And then the man slowly raised his hand and pointed — not at them — but behind them. They turned. And there, silently emerging from another store — were two more of them.

Same look. Same vacant smiles. Same slow humming begins to rise.

"Fall back!" Bellamy barked.

But the humming grew louder. A low, vibrating resonance that seemed to bleed into the walls.

Jennifer's eyes widened.

The infected below — the fifty in the concourse — they started to turn. Slowly. All of them. Away the symbol. Then one by one, they looked up. Straight toward the upper floor. Straight at Jennifer's team.

"Go!" Bellamy shouted.

The humming turned to a shriek — sharp, mechanical, and high-pitched — echoing through the upper level like a siren built into a throat. The three figures lunged.

The first moved like a snake uncoiling — fast, deliberate, too smooth for anything human. Bellamy fired once, the shot slamming into the figure's shoulder. It barely flinched. Still grinning.

"Down it!" Bellamy shouted.

Jennifer opened fire — three shots centre mass. The figure staggered back, but didn't fall. The other two leapt forward, shrieking with that same unnatural pitch, charging Ortega and Erin.

"Contact!" Ortega yelled, swinging his rifle like a bat as the closest attacker got within striking distance. Anne fired a burst into the second figure's side. Flesh tore — but again, no scream. No hesitation. They kept moving like puppets with their strings yanked too tight.

—

"Something's happening," Lee said, backing away from the symbol.

The zombies, once frozen and silent, were now turning — eyes rising, limbs twitching. One fell to its knees. Another tilted its head like it had just woken up. Then, one by one, they looked up toward the mezzanine.

"Shit—" Daryl raised his crossbow.

The first of the zombies screamed — not a groan, not a moan — a shrill, guttural cry. Then the rest joined in. Fifty mouths howled as one. And the entire horde exploded into motion.

"Fall back! Fall back now!" Maggie shouted.

Ashley grabbed Sarah's arm and yanked her behind the shattered Pret counter. The stampede began — feet slamming against tile, bodies crashing through debris, glass shattering under the surge. It was no longer a group of shambling undead. It was a mob.

—-

Jennifer ducked as the third attacker lunged, slashing at her with rusted shears. The blade grazed her shoulder, tearing cloth, drawing blood. Erin opened up with her sidearm, firing point-blank into its jaw. Bone shattered — but the figure didn't stop. It tackled Erin, slamming her into a glass display that exploded beneath her. Ortega tackled the creature off her, wrestling it to the ground, driving a knife up under its chin. Finally, it stopped moving.

"They can die!" Ortega roared.

Bellamy and Anne put down the second — headshots only. Nothing else worked. The first figure, the one with the smile, charged again — Jennifer fired into its face. This time, the bullet found its mark between the eyes. It dropped like a sack of bricks.

Silence.

Three bodies twitched on the ground. Black fluid leaked from their mouths.

Erin gasped, bleeding from her scalp. "The hell were those?"

"I don't know," Bellamy said. "But they're not zombies. They're something else."

From the floor below — they heard the chaos erupt.

"Run!" Daryl screamed, loosing bolts into the surge.

The infected were faster now — not reaper-fast, but faster than they'd ever seen zombies move. Driven by something beyond hunger. Lee fired blindly behind him as they retreated, drawing the horde into bottlenecked paths between kiosks. Sarah tripped — Maggie pulled her up just in time. Ashley tossed a smoke flare behind them. Red fog filled the corridor, disorienting the undead briefly. But it didn't last. The horde was adapting. Working around obstacles. Some even began climbing up broken shelving to reach over barriers.

"Where the hell is Bellamy?!" Ashley shouted.

Lee's voice broke through the panic. "We need to fall back to the service corridor — link up with the others or we're gonna be torn apart!"

—-

The group stood over the corpses of the three smiling attackers.

Jennifer's voice was cold. "They triggered it. The symbol. The humming... it wasn't random."

Bellamy's face was stone. "We just walked into a goddamn ritual." He turned to the others. "We move now. Regroup with the others. Fight our way out if we have to." He looked down over the railing at the chaos erupting below. And then — his eyes locked with something. Something standing in the centre of the carnage. A tall, thin shape... not moving, just watching. Not infected. Not alive. Wearing a white mask. It didn't flee. It didn't charge. It simply lifted one pale, gloved hand... and pointed up at him.

—-

The service corridor reeked of dust and mold, the strip lights flickering as Jennifer's group sprinted in from one direction, boots thudding heavily on the cracked concrete.

At the same time, Lee's group barreled in from the opposite end — Lee shouting back over his shoulder as distant growls echoed behind them.

"Go, go, go!" Daryl barked, helping Ashley limp through the doorway.

The teams collided in the middle, weapons raised until they saw one another — dirty, blood-smeared, wide-eyed.

"They're behind us!" Maggie shouted.

Bellamy didn't hesitate. "Up the stairs — now!"

The metal stairwell groaned under their weight as the entire group thundered up, the narrow corridor behind them already filling with snarls and slapping footsteps. The double doors burst open as both groups — battered, breathless — reunited on the shopping centre floor. Groans echoed behind them, the sound of the horde hot on their trail. But something was still wrong.

The undead weren't attacking in their usual frenzy. They were coordinated, eerily in sync — still moving fast, still hunting, but not chaotic. It was controlled.

Ortega slammed the service hallway door shut behind them. "They're still coming!"

"No time to regroup," Bellamy snapped. "Move!"

Then Jennifer saw it — halfway up on the first-floor balcony. The figure. White porcelain mask. Tactical black gear. Perfectly still. And smiling. Unmoving as dozens of infected streamed past below, crashing into walls, stumbling over counters — but never touching it. It was like they didn't even see it.

"Same one," Daryl said. "I saw it before—watching."

Jennifer raised her rifle.

"No," Bellamy said grimly. "Let Ortega and Daryl take it."

They stepped forward together.

Daryl's crossbow bolt zipped upward — it clipped the mask, slicing a jagged crack across the cheek. The figure didn't react. It simply turned its head... and let out a low, guttural growl — a sound too deep, too unnatural for any human throat. The horde screeched in reply. They surged forward in unison.

"Take the shot!" Bellamy roared.

Ortega adjusted, exhaled, and fired.

Thunk.

The bolt embedded deep in the centre of the mask — straight through the head. The figure jerked violently and collapsed backward, vanishing from view. For a moment — silence.

And then...

The change was instant. The pursuing horde stumbled mid-stride — snarls cut short. Hands twitched. Feet faltered. Dozens of undead collapsed to their knees or spun in disoriented circles. The coordinated rage drained from their eyes. Groans returned. Slack jaws hung low. The sprinting stopped. Now they shuffled. They moaned. Staggered. Drooled. The hive-mind fury — gone.

Ashley lowered her weapon slowly. "What the fuck just happened?"

"They were being controlled," Jennifer muttered, heart pounding. "That thing... it was the source."

Bellamy stepped forward. "Doesn't matter. They're still dangerous."

He turned to the group. "Get into that store. Now."

They flooded into the back of a looted Iceland, slipping behind counters and storage crates. Bellamy pointed toward the metal refrigeration units along the back.

"We draw them in. Seal the door. Trap them."

Maggie, Lee, and Sarah banged old cans along the corridor walls — just enough noise to draw a dozen of the newly reverted zombies toward the store. They stumbled in slowly. Shuffling. Moaning. Back to what they were — mindless and hollow.

Jennifer and Ortega moved behind the door as the last few entered.

"Now," Bellamy ordered.

SLAM.

The door shut hard.

CLUNK.

Latch engaged. From inside — fists beat the walls. Moans echoed. But no screams. No patterns. Just noise. Just the dead again. Contained. Silverburn had fallen quiet.

But something far worse had just begun.

—

The team moved slowly now — exhausted, scraped up, and still processing the chaos that had unfolded. The groans of the trapped infected in the refrigeration room had faded into muffled echoes. For the moment, the shopping centre was still. They followed the faint, rhythmic banging echoing from further inside — metal on metal, deliberate.

Jennifer's pulse kicked again. "That's them."

Through the shattered remnants of a travel agency and past an upended cash machine, they reached the bank. The door to the main branch was barricaded with overturned chairs and a broken sign. Behind it, the vault stood closed... but not sealed.

The rhythmic bang sounded again — hollow but strong.

Bellamy banged twice in return. Silence. Then the vault door slowly creaked open. And there they were. Derek and Jillian, dirty, tired, and squinting against the sudden light.

Jennifer didn't wait. She dropped her weapon and threw her arms around Derek, squeezing him tight enough to make him grunt. "I thought you were dead," she whispered.

"Not even close," he said with a crooked smile.

Then Jennifer hugged Jillian too — just as tightly. "You okay?" she asked.

Jillian nodded, eyes red. "We are now."

Inside the vault was a small stash of scavenged supplies — bottles of water, canned beans, a flashlight, and a few energy bars. It was just enough for them to hold out.

Derek leaned against the doorframe, exhaling slowly. "They came right after Lee and Sarah left. First it was quiet... then the infected started acting weird."

Jillian added, "They all stopped. Just stopped moving. Like they were waiting for something."

"We figured it was a chance to slip out," Derek said. "Made it to the top floor, but two of those... things chased us. Fast. Quiet. Smiling."

"We killed one," Jillian said, a tremor in her voice. "Threw it from the upper floor."

"Managed to lose the other one in a pharmacy," Derek continued. "We doubled back, found the vault still unlocked. We'd salvaged food earlier... figured it was the safest place to wait. And hope someone came."

Jennifer nodded. "You made the right call."

Bellamy glanced down the hallway. "Time to move."

The sun was beginning to rise behind the clouds as the group emerged from the mall, shadows stretching long across the cracked concrete. They stepped out past the security shutters and broken display glass, weapons lowered, senses still on edge. But the car park — where once a massive horde had waited, motionless and terrifying — was now empty.

Not a single zombie in sight. Just abandoned cars, torn bags, and puddles of standing rainwater.

Bellamy scanned the horizon. "Where the hell did they go?"

No one answered.

Because no one knew.

Jennifer looked at Derek, then at the others. Everyone is alive. Everyone accounted for. But something had changed. Something deep. And as they walked back toward the vehicles in silence, the image of that smiling mask still lingered in all their minds.

Chapter 18

Flashback

Not long after Lee and Sarah left. The sounds of the horde had long faded. But the silence that followed wasn't comforting — it was suffocating. Derek and Jillian moved carefully through the service corridor on the second floor, every step deliberate, boots whispering against the floor tiles.

"Just need to find a place to wait it out," Derek whispered.

They eased into an adjoining store — a gutted clothing shop with shelves torn down and mannequins shattered across the floor. Toward the back, they found a supply box cracked open — inside, a few energy bars, some canned drinks, and half a packet of crackers.

Jillian opened a bottle of water and handed it to Derek. "Think they're still out there?"

"Oh, they're out there," he said grimly. "But something's changed."

As they moved toward the service stairwell, Derek paused. He froze mid-step. Three figures stood across the corridor — just beyond the display windows. Still. Silent. Smiling. All three wore tattered black gear, pale faces stretched by unnatural grins. Their heads tilted slightly, as if curious.

"They're not zombies..." Jillian whispered.

"No," Derek said. "They're worse."

He slowly stepped back, pulling Jillian with him. That's when they moved. Fast. No sound. No warning. The first lunged — claws swiping, just missing Derek's face by inches as he ducked. The second sprinted straight for Jillian — arms out, eyes wide.

"Jill—down!" Derek grabbed her by the shoulder and yanked.

The creature overshot — stumbled — and toppled over the balcony railing. Crack. It hit the floor below in a twisted heap.

"Go!" Derek shouted, pulling her toward the closest store.

They dashed inside — a pharmacy, shelves overturned, boxes scattered. They sprinted through the aisles, knocking over racks as they ran into the back storage area. Derek slammed the supply room door shut behind them, wedging a mop handle through the metal hinges. Silence. Then... Creak. The door handle turned. The figure was out there.

Searching. Breathing. Moving without footsteps.

Jillian pressed her back to the far wall, eyes wide. Her gaze dropped. A hole in the floor — maybe where the maintenance team had been pulling up tilework. It led directly to the lower level. "Derek—here!"

They knelt, slipped down carefully — landing hard on the first floor. Groans echoed in the distance, but no fast movement. No shrieking. The reaper-like figure hadn't seen them drop. Sticking to the wall, they edged along the concourse, ducking behind displays, sidestepping overturned tables. Then they saw it.

The bank. The vault door was open. They ran. No second thoughts. They stepped inside, Derek pulling the door closed behind them — not all the way, but enough to block light and sound. The heavy metal sealed them in, locking out the chaos.

And for the first time in hours...They breathed.

Silence followed.

Not the peaceful kind — but a deep, exhausted kind. The kind that seeps into your bones after you've been running for your life. Jillian collapsed to the floor, her back against a metal shelf filled with dusty banking forms and rusted file boxes. Derek sat down beside her, his chest rising and falling, sweat sticking his shirt to his skin.

They didn't speak for a while. Just breathed. Listening. Waiting. Then Jillian shifted closer, wrapping her arms around him and burying her face into his shoulder.

"Thank you," she whispered. "For pulling me out of the way. For not letting me die."

Derek exhaled slowly. "It's all part of the job," he said, trying to sound light.

But there was no humour in her eyes when she pulled back.

Her hand lingered on his chest. "No, seriously. I'd be dead without you. You've always—"

She stopped. Their eyes met. And the silence stretched between them — thick, heavy, charged. The world outside was burning, rotting, breaking apart. But at that moment, there was only the two of them. The closeness. The heat. The fear. The relief.

"I honestly would be dead without you," she repeated softly.

And before she could say anything else, Derek leaned forward and kissed her. It was sudden. Not rough. Not frantic. But real. Firm. Full of everything they'd buried and bitten back for months. Jillian didn't pull away. Her hand slid up the side of his face, fingers curling into his hair.

And for a moment — just a moment — the end of the world didn't matter.

They were alive. Together. Still human. And both thought the same thing, this could be where they die!

—

Back at New Haven. It had been three days since the Silverburn mission. Three days since the masked figures. Three days since everything changed. Inside the former Warden's Office — now converted into New Haven's council chamber — the twelve seated members gathered around the heavy oak table. Sunlight filtered weakly through the narrow window slits. Maps, reports, and weapon logs littered the surface.

Derek, Jennifer, Jillian, Callum, Lee, Daryl, Bill, Bellamy, Munroe, Maggie, Anne, and Dr. Aria Hensley formed the full council. Each carried fresh bruises, dark circles, and the weight of responsibility.

Bellamy opened the meeting with a tired breath. "Let's get to it. What happened at Silverburn can't be ignored."

Jennifer leaned forward, her expression hard. "We saw them. Not zombies — not exactly. People... or what used to be people. Standing still. Silent. Smiling."

"Then giving orders," Callum added. "The horde didn't move until one of them growled. They were acting like... soldiers."

"Coordinated," Daryl said. "We've seen aggression. We've seen speed. But this? This was strategy."

"They made them wait," Jillian said quietly. "To trap us."

"Then once that last one was killed," Lee added, "everything changed. It was like someone flicked a switch. The infected went dumb again. Wandering."

"Back to normal," Maggie said. "If we can even call that 'normal' anymore."

"We need to assume those masked figures are a new phase," Anne said. "Or a new faction. Someone has succeeded where Ellis failed."

Everyone turned to Dr. Hensley, who had been quiet until now.

"They weren't just anomalies," she said. "The Chimera strain was always capable of evolving. But this... this isn't just mutation. This is design. Or manipulation. Someone's controlling them. Enhancing them."

"And testing them," Bill muttered, arms folded tight.

Bellamy nodded once. "Effective immediately, Silverburn is off-limits. Doesn't matter what supplies are left. It's compromised."

"There's still the freezer," Callum said reluctantly. "But we've got enough from the earlier hauls to stretch three months — four, if we ration the new bread line."

"We can thank Sarah and Vicki for figuring out how to use the flour," said Munroe. "But that's just buying time."

"We can't keep playing defence forever," Derek said, eyes scanning the table. "We need to figure out where those masked freaks came from. And how many more are out there."

"And fast," Jennifer added.

"We reinforce the walls," Lee said. "Expand patrol range. Add more solar motion detectors. I'll start sketching upgrades today."

"And scouts," Daryl added. "We send a team south — quiet. See if Silverburn was a fluke or the start of something worse."

Bellamy looked around the room. "Agreed?"

One by one, the council members nodded.

Hensley's voice cut through the tension like a scalpel. "We've survived Phase One. These smiling ones?" She paused. "This is Phase Two."

Silence fell over the chamber. And the war, they all knew, was far from over.

The heavy door of the council chamber creaked open as the members filtered out, one by one. Outside, the prison-turned-sanctuary of New Haven hummed with life. The clang of metal, the bark of orders, and the scent of freshly baked bread drifted through the early morning air. Life was continuing — cautiously, nervously — but continuing.

In the Courtyard. Derek sat on one of the old stone benches, elbows on his knees, staring at the ground. Jennifer approached and sat beside him without a word. For a while, neither spoke. Then:

"You okay?" she asked softly.

Derek didn't look up. "I keep thinking about Silverburn. How close we came."

Jennifer nodded. "You and Jillian were lucky."

"That's just it," Derek said. "It wasn't luck. It was something else. That figure... if it hadn't slipped, if it hadn't hesitated..." He trailed off.

Jennifer placed a hand on his shoulder. "You're alive. That's what matters."

He glanced at her, eyes tired. "We can't afford to wait for them to slip next time."

—-

Inside the Medical Wing. Jillian sat on the edge of a cot, unwrapping the gauze on her forearm where a deep graze was healing. Dr. Aria Hensley examined her with clinical detachment, but her tone was soft.

"You were in close proximity to two of them," Aria said. "You're lucky you weren't scratched."

"I don't think they were trying to turn us," Jillian murmured.

Aria paused. "What do you mean?"

"They weren't... hungry. Not like the others. They wanted us to be afraid. They watched us." Jillian explained.

Aria noted something in her journal. "Psychological dominance. Like wolves testing prey."

Jillian looked at her. "We killed one. Threw it off the second floor. The other one followed us like it knew us."

"That might be more dangerous than hunger," Aria said.

—-

Out along the eastern perimeter, Lee was already halfway up a scaffold, checking motion sensors and repositioning floodlights. Daryl stood at ground level, chatting with Callum and pointing to a map.

"We should reinforce the treeline, at least twenty meters out. Clear the brush. If anything like those figures shows up again, I want a clear shot."

Callum nodded. "We'll need more arrows, traps, maybe rotating patrols."

"We'll make it happen," Lee called down. He glanced out over the horizon. The woods were still. Too still.

—-

Maggie leaned against the bunkhouse doorframe, arms crossed, watching Anne pack up scavenged medical kits into storage crates. "You think they'll come again?" she asked.

Anne didn't pause. "They didn't come to Silverburn by accident."

"So what, we're targets now?" Maggie asked.

Anne zipped the final kit shut. "We were always targets. Now we just know it."

—-

As the day gave way to dusk, Bellamy stood atop one of the northern guard towers, binoculars pressed to his face. The forest swayed in the wind. Quiet. Peaceful. Deceiving. He scanned slowly. Then stopped. A flicker of white. Just at the edge of the treeline. Not moving. Just watching. A shape in black, with a sliver of something pale — a grin? He blinked. It was gone.

The next day Derek was just stepping out of the tool shed when Daryl and Ortega flagged him down. Both were geared up already — rifles slung over their backs, hands marked with grease and dirt from earlier checks on the perimeter.

"We've got an idea," Daryl said. "About reinforcing the treeline."

Derek wiped sweat from his brow. "Alright. What've you got in mind?"

"There's a storage room in the prison basement," Ortega explained. "Full of razor wire coils, gloves, nail hooks. Probably leftover from before this place fell. We're thinking: secure the treeline using all of it. Stretch the wire across the back end as far as it'll go. Spike traps between the trees."

Daryl added, "As a last line of defense, we could even dig a moat. Deep enough so nothing crosses it without using the roads. Funnel them into choke points."

Derek considered it for a moment, then nodded. "Good thinking. The moat idea's solid, but we'd need equipment — diggers, maybe a crew. That's something we'll plan for."

He turned to Ortega. "The treeline and traps, though — start immediately. Draw up the layout. I want the plan on my desk within the hour."

"You got it," Ortega said, already turning back toward the yard.

Daryl lingered. "You alright, boss?"

Derek gave him a half-smile. "Since when did I sign up for this job?"

Daryl shrugged. "Since we all started surviving because of you."

—-

The sun was starting its descent behind the trees, bathing the compound in fading gold. Derek stepped out onto the admin block rooftop — his quiet place. From here, he could see the main yard, the walls, the distant forest line... and the pressure sitting on his shoulders. He heard soft footsteps behind him.

Jillian. She didn't say anything at first — just leaned on the ledge beside him, arms folded, watching the sky turn amber. "You've got the whole place spinning around you now," she said.

Derek smirked, but it didn't reach his eyes. "Yeah. Lucky me."

Jillian was quiet, then said softly, "You saved me back there."

"You would've done the same."

"Still," she said, turning to him. "Thank you. For pulling me out of the way again. For getting us through that."

Derek looked at her. "It's what I do Jill. You're family to me just like Jennifer. There's nothing I won't do to protect you both." He didn't mention the kiss in the vault, neither did she, but both knew this would come to a head eventually.

New Haven had settled into an uneasy quiet. The clang of tools had faded. The children had been called in. A few guards still patrolled the walls, their silhouettes shifting in the golden wash of the sunset.

Up on the rooftop, Derek and Jillian stood side by side, resting against the rusted railing. The view stretched far — beyond the high concrete walls, over the treetops, into the horizon where the sun began to melt into amber and crimson.

The silence between them wasn't awkward. It was earned — forged through fire, blood, and shared secrets. Jillian leaned her head lightly on Derek's shoulder. He didn't pull away. The breeze was soft, warm. The world, for the first time in days, felt still.

"I used to hate sunsets," Jillian murmured. "They always felt like endings."

Derek glanced sideways at her. "And now?"

She smiled faintly. "Now they feel like breathers. Little pauses between battles."

He nodded, his eyes fixed on the edge of the forest. "We'll take every one we can get."

They stood there for a long time, saying nothing else. Just two survivors on a rooftop, watching the light die slowly, knowing darkness would come again...

...but not just yet.

Chapter 19

The sky had barely begun to shift from charcoal to pale blue when Daryl tightened the final post knot. The sharp twang of tensioned wire echoed softly through the treeline as Ortega straightened up, wiping sweat from his brow with the back of a gloved hand.

"We've got enough for three full rows," Ortega said, checking the tension. "Should stretch the entire treeline if we use the gaps right."

"Let's make it four," Bellamy muttered from a few paces down. "We've got the metal. Let's make damn sure nothing walks through it."

Maggie and Munroe moved in sync nearby, driving more posts deep into the earth while Steph, standing sentry at a clearing, scanned the woods with sharp, cautious eyes. Her rifle hung loose in her grip, but her eyes were fixed on the shadows. Birds began to chirp in cautious bursts — the hesitant signs of a world trying to pretend it was normal again.

—-

While the rest of the settlement stirred and came to life, Derek hadn't moved. He'd been standing there all night — still, silent, watching the treetops shift in the wind like the restless ghosts of everything they'd lost. The incident at Silverburn played on a loop in his mind. The smiling figures. The dead standing still. The moment the horde dropped like puppets with their strings cut. The food they'd left behind. The lives they nearly lost.

The cold vault. The pounding on the door. Jillian's voice in the dark. Her body pressed against his. The kiss. The weight of her hand in his. He hadn't meant for it to happen again. But it had. And worse, part of him hadn't wanted it to stop. And Jennifer... her arms around him when they were found. Her warmth. Her loyalty. Her faith in him.

He felt like a man split in two.

He gripped the railing tighter, his knuckles whitening. Below him, New Haven stirred. Fires were being lit. Morning patrols called out reports. Kids laughed faintly in the courtyard as water was drawn. Life was moving forward. But Derek? He was still stuck in that corridor, staring into the eyes of something not quite human. And wondering when it would come back.

—-—

The sound of boots on concrete broke the silence, slow and deliberate. Derek didn't have to turn. He already knew who it was. Callum stepped up beside him, saying nothing at first. He stood just far enough away to give Derek space, but close enough to be heard over the soft wind sweeping across the roof. For a long moment, neither spoke. Below them, New Haven was fully waking. Smoke curled from chimneys, patrols rotated positions, and the early morning drills had begun in the yard. Eventually, Callum broke the silence.

"You haven't been sleeping."

Derek gave a dry, humorless chuckle. "Didn't realize you were keeping tabs."

Callum shrugged. "I wasn't. But I know the look. Had it myself after Kinross."

Derek's jaw tightened. "It's not just what we saw."

"I know." Callum replied.

More silence. Then:

"Everything okay with Jennifer?" Callum asked, cautious.

Derek hesitated. "She hasn't asked. I think she knows something's off... but she hasn't pushed."

Callum nodded slowly. "And Jillian?"

Derek turned to look at him, finally. "We didn't mean for it to happen again."

Callum didn't flinch. Didn't judge. He just sighed. "I figured."

"I'm not proud of it," Derek admitted, his voice low.

"I'm not your conscience," Callum said. "But I am your friend. And whether or not you meant for it to happen... you've got to stop carrying it like you're the only one breaking."

Derek looked out at the woods again. "Feels like if I take even one breath for myself, everything's going to fall apart."

"You're not Atlas, mate," Callum said. "You don't have to hold up the whole sky."

Derek smirked slightly. "Tell that to the council."

"I'll tell them once I've had my coffee." Callum joked.

For the first time that morning, Derek let out an actual laugh — tired, but real.

Callum clapped him lightly on the shoulder, then turned to leave. "When you're ready, the crew at the treeline could use a set of eyes. They're almost halfway with the wire."

Derek nodded, watching his friend disappear down the stairwell. He stayed a little longer — just a man with too many thoughts and too much weight. But for the first time in days... he didn't feel entirely alone in it.

The chapel was quiet, as it always was in the early hours. Tucked inside what had once been the prison's visitation hall, it had been repurposed by survivors who needed something — anything — to hold onto. Rows of scavenged chairs faced a modest wooden altar built from broken benches and floorboards. A faded cross, hand-carved and uneven, hung crookedly on the wall behind it. Candles flickered gently in the corners. Father Thomas stood at the far end, his sleeves rolled up, scrubbing at a wax-stained cloth as if cleansing it would somehow wipe away the rot of the world. When Derek entered, the priest looked up, offering a calm, weathered smile.

"You look like a man who didn't sleep again," Father Thomas said.

Derek managed a tired nod and sat heavily in the front row. His voice was low, almost strained. "I didn't come for a sermon."

"You never do," Thomas replied, placing the cloth aside. "But you always leave with something."

A long silence followed. Then Derek spoke — voice raw, heavy.

"I can't stop seeing their faces," he said. "Those things. Smiling like they enjoyed what they were doing. Watching us panic. Watching us run."

Father Thomas listened, saying nothing.

"I keep thinking..." Derek swallowed hard. "What if we hadn't made it? What if Jennifer had come back and found our bodies? What if Jillian... what if she'd—" He stopped himself. Pain clenched in his chest like a vice. "I'm supposed to protect them all," he said. "But I don't know what we're even fighting anymore."

Father Thomas sat beside him, resting his weathered hands on his knees. "It's okay to be afraid, Derek. Even the strongest shepherd sometimes doubts the path."

"I'm not a shepherd," Derek muttered.

"You are to them." Father Thomas said.

More silence. Then a thought — wild, sharp — broke through Derek's clouded mind. His voice was quiet at first. "What if we went back?"

Father Thomas looked over, his brow creasing slightly. "To Silverburn?"

Derek nodded. "We get the food. All of it. The freezer haul. Every scrap. And then..." He exhaled hard, jaw set. "We burn it to the ground. All of it. The figures, whatever was drawing them there — destroy it. So the bastards never come back."

Father Thomas didn't speak right away. Then he said, simply, "Vengeance and justice often wear the same face, Derek. Just be sure you know which one you're chasing."

Derek stood. "I'm not chasing either. I'm trying to make sure no one else ends up trapped with monsters grinning at them from the dark."

And with that, he turned and walked out of the chapel. An idea now burning in his chest like a fuse.

—

The buzz of chatter and the clink-clink of tools greeted Derek as he made his way across the yard and through the rear gate. The morning haze had burned off, revealing a clear blue sky above the surrounding forest. At the edge of the eastern treeline, a half dozen figures were hard at work.

Daryl and Ortega were tying off the final lines of razor wire, threading it with careful precision between thick wooden posts. The wire gleamed silver under the sunlight, taut and sharp as a scalpel.

Further down the line, Munroe was pounding spikes into the ground to mark out pressure traps while Bellamy coordinated placements for the metal spike beds. Maggie and Steph were stacking the remaining coils, already preparing to begin the second row.

Derek approached with purpose, his boots crunching through grass and loose gravel.

Daryl spotted him first. "Hey, boss. About time you got out of your head."

Derek gave him a half-smile. "That obvious?"

Ortega grinned while adjusting a tension brace. "You've got the face of a man who's been fighting zombies and thoughts."

Derek surveyed the setup. "This is good. Real good."

Bellamy joined them, wiping sweat from his brow. "We're halfway through the second row. If all goes well, we'll have three done by sundown."

Steph added from a few feet away, "We've already marked the spike zones. By next week, nothing's coming through here without losing half its body mass."

Derek nodded approvingly, arms folded. "It's solid work. Might be what saves us." He paused. "After this," he said quietly, "we're going to need that kind of preparation everywhere."

Ortega looked up. "Something on your mind?"

"Yeah," Derek said. "But first, I need to call the council together, everyone needs to hear this."

There was a slight hush among the crew, a shift in tone. Everyone knew that back-to-back council meetings meant something big.

Daryl glanced at Ortega. "That about the food run?"

"Not just the food," Derek said. "It's about finishing what we started." He turned to leave, but not before looking over the field of metal, traps, and wire. "You all keep going. This line — it matters." Then he walked back toward the compound, the weight of leadership heavy again... but this time, purpose driving him forward.

—-

The corridors of New Haven were quiet, lit only by the pale sunlight spilling through the reinforced windows. Derek walked with purpose, steps firm, mind racing with the plan he was about to put before the council. He rounded the corner toward the meeting room— And stopped short. Jennifer was waiting. Arms crossed. Eyes soft, but unreadable. She didn't look angry — just... tired. Tired in the way only someone who loved deeply could be.

"Heading to the council?" she asked.

Derek gave a faint nod, trying to step past her.

She blocked him gently with one hand. "Derek..." He paused. Looked at her. "Please don't be distant with me again," she said, her voice low but steady. "I understand that you and Jillian went through something horrifying. Life-threatening. I'm not pretending I know what it felt like." She took a breath. "But shutting me out isn't the answer."

Derek looked away, jaw tense. "I'm not shutting you out."

Jennifer gave a small, sad smile. "You're trying not to. But I can feel you pulling away. Like you're afraid if I get too close, I'll see something you don't want me to."

Silence lingered.

Then, quietly, Derek spoke. "We were trapped. I thought I'd never see you again. I thought we were going to die in that building. And all I could think about was... what I hadn't said. What I hadn't fixed." He looked at her now, finally. "And now I'm back, and you're here, and I don't know how to be around you without feeling like I failed."

Jennifer stepped closer, placing a hand on his chest. "You didn't fail. You came back. That's what matters." Derek's eyes dropped to the floor. "I love you, Derek," she said softly. "But I can't fight to keep us together if I'm the only one showing up."

That hit deeper than he expected.

"I know," he said. "You're not."

Jennifer gave him one more searching look, then leaned in and kissed his cheek. "Come back to me when you're ready." She turned to go— But Derek reached out and caught her by the wrist, gently but firmly. She turned just as he pulled her toward him, closing the space between them in a heartbeat. Their lips met — not cautiously, not gently — but with all the fear, longing, guilt, and love that had been buried since Silverburn.

A kiss full of fire and pain, and promise. When they finally parted, Derek rested his forehead against hers, his voice barely above a whisper.

"I've loved you since the day we met," he said. "And I'll love you for the rest of my life... no matter what happens."

Jennifer's breath caught, tears building in her eyes — not from sadness, but from the weight finally lifting. She nodded. And this time, when they turned to walk into the council room — they walked in together.

The council room inside the admin block buzzed with quiet conversation as members took their seats around the old, scarred oak table. Papers, maps, and updated supply logs were scattered across its surface.

Present were: Derek, Jennifer, Jillian, Callum, Lee, Daryl, Bill, Bellamy, Munroe, Maggie, Anne, and Dr. Aria Hensley.

The air was heavy with anticipation. Derek stood at the head of the table. He didn't waste time. "We're going back to Silverburn," he said. The murmurs stopped instantly.

Bellamy leaned forward. "You serious?"

Derek nodded. "We left a fully stocked industrial freezer behind. Enough food to feed New Haven for months — meat, veg, preserved goods, frozen water. That supply could make the difference come winter."

"We barely made it out alive," Anne said, eyebrows raised. "That place is cursed."

Jillian sat back, arms crossed, her eyes watching Derek carefully.

Callum cleared his throat. "What's the plan, exactly?"

"We go in, extract the food, and then..." Derek hesitated for only a moment. "We destroy the entire site. Burn it down. Take no chances."

Dr. Hensley folded her hands. "You think burning the site will stop the smilers?"

"I don't know," Derek admitted. "But I know this: something unnatural is happening there. Those figures were controlling the infected. They commanded them to wait. To kill. To freeze. And the moment they died, the horde returned to normal. Whatever that was — I don't want it taking root."

Lee looked up from the map. "You think the figures are gone?"

"I think we have to act like they're not," Derek said. "This isn't just a food run. It's about removing a threat before it grows into something worse."

There was a pause. The weight of the decision hung in the room like thick smoke.

Bellamy broke the silence. "What's the extraction plan?"

"We send a small strike team — fast, quiet. Two trucks. In and out. The moment we load the food, we plant accelerants and detonate the interior. The fire should take care of the rest."

Munroe whistled low. "That's gonna draw a crowd."

"Which is why we make damn sure we're gone before the fire peaks," Derek replied. "We'll set traps behind us. Force anything following to slow down."

Bill looked hesitant. "And if the figures come back?"

"Then we finish what we started." Derek replied. A quiet settled again. All eyes were on Derek.

Finally, Jennifer spoke. "You have my vote. We owe it to the people to make sure that place can never hurt us again."

Callum nodded next. "Same here."

One by one, heads turned and nodded in agreement. Until all twelve council members were unified.

Derek exhaled. "Then we move tomorrow at first light. I'll lead the team."

The vote had been cast. Agreement reached. But the room didn't breathe easier — not yet. Derek stayed on his feet, pulling a hand-drawn map of Silverburn from the pile and laying it flat on the table. "Alright," he said, tapping the layout with his finger. "Here's how we're doing it." The council leaned in. "There will be three teams," Derek began. "Each with a different job, all working in sync."

—-

Team one will be the strike team. "Myself, Callum, Bellamy, Jillian, and Lee," Derek continued. "We go into Silverburn. We'll take both trucks and as many large crates as we can carry. The mission is in and out — fast, no detours. We hit the service corridor again and load the freezer contents."

"We'll take firebomb kits and accelerants," Bellamy added. "Propane tanks, fuel canisters, tripwire charges. I'll set the burn pattern to trigger when we're on our way out."

Lee nodded. "Silent entries only. No gunfire unless absolutely necessary."

Team two is on freezer retrieval "While we're out, I want Daryl, Reggie, Maggie, and Ashley at the industrial block across town. We know there were chest freezers in storage there — I need at least six, more if possible. Prioritize ones with strong seals."

Daryl leaned back in his chair. "You'll get them."

"Jennifer and Abby will coordinate the logistics and get the storage zone inside New Haven cleared and ready," Derek added.

Team three will be sorting power, he went on, looking at Dr. Hensley, Munroe, and Bill. "You'll need to rewire a few of the isolated solar panels and divert them to a separate battery array. Freezers draw power and we can't have them leeching from our main grid."

"Agreed," Dr. Hensley said. "We'll isolate the prison's west panel cluster and reroute it to an off-grid battery bank. I'll need volunteers with tech experience."

"Take Scott and Felix," Jennifer offered. "They've been doing maintenance all week."

—-

Derek tapped the corner of the map. "Once the strike team extracts the food, we leave the fire traps behind and detonate from the outside. Bellamy's overseeing the fire pattern — when it goes up, I want that place reduced to rubble."

Jillian spoke for the first time. "What if something's still inside?"

"Then it burns," Derek said coldly. "Whatever those smiling freaks were... I don't want even their memory left standing."

Silence followed. Not from doubt — but from the sheer weight of what they were about to do. A return to hell. A mission to take something vital and erase something even more so.

Jennifer finally broke the tension. "We've all been through worse. But this time, we go in smart. We come back smarter."

Derek nodded, his voice firm. "We move at dawn."

—-

The air had cooled with the approach of evening. The sky overhead burned orange and purple as the sun dropped behind the distant hills. A faint breeze carried the scent of freshly turned soil from the vegetable plots near the wall. Derek found Jennifer alone, kneeling beside one of the smaller planter beds, gently pulling weeds from between rows of carrots. Her hair was tied back, her sleeves rolled up, and despite everything — the vote, the danger, the unspoken tension — there was a calmness to her that eased something inside him.

He stopped a few feet away and said softly, "You always come out here when things get heavy."

Jennifer didn't look up right away. "And you usually bottle it all up until you explode," she replied gently.

A smile tugged at the corner of his mouth. He stepped closer.

She finally glanced up at him. Her eyes were tired, but warm. "You okay?"

He crouched beside her. "Not really," he admitted. "But I'm getting there."

Jennifer studied him. "Are you sure you're up for this? Going back to Silverburn... especially so soon?"

Derek looked away for a moment. "It's not about being ready. It's about doing what has to be done."

"But you're the one going in. After what happened..." Her voice faltered slightly. "You barely made it out."

"I know," he replied.

She brushed dirt from her fingers, then gently touched his arm. "Then tell me the truth — are you doing this because it's right... or because you're still punishing yourself?"

That question hit deeper than he expected.

Derek turned to face her fully. "I keep thinking... what if we'd died in there? What if I'd never seen you again? I can't let that happen — not to us, not to anyone here. So yeah, maybe part of me is doing this to make up for the fear I couldn't shake when I was trapped in that vault. But mostly... I'm doing it because we need to end this."

Jennifer's expression softened. She reached up and cupped his face. "You came back to me, Derek. That's what matters. You don't have to prove anything."

"I'm not trying to prove anything," he whispered. "I just want to make sure we all have a future."

She leaned forward and kissed him — slow, tender, and grounding. When they pulled apart, she rested her forehead against his. "Come back to me again. No matter what."

"I will," he promised. "Always."

They sat there for a while longer, watching the sky fade, saying nothing — two people carrying the weight of a hundred lives, but finding a little peace in each other.

Chapter 20

The cold crept in early. Thin fog hung across the courtyard, swirling around boots and crates as figures moved with hushed purpose. The compound's lights glowed faint amber, casting long shadows across the yard where trucks were being loaded, weapons checked, and last-minute supplies handed out. The strike team gathered near the eastern gate—Derek, Callum, Jillian, Bellamy, and Lee. Each wore lightweight armour, knives strapped tight, rifles slung across their backs, and radios clipped to their vests. Their expressions were grim but focused.

Across the lot, Daryl, Reggie, Maggie, and Ashley prepped one of the flatbeds for the freezer retrieval run. Steel ramps had been welded on the rear. Heavy canvas tarps were folded in the back, ready to wrap anything they recovered.

Near the solar array station, Dr Aria Hensley, Bill, and Munroe were double-checking schematics with Scott and Felix, loading battery packs onto a utility cart that would follow them to the west side later in the morning.

It was a well-oiled machine—the product of a settlement that had learned how to survive. Derek stepped back from his team for a moment, scanning the yard. Jennifer approached from the walkway above, wrapped in a jacket. Their eyes met, and no words were needed. He gave her the faintest nod, and she returned it with a soft smile—quiet strength behind tired eyes.

Bellamy slung his pack into the truck bed. "Fuel, detonators, wire, two timers, and enough burn kits to turn that mall into a firestorm."

Callum patted the side of the truck. "If we're lucky, we'll be out before it gets too loud."

Jillian checked her sidearm, then looked toward Derek. "Still want me on this?"

He didn't answer immediately. Then he nodded. "You're with us. All the way."

Lee tightened his vest straps. "Clock's ticking. Let's make this count."

Nearby, Daryl started the engine of the flatbed. The low rumble echoed against the walls. Maggie climbed into the passenger side, Ashley and Reggie hauling the last crate into the back.

Over at the solar setup, Dr Hensley turned and gave a small wave to the strike team. "We'll be operational by noon. Just make it back."

Derek checked the time.

04:57. He exhaled, nodded to Bellamy, and climbed into the lead truck. Jillian slid into the seat beside him; Callum and Lee jumped into the second truck as it roared to life behind them, Bellamy at the wheel.

As the eastern gate rolled open and the team disappeared into the fog beyond, New Haven stood still—watching its best gamble roll out into the unknown.

The world outside was unnaturally still. No wind. No birdsong. Just a silent grey morning hanging low over a ruined land. The motorway was cracked and overgrown in places, faded white lines barely visible beneath creeping moss and dirt. On either side, abandoned cars sat half-swallowed by weeds and ivy—rusted-out shells of a world long gone. The two trucks moved in cautious formation, keeping distance but never straying too far.

Inside truck one, Derek and Jillian rode in heavy silence, broken only by the faint rattle of gear in the back and the low hum of tyres on worn asphalt. Jillian stared out her window, fingers clenched in her lap. She hadn't spoken since they left New Haven. Derek gripped the wheel, eyes scanning the road ahead with rigid focus. He wasn't just watching the road—he was bracing for something. Anything.

"I had a dream last night," Jillian said suddenly, barely above a whisper.

Derek didn't respond right away.

"I was back in that corridor at Silverburn," she continued. "But this time, when I turned around, everyone was gone. Just... gone. No sounds. No blood. Just those things—standing there, all smiling."

Derek's hands tightened around the wheel. "It was just a dream."

"Felt real," she whispered. "They weren't like the others. They didn't want to feed. They wanted us to watch them. Like we were the performance."

He glanced at her, his jaw clenched. "Let's just focus on the mission."

Jillian gave a small nod, but her eyes didn't leave the window. The road ahead curved slightly—and in the distance, just barely visible through the thinning mist, the jagged silhouette of Silverburn Shopping Centre began to emerge.

Inside truck two were Bellamy, Callum, and Lee.

"Something feels off," Lee muttered from the passenger side, peering out at the treeline. "Even more than usual."

Callum, sitting in the back, cleaned the edge of his blade for the fifth time.

Bellamy didn't take his eyes off the road. "Yeah. No birds. No movement. It's too damn quiet."

"You think they're still there?" Callum asked flatly.

"If they are, we deal with it," Bellamy replied. "If they're not... we deal with that too."

Lee rubbed at the back of his neck. "I keep waiting for something to move. Even a single shadow. This stillness feels like the world is holding its breath."

Bellamy's grip on the steering wheel tightened. "Or maybe it's already exhaled."

The radio crackled briefly. Static. Derek's voice came through, calm but firm: "Eyes up. Silverburn in sight."

As the trucks crested the final rise, the car park came into full view—the broken remains of scattered vehicles, shattered glass glittering in the dirt, and the empty shell of the shopping centre, looming silent in the gloom like a carcass. Not a single zombie in sight. But the feeling in everyone's stomach was dread.

—-

The trucks rolled to a stop just off the broken edge of the eastern car park, near the old service entrance where Derek and Jillian had fled days before. The early morning light filtered weakly through the cloud cover, casting long shadows across the debris-strewn lot. Derek killed the engine and sat still for a moment, just listening. No wind. No moans. No shuffling.

Jillian unbuckled slowly. "Too quiet."

He nodded. "Stay close. Say nothing unless you have to."

Behind them, the second truck stopped. Bellamy, Lee, and Callum climbed out silently, all of them checking weapons and gear. Bellamy moved quickly to the back, unstrapping one of the larger duffel bags filled with accelerants and charges. Lee looked up at the shopping centre's second-floor windows.

"Looks empty," he said, not sounding convinced.

Derek led the group to the service entrance—the same metal door they'd escaped through before. It hung open slightly, its lower edge stained with soot and blood. He gestured for Bellamy and Callum to cover the rear while he tested the door. It groaned faintly as it opened. The service hallway beyond was dark and musty. Nothing moved inside.

Derek turned to his team. "Same path in. We head to the corridor behind the freezer zone. Bellamy—plant fire points on the way in, but don't arm them yet. We do that after the load."

Bellamy gave a nod. "I've got charges set for corridor junctions, plus a timer rig in case we need to light it remotely."

"Good. Let's move," Derek said.

Inside the Service Corridor. The group moved in tight formation. Their boots echoed faintly in the silence as they passed mould-stained walls and scorched floor tiles. Every corner, every doorway was cleared twice. Guns raised. Hearts pounding. Jillian walked just behind Derek, her breathing shallow. The further they went in, the stronger the scent of rot and old ash became. But there were no signs of movement. No groans. No shambling. Not yet.

They reached the back corridor behind the food court—the place where the freezer was located. The metal doors were still half open, cold mist clinging to the air around them. Bellamy signalled for a halt and immediately began setting his charges along the hallway junction.

Derek turned to Lee and Callum. "Get inside. Load fast. Prioritise protein packs and sealed goods."

Jillian moved to help, eyes scanning constantly. Inside the storage room, the industrial freezer still hummed softly—powered by its own backup solar panel rig that hadn't been scavenged yet. Frost clung to the walls and the floor was slick.

Callum gave a small whistle. "Still running."

They began loading crates into a trolley as quietly as possible.

Bellamy's voice came softly over the radio: "Charges set. Perimeter stable. No movement. For now."

The first two crates were loaded without incident. Callum and Lee moved fast, stacking sealed meat packs and bags of dried vegetables into the trolley. Jillian sorted labels quickly, prioritising anything vacuum-packed or calorie-dense. Derek stood just outside the freezer room, watching both ends of the corridor, his rifle lowered but ready. The silence still hung like a blanket—oppressive, but oddly soothing. Bellamy knelt near the hallway junction, double-checking the primer on the incendiary gel strips.

"If we keep this pace," he muttered, "we're out in twenty."

"Fifteen," Derek replied, quiet and controlled.

Three full crates now. The trolley wheels creaked softly as Callum and Lee rolled it into position for final loading. Derek tapped his radio.

"Bellamy—all clear on your end?"

A moment of static. Then: "All clear. Not a breath down here. I'm going to prep the fire line near the exit."

Derek gave a short nod. "Copy. Stay sharp."

Jillian glanced at Derek, lowering her voice. "Feels... wrong."

"What do you mean?"

"This," she whispered. "It shouldn't be this easy."

He didn't answer right away. Because she was right.

The final crate was almost full. Jillian sealed the lid while Callum checked the straps. Lee kept his eyes on the shadowy corridor, chewing his lower lip out of habit.

Then it happened.

A sound.

Soft. Metallic. Far down the main corridor. Not a moan. Not a growl. A clink—like something being dropped or shifted. Derek raised a fist silently. Everyone froze.

Bellamy's voice whispered over the radio. "...did anyone just move something near the food court?"

Derek clicked his radio twice in response—negative.

Then came another noise—this time closer. A faint dragging sound. Something light. Like fingertips scraping glass or a dull blade being pulled across the tiled floor.

Callum looked at Lee.

Lee swallowed hard. "Please tell me that was the wind."

"There is no wind in here," Callum whispered.

Derek turned to Jillian. "You and Lee roll the carts to the trucks. Quiet and quick."

"What about you?" she whispered back.

"I'm going to check it out."

—-

The team split. Jillian and Lee began carefully rolling the loaded trolley back through the service corridor, navigating over cracked tiles and bloodstains long since dried. Callum stayed just behind Derek, rifle raised, both men moving silently toward the noise. They reached the far end of the hall—where the corridor opened into the first-floor junction.

There was nothing.

Just the familiar rot-stained walls, broken signage, and a few discarded display racks that hadn't been moved in years.

Derek took a step forward. Something was different. A piece of graffiti on the far wall. Was that there before? A crude smiling face in smeared black soot—jagged teeth, wide hollow eyes.

Fresh.

—-

The last crate was locked in place. Lee slammed the tailgate closed and double-checked the latches. Callum climbed into the second truck, Bellamy behind the wheel, engine idling low. In the lead truck, Jillian was already in the passenger seat, eyes fixed straight ahead. Derek stood still beside the driver's door, staring up at that second-floor window. The silhouette was gone. He scanned the rooftop. Nothing.

The wind picked up slightly, just enough to make the debris on the asphalt shift—plastic wrappers, a half-buried shopping bag. The rustle was subtle, but after the long silence, it sounded deafening. Derek finally climbed in and shut the door.

"Something's watching us," Jillian said quietly.

"I know," he replied, starting the engine.

The two trucks rolled out slowly, tyres crunching over loose gravel and glass. No words were exchanged over the radios. They passed the far corner of the building—the site of the smiler's first appearance days ago. The ground was still scorched there. Blackened. Burnt corpses in melted clothing remained piled in corners, unmoved. Yet none of the bodies had shifted. No dragging. No missing pieces. As if nothing dared return.

The trucks picked up speed as they reached the ramp leading back to the motorway. The two trucks rumbled over the broken stretch of motorway, the wreckage of Silverburn finally falling behind them in the distance. Inside the lead vehicle, Derek keyed the radio.

"Bellamy. Light it up."

"Copy," Bellamy said, flipping the safety off the remote detonator. He pressed down.

A dull click.

And then all hell broke loose.

—-

From behind, Silverburn's interior detonated in a shockwave of fire and force, the fire kits igniting the corridors, the freezer area, and the rigged escape hallways. But what followed wasn't supposed to happen. The explosion spread underground, then upward—a thunderclap beneath the motorway itself. The tarmac cracked with a violent jolt. The concrete pillar holding the overpass up blew out in front of the trucks and then collapsed. Half the overpass caved in, dropping flaming wreckage down onto the old rail bed below. One of the military trucks they'd seen abandoned on the approach vanished into the fiery hole without a sound.

Jillian screamed as debris smacked the truck's roof.

"Go, go, go!" Derek roared, slamming the truck into a 180 and heading the wrong way down the motorway.

Behind them, Bellamy followed suit as the second truck bounced over the fractured roadway, a twisted length of rebar slamming into the hood.

Inside the cab, Callum shouted, "What the hell was that?! That wasn't just the mall that blew!"

Bellamy didn't answer. His face had gone pale. Smoke thickened, trailing off as the trucks moved along the motorway.

But what greeted them wasn't open road.

It was a wall of the dead. Hundreds of zombies packed across the tarmac, shoulder to shoulder—still. Silent. Waiting. And in front of them—

Three smilers. One stood with hands clasped behind its back, eyes locked onto the approaching vehicles. Another crouched low like an animal, grinning up at them with teeth like broken glass. And the third simply stood still, blood trailing down its neck, smiling wide—that same inhuman, empty smile.

"Jesus," Jillian whispered. "They knew. They planned this."

Derek stared forward, hands trembling on the wheel. His brain raced, running through the placement of charges, the blast patterns, the weight—There were no charges under the bridge. That wasn't their setup. A charge was moved. Intentionally.

Jillian said it before he could. "They... set this up."

Lee leaned forward. "You're telling me that bridge didn't just collapse?"

"No," Bellamy muttered. "That was a charge that was meant to be in Silverburn."

Callum's voice was cold. "They forced us into this road. Straight into the trap."

Derek hit the brakes and stared at the horde. Smilers didn't flinch. They just smiled.

"I'm not playing their game," he growled. He hit the radio. "We're backing off. Cut through the east embankment—there's a service road near the old petrol station. It'll be tight, but it avoids this death trap."

"Copy that," Bellamy replied.

The trucks reversed fast, tyres skidding as the smoke from the explosion still drifted across the road.

As they pulled away, Jillian looked back. The smilers hadn't moved. But she could feel it. They were smiling because this was just the beginning.

The two trucks bounced violently as they veered off the main road, tyres kicking up ash and broken glass. The sound of cracking branches and crunching debris echoed through the open windows.

Behind them, the horde remained, unmoving. The smilers still stood in formation, watching like sentinels. They hadn't followed. Not yet. But it was clear now—they could choose when to. That was worse. Much worse.

Inside the lead truck, Derek flicked his thumb over the comm switch. "Bellamy, we should split up."

"Split?"

"Yeah," Derek said. "We don't know how far they can track. I'm not risking both trucks leading that shit back to New Haven." Jillian's eyes flicked to him but she said nothing. "We'll take the east service road and loop round the old back lane through Shawfield," Derek continued. "You go south, then cut west past the water plant. We'll meet outside the cemetery, then circle in together. Radio silence after this. Only reconnect if you see hostiles. Good luck."

"You too, brother."

And just like that, the two trucks split—one veering off to the left, bouncing down a narrow gravel lane between trees; the other disappearing south into a tighter, more wooded track that barely resembled a road at all.

The forest closed in fast. Branches clawed at the sides of the truck. Jillian kept her eyes out the side window, shotgun resting on her lap. Her breathing was shallow, and she didn't realise until now just how hard her hands were shaking. Derek kept his focus on the path ahead.

"Do you think they're following?" she asked finally.

Derek didn't answer at first. "I think... they want us to wonder."

She looked at him. "That's worse than following."

He nodded. "Exactly."

In the second truck, Callum tightened the strap on his rifle while Lee scanned the treeline ahead.

"Can't believe they turned our exit into a trap," Lee muttered.

Bellamy's knuckles were white on the wheel. "They're not just smart. They're organised."

"And if they moved those charges..." Callum added grimly, "it means they were already in Silverburn. Probably watching us the whole time."

Silence followed. The weight of that thought landed heavy.

They cleared the dense trees as the sun finally began to break through the thinning cloud. Ahead, the old cemetery gate came into view—a rusted iron arch nearly hidden by overgrowth. It sat just east of New Haven's outer checkpoint. Derek slowed the truck. No signs of pursuit. No signs of life.

Jillian finally exhaled, rubbing her face. "We made it."

"For now," Derek replied, checking his watch. "Let's wait for the others. If they're not here in ten, we head in and raise the guard."

He stepped out of the truck and scanned the horizon. Wind tugged at his jacket. His eyes drifted back the way they came. Still no movement. But that didn't settle him. Because in his gut, he knew—this wasn't the end of it. It was just the first move in whatever came next.

The rising roar of an engine broke the still morning. Derek turned toward the bend—and there it was. Bellamy's truck, fishtailing up the road, one tyre spitting smoke. Seconds later, the shapes emerged behind them. Dozens of infected, fast and snarling, pushed through the treeline in pursuit.

Then came the voice over the radio, cracked and frantic.

"They found us! That freak—it followed us. It was waiting!" Bellamy's voice, hoarse and urgent. "It had circled around and sent the horde right at us—we can't take them to New Haven, Derek! We can't!"

Derek didn't hesitate.

He grabbed his mic. "Bellamy, go to fallback location Echo. Don't stop. Don't slow down. We'll meet you there."

The truck ahead skidded hard, tyres squealing. At the split in the road, Bellamy yanked the wheel left—a violent turn, too sharp—the vehicle tipped for a breathless second—then slammed back down, roaring into the woods toward the south trail. The zombies chased after like a tide.

Derek watched until the trees swallowed them all.

Inside the lead truck, Derek hit the accelerator, hands tight on the wheel, and picked up the radio again—this time to New Haven. "Control, this is Derek. Do not open the cemetery gate. Bellamy's team was followed by a smiler and a small horde. They've diverted to fallback. We're en route to intercept. Repeat—do not open any gates until we signal."

Static.

Then Lee's voice came back, tense. "Understood. Stay sharp, boss."

Jillian broke the silence as the truck rumbled off-road, taking a southward trail through wild brush. She turned to him, eyes narrowed. "Fallback location? What location? I didn't know we had one."

Derek nodded once, eyes scanning the road. "It's new. Found it with Callum and Munroe two weeks ago on a scavenging run. An old primary school, out past the far woods."

"Why there?" she asked.

"Solid walls. Metal security gates. It's half-overgrown, easy to miss. We've been quietly stocking it—meds, water, canned food. Just in case."

Jillian raised an eyebrow. "Smart."

Derek didn't respond. His eyes were hard now. Focused. He was already thinking three steps ahead. The smilers weren't just wandering anymore. They were coordinating.

The truck rumbled to a halt on the cracked, overgrown road outside the school's rusting front gates. The sun had burned through the worst of the smoke. The trees here stood tall and still. Birds chirped distantly—the first natural sound in hours. To Jillian, it looked almost... normal.

She peered out the window. "Looks innocent and peaceful enough."

Derek didn't answer. He stepped out first, boots crunching on gravel, rifle slung across his shoulder. Jillian followed, cautiously approaching the crooked fence. But before she could get far, Derek reached out and snatched her arm, stopping her in her tracks. His voice was low but firm. "Careful."

She blinked at him, caught off guard.

He gestured ahead. "When we found this place, someone had already started turning it into a fort. There are pit traps and spike beds all over the front lot. Most are buried shallow. If you step off the path..."

He didn't finish.

Jillian swallowed hard. "Someone else did this?"

He nodded. "Long gone. Or dead. We never found them."

He knelt beside a large, moss-covered rock near the gate, shifted it aside, and pulled out a folded plastic-wrapped map, dirt-stained and brittle along the creases.

Opening it, he pointed. "This line here—that's the cleared path. Watch for the red cloth markers on fence posts. Stay between them and step exactly where I do."

She nodded, tension slipping back into her shoulders.

The playground beyond the rusted gate was eerie in the early morning light. Overgrown grass, broken seesaws, a slide cracked in half. But now that she looked again—

She spotted one: a patch of disturbed earth, slightly sunken.

Another had a thin metal pole sticking up with faint red cloth tied to it, frayed but deliberate.

"Jesus," she muttered.

Derek checked the angle of the map to the field ahead. "Come on," he said without looking back. "Bellamy won't be far behind. Let's make sure it's safe when they get here."

They crossed into the playground, every step a calculation.

The silence that hung over the school wasn't peaceful.

It was waiting.

—-

The heavy side door creaked open as Derek pushed through, his torch beam slicing through the dark. Dust danced in the stale air. The building had clearly been untouched for months—maybe years. Faded school posters still clung to the walls, edges curled and yellowing. A mural of stick-figure kids holding hands had peeled halfway from the corridor. Jillian stepped in behind him, shotgun lowered but ready, her eyes scanning every doorway. The sound of their boots echoed faintly against the tiled floor.

"We cleared two floors last time," Derek said softly, his voice bouncing gently through the space. "West wing was locked down. Didn't want to force it without a reason."

Jillian nodded, brushing cobwebs from her jacket. "You really think whoever was here before just up and left?"

He paused near the end of the hall, where faint light filtered in through narrow windows. "No bodies. No sign of a struggle. Just... vanished." He pointed toward a side room. "We'll use this room to rest. Only place with full windows and a metal lock."

He led the way in. It had once been a classroom—now stripped of desks, but with two rusted camp cots set up in opposite corners. A few plastic crates were stacked along the back wall, marked with scavenged supplies. Derek lowered his gear and sat on the edge of one cot.

Jillian lingered near the door, staring out through a grimy window toward the treeline. For a while, neither said anything. It was peaceful. Too peaceful.

"You think they'll make it here okay?" she asked.

Derek nodded slowly. "Bellamy's smart. He'll know how to lose them."

Another beat of quiet passed. Jillian crossed the room and sank down onto the opposite cot. "I hate that we need a place like this."

"Me too."

She looked over at him, softer now. "I know this isn't the time to say it but... when I thought we weren't gonna make it out of that mall..." She hesitated. "I was ready to die with you. You know that, right?"

Derek looked up. Their eyes locked again, same as they had in the vault. A moment that said everything and nothing at once.

But this time, Derek didn't say a word. He just nodded, once.

They both sat back. Waiting.

—-

The engine groaned in protest as Bellamy kept his foot heavy on the accelerator, tyres kicking up mud and dry leaves along the winding forest path. Branches slapped the windscreen, some snapping with loud cracks, others scraping like claws. Callum sat in the back, a deep cut running along his temple, blood dried at his jaw. He pressed gauze against it, breathing heavy.

Lee leaned forward, eyes glued to the side mirror. "They're still back there."

Bellamy glanced to his right. "How many?"

"Too many," Lee growled. "They're not giving up."

A faint rumble trembled through the chassis—not from their truck, but from the dozen or so infected pounding after them through the trees. Smiler-led. Smart-led. They were faster. More coordinated. And somehow... They didn't fatigue.

Callum swore under his breath. "I don't get it. We took side roads, doubled back twice—how the hell are they still on us?"

Bellamy clenched the wheel tighter. "They knew where we were going."

Lee looked at him, surprised. "You think they know about the fallback?"

"Not exactly. But they set up the explosives. They herded us. They're not just reacting anymore." He stared ahead. "They're planning."

Callum reached for his radio. "New Haven, this is Echo Team. Still being tailed. ETA to fallback: ten minutes. Will attempt to lose them at the fork near Ash Creek."

Static.

Then a garbled voice. Possibly Lee from the gate. "Copy. Good luck."

Bellamy cursed softly. "Hold on."

Ahead, the road forked—one path deeper into dense trees, the other heading around a small, dry creek bed lined with thick mud and rocks. He spun the wheel left. The truck skidded, slammed over the shallow ditch, and bounced back up onto a moss-covered slope, barely resembling a road. The horde behind them hesitated. Some stumbled into the creek bed.

But the smiler didn't stop.

It simply stepped onto a fallen log and waved an arm once—eerily precise. The zombies behind it regained direction like a compass reset. And they came again.

Lee watched them gaining again. "They're adapting."

Callum, grimacing from the pain, said what no one wanted to. "If we lead them to the school, it's over."

Bellamy's jaw tightened. "Then we don't." He yanked the wheel again, heading for a broken utility road that veered wide—away from the fallback zone. "Get ready to bail when I say."

"What?!" they both said.

"We're splitting again. Just like Derek did. One of us lures them. The others double back."

The trees swallowed them whole again, the forest echoing with their own heartbeat. The truck burst from the treeline onto the narrow bridge—its wooden frame rotted and sagging, iron bolts rusted to dark orange. Water rushed below in a steep drop to the rocks and riverbed, fifty metres down.

Callum leaned forward. "This doesn't look safe."

"It's not," Bellamy muttered, eyes wide.

The front third of the bridge had collapsed, the wooden planks snapped and dangling. The middle was a gaping hole, maybe ten feet across. No time. No options. Without hesitation, Bellamy floored it.

"Hold on!"

The engine screamed. Mud spat from the tyres. The truck jolted hard as it struck the ramped edge of the broken decking. For a moment—it flew. A sickening crunch rang out as the front wheels cleared the gap, landing violently on the other side. The back end slammed down hard, nearly bottoming out, but the truck made it, skidding to a stop in a cloud of dirt. Inside, everyone was shaken, adrenaline pumping.

"Jesus Christ," Callum wheezed. "Tell me that was the worst of it."

But it wasn't. Behind them the horde reached the shattered bridge. They paused. Confused. Then the smiler emerged from the trees, its pale face blank, eyes fixed forward. It ran full speed toward the gap—and leapt. It flew farther than any of them expected, landing fingers-first on the broken wood, legs dangling over the void. It hung there, grinning wide. Pulling itself up.

Until—boom.

A shotgun blast thundered through the canyon. Lee had already jumped from the truck, acting on instinct. He stood near the edge, shoulders squared, his shotgun smoking. The smiler twitched. Then it lost its grip. It fell. Fifty metres down, past stone and river mist, its body smashed into the rocks below with a muted, final crack.

For a second, the horde hesitated. A few snarled. One stepped forward—and then they began to fall. Mindless now. Leaderless. One by one, they stumbled forward, tumbling off the edge of the bridge like ants over a cliff.

Lee stood there, still pointing the shotgun, chest rising and falling.

Bellamy climbed out, stunned. "That was..."

Lee turned, half dazed. "...the first time I didn't think. I just did it."

Callum laughed breathlessly from inside the truck. "Good thing you did."

Bellamy clapped a hand on Lee's shoulder. "That just bought us our way out."

They were safe. For now.

As Bellamy started the truck again, Lee gave the ravine one last glance—the smiler's body now just a pale speck among jagged rocks. Then they turned and headed for the school.

Chapter 21

"Control, this is Derek. Do not open the cemetery gate. Bellamy's team was followed by a smiler and a small horde. They've diverted to fallback. We're en route to intercept. Repeat—do not open any gates until we signal."

For one breathless moment, the world seemed to freeze. Then—New Haven ignited. The alarm bell tolled: two short clangs, one long. Lockdown protocol. Within minutes, families moved quickly. Volunteers escorted the elderly and children toward the fallout shelter entrance, their pace urgent but controlled. People didn't ask questions—they just moved. The weight of the warning in Derek's voice made that unnecessary.

Jennifer was already in position. Rifle strapped tight, eyes locked on the treeline past the wall. She didn't flinch, didn't fumble.

But inside, she was trembling.

Munroe, Bill, Daryl, Steph, Anne, and Maggie flanked her—armed, ready, eyes steeled.

Daryl stood on the lookout perch, scanning the empty road. "Nothing yet."

"They'll come through the fallback route," Jennifer said, not looking away from the horizon. "Unless they don't make it."

"They'll make it," Maggie murmured.

Jennifer's knuckles whitened around her radio.

At the south gate, Ortega had taken command. Ashley, Mary, Michone, Finn, Roary, Felix, Jonas, and Reggie lined the perimeter in a defensive semicircle. Roary adjusted the scope on his rifle with shaking hands.

Ortega noticed but didn't call it out. Instead, he barked toward the tower, "No movement west or south?"

Jonas called back, "Not yet. Still watching."

Inside the admin block, the infirmary had come alive. Erin, New Haven's appointed medical lead, directed the preparation with a precision honed by months of emergency care. Ali, Abby, and Scott worked with quiet urgency—IV bags unwrapped, stretchers prepped, morphine and antibiotics checked.

"We treat this like a war zone," Erin said, loading syringes into a case. "Expect multiple trauma cases. Blunt, bites, burns. Assume nothing."

Ali wiped her forehead. "If Bellamy's team was tailed... they might come in hot."

Scott added, "If they come in at all."

The heavy hatch of the fallout shelter was nearly closed. Inside, children clung to parents. The elderly sat along benches, waiting in silence that pressed on the ears like weight. A single lantern cast flickering shadows against the wall.

A small boy leaned close to his mother. "Will the monsters get in?"

Her voice cracked. "Not today, sweetheart."

Back at the main gate, a soft breeze drifted through the compound. For a moment, there was nothing—just the whistle of wind over concrete.

Bill spoke quietly. "You think this is the one? The time it finally breaks us?"

"No," Jennifer said, calm. "Because if it was—Derek wouldn't have told us to wait."

She lifted her radio again, thumb hovering over transmit. Then she put it down.

And waited.

—-

At the school, the sharp screech of tyres echoed through the open yard. Derek was outside already, crouched beside the rusted swing set near the entrance, rifle aimed toward the gravel path. Jillian flanked him, tense, ready—the silence of the past hour hanging like a weight over them both.

Then—the rumble of a diesel engine cut through the morning.

A battered truck burst from the misty treeline, front grille dented, windscreen cracked. It swerved hard onto the drive, tyres skidding over cracked pavement before jolting to a stop.

Bellamy's truck.

Derek was moving before the engine fully died. The passenger door burst open—Lee jumped out first, eyes wide, covered in dirt and sweat. Callum followed, limping slightly but alive. Bellamy climbed out last, scanning every angle, hand still on his sidearm.

"You made it," Derek said, reaching them.

"Barely," Bellamy rasped. He glanced to Jillian, who stepped forward to steady Callum.

"What the hell happened?" Derek asked.

"They chased us the whole way," Bellamy said. "A smiler was leading them—fast, aggressive. It pushed us straight to Ash Creek Bridge."

Derek's expression hardened. "That bridge was gone. How the hell did you cross it?"

Lee spoke next, voice tight. "Bellamy floored it—we jumped the gap. Just made it. The horde would've caught us if we hadn't."

Derek looked at the truck. "You jumped the gap?"

Callum gave a dry chuckle. "Not exactly a smooth landing, but yeah."

"And the smiler?" Derek asked.

Lee stepped forward, jaw tense. "It jumped after us. Missed the edge. Grabbed the ledge. I didn't think. I just—" He mimed raising his shotgun.

"You put it down," Derek finished.

Lee nodded. "It fell. Hard. Hit the rocks at the bottom. I don't think even those freaks get up from that."

"And the rest of the horde?" Jillian asked.

"Stumbled. Disorganised," Bellamy said. "Like something shorted the second that smiler went down."

"Just like Silverburn," Derek murmured.

They moved inside the old school—secured, reinforced—an eerie calm settling over the dusty halls. In what used to be a teachers' lounge, they gathered around a table cluttered with maps, a candle, and Derek's handwritten fallback instructions. Outside, birds had returned to the trees. The quiet was almost surreal.

Bellamy drank deeply from a flask. "We shouldn't stay long."

"No," Derek agreed. "But we rest first. Then we figure out how far their reach goes."

"They're not chasing anymore," Callum said, leaning back in a broken chair. "Doesn't mean they're gone."

"We'll head back by dusk," Derek said. "That food won't stay frozen forever."

They settled into brief stillness. Sunlight through grime-streaked windows painted long beams across the floor. The room smelled of old coffee, burnt plastic, damp wood—the scent of abandonment.

Callum broke the silence. "We should check out the west wing."

All heads turned.

"Now?" Lee asked.

"Yeah," Callum said. "It was locked up tight when we first came. With all of us here, it's time to clear it properly."

Bellamy smirked. "Christ, lad. Got ants in your pants? Can't sit still for five minutes, can you?"

"I don't like blind spots," Callum said. "Not after what we've seen."

"He's right," Jillian said. "If someone started setting this place up before us... we don't know what could still be in there."

"Better we clear it now while we've got numbers and daylight," Lee added, pushing up with a grunt.

Derek rubbed his temples, then stood. "Alright. Gear up. Slow, quiet, clean."

Bellamy stood last, tossing a carved piece of wood onto the table—a rough wolf's head. "Let's go ghost-hunting, then."

—-

The corridor to the west wing was darker. Colder. Dust swirled with every step. Curled linoleum made each footfall echo like thunder in the silence. Derek led, rifle up; a vest torch cut a beam through the gloom. Jillian was close behind, pistol raised, scanning side rooms. Callum walked just ahead of Lee, shotgun lowered but ready, while Lee kept checking their six. Bellamy brought up the rear, machete drawn, jaw tight enough to crack.

At the end of the corridor: a heavy double door, chained and padlocked. Faded lettering above:

ADMINISTRATION – WEST BLOCK

The lock was old but strong. Someone had wanted it sealed.

"This wasn't just to keep looters out," Callum said, running fingers along the chain.

"Could've been to keep something in," Bellamy muttered.

Derek checked the floor. Dust undisturbed. "No prints. No sign anyone's been through recently."

"No scratches. No blood. No scorch marks," Jillian added, scanning the frame.

Lee raised the bolt cutters. "Still want it open?"

Derek hesitated. Then nodded. "Do it."

SNAP.

The padlock cracked; the chain fell. The doors groaned wide, revealing deeper black untouched by light for years.

They moved in slowly, lights dancing across the room. Filing cabinets. Broken desks. Overturned chairs. A torn Scottish flag sagged behind a crumbled reception counter. Mildew clung to the ceiling tiles.

"Office wing?" Callum asked.

"Could be," Jillian said, sweeping left. "Door marked 'RECORDS'. Another 'STAFF ROOM'."

"We clear room by room," Derek said. "Anything locked, we leave for last."

"Famous last words," Bellamy muttered.

They split into pairs, moving through sectioned offices. The building groaned faintly in the breeze, like something ancient shifting in its sleep. Lee opened a supply closet: empty. Callum found a room with cots and blankets. "Someone used this—recently." He gestured to a crushed packet of biscuits and a half-burnt candle.

"These blackout curtains weren't put up by teachers," Jillian said, crouching by a window.

Derek said nothing, but his instincts were loud. This wing had seen recent, deliberate use.

A sharp metallic clink echoed deeper inside.

They froze.

"That wasn't one of us," Jillian whispered.

"Definitely not," Bellamy said, raising his machete.

Derek signalled: advance—quiet—weapons up.

Dust motes drifted in angled sunlight. Desks lay scattered—some broken, others stacked as barricades. Shelves of water-damaged books sagged with neglect. Torn lesson posters clung to the walls: multiplication tables, a map of Scotland, faded motivational quotes.

At the far end: a camp.

A bedroll on two rugs. Dented tins and crumpled wrappers. A half-full plastic water jug. A chemical toilet tucked behind stacked chairs. A coat, still damp, over a chair back.

On the floor, a crowbar spun lazily to a stop with a soft metallic clink.

"They heard us coming," Lee whispered.

Derek advanced, rifle lowered but ready. He knelt by an unopened tin. "Not old. Expires in six months. Someone's still living here."

"Window's cracked but barred," Callum said. "They didn't get out that way."

Jillian ran a palm over mesh on the back wall. "No footprints. No blood. They're still inside."

A faint cough. Soft. Muffled. Nearby.

Derek's head snapped up. He called, voice calm, firm. "We're not infected. We're not here to hurt anyone. We're from a safe community."

Another cough.

A cupboard creaked open—slow, cautious.

A thin girl—maybe fourteen—stepped out, trembling. Dark hair. Pale skin. Eyes flicking to each of them. Layered, oversized clothes. Hands empty, raised slightly.

"It's okay," Jillian said, lowering her pistol. "What's your name?"

A beat. "...Emily."

"Are you alone, Emily?" Derek asked gently.

She hesitated... then shook her head. "Come on," she whispered. "They're... in the next room."

The door ahead was heavy, braced from inside. Derek knocked twice. "This is Derek. We found Emily. We're from New Haven—a secure settlement. We're here to help."

A scrape. Something dragging. A bolt clicked.

The door cracked. A teen girl, about seventeen, stood there, a hammer clutched in both hands. She stared like a stray—tense, on edge. Grimy clothes. Protective stance.

Seeing Emily, her shoulders sagged. "Jesus... you're okay."

She pulled the door wider. Inside, six more kids huddled—dirty, tired, armed with whatever they'd found: planks, pipes, kitchen knives. The youngest looked no older than eleven. They stared like they hadn't seen another adult in weeks.

"Dear God..." Jillian whispered.

"How long have you been here?" Derek asked.

"Weeks," the older girl said. "Maybe more. We... lost track."

"What's your name?"

A pause. "...Skye."

A tall, wiry boy—maybe fifteen—stepped forward, voice sharp. "Don't trust them, Skye. They'll take us like the others."

"Robbie—" Skye began.

"They're not coming back," he pushed on. "The grown-ups. My mum, your dad—they're gone. They left us!"

A younger kid started to cry. Skye stepped between him and the others. Her voice shook, but she held her ground. "They didn't leave us. They went to stop the smiling men."

The words chilled the room.

"...Smiling men?" Jillian asked.

Skye nodded. "They came a few days after everything went quiet. They didn't growl or chase. Just stood there. Watching us. Always smiling. I don't know how many... too many."

She glanced at the bolted windows. "Our parents locked us in, said they'd come back when it was safe." Her eyes met Derek's. "They never came back."

Silence.

"You've all been unbelievably brave," Derek said. "But it's time to come with us. New Haven is safe. Protected. You won't be alone anymore."

"Is it really safe?" Skye asked, voice cracked.

"It is," Jillian said. "We promise."

Robbie scowled but stayed quiet.

Finally, Skye nodded. "Okay. We'll come."

Derek let out a breath he hadn't realised he was holding. "Pack what you need. We leave soon."

The kids gathered what little they had—worn backpacks, dented water bottles, torches, scraps of food. A few drawings were taped to the walls: crooked crayon shapes, faded by time. They peeled them down carefully, unwilling to leave even those memories.

In the hall, Jillian knelt to help a boy named Leo—maybe twelve—knot a torn coat sleeve. He didn't say thank you, but when she stood, he grabbed her sleeve and didn't let go until they rejoined the others.

Derek stood at a window, arms folded, watching sunlight glint on rusted swings. The same playground these kids had stared at for weeks, hoping their families would walk back into view.

"They were just kids," he said as Callum joined him, handing over lukewarm tea.

"Still are," Callum replied.

"They shouldn't have gone through this."

"That's why we're here now," Callum said. "So they don't have to anymore."

Bellamy checked the doors, securing their path out. He handed Skye a small pocketknife. "Just in case."

She nodded, gripping it tight.

Outside, the sky turned a muted grey. A soft, cool wind picked up. Somewhere distant, a single bird called. Derek gathered the group at the door. "Two trucks. Slow and quiet. You'll ride with us—windows covered. We won't let anything happen to you."

Skye nodded. Robbie hovered, suspicious eyes flicking to every adult.

A younger girl with a unicorn hairband tugged Jillian's sleeve. "Will there be a bed?"

Jillian smiled. "Yeah. There'll be a bed."

Derek opened the front door. "Let's bring them home."

—-

The trucks idled at the curb, windows darkened, engines low. The gate creaked as Bellamy and Lee removed the last wire traps they'd reset the night before. Callum stood by the front tyre, trying to raise New Haven.

Static.

"Control, this is Callum. Do you read?"

More static.

"Nothing. Dead," he said, frowning.

"Keep trying," Derek said. "We'll switch to the emergency band once we clear the hill."

One by one, the kids climbed into the first truck. Jillian followed, soothing, practical—belts, water, soft words. Skye was last. She looked back at the school—the broken windows, the playground, the crumbling brick. Then she climbed in, and Jillian shut the door.

Callum, Bellamy, and Lee loaded into the second truck.

"We'll stay ahead," Derek said. "Eyes open."

"Always," Bellamy answered, sliding into the driver's seat.

Derek climbed in beside Jillian. He checked the mirror. The school's cracked doors swung shut on the breeze like the end of a long, terrible chapter.

They rolled out. The gates closed behind them.

They were going home.

—-

The road stretched ahead in solemn quiet. Grey clouds hung low, heavy with the threat of rain. Both trucks moved steadily, tyres humming over cracked asphalt. No signs of life. No signs of death either—just the in-between silence that had become familiar.

In the lead truck, tension ebbed into a tired hush. Kids huddled under blankets Jillian had passed out, eyes flicking between windows and adults.

"Still nothing on either frequency," Callum's voice crackled through. "Not even static this time."

Derek nodded, eyes on the road. "We knew this was possible. We stick to protocol."

He turned, voice gentle. "You're probably nervous. Here's how we get home. New Haven isn't like other places. It's hidden. Protected. We don't go through the main gates unless we're sure it's safe. Instead, there's a tunnel. It starts in an old cemetery near the edge of town."

Some of the younger kids were tense. A boy shrank into the corner.

"It's not scary," Jillian said warmly. "Short tunnel, reinforced. Lit, secure. There's always someone waiting on the other side."

"A cemetery?" a girl whispered.

Skye squeezed her hand. "It's okay. We've seen worse, right?"

"Way worse," Robbie said, deadpan—but the little ones settled.

"You'll see other kids at New Haven," Jillian added. "A lot of them. You'll make friends. We'll look after you."

"We'll also do everything we can to find your families," Derek said. "We have records. Patrols. We don't stop looking."

"You really do that?" Skye asked.

"Every day."

Quiet fell again—this time, a weary kind of hope.

Up ahead, the cemetery wasn't far now.

—-

Hours since the alarm. The outer defences stayed still. A handful of strays were dropped quietly near the fence. No smilers. No hordes. No radio contact. No trucks.

Jennifer had stood at the south gate for nearly two hours before Munroe convinced her to rotate out. Now she was deep underground, checking in on the elderly, the children, the vulnerable—huddled in the reinforced shelter beneath the prison complex. The air was thick with tension, whispered questions, forced reassurances.

"They'll be back soon. Derek knows what he's doing. Bellamy's team can handle themselves."

She smiled for others' sake, but it didn't reach her eyes. Thoughts raced.

Maybe they're lost. Maybe another horde. Maybe they're dead.

She placed a hand on a child's shoulder and turned toward the surface.

A sharp bang echoed through the access tunnel.

She froze. The shelter went quiet. Children clung to guardians. Panic rippled.

Another bang. Then another. Heavier. Closer. Urgent.

Jennifer raised her rifle, steadying her breath. She keyed her radio. "Daryl, Bill—tunnel entrance. Now."

She stepped toward the steel bulkhead at the corridor's end. The reinforced access tunnel protected New Haven's fallback route. No one should be coming through unless expected.

The banging returned—more frantic. Then a voice—muffled, desperate, unmistakable:

"Open up! We have kids here with us—it's Bellamy!"

Jennifer's heart kicked hard. Daryl and Bill sprinted down the hall behind her, weapons up, hope in their eyes. Jennifer gripped the release lever and cranked. Bolts hissed. The door swung inward—

And there they were.

Bellamy—sweat-slick, bruised, standing tall. Lee, guiding a younger boy through. Callum—wearied, steady. Jillian, flanked by three kids, a hand on a girl's shoulder. More children behind—wide-eyed, alive.

And at the back—as always—Derek. Rifle slung, ash-dusted, eyes locking with Jennifer's.

She didn't wait. She ran into him and hugged hard. Tears stung; she held them back.

Murmurs turned to gasps as the shelter saw the children. The new survivors. Alive.

Daryl lowered his weapon and exhaled. "Holy shit. You made it."

Jennifer stepped back, still holding Derek's arm. "You brought them back."

Derek nodded. "We're home."

—-

Dusk cast long shadows across the worn table. Every seat was taken. Derek stood at the head, dirt still on his sleeves, strain under his eyes. He hadn't changed. He hadn't stopped.

Around the table: Jennifer, Jillian, Callum, Lee, Daryl, Bill, Bellamy, Munroe, Maggie, Anne, Dr Aria Hensley—the core of New Haven's leadership.

"The Silverburn mission was a success," Derek said.

Relief flickered—then faded.

"The centre was destroyed. Bellamy lit the charge. We collapsed the structure, buried the rest of the food we couldn't take." His eyes darkened. "But that's not the full story."

He leaned onto the table. "Before we made it home—the motorway overpass blew. Collapsed entirely."

Lee's jaw tensed. He nodded, remembering.

"It wasn't us," Derek said. "Our charges were on the shopping centre only. After it went up and we started back, the overpass went next."

"We found remnants," Bellamy said. "Wiring. Fuse caps. Our materials."

Derek nodded. "The smilers moved some of the explosives. Planted them at the overpass."

Shock rippled.

"They knew our plan," Lee said quietly. "Used it against us."

"They herded us," Derek confirmed. "Forced a trap. We nearly didn't make it."

"We were followed," Bellamy added, voice hard. "A smiler tracked us. Sent a small horde. Lee took it out—shot it clean off a collapsing bridge. The horde fell with it."

"So they're not just learning," Maggie said. "They're planning."

"We're facing a different enemy," Dr Hensley said. "Smilers aren't just variants—they're commanders. Manipulators."

Derek let that settle, then turned to Munroe. "Your moat idea."

Munroe blinked. "You sure?"

"As sure as I've ever been," Derek said. "We start tomorrow. We dig it deep. Line it with spikes. Fill it if we can. Only access through north and south gates. We funnel everything—and everyone—through controlled points."

"This buys time," Callum said. "Eyes on every entrance. No more surprises."

Jennifer, quiet until now, spoke. "How long before they adapt to this too?"

Derek met her gaze—tired, resolved. "Then we adapt faster."

He straightened. "Meeting adjourned. First light."

No one argued. They rose with the quiet resolve of people who'd seen the edge and stepped back from it.

New Haven would survive.

But not passively.

Chapter 22

The earth groaned under metal and sweat. Near the treeline outside New Haven, shovels bit deep into the dirt. The air was thick with the sound of clanking tools, shouted instructions, and the occasional backfire from the old repurposed digger clawing out trenches. This was no ordinary fence repair or wall extension. This was the beginning of something much bigger.

A moat.

Ortega and Munroe had rallied the work teams at first light, mapping the perimeter and marking dig zones with scrap piping and strips of coloured cloth. Razor wire rolls lay stacked like coiled serpents, ready to be strung along the inner edge of the future trench. A final line of defense. Derek had been walking the perimeter in silence. Checking progress. Watching the line between forest and prison, and thinking. Always thinking. Not just about the moat, or the fences, or the food supplies now dwindling faster than they liked. But about Silverburn. About the grinning figures. About Jillian.

He left the crew and made his way back toward the main compound.

—-

Inside the converted admin wing, the air was quieter. The children rescued from the abandoned school were finally starting to settle in. Blankets had become forts. Filing cabinets became makeshift toy chests. The older ones helped the younger — Skye, ever the protector, calmed nerves while Robbie watched the windows.

Derek stepped in, his shadow stretching along the floor. "How's everyone doing?" he asked softly.

Skye stood up. "Better today. Still scared, but... they're starting to smile again."

He nodded. "That's good. You're doing a hell of a job."

Robbie didn't look up from the small piece of wood he was carving. "You think our parents are still out there?"

Derek hesitated. "We don't know. But we'll keep looking. That's a promise."

Elsewhere, near the South Gate, Daryl and Munroe leaned against a stack of supply crates, watching the moat crews dig.

"You know," Daryl said, adjusting the brim of his cap, "I never thought we'd be digging trenches around a prison."

Munroe grinned. "Better than digging graves."

They shared a laugh, low and genuine. Over the past few months, the two had grown from wary allies into something like brothers. They worked well together — Daryl's caution balancing Munroe's impulsiveness.

"Still," Munroe said, watching the treeline, "this place feels different now. Like something's coming."

"It always is," Daryl replied, then clapped him on the shoulder. "We'll be ready."

—-

At the training yard, Bellamy was drilling a group of civilians — teaching them how to handle weapons, run drills, hold formation. "Keep your muzzle up!" he barked at one of the younger trainees. They responded quickly. The people of New Haven were learning. Bellamy had insisted they had to — especially after what happened with the Smilers. He walked the line, correcting stances, offering encouragement. "You're not soldiers," he told them, "but that doesn't mean you can't fight. We fight smart, we fight together. That's how we survive."

—-

Jillian sat alone near the upper watchtower, watching Derek from afar. He was always moving, always focused — barely speaking more than a few words at a time. She sighed, fingers tightening around the railing. She remembered the vault, the kiss, the moments they shared. But lately... he was distant. She didn't want to push. She knew what he carried. But her heart ached all the same. "How do I bring you back?" she whispered to herself.

—-

Inside one of the converted classrooms, Jennifer stood at a chalkboard, guiding a group of nearly twenty children through simple lessons — reading, numbers, some geography. She smiled as hands shot up to answer her questions, but her eyes were tired. She glanced out the window, catching a glimpse of Derek speaking to Ortega by the main gate. He was taking on too much. The weight of the council, the defense, the people. He was closing himself off. And Jennifer felt it, in the quiet moments at night, in the way his eyes never lingered anymore. She kept teaching, for the kids' sake — but her heart was heavy.

—-

Near the clinic, Callum sat on a bench beside Anne. She rested a hand on her stomach, glancing around to ensure no one was listening. "I think we should tell them soon," she whispered.

Callum smiled, taking her hand. "Not yet. Let's wait until things calm down a little. A couple more days."

"You really think things will calm down?" She asked.

"No," he admitted. "But we'll make time for this. For us."

They sat in silence, the weight of their secret nestled between them.

—-

Later, Derek was returning to the council block when the north lookout called through the radio.

"Movement on the main road. Group of five. On foot."

The gate crews prepped quickly. The kill zone was set. Everyone was alert. The five figures were ragged, dirt-covered, walking slow. One held a makeshift white flag. The exterior gate opened only halfway. A woman stepped forward. Sharp-eyed. Burned but not broken.

"We're not here for food," she said. "My name's Nia. We came from a settlement called Halestow."

Derek frowned. "Where's that?"

"Southwest. Near the old canal routes. It's... surrounded. We managed to slip out." Nia looked behind her, then back. "We came to warn you."

Jennifer had joined them by now. Bellamy too.

"Warn us about what?" Derek asked.

"The things with the smiles. We call them Grinners."

The group stiffened. Jennifer exchanged a look with Derek.

"They're coordinating," Nia continued. "They're not wandering aimlessly. We saw three of them. At once. Each controlling a different group of infected. Pushing them, like herding animals."

Bellamy's jaw clenched. "Like what happened at Silverburn."

Nia looked between them. "You've seen them too."

Derek gave a slight nod. "We've had run-ins."

Jennifer asked, "How did you find New Haven?"

Nia replied, "We stumbled on it by accident. Heard the sounds of digging and machinery — followed the noise. Honestly, we were just looking for somewhere that wasn't crawling with the dead."

—-

Derek looked to the others. Then to the gate. "Open both gates. Bring them in. But keep your eyes open. And someone find Callum. We're calling a council meeting."

Around the table sat the core of New Haven's leadership: Derek, Jennifer, Jillian, Callum, Lee, Daryl, Bill, Bellamy, Munroe, Maggie, Anne, and Dr. Aria Hensley. Today, there were more chairs. Skye sat near the end of the table, her hands folded, a touch of nerves on her face. She'd been asked to join — not to vote, but to listen, learn, and relay information back to the other kids in a way they could understand. Across from her sat the newcomers: Nia, Joe, Henry, Lexi, and Sam. All looked tired, their clothes torn and dusty, but their posture told the room they'd come with purpose.

Derek stood, palms on the table. "You said you came from Halestow. It's surrounded. And that you've seen them — the ones we call Smilers."

Nia nodded. "We call them Grinners. Doesn't matter the name, I suppose. They're not mindless. Not anymore."

Joe leaned forward. "We held out for months, had walls, watch rotations, backup plans. But then they started showing up — not just the zombies, but them. The Grinners."

Lexi picked up where he left off. "They'd watch us from the treeline, just out of range. Then one day... They sent two hordes at once. From opposite sides."

Sam added, "They knew where to hit. It wasn't random."

Derek looked to his council. "This matches what we saw at Silverburn. The coordination. The silence. The control."

Dr. Hensley scribbled notes. "This level of organization... it's evolving faster than anything I've studied."

Jennifer asked, "Did Halestow fall?"

Nia shook her head. "We don't know if it has. We escaped before it was too late. There were still people fighting when we left, but... it didn't look good."

Skye raised her voice, a little timidly. "What do they want? Do they want to kill us?"

Henry glanced at her, then said softly, "They want us to suffer. That's what it feels like. Like they enjoy it."

Silence settled over the room.

Finally, Bellamy broke it. "So what do we do?"

Derek looked down at the table. "We listen. We plan. And we make sure that whatever happened at Halestow, whatever is coming — it doesn't reach our gates." He looked to Skye and gave a small nod. "Everyone in this room has a part to play. And now, so do you." She straightened, a flicker of pride softening her nerves.

Outside, the digging continued.

—-

The silence that had settled over the room was broken by Nia's voice — steady, but laced with emotion. "We're not asking for much. But we need to know. Can you send someone to Halestow? We left them... and we don't know if anyone made it. If the Grinners took it or not." She looked directly at Derek. "Please."

Before anyone could respond, Lexi leaned forward in her chair, her voice cracking slightly.

"My sister... she was there. She's only sixteen. We have friends, family — people we grew up with. We need to know if they're alive... or if they're dead. Or worse."

The weight of the room shifted again — from strategy to humanity.

Callum glanced to Derek, then to the rest of the council. "If there's even a chance people survived, we have to try."

Munroe nodded slowly. "We're building defenses here, but if Halestow still stands, they'll need support. And if it's gone... we need to know what we're up against."

Dr. Hensley added quietly, "And if anyone was taken by the Grinners rather than killed, that may tell us even more. Especially if they have been taken alive."

Derek's jaw clenched as he looked around the table. "I won't send anyone unprepared. But we'll scout it. Quiet. Fast. Small team." He turned back to Nia and Lexi. "We'll find out what happened."

Lexi exhaled, nodding gratefully as emotion brimmed in her eyes. "Thank you."

—

Derek leaned forward, his voice calm but decisive. "If we're doing this, it's got to be fast and clean. I'll go. Daryl, you're with me. Ortega too." He glanced around the room. "Nia, Joe — you know the area. We'll need your eyes."

Before he could say more, Jillian spoke up. "I'm coming too." A few eyes shifted toward her. She stood, not defiant — just steady. "I've been training. I'm not needed here. And I'm good with a crossbow now."

Daryl nodded without hesitation. "She's not wrong. She's got a calm hand. Doesn't flinch."

Derek hesitated, then nodded. "Ok you're on the team too."

He turned to Nia. "I'll need you to mark out the best route — in and out. Quiet roads. Landmarks. Everything you remember."

Nia gave a sharp nod. "I can do that."

Derek stood and addressed the rest of the council. "Callum, Jennifer — you're in charge while we're out." Jennifer gave him a measured look but nodded, her hand resting on the table. "The moat is top priority," Derek continued. "We need it to stretch the full perimeter. Get Lexi, Sam, and Henry involved. If they're willing, put them on it." He paused, making sure every word hit. "If you're not training or healing, you're digging. Even the older kids. We're not surviving this because of walls — we're surviving it because everyone pulls weight."

Bellamy gave a soft chuckle. "You've turned into quite the motivational speaker."

Derek gave him a look. "Keep an eye on them."

Bellamy nodded, his face serious now.

"Everyone clear?" Derek asked.

The room murmured in agreement, chairs shifting, boots scraping the floor as people rose. The next phase was in motion.

—-

The council chamber had emptied, voices and footsteps fading down the corridor. But Derek remained, seated at the table with his notes spread before him, pen scratching across the paper. Jennifer lingered by the door, arms folded as she watched him for a moment before speaking.

"You really should get someone to do that while the meetings are happening," she said, a gentle smile playing on her lips.

Derek looked up, the tension in his face easing just slightly. He gave a tired nod. "Yeah. You're probably right."

She stepped closer, her voice softer. "You've been closed off lately. And I get it. After everything that's happened — Silverburn, the Smilers, the kids — it's a lot. But Derek... you're doing a great job. New Haven will hold."

He met her eyes, guilt and gratitude flickering behind his own. "I just don't want to lose this place. We've come too far. I can't let it fall. Not after all we've been through."

Jennifer stepped in, gently placing her hand on his. "Then trust what we've built. Trust us. We've got your back."

Before she could say anything else, Derek stood and pulled her into a deep, sudden kiss. She melted into it, arms wrapping around him, the weight of the world temporarily forgotten.

When they parted, he rested his forehead against hers.

"When I get back... when things calm down, why don't we carve out some alone time?"

She arched an eyebrow, smiling. "Alone time?"

"I know a lovely segregation cell — peaceful, good acoustics." He smirked.

Jennifer gave him a playful slap on the arm. "I'll hold you to that."

They shared one last look before parting. Derek grabbed his gear and stepped outside into the crisp air of the courtyard. Nia, Joe, Ortega, Jillian, and Daryl were already geared up and waiting near the truck. Weapons checked. Packs loaded. Derek approached, glancing one last time over his shoulder. Jennifer stood next to the truck to see them off.

Derek walked up behind her, leaned in, and kissed her once more — firm, deliberate.

"Stay safe," she whispered.

"You too," he replied, then climbed into the passenger seat.

Jennifer raised her voice. "Open the gates!"

The steel doors of New Haven creaked and groaned as they slid open. Dust lifted into the air. The truck rumbled forward, wheels crunching over gravel as it rolled out of the safe zone and into the unknown.

Destination: Halestow.

—-

The sun was climbing higher, casting long shadows from the outer wall and scaffolding set up around the moat construction. Dust hung in the air, kicked up by the rhythm of shovels and boots. The sound of work was constant — digging, hammering, murmured conversation. Jennifer sat on the edge of an overturned supply crate, her water flask resting between her hands. Callum approached, wiping sweat from his brow, eyes scanning the busy work crews.

"Everything alright?" he asked, nudging her gently with his boot.

She hesitated, then looked up at him, eyes full of unease. "I don't know," she said quietly. "I keep trying to tell myself it's just the stress... but something feels off."

Callum sat beside her. "What do you mean?"

She looked toward the gate where Jillian had last been seen leaving with Derek. "I think something's going on between them... Derek and Jillian."

Callum was quiet for a moment. He exhaled slowly, rubbing the back of his neck. "Jen... no. I mean, Jillian's always tried to be helpful. She's been through a lot too. Maybe she's just leaning on him."

Jennifer gave a half-hearted shrug. "Maybe. But she looks at him like... like I used to. Like I still do. And I don't know, Callum... he's different around her. Lately."

Callum offered a small, reassuring smile. "You know Derek. He carries everything on his shoulders — especially guilt. If something happened, he'd tell you."

Jennifer wanted to believe that. She nodded slowly, but the worry still lingered behind her eyes. What Callum didn't say — what he didn't want to admit — was that he'd seen it too. A look, a moment too long when they thought no one was watching. He didn't have proof. And he didn't want to believe it either. Before the silence between them grew heavier, a shout rang out from the outer wall.

"Zombies! Roadside — maybe twenty of them!"

Jennifer and Callum both sprang to their feet, rushing to the nearest ladder up to the guard tower. From the perch, they saw them — a small pack, staggered and shambling. Fifteen, maybe twenty. Classic zombies. Sluggish. Mindless. But something about it didn't sit right. Daryl was already barking orders near the gate, directing some of the younger adults to the wall with bows and spears. A few others moved to reinforce the fence line. Within minutes, the zombies were dispatched — efficient and quiet. Not a single one made it within ten feet of the outer trench.

But that wasn't what left Jennifer's skin crawling. "They're testing us," she muttered.

Callum looked over. "What?. Who?"

Jennifer's voice was low. "The Smilers. Grinners. Whatever they are. They're testing our defenses. Watching how we respond. How fast we move. What we use."

Callum didn't disagree. He scanned the treeline again.

"Then we make sure the next time they look, we're ready for them."

Jennifer nodded, jaw tight. "Because next time... it won't be twenty zombies."

—

Maggie leaned over the trench wall, sweat beading on her forehead. She'd been digging since sunrise, sleeves rolled to her elbows, hands raw inside leather gloves. She paused only when Anne brought over a canteen of water.

"You're pushing too hard again," Anne said softly, handing her the drink.

"I've got two teenage girls watching me," Maggie replied. "If they see me slacking, I lose the right to tell them what to do."

Anne smiled, resting a hand briefly on Maggie's shoulder. "They already look up to you. You don't have to be a machine."

Maggie gave a tired laugh. "Don't I, though? Machines don't break."

—

Roary was seated beside Finn and Michone, the three of them maintaining a stack of salvaged gear near the southern guard post. Rope, spare nails, barbed wire, sharpened wood. Every piece counted.

"Think we'll have enough wire to do the other side?" Finn asked, wiping grease from his hands.

Roary shrugged. "Depends on if Ortega's math was right. And if nobody steals more to build another damn chicken coop."

Michone snorted. "They're not stealing, Roar. They're surviving. Chickens wander, they need somewhere to be secured."

Roary gave a quiet grunt and went back to hammering a metal stake into a wooden board. Still, he watched the road more than his work — the thought of another Smiler showing up gnawed at him like a splinter under skin.

—

In the lower yard near the chapel, Ali was helping Erin and Abby sort through a stockpile of meds and bandages. After the last scare, Erin insisted they redo the inventory from scratch.

Ali held up a dusty bottle. "What even is this?"

Erin glanced over. "Expired three years ago. Keep it. Might still work for pain."

Abby leaned in. "What happens if they come again? With another horde?"

Erin looked up, eyes dark but steady. "Then we patch who we can. And bury who we can't."

It was the kind of truth only a medic could say and not flinch.

Felix and Jonas were at the west watchtower, both taking turns watching the treeline with binoculars. Below them, Reggie sketched quick diagrams of the defensive lines — how they'd reroute the trenches, where to place wooden barriers, how to make the spikes more effective.

"I don't like this waiting," Felix muttered. "They're out there. I can feel it."

Jonas didn't reply right away. He just kept scanning the horizon. After a while, he said, "They're always out there. The question is — when are they going to try get in?"

—-

Back in the courtyard, some of the older kids played a game Jennifer had taught them — something simple with chalk and numbers. Laughter still echoed, faint but real. A reminder of what was being protected. In the shade of the guard tower, Lexi leaned against the wall, arms crossed. She was supposed to be helping dig, but her thoughts were elsewhere. Every few minutes, her eyes flicked toward the northern hills — where Halestow lay somewhere behind the trees and mist.

Beside her, Sam was pacing again, chewing his thumb.

"They'll come back," Lexi said. "Derek's smart. They'll be fine."

Sam nodded, but said nothing. Because until they saw the trucks again — silence would always mean fear.

That evening, as the sun dipped low beyond the treetops, a heavy quiet fell over New Haven. The wind dragged dust across the nearly finished trench, and the smell of dirt and sweat clung to everything. Jennifer stood at the northern wall, arms folded, eyes scanning the distant treeline as if willing Derek's truck to appear. But there was only stillness. Below her, the children played quietly. Nearby, Abby hummed as she repacked the med tent's supplies. Bellamy drilled another group in basic marksmanship with Roary barking corrections from behind. The rhythm of survival carried on — but tension clung like mist.

Some of the other adults were moving supplies into the shelter, enough for everyone to hold out for a few weeks at least. Just in case they needed to use it. Atop the admin block, Munroe oversaw construction, arms crossed, barking orders down to the crews shaping the earth. With every foot of trench and every sharpened stake, he hoped they were buying more than just time. New Haven was holding.

But everyone knew the real storm was still coming.

Chapter 23

The truck rumbled through the narrowing woodland trail, branches scratching along the sides like skeletal fingers. Inside, the six of them sat in silence, tension thick between every breath. The vehicle bumped along uneven earth as the trees began to thin ahead. Nia was still behind the wheel, eyes locked forward. Derek sat beside her, arms crossed, jaw set. Behind them, Jillian sat by the window, watching the trees blur by, while Ortega, Daryl, and Joe bounced in the rear bench, weapons ready, packs at their feet.

"You said it was called Halestow?" Derek asked, breaking the quiet.

Nia nodded. "Yeah. It was supposed to be a self-sustaining community. Started a few years before everything went to hell. Green energy, off-grid systems. Solar panels on every roof. Big emphasis on security and privacy."

Derek raised an eyebrow. "Smart move. And it held?"

"For a while," Nia replied. "Ten-foot walls, three feet thick. One road in, same road out. Fenced the top edge of the walls to make it harder to climb. There were only about fifteen houses inside, but each had independent power and water from a filtered section of the river nearby." She paused, her jaw tightening as memories surfaced. "We had gardens, water collectors. Even had hot showers for a time. We took in stragglers when we could, screened them, helped them fit in. It was working. It was really working."

Derek listened, quietly impressed.

"But then," Nia continued, "two months ago... the grinning ones showed up. Just... standing in the treeline. Like statues. Sending the dead toward us, over and over. Never attacking themselves. Never saying anything. Just watching. Smiling."

"They never came close?" Derek asked.

"No," Nia said. "They just... pointed. Directed. Like shepherds sending in wolves. We held them off for weeks. Then we ran low on ammo. Food. People started panicking. And then..." Her voice trailed off.

"That's when you left?" Derek asked gently.

"Yeah. A group of us made a run for help. We were supposed to circle around and find allies. Bring people back to help clear them out. Reinforce the walls." She paused. "But we don't know what we're going back to. Could be nothing. Or..."

Derek nodded. "Could be worse."

Behind them, Jillian leaned forward in her seat, having overheard. "Let's just hope someone held the line."

Nia's knuckles whitened on the steering wheel. "I hope so too."

The trees began to thin. The path widened slightly, the distant glint of sunlight on metal hinted at something up ahead. They were getting close.

"How far do you think we should go before we stop and scout?" Ortega asked.

Derek turned his head slightly. "Once we break the treeline and get a visual. We don't go barreling in blind."

Joe shifted nervously. "What if it's already gone? If we're too late?"

"We're not here to take it back," Derek said. "Not yet. We're here to see."

Joe didn't respond, but the way his hands flexed on his rifle said enough. The truck grew quieter again as the canopy began to part. Sunlight spilled across the cracked road ahead — and beyond it, in the distance, they caught their first glimpse of Halestow. Just as Nia had described — a wall, maybe ten feet high, weather-stained and solid. It stretched wide, curving gently to follow the layout of the community inside. Fencing curled along the top, rusted but intact. A wooden barricade framed the single entry point where the road met the wall — a reinforced gate built of steel and timber. And beyond that gate... nothing. No sound. No movement. No smoke. They stopped in the cover of trees about 200 meters out.

Derek climbed out, shouldering his rifle and crouching beside the hood to get a better view. "Alright. We walk the rest of the way in. Quiet and slow." The group moved in tight formation, weapons ready, every footstep deliberate. For a long beat, no one spoke. Jillian stepped down, cocking her crossbow. Joe hopped out, eyes locked on the gates. "If they're still in there, they'd have seen us by now."

"Looks intact," Daryl finally said. "Too quiet."

"Way too quiet," Ortega noted.

"Unless they can't," Nia says "Or won't," she added.

The group moved in tight formation, weapons ready, every footstep deliberate.

Dry leaves crunched under their boots as they emerged from the trees and stepped onto the overgrown road leading straight to Halestow's main gate. The air was unnaturally still — no birdsong, no wind. Just the distant creak of old wood under pressure and the occasional rustle from deeper within the trees.

The ten-foot wall loomed over them. Faded hand-painted signs still clung to it — SAFE HAVEN, SURVIVORS WELCOME, WE PROTECT OUR OWN. The once-welcoming words now felt like echoes from another time. Derek reached the gate first, pressed a hand to the heavy wooden crossbars, and gave a solid push. Nothing. He tried again — this time with more force — but the gate didn't even shift. "It's solid," he muttered. "Barred from the inside."

Nia stepped up beside him, breath catching slightly. "That's... that's a good sign, right?" She looked back toward Joe, eyes betraying a flicker of hope. "Someone could still be in there." Joe gave a tense nod. Then — before anyone could stop her — Nia cupped her hands and shouted, "It's us! It's Nia and Joe! We made it back!"

The words echoed off the trees like a siren, far too loud in the dead silence.

Derek's grip tightened around Nia's arm, his voice low and urgent. "Are you daft?" he hissed. "Keep your voice down!"

"But—" she stammered.

"We don't know what's watching these walls," he growled. "Those things could still be out there—or worse, already inside."

She fell silent, nodding reluctantly. And then— A howl. Low. Guttural. Inhuman. It echoed from deep within the forest behind them. Not an animal. Not natural. A sound they had all heard before, one that sent a shiver through the marrow.

Nia's face went pale. "It's them..." she whispered. "The Grinners."

Everyone turned. From the dark line of trees beyond the road, three shapes emerged — tall, thin, bodies twitching unnaturally, their grotesque, stretched grins locked in place. Behind them... came the zombies. Dozens of them poured out from the trees, shambling forward, slow at first — but drawn with unmistakable intent. Yet the smilers didn't move. They just stood, arms spread wide, as if conducting an orchestra of rot and death.

"They're sending them!" Nia gasped.

Derek didn't hesitate. "Weapons up! NOW!"

The group turned as one, guns raised, crossbows cocked. The forest erupted in groans and snapping twigs as the first of the horde broke into a clumsy run.

"Form up!" Derek bellowed. "Hold the line!"

And then—The dead charged.

—-

Gunfire cracked through the air as Derek's group unloaded into the oncoming dead. Crossbow bolts flew, Ortega's machete was already slick, and Jillian stood shoulder to shoulder with Daryl, dropping zombies one by one. But there were too many. The smilers didn't flinch. They stood tall at the treeline, silent commanders orchestrating a living wall of death. Then— A loud metallic creak echoed behind them. The massive gate to Halestow groaned open just a few feet — just enough.

"GET INSIDE!" a voice shouted from within. "NOW!"

"Move!" Derek roared.

The team fell back, still firing as they backed toward the gate. Ortega and Daryl covered the rear, Derek dragging Nia by the arm as she stumbled in shock. Joe helped Jillian, who had twisted her ankle on the uneven ground. One by one they dove through the narrow opening. As the last boot cleared the threshold, the gate slammed shut with a thunderous clang, followed by the sound of wood and iron braces being slammed into place. The groans of the dead were right behind them, now pounding and slamming against the reinforced gate.

Inside, Derek spun around, rifle raised— Only to see a young man, maybe mid-thirties, holding up his hands, breath ragged. His clothes were filthy, but his eyes were alert.

Nia gasped. "Paul! You're alive!" She rushed forward and threw her arms around him. He hugged her tight, his voice cracking.

"Didn't think I'd see you again."

After a moment, she pulled back, beaming. "Everyone — this is Paul. He helped build Halestow from the start."

Paul nodded to the others, breath still shaky. "Come on, we'll talk inside. No point standing here with all that noise."

Once they moved beyond the gate's inner defenceline, NiaThe noise of the zombies hammering at the gates faded to a distant, muffled thump as Paul led them into the heart of Halestow.

The community was quiet — too quiet. As they passed between rows of makeshift homes and converted cabins, faces peeked out from behind curtains. Tired eyes. Hollow cheeks. The kind of quiet that came from too many sleepless nights and not enough full stomachs They reached an old stone church at the centre of the community. Its stained-glass windows were cracked, but sunlight still filtered in through coloured shards, casting dull rainbows salvaged part

—

The midday sun beat down over the prison-turned-sanctuary as the clang of shovels and the low rumble of machinery echoed through the air. Dust hung in golden clouds as the moat continued to take shape — a wide trench that now stretched nearly three-quarters of the way around the outer wall. Piles of overturned earth lined its edges, and the gleam of reinforced spikes lay neatly bundled, ready for placement.

At the western edge, Callum stood shirtless and mud-streaked, coordinating with Reggie and Jonas on trench depth. Nearby, Lexi and Sam hauled bundles of barbed wire, sweat dripping from their brows. Even some of the older kids were pitching in under supervision — filling sandbags, passing tools, or ferrying supplies between stations.

Jennifer stood at the overlook of the admin block with Munroe and Maggie, watching it all unfold.

"It's coming together quicker than we thought," Munroe said, shielding his eyes from the sun with a gloved hand. "Another day, maybe two, and we'll have a full circuit. After that, we fill parts of it with barbed wire and lay the spikes."

"How many zombies today?" Jennifer quietly.

"Just five. Came from the east road. Michone spotted them before they even got near the wall," Munroe replied. "Felix and Roary dropped them with no fuss."

Jennifer offered a small smile. "Good. That's good."

But her eyes drifted back toward the horizon. Still no sign of the truck. Still no word.

—-

Bellamy stood in the former rec hall with a growing group of armed civilians — some new, some veterans of the prison since the beginning. He barked orders with clarity and precision, stepping between rows of people holding crossbows, machetes, and a few refurbished rifles.

"Again!" he shouted. "If it's not second nature now, it'll cost you when it matters."

The group responded in sync — raising weapons, aiming, backing up into defensive formations. Abby handed out water between drills, while Scott adjusted someone's grip on a homemade spear. Bellamy paused beside a young woman — Alice, one of the newer residents who'd joined just weeks ago. Training was going well. The people of New Haven weren't soldiers — but they were willing, and that mattered more.—

Later, near the chapel, Callum and Anne sat under a patch of shade, sharing a quiet moment with their hands clasped between them.

"You think they're okay?" Anne asked softly.

Callum nodded, though the crease in his brow betrayed his doubt. "If anyone can handle it, it's Derek and Daryl. But I still don't like not hearing from them."

Anne leaned against him and whispered, "We need to tell them soon."

He looked at her. "Yeah. We do."

But for now, all they could do was wait — and dig.

The pounding at the gate had finally stopped. The air hung heavy with silence — not peace, but the taut, unnatural stillness that only came when something was watching you. From the top of the watchtower, Derek stood with one hand on the rail, the other gripping a battered pair of binoculars. He scanned the treeline ahead. And there they were.

Three of them. The Smilers — or Grinners, as Halestow called them — stood just beyond the brush. Unmoving. Faces stretched into those eerie, unnatural smiles. Eyes like empty sockets in porcelain masks. One slowly cocked its head, as if it knew Derek was watching.

"Creepy bastards," Daryl muttered, stepping up beside him. He adjusted the strap on his rifle, shouldered it, and aimed through the scope. "Let me take one of them out."

Derek didn't answer. Daryl steadied the sight, finger curling around the trigger. Click. Derek's hand landed on the barrel and slowly pushed it down.

"Not yet," he said, quietly.

Daryl looked over, annoyed. "You waiting for them to send invitations next time?"

"Just look," Derek replied, handing him the binoculars. "To the west. Past the treeline."

Daryl huffed, but raised them to his eyes. And then he saw it. Tucked behind the trees, maybe 200 meters away, sat an old petrol station, nearly swallowed by foliage. Its sign half-fallen, rusted. But beside it— A tanker truck. Still intact. The faded blue logo on the side was barely visible beneath grime and ivy, but the tank itself was unruptured. No bite marks. No blood smears. No sign of looting.

"If that's full..." Derek began.

"...we could use it to blow them sky-fucking-high," Daryl finished, lowering the binoculars with a wicked grin.

They looked at each other, and for the first time in days, there was fire behind both their eyes.

But then Derek's expression darkened again. "We can't just go in blind. That station's out past the treeline. Could be swarming. Could be booby-trapped. Could be a trap itself."

"We'll need eyes. A stealth check," Daryl said, already mapping it out in his head. "Take Joe. Maybe Nia. Quick and quiet. Just to see what we're working with."

Derek nodded slowly. "We talk to Paul. See what Halestow can spare. If that tanker is usable, we've just found ourselves a way to send a message."

He turned back to the Grinners. Still standing. Still watching. And for the first time...

Derek smiled back.

Derek and Daryl stepped off the watchtower, gravel crunching beneath their boots as they moved with purpose across the courtyard. The Grinners still lingered at the treeline like statues, silent and still... watching. Inside the old church-turned-command-post, Paul was hunched over a makeshift map table, noting shifts in the patrol routes and rationing schedules. His head lifted as the door opened.

"Trouble?" he asked.

"Not yet," Derek replied. "But we might have found an opportunity."

Paul leaned forward. "Go on."

Daryl wasted no time. "That petrol station to the west — we spotted it from the tower. There's a tanker still parked out front."

Paul's brows furrowed with recognition, then softened with a regretful nod. "Yeah. It's ours... or was. We were pumping some of it into reserve barrels when the Grinners first showed. Had to bail fast. The tanker's still mostly full — maybe ninety percent, give or take."

"You haven't sent anyone to retrieve it?" Derek asked.

Paul shook his head. "We tried once — small team — but a Grinner appeared halfway down the road before they even got close. We didn't risk it again."

Daryl crossed his arms. "If it's untouched, that could give us serious firepower. Enough to torch a good chunk of the dead. Maybe even get rid of a Grinner or two."

Paul hesitated, then nodded. "Yeah. That's what we thought too."

"We'll need a guide," Derek said. "Someone from your people who knows the area."

Paul thought for a second. "Mason's your best bet. Quiet, quick on his feet, knows those back roads better than anyone. I'll speak to him. He'll go."

Derek gave a single nod. "We move at first light. Quiet and fast. No screw-ups."

Paul pointed at the map, tracing a thin red line with his finger. "There's a service path that'll get you within a few meters of the station. Overgrown, but if you stick to it, you should avoid most of the open ground."

Daryl grinned. "Sounds like a plan."

As the three of them leaned over the map, going over paths and back up signals the undead were all away from the gates.

But at the treeline, the Smilers remained. Still watching. Still smiling.

Chapter 24

The air inside the old Halestow chapel was thick with smoke and silence. Derek stood over a hand-drawn map laid across a wooden table, cigarette burning low between his fingers. Daryl was pacing beside the pews, crossbow slung low, eyes scanning the stained-glass windows as if the Grinners might burst through them at any moment. Paul leaned over the map, brow furrowed in thought.

"Here's the plan," Derek began, stabbing his finger at a sketch of the settlement. "We send a team—two or three people—out the east gate. Loud, obvious, make it look like we're abandoning Halestow. Our trucks parked just a few hundred metres away, if they can get to that then they can get away."

Daryl raised a brow. "And the Grinners bite, follow them?"

"That's the hope," Derek said grimly. "If they move the horde even slightly, that gives us our window."

Paul added, "The west wall's still got that crawl space under the old compost yard. No eyes there—just thick overgrowth. If you hug the trees and stay low, you can make it to the petrol station in fifteen, twenty minutes."

Derek nodded. "We sneak out. Me, Daryl, and Mason. We've got enough C4 left to do the job, but no detonators to blow it remotely. So…"

"So someone has to shoot the c4 perfectly," Daryl muttered, running a hand over his beard. "Hell of a plan."

"Not ideal," Derek admitted, "but if it works, we take out a big chunk of them. Maybe enough to finally shake them loose from these walls."

Paul tapped the map again. "The downside is the fire. That tanker goes up near the woods and we're looking at a blaze. We don't have the means to put it out."

Derek glanced out the nearest window. The forest loomed — silent, ancient, and dry. "It's a risk," he said. "But the longer those things watch from the treeline, the more we bleed inside these walls. We hit them hard. Fast. We burn the infection from the roots."

No one spoke for a moment.

Then Daryl sighed. "Guess we light the fuse."

The tension hung like static as Joe double-checked the makeshift noise rig they'd strapped to the rear of an old quad bike. A pair of battered metal pans, a few lengths of chain, and a plastic sheet rigged to catch wind — all of it guaranteed to make a racket once they took off. Nia stood nearby, tightening her gloves, her jaw clenched.

"You sure you're up for this?" Paul asked, concern etched in his voice.

"We just have to get their attention and lead them east. No heroics," she said. "Just noise and movement."

Joe gave a nod. "We'll take the long route. Loop around the far ridge. If they follow, we'll know it fast."

Paul looked out past the gate — where the trees began to sway and distant, silent silhouettes still lingered among the trunks.

"No lights," he warned. "If they see the quad coming too clearly, they might get clever."

"We'll keep it loud and stupid," Nia replied, then cracked a small grin. "Like Daryl."

From atop the gate, someone gave the signal. The doors opened just wide enough to let them through. The quad engine sputtered, caught, and roared into life — and with a burst of sound and clatter, Nia and Joe shot down the path. Chains clanged wildly. The forest shook.

Three Grinners turned. And then — they followed.

—-

Derek exhaled slowly as he dropped to his belly and slid beneath the broken stone lip of the west wall. Mud sucked at his jacket. Twigs snapped under his boots. Behind him, Mason grunted and squeezed through the gap, eyes scanning the overgrowth. Daryl followed last, crossbow in hand, his movements slower but deliberate. They emerged into the thick underbrush. Towering ferns, brambles, and rot-thick trees surrounded them like a barrier of their own. Derek lifted his hand, signaling silence, and the three men crept forward — low, methodical, every step measured. Insects buzzed in the heat. Up ahead, just barely visible through a thin veil of vines, the rust-red shell of the petrol station loomed. The tanker was still there — slumped beside the pumps like a sleeping beast. A few zombies were on the forecourt but nothing they couldn't handle.

Daryl let out a breath through his teeth. "There she is."

Mason looked to Derek. "You think they took the bait?"

Derek peered back through the brush. Far behind them, down the hill and through the trees, faint shapes were shifting east — away from Halestow. "Looks like it."

They moved quickly now. The closer they got, the more silence pressed in. No birds. No wind. Just the hiss of heat off asphalt and the distant, whispering groans of the dead.

From the watchtower atop Halestow's battered north wall, Joan squinted into the sun-glared treetops, binoculars locked tight to her face. She'd tracked them — the horde trailing Joe and Nia, a slow-moving, groaning wave funneled down the old railway path. Until now. "Wait..." she whispered, adjusting focus. A shadow peeled away from the treeline. Then another. One of the Smilers turned. And then the horde followed.

"Oh no..." Her voice caught in her throat before bursting loose. "They've turned! THEY'VE TURNED!" She grabbed the flare-flag and waved it hard toward the western treeline. "They're heading for the petrol station!"

Below, Paul rushed to the inner wall edge, waving his arms, trying to catch any glimmer of reflection from the team's position. "DE-REK! They're coming your way!" But the smoke haze and distance swallowed his voice.

—-

The last zombie slumped down hard onto the gravel, a bolt through its eye.

Derek, Daryl, and Mason stood among a few fresh corpses, breathing heavy, blood splattered across their arms and torsos. The station — an old two-pump depot — sat silent, the tanker still gleaming in the sunlight.

Derek wiped sweat from his brow, glancing to the treeline. "That should be all of them. Let's finish this."

The C4 was nearly set — rigged across the tanker's undercarriage, with a dead man's trigger wired up in the cab. A crude but effective explosive that would make this entire patch of road a memory.

As Derek strapped the final charge near the rear axle, Mason looked up — eyes squinting.

"Wait... is that a flag?"

He turned, hand shielding his face. There, waving over the trees, a red flare-flag flapping wildly — Joan's warning. Then came the sound. Low. Dull. Building like distant thunder.

Daryl's head snapped toward the woods. "Shit. They're coming."

The trees shivered — and then they saw them: dozens, maybe hundreds, with one Smiler at the front, mouth agape in its permanent grin, eyes locked dead ahead.

"Go!" Derek shouted.

But Mason was already inside the tanker, doors locked, engine revving.

The growl of the motor roared as the massive vehicle lurched forward — a beast built for fuel, now turned into a bomb on wheels.

Mason gave them a nod through the cracked windscreen. Then — he was gone, the tanker plowing through low brush, straight for the approaching horde.

From the watchtower, Joan had her binoculars fixed on the treeline, barely breathing.

Beside her, Paul gripped the ledge tight enough to whiten his knuckles.

"Come on... come on," he muttered.

Down the ridge, the tanker thundered forward — engine roaring like a beast unleashed.

And now... all three Smilers had emerged from the treeline, standing perfectly still but perfectly commanding — arms outstretched, fingers twitching. And the horde obeyed. Dozens, then hundreds, shambled and surged toward the approaching truck, funneled like cattle through a controlled gate.

"They're guiding them," Joan whispered, chilled. "They know the truck's coming."

A short distance from the treeline, Daryl was perched on the rusted hood of a wrecked pickup, he had Derek's rifle raised and aimed squarely at the tanker's belly.

Derek stood behind him, tense, eyes scanning the movement.

"He's not slowing down," Daryl said. "He's not gonna jump."

Derek didn't respond. He couldn't. They both watched as the horde surged, Smilers directing them like generals, and Mason — brave, stubborn Mason — drove on.

"We can't wait much longer," Derek finally said, voice cracking from the weight of it.

Daryl glanced down his scope. Still no sign of an exit. No door opening. No leap for safety. Just a steel coffin on wheels. And a man who refused to let his home fall.

—-

Mason had the wheel gripped tight, knuckles raw against sun-heated metal. Zombies smashed against the windshield, bones snapping under tires. The tanker shuddered with each kill. And yet still — no bullet. Still no explosion. "Come on," he whispered, watching the horde grow thicker, watching the Smilers' eyes widen. "Shoot, dammit... end this—" His voice broke. "I'm sorry, Clare...It came like a breath, barely a sound. He closed his eyes.

—-

"Now," Derek said. "He's reached the smilers."

And Daryl pulled the trigger. The rifle barked once. The round ripped through the space between them — and hit dead centre on the C4 charge strapped beneath the tanker's belly.

—-

The world went white.

A thunderous explosion erupted from the forest's edge, like a bomb dropped from the heavens. A shockwave of flame and force rolled through the trees, hurling the dead into the air like leaves in a storm. The three Smilers didn't even have time to react. They were caught in the first wave — blown to pieces, their grins the last thing visible before the fire swallowed them whole. The forest ignited, flames racing through the underbrush and curling into the treetops. From Halestow's walls, the light was blinding. The sound was deafening. Joan ducked behind the tower beam as a wave of hot wind slammed through.

Paul just stared, mouth open, ash raining down around them.

—-

Derek shielded his face as debris rained around them. Daryl slid down off the hood, winded but alive. Smoke billowed into the sky. Silence followed... just for a moment.

"Jesus," Daryl muttered, coughing. "He... he didn't jump."

"No," Derek said softly, lowering his hand from his eyes. "He made sure he got to the centre, to the smilers."

—-

The blast had hit like a tidal wave of flame and thunder. From the watchtower, Joan's ears rang with a high-pitched whine. She could barely hear Paul yelling her name as he pulled her back to her feet. Her vision blurred — heat shimmered in the air, and a thin drizzle of ash began falling like snow. Below them, men and women ran from the church, from gardens, from behind barricades — people who'd braced for the worst now blinking in confusion at the sudden silence.

The Smilers — the ones who'd haunted the treeline for weeks — were gone.

Paul gripped the railing and stared. Smoke curled upward in a dark, rolling plume above the western forest. A few stray flames still danced in the trees, but much of the horde had been obliterated, reduced to chunks of flesh and scorched bone. "What the hell did they do..." he muttered, half in awe, half in fear.

Joan dropped her binoculars and ran to the ladder. "We need to open the gates. Get them back inside. If they're still alive—"

—-

Nia, Joe, and several others were already sprinting toward the outer wall, weapons still raised from the earlier chaos.

Paul met them there, shouting, "Get this unbarred now!"

They worked quickly — iron latches groaning, chains rattling. With a hard pull, the main gate creaked open. Out beyond the scorched field, through the curling smoke...

Two figures emerged — one limping slightly, both covered in soot, ash, and blood. Daryl held a rifle over his shoulder. Derek carried a pack that looked like it had taken shrapnel. No words were said at first. Just faces. Nods. And a few stunned gasps from Halestow's people.

Then Joan called down from the tower: "No movement! Nothing's coming! I think it's over!"

A cheer rose up from within the walls — not loud, not full-throated, but relieved, worn, real. She ran to Derek, stopping just short of throwing her arms around him.

"You made it," she said, wide-eyed.

Derek gave a nod, breathing hard. "Mason didn't."

The celebration quieted at that.

Paul stepped forward, his voice soft: "He drove the truck?"

Daryl gave a slow nod. "All the way into the middle."

Silence fell again — this time deeper. But it was a respectful silence. One earned.

Paul placed a hand over his heart. "We'll remember him."

—-

From the forest's edge, the fire still burned. The smilers were gone — for now. But the flames had only cleared the way for what came next. Inside Halestow's small infirmary, the air was thick with antiseptic and dust. Beds lined the walls — some used, most empty. The pale light filtering through frosted windows did little to soften the weight hanging over the room. Daryl and Derek limped in first, soot-streaked, shirts torn from the heat of the blast. Joe and Nia trailed behind them, quiet and shaken but alert, every glance checking corners, watching for movement that wasn't there.

Outside, in the courtyard just beyond the open door, Paul stood with his arm around a woman, trying to steady her shaking frame. Derek stopped halfway into the room and turned to Nia.

"Who's that?" he asked, voice low.

Nia hesitated, jaw tight. "That's Clare. Mason's partner."

Derek's throat went dry. He'd barely had time to register Mason's sacrifice, but the reality of it struck hard now. He looked away — not out of shame, but respect. Inside, they collapsed into the nearest chairs — bones sore, muscles burning. Derek's ribs ached with every breath. Daryl cradled his wrist, already swelling.

Moments later, Paul stepped inside and closed the door softly behind him. "I need to ask," he said gently. "About Mason."

Derek looked up, grim.

But it was Daryl who answered. His voice came out raw. "He... he locked himself in the truck. Right after I finished setting the last charge."

Paul didn't flinch. He nodded once. Kept listening.

"He started it, wouldn't let us in," Daryl continued. "He just... drove. Straight into the middle. Through the bastards. The plan was to jump out just before—" He stopped. Looked away. "He didn't jump."

Paul was silent for a long moment. Then nodded again, slower this time. "Clare will want to know," he said. "That's why I asked."

—-

The door burst open. Jillian, hair tousled from sprinting, skidded into the room.

"Derek!" she called, breathless.

Her eyes flicked over his face, his frame — taking in the scrapes and bruises, the soot, the blood. She crossed the room in three quick strides and dropped beside him, checking his side, then his shoulder, then cupping the back of his head like he might disappear if she looked away.

"I'm okay," Derek murmured. "We're okay."

She didn't say anything. Just let out a shaky breath and nodded. Her hand lingered on his chest a moment longer before she stepped back, glancing at Daryl too. "You?"

"I'm alive," Daryl said gruffly, wincing as he adjusted in the seat. "Ask me again tomorrow."

The faintest smile touched Jillian's lips.

Outside, the air was still heavy with smoke and silence, but within Halestow's walls, something new had begun to settle. Not just relief. But resolve. Because Mason's sacrifice had bought them something rare: Time. Time to regroup. To plan. To fight.

And in the quiet between the echoes, Halestow began to breathe again.

—-

A few hours had passed and from the watchtower, Joan lowered her binoculars and let out a slow breath. "It's dying down," she murmured.

Beside her, Mark nodded, eyes still fixed on the scorched treeline where the fire had once raged. Smoke curled into the air, black fading to grey, then nearly gone. "It didn't spread like we thought it would," he said.

"Yeah..." Joan replied. "Could be the soil. Could be the wind. Could be dumb luck."

Below them, the forest's edge glowed in patches — smouldering and cracked, like the earth had been split open by rage. The corpses that once swarmed now shuffled clumsily, maybe twenty at most, no longer marching in time. No eerie grins. No purpose.

The smilers were gone.

At least for now.

—-

Elsewhere in Halestow, Derek stood in a quiet corner of the courtyard, beside Paul, both facing a woman who hadn't said a word since they'd approached. Clare sat on a bench with her hands folded in her lap, a scarf half-clenched in her fist. Her eyes were swollen but dry. No more tears left.

Derek knelt down, resting his arms on his knees. "He saved us," he said. "All of us."

Paul nodded slowly. "He didn't hesitate, Clare. He made the call so no one else would have 'to."

She didn't look up. Just closed her eyes and nodded once. Derek wanted to say more — something noble or comforting — but the truth was, nothing he could say would ever fill that hole. So he rose and quietly stepped away, leaving Clare to the stillness.

—-

Later, as the sun dipped below the walls of Halestow, Jillian wandered the corridors of the main hall until she found him — Derek, sitting alone in one of the unused rooms, door ajar. He was hunched over on a bench, elbows on knees, hands clasped. The orange light from outside cast long shadows across his face.

"You always disappear after," she said gently from the doorway.

Derek didn't look up. "Just... needed quiet."

She stepped inside, closing the door behind her. "You did good today," she said. "You all did." He didn't reply. After a moment, she crossed the room and sat beside him. They sat together in silence as Halestow held its breath around them.

Chapter 25

It had been two days since the sky turned orange and the ground shuddered beneath them. The once-raging fires along Halestow's western edge had finally weakened, now little more than smouldering black earth dotted with occasional wisps of smoke. The scent of burned wood and charred flesh still clung to every breath.

Inside Halestow, people moved with a wary calm. Relief, exhaustion, and grief mixed in equal measure.

—-

Derek sat on the edge of a bed inside the infirmary, his arm wrapped in fresh bandages. His side ached with every breath. Across the small room, Daryl lay propped up, reading an old tattered book someone had dug out for him.

Derek glanced at him. "You ever gonna finish that page?"

Daryl didn't look up. "Maybe I just like the words. Stop staring."

Derek managed the faintest smirkIt had been over six days since Derek and the others had left for Halestow.

—

Each sunrise felt longer than the last, the quiet nights filled with the wind rattling through half-finished barricades and the echo of distant groans beyond the walls.

In that time, Lexi and Sam from Halestow had become familiar faces inside New Haven. Under Lee's watchful eye, they helped fortify guard posts, pass out water, and carry supplies — Lee rarely straying more than a few steps from them, protective but fair.

A heavy air hung over the main meeting room as the council gathered. The makeshift table — an old conference slab salvaged from an office — was littered with maps, half-finished plans, and a few empty water cups.

Present today: Jennifer, Callum, Lee, Bill, Maggie, Anne, Dr. Hensley, Bellamy, Munroe, and Lexi (younger). Lexi and Sam from Halestow sat off to the side, invited to observe and give input.

Callum stood, leaning forward, his rough hands braced against the table edge. "The moat should be finished within the next two hours," he began. His voice, steady and measured, carried easily in the small space. "But it's not enough on its own. We need to start organizing supply teams — food, weapons, ammo. Anything that gives us an edge if something like the Smilers or a horde shows up."

Maggie nodded, eyes tired but sharp. "We've been on half rations too long. We can't keep going like this."

Munroe shifted in his seat. "We also need more traps. Spike traps, snare lines. Anything that can slow them down before they even hit the moat."

Bill, usually quiet, added, "We have a list of old warehouses and small towns south of here that haven't been cleared. We could split into two or three groups, cover more ground."

Jennifer leaned back, folding her arms. Her face showed worry beneath the composed surface. "We need to remember: every person we send out is someone we risk losing. But we can't hole up and starve either."

Lexi from Halestow looked up, hesitant but determined. "Back at Halestow... we had scouts travel in pairs. Always one to watch the other's back. It worked — until the Smilers came. But for normal runs, it helped."

Sam chimed in beside her. "We can help plan. We know some of the nearby backroads. Might avoid the worst of the undead."

Callum nodded "Good. We'll need that."

Anne shifted forward, glancing around the table. "We also need to figure out what to do if we're hit hard. Where do we fall back? Who stays to hold? Who gets the kids into the shelter?"

A beat of silence passed.

Finally, Jennifer exhaled, nodding slowly. "Alright. Let's start drafting these teams now. No more waiting."

The room filled with scribbles, low voices, and tense planning — each name a gamble, each route a risk. Outside, the final shovels scraped at the last stretch of dirt, the moat nearly complete. And in that still air, New Haven held its breath, waiting for news from the road... and preparing for the moment when silence would break again. The scratching of pencils and the rustling of old maps filled the room. Tension simmered beneath every word

— a silent reminder that every decision might determine who lived through the next season.

Callum stood at the head of the table, voice steady as he listed the newly formed teams:

—-

Team one is on the food run, Maggie, Anne and Reggie

Team two is on ammo & weapons Lee, Bill and Felix.

As the teams were confirmed, a low murmur passed through the room — names written on paper, but each one heavy as stone. Jennifer tapped her pencil against the map, eyes tracing escape routes and fallback paths. That's when Bellamy, who had been leaning against the far wall, pushed off and stepped forward. His voice, calm but certain, cut through the room.

"We're missing something," he said.

All eyes turned.

"Everyone knows the plan if the walls fall — we grab what we can and head to the shelter, then through the tunnel to the cemetery," Bellamy continued. "But what happens after we're standing there? With over a hundred people, most of them kids and elders? We can't just scatter into the woods and hope."

Silence.

He let the words settle before going on. "We need vehicles — trucks, buses, anything that runs. We need a fallback location, somewhere we can regroup or shelter long enough to decide the next move. Right now, if that day comes, we're walking. That's suicide."

Callum nodded slowly, brow furrowed. "He's right. We need more than just a tunnel escape. We need a real contingency."

Jennifer looked at Bellamy. "Where would you even start scouting?"

Bellamy rubbed his chin. "We've got that industrial yard south of here — might be some buses or large vans left. Beyond that, there are a few old ranger stations along the forest edge. Could be cabins, garages, storage. We'd need to send a team to check them out and start marking them as fallback options."

Maggie glanced at the map. "And we'll need fuel. Stockpiles near the tunnel exit."

Munroe leaned forward, tapping a point on the map. "We could designate one of the south roads as an emergency convoy route. Block it off from zombies as best we can. Even simple barricades would help."

Lexi from Halestow nodded. "If we have time to prepare, we can stage supplies — water, tools, medical kits. Little caches. That way even if the worst happens, we're not totally blind and empty-handed."

A heavy silence settled again — but this time, there was a strange flicker of resolve behind it.

Jennifer finally looked up. "Alright. We finish the moat today. Then we send out the scouting teams tomorrow."

Bellamy gave a tight nod. "I'll lead it. Take Roary and Steph. They've got sharp eyes, and they don't rattle easily."

Callum glanced around the table. "Any objections?" Heads shook slowly, each movement another quiet commitment. "Ok then, Bellamy you are team three with Steph and Rory, search for transport and fall back locations."

Jennifer sighed, but it was a steadying breath. "Then let's get to work."

—-

The council disbanded, voices rising in low chatter, boots echoing down the corridor as each person moved to their assigned tasks. New Haven had survived this long by thinking ahead. Now, they'd take one more step — preparing for the day they hoped would never come. As the final voices from the council faded down the corridor, Callum hung back, motioning to Jennifer and Anne to stay a moment. His face was calm, but there was something deeper in his eyes — a weight he hadn't shown during the meeting.

Once they were alone, he glanced around, then lowered his voice. "I didn't want to say this in front of the others," he began, "but Anne's not going out on the run."

Jennifer raised an eyebrow, confused. "Why not? She's one of our best scouters."

Callum looked to Anne, who gave a quiet, nervous smile. Then he spoke softly, with pride in his voice. "She's pregnant."

Jennifer blinked, stunned for a moment before a smile bloomed across her face. "Are you serious?" she whispered, then immediately pulled Anne into a warm, heartfelt hug. "That's incredible news."

Anne let out a shaky laugh, clearly relieved to have someone else know. "We were going to wait until things calmed down... until it felt safer."

Jennifer nodded, her voice gentle. "Well, it's a hell of a time to start a family — but maybe that's what we all need. A reason to fight harder."

Callum smiled slightly, the edge of his worry softening.

Jennifer stepped back and glanced toward the door. "I'll take care of the team swap. Michone's been practically pacing a trench into the dirt waiting for a chance to head out. She'll be over the moon."

Callum exhaled, grateful. "Thanks. Only Erin knows, aside from you now. We just need to get through the next few weeks."

Jennifer looked between them. "We will. And we'll make damn sure this bairn is born in a world that's trying to heal, not just survive."

Callum gave a short nod, then kissed Anne's temple and slipped out of the room.

Callum found Michone sitting on the edge of a supply trailer, fidgeting with the strap of her rifle. When she saw him approaching, she hopped down, hopeful. "Well? Am I in?"

He gave her a knowing smile. "You're in. You're on the food run with Maggie and Reggie."

Her eyes lit up. "Finally."

"You're replacing Anne," he added. "She's staying behind on medical."

Michone gave a quick, respectful nod. "Understood. I'll be ready in five."

Callum watched her go, then turned back toward the yard, his expression thoughtful. The world was still burning in places — but here, right now, new life was taking root.

—-

Back in the now-quiet council chamber, Anne sat down heavily on one of the benches, her hands resting just over her stomach. The firelight from the wall sconces flickered gently across her face, painting her in a softer glow than Jennifer had seen in weeks.

Jennifer pulled a chair over and sat beside her, her voice quiet, thoughtful.

"How far along do you think you are?"

Anne exhaled slowly. "Three months at most. Maybe a bit less. Erin's not been able to give me much more than a best guess. No proper equipment."

Jennifer leaned forward, elbows on her knees. "Then we need to try and source an ultrasound machine. I'll speak to Maggie before they head out — there's that wee family planning clinic not far from here. Or even a vet's. I read somewhere they use similar machines for animals."

Anne looked up, her eyes glassy but smiling. "A vet's?" she said with a small laugh. "Only in the end of the world."

Jennifer grinned softly. "Hey, if it works, it works. We'll find something. I'll have Maggie and Michone check both places."

Anne nodded, the emotion catching up to her. "I'm so glad we told you. I've been walking around like I've been hiding a secret in plain sight."

Jennifer placed a gentle hand over Anne's. "You've got nothing to be afraid of here. You're not alone, not for one second. This place... what we've built — it's for things like this. A future. Not just survival, but life."

Anne's voice was small, hopeful. "I just hope that when the time comes, it's not as crazy as it is now. I want... I want to bring the bairn into a world where people still smile. Where they're not afraid every time they hear a noise."

Jennifer squeezed her hand, steady and certain. "Then that's the world we'll make, Anne. One day at a time. And your baby's going to be part of the reason we fight so damn hard to make it real."

A silence settled between them, but it wasn't heavy. It was warm — the silence of shared hope, quiet understanding, and the faintest glimmer of peace in a world still clinging to chaos.

—-

As the sun dipped low in the sky, casting burnt orange hues across the horizon, the final coils of barbed wire were fastened into place. The last of the sharpened spikes driven deep into the earth. The moat — two metres wide, six feet deep, bristling with steel and fury — was finally done. It wasn't just a ditch. It was a message. To the dead. To the Smilers. To anything that dared come for them. They would not fall easily.

A quiet murmur passed through the courtyard as tools were laid down and shoulders slumped in shared relief. Laughter returned in small bursts, cautious but genuine. Meals were shared under firelight, guards took up their rotations with just a little less tension in their steps.

New Haven exhaled. For the first time in days, it felt like they'd built more than just defences — they'd rebuilt a little hope.

Later that night. Most were sound asleep — worn out from digging, welding, hammering.

But Jennifer couldn't rest. Boots crunching softly along the perimeter path, she walked the top of the wall alone. Her eyes scanned the darkness beyond, though she knew nothing could be seen. Just shadows and trees and endless black.

She wasn't looking for threats.

She was looking for headlights.

Her fingers wrapped tight around the radio on her hip. Silent. Still no word. Derek was out there. So was Jillian. Daryl too. Six days. She knew they were capable — some of the best they had. But still... the silence gnawed at her.

Jennifer paused at the northern tower. She placed a hand on the cold concrete and whispered into the wind, not for the first time that week:

"Come home. Please, just come home."

Above her, the stars blinked cold and distant. And New Haven, wrapped in its newly-earned stillness, slept a little deeper that night.

—-—

The gates were closed, the fires were long gone, and the smilers hadn't returned. Not since the blast. What few dead had trickled out of the woods in the days after were cut down easily by the watch rotations now in place.

Halestow stood strong.

Inside the small church that served as its heart, Derek, Jillian, and Daryl gathered their gear and checked over their supplies one last time. The bruises had faded, the burns had scabbed. They weren't exactly fresh, but they were strong enough to travel.

"Seven days," Derek muttered as he buckled his belt. "Feels longer."

"People'll be getting worried," Jillian added, her voice soft.

"Especially Jennifer," Daryl said. "She doesn't take silence well."

Derek nodded but didn't reply.

Outside the gates, Paul and Nia were already waiting, their faces lit by the early sun. Joe stood nearby, leaning against the wall, arms crossed, doing his best not to look like he didn't want to say goodbye.

"We've packed what we could spare," Paul said, handing over a small crate of tinned food and painkillers. "We're still low, but... call it a thank-you."

Derek nodded gratefully. "We'll return the gesture when we can."

"I meant what I said before," Nia cut in, looking between the three of them. "We want to stay in touch — not just for supplies or info. For backup. What you did here... it saved lives."

Daryl stepped forward. "You've got something solid here. Real defences, people who give a damn. You keep going like this, Halestow's going to last."

"And if New Haven stands too," Paul added, "maybe we can do more than just survive. Maybe we build something worth defending. Together."

Derek offered his hand. "Then let's call it what it is."

"An alliance?" Paul asked.

"A start," Derek replied. "We'll work out the details soon — maybe even get some trade routes running, share patrol intel. But right now, we need to get home."

"Fair," Paul said, shaking his hand. "Go. We'll be listening for your signal."

As the truck doors slammed shut, Jillian looked back at the gate one last time, where Paul, Nia, and Joe stood waving. "You think it'll hold?" she asked.

Derek didn't answer straight away. He stared down the long path toward the horizon. "It has to," he finally said.

Daryl lit a cigarette and blew smoke out the window. "Let's go home."

The engine rumbled to life, tires crunching dirt as they pulled away from Halestow. Ahead lay the unknown. Behind them — something new. Something hopeful.

—-

As the sun rose above the horizon. The south gate of New Haven creaked open as Maggie, Michone, and Reggie rolled out in the small blue pickup they'd prepped the night before. A cloud of dust trailed behind them as they took the winding road through the woods, bound for the west side of the town where old retail parks and food wholesalers had once stood. They had avoided this part of town as there were always a lot of zombies nearby but they needed food.

"Keep eyes up and radios on," Maggie said, her tone steady. She sat in the passenger seat, a map open on her lap. "We're going to check the family planning clinic first, then the vet clinic if we have time. After that, the wholesale food depot."

"Got it," Michone replied, driving one-handed, a crowbar resting between her seat and the door.

Reggie, sitting in the back with the supplies, added, "I'll keep the gear checked and ready. If we run into anything, I've got the molotovs prepped."

The roads were quiet. Eerily so. Since the horde incident at Silverburn, even the usual wandering dead seemed fewer.

—-

They stopped outside what had once been a tidy little building painted in soft pastels. The windows were smashed, but the walls still stood. Vines had started to creep up the sides. Michone stayed at the truck while Maggie and Reggie went in. Inside, it smelled of damp paper and mildew. Old posters about prenatal care still clung to the walls. Drawers were ransacked, but the back room was mostly intact.

"Ultrasound machine?" Reggie whispered.

Maggie pointed. "There. A portable one, too."

They checked it over. It was dusty, but the unit looked intact.

"We'll bring it back and let Erin check it out," Maggie said. "Might actually work."

They loaded it into the truck quickly, not wanting to linger. Michone scanned the treeline, her fingers tightening on the wheel. "We good?" she asked.

"Good," Maggie confirmed. "Next stop—vet clinic."

—-

The vet's office was less fortunate. Half of it had collapsed, and there were signs a fire had raged through at some point. Still, they scoured what remained.

"Couple bags of dog kibble," Reggie muttered, holding up a soot-stained bag. "Worst-case scenario."

"Take it," Maggie said. "Protein's protein."

They found a few medical supplies in an undamaged drawer and bundled them up. No second ultrasound, but some of the diagnostic tools might be useful. Back in the truck, Maggie tapped the map.

"Last stop—food depot by the roundabout. If there's anything left, we'll take what we can."

—-

They parked a block away from the wholesale dealers and approached on foot. The metal shutters were half-down, pried open just enough to slip through. Inside was dark, cavernous, and unnaturally quiet.

"Split up but stay within shouting distance," Maggie instructed.

They moved cautiously. Canned goods were sparse, but they found a stash in a sealed breakroom—tinned meats, powdered milk, a few bottled juices.

"Score," Reggie grinned.

They'd just finished loading when Michone gave a low whistle from the front.

"Incoming. Three zombies. Slow."

Maggie waved them out. "Let's not fire unless we have to."

The trio dispatched them quietly with blades, and within minutes, they were on the road again.

As the truck bounced back toward New Haven, Reggie leaned back, grinning.

"I think we did alright."

Maggie nodded. "We'll see what Erin says about that machine. If it works... might be the best find of the day."

Michone, eyes still scanning the road, smiled faintly. "It's good to be useful again."

And for a moment, as the wind rushed through the cracked windows and New Haven grew closer on the horizon, it felt like hope was something they could carry home with them.

—-

Lee, Bill, and Felix had driven for hours through cracked roads and overgrown highways, finally reaching the military base nestled deep in the wooded outskirts. It had taken this long to get there, but the payoff was hopefully worth it. The compound was old, rusted in parts, but still standing. Most of the dead here had long since rotted into piles of tattered bones and moss-covered gear.

The base had been quiet. Still.

Lee signaled for silence, raising his hand as they approached the perimeter fence. It took some effort to pry open a loose section of the chain link, but once through, they made it straight for the armory building.

Inside, they found exactly what they came for.

"Jackpot," Bill muttered as they uncovered crates of ammo — 9mm rounds, shotgun shells, and even a few magazines for rifles. Felix hooted softly under his breath, already grabbing an empty duffel bag from his pack. They got to work, loading up as much as they could carry and then some.

"Let's make this quick," Lee warned. "I don't like how quiet it is."

That's when Felix, glancing through a narrow window toward the adjacent hangars, paused. "Uh... guys?"

Lee and Bill followed his gaze.

Across the cracked tarmac stood several long hangars, their wide sliding doors pulled shut but weather-worn. One had a torn canvas tarp caught on a corner, flapping lightly in the wind.

"We've got what we came for," Lee said, but Bill was already shaking his head.

"If there's something in there... Might be worth a look."

With weapons drawn, the three of them crossed the tarmac, every footstep echoing just a little too loudly. They reached the hangar. Lee and Felix pulled the door slowly aside.

Dust and stale air greeted them — along with a familiar shape.

"No way," Felix said.

A helicopter.

Covered by a tarp and camo netting, the military chopper sat nestled in the gloom like a sleeping beast. Its rotors were intact. The landing gear looked solid.

Lee approached carefully and peeled back more of the tarp. "She's old, but this might actually work."

"Would it even fly?" Bill asked.

"We'd need fuel. Batteries. But yeah... it's possible."

"We tell the council. This changes everything," Felix added.

They marked the location carefully on their map, took photos with the small solar-powered camera from Bill's gear, then closed the hangar back up.

"Alright," Lee said. "Let's get the ammo loaded and get the hell out of here."

As they rolled away from the base, hearts racing with excitement, none of them noticed the slow figure watching from the treeline — its mouth curled into an unnatural grin.

Chapter 26

Team three were the last of the three supply teams to leave New Haven. The early morning light broke over the treetops as the trio drove out past the southern gate, leaving behind the now-fortified walls and freshly dug moat. The community had slept a little easier the night before, but the fear never truly left. Not with the world still in ruins and the Smilers still lurking somewhere beyond the trees.

Jennifer had seen them off personally, standing at the gate with Munroe and Callum. She'd given Bellamy a nod of quiet encouragement, her eyes still shadowed with concern over Derek, Jillian, and Daryl not yet returning from Halestow. But she didn't let it show. Leadership demanded calm. Hope. And she was determined to hold the line until they returned.

—-

The truck rumbled down the cracked roads, weaving past abandoned vehicles and overgrown hedgerows. Roary was quiet as he drove, one hand on the wheel, the other resting on the butt of his rifle.

"So what's the plan?" Steph asked from the backseat, leaning forward between them.

Bellamy unfolded a worn map across his lap. "First, we head to the old industrial estate east of Millhaven. Check the garage lots, see if there's anything salvageable. Then maybe north — the fire service training compound. Might be something there we can repurpose. If not…"

"We keep moving," Roary said. "We'll find something. Can't go back empty-handed."

Bellamy nodded, though his jaw tightened. "We're not just looking for trucks or buses. We need a fallback point. Somewhere we can move the whole community if it comes to that. Over a hundred people. We'll need space, shelter, water… and something defensible."

"A needle in a haystack," Steph muttered.

They passed through a small town an hour later — or what was left of it. Burned out shops, rusting vehicles, and the skeleton of a collapsed petrol station. No movement. No sound.

Bellamy signaled to stop. "We sweep on foot. Just in case."

Weapons drawn, they moved street to street. A few shambling zombies drifted around the square — easy enough to put down. But there was nothing here. No food. No power. No people.

"Same story everywhere," Roary said as they returned to the truck. "This place is dead."

Bellamy glanced toward the horizon. The mainland had become nothing but danger — roads clogged with undead, roaming packs of infected, and worse. Places that had once offered safety were now crumbling ruins or overrun. Even if they found transport, where would they go?

"We might need to think bigger," he said.

Steph raised an eyebrow. "Bigger?"

"Different," Bellamy replied. "Out of reach. Somewhere the dead can't easily get to."

"You thinking what I think you're thinking?" Roary asked.

Bellamy nodded slowly. "An island."

Roary whistled. "That's ambitious."

"Yeah," Steph agreed. "But it might be the only real chance we've got."

—-

They piled back into the truck and drove on, the conversation still hanging in the air. They didn't say it, but all three of them knew: every new place they searched on the mainland made the idea of the island more appealing. The world had changed. Maybe it was time their strategy did too.

The road curved around a low hill, the landscape thinning out into rows of empty industrial lots and rusted signage. The air was still, the kind of stillness that made your instincts prickle.

Roary was behind the wheel, scanning both sides of the road with quiet focus. Steph sat shotgun, a battered map open on his lap, though they hadn't needed it for a while. Bellamy, silent in the backseat, kept watch through the rear window.

As they crested a gentle rise, the landscape changed.

"Bus depot," Roary murmured, pointing ahead.

Beyond a chain-link fence, a wide yard sprawled out—cracked tarmac, weeds pushing through, the remains of painted parking lines. And beyond that, nestled toward the far wall, rows of red double-decker buses. Maybe ten of them, some listing to the side, others looking mostly intact.

"Holy shit," Steph muttered. "Two of those could carry everyone."

Bellamy leaned forward. "Pull in slow. Don't want to stir up anything hiding."

They rolled up to the fence, which had already been peeled back at one corner. Roary drove through, tyres crunching over gravel. The depot building itself was a crumbling office block to the left, its windows smashed and the door long gone. But the buses...

They were lined up like sleeping giants, engines silent, paint dulled but mostly untouched. At least two near the back seemed in surprisingly good condition—no shattered windows, tyres still holding air.

The three men stepped out of the truck, weapons raised, eyes scanning.

"No sign of zombies," Steph said quietly, "but this is too good to just walk into. Let's check the office first."

Bellamy nodded. "Roary, watch the entrance. Steph—on me."

They advanced toward the office block, careful over the broken glass and tangle of weeds. Inside, the air was musty. Old rot, paper mould, and engine oil. Desks had been overturned, chairs stacked against the far doors as if someone had once tried to barricade themselves in.

But it was empty.

Nothing stirred.

They returned to the yard and regrouped at the buses.

Bellamy approached one cautiously, peering through the window. "Seats are clean. The engine panel's rusted but not wrecked. If the fuel tank's not bone dry, we might be onto something here."

Roary had already popped open a side panel. "Looks like someone tried to siphon it at some point," he said, frowning. "But not all of them. We might get one or two running if we can find diesel and battery packs."

Steph circled one of the larger buses, whistling low. "Even if we can't drive them now, just having them parked near the cemetery exit—ready to load up—is a game-changer."

Bellamy gave a tight nod. "We flag this place. Get it logged. Then we report back and come with mechanics, batteries, fuel. Maybe even move a few here now and get them prepped in advance."

Roary looked across the lot. "We should sweep the area. If it's clear, we could use this whole depot as part of the fallback plan. Park more vehicles. Maybe set up a fuel cache."

Bellamy's eyes followed the fence line and the treeline beyond it. "Let's be quick. Sweep, mark what we need. Then on to the next site."

Steph was already moving again. "Still think an island's our best bet long term," he said. "But something like this? Could be what saves everyone in the meantime."

The sun had dipped behind a thick bank of clouds, casting long shadows across the depot yard. The silence stretched unnaturally, broken only by the wind whispering through broken glass and twisted fencing.

Bellamy motioned with two fingers.

"Clear the area. Office first. Then the buses. We don't split up more than ten metres."

Steph nodded, already moving toward the rear office block. Roary followed, shotgun raised, sweeping side to side.

Inside, the building was dim and hollow, shelves stripped, filing cabinets wide open and empty. They worked quickly, room by room. In what used to be the manager's office, Steph rifled through a cracked metal drawer.

"No keys," he muttered, tossing aside a clipboard. "Just old logbooks."

Roary checked the underside of the desk. "Not even a damn spare taped under here."

He stood and glanced at Bellamy. "Hopefully they're still in the buses."

Bellamy gave a grim nod. "Let's check them one by one. Keep it tight."

—·—

The trio moved back out into the open lot, heading toward the nearest line of buses. Moss clung to the windows. A few were so sunken on their tyres they'd be no use. Others, though, looked promising.

Steph climbed into the first bus, slowly stepping down the aisle.

"Empty!" he called out. "No keys though."

Roary tried the second one. "Same."

The third bus had a loose driver-side door. Roary climbed up, checking under the visor, around the seat, even in the cupholder.

As he exited, he called over his shoulder, "Maybe they stored them all in a box or something—"

His voice cut off with a startled yell.

He'd turned the corner of the next bus and walked straight into two figures — half-rotted, grey-skinned, jaws slack and arms already reaching. One had a twisted construction vest barely hanging off its ribs. The other, face half gone, was faster than it looked.

They grabbed Roary in an instant.

He raised the shotgun but wasn't fast enough.

Teeth sank deep into his arm — once, then again.

"ROARY!" Bellamy's shout ripped through the yard as he sprinted forward.

Steph was there a second later, slamming one walker against the side of the bus with the butt of his rifle. Bellamy grabbed the other and fired point-blank, sending bone and blood spraying across the side of the vehicle.

Roary writhed on the ground, sweat already pouring from his brow as shock set in.

"The bite's too deep," Steph said, voice trembling. "It's right through the muscle—"

Bellamy cut him off, grim and certain. "We amputate. Above the elbow."

Roary blinked up at them, teeth gritted. "Fuckin' do it."

Bellamy didn't hesitate. "Steph — your axe. Now."

Steph pulled the compact hand axe from his belt. His hands shook.

"Keep him still," Bellamy said. "Steph, when I say go, you bring it down hard. Clean as you can. Then cauterise immediately."

Roary looked from one to the other, breathing fast. "Tell Maggie I wasn't scared."

"You'll tell her yourself," Bellamy replied, steel in his voice.

They laid Roary back, wedging a chunk of wood from a broken pallet between his teeth. Steph raised the axe.

"Ready?" Bellamy asked.

Roary nodded once.

"Do it."

The axe came down with a sickening thud. Blood sprayed across the dirt. Roary let out a muffled scream as Bellamy immediately pressed the hot end of a scavenged exhaust pipe — heated on a small blaze Steph had prepared — against the open wound.

The smell of seared flesh filled the air.

Roary passed out.

—-

Moments later, he was strapped into the back seat of the nearest working bus, arm tightly bandaged and elevated. Bellamy was at the wheel, hands clenched, knuckles white. Steph sat behind Roary, checking his pulse every few seconds.

"He's alive," Steph muttered. "For now. But we've got to move."

Bellamy nodded. "Radio's still dead, We need to drive straight back. Top speed. Hold on."

The old engine growled to life. The depot gates creaked open, and the bus pulled out onto the overgrown road, tyres crunching gravel and glass.

"We get him home," Bellamy muttered under his breath. "Whatever it takes."

—-

The sun hovered low in the sky, spilling orange and amber across the landscape. Up in the watchtower, Jennifer adjusted the binoculars, her gaze sweeping across the treeline. Anne stood beside her, quiet, alert.

It had been over seven days since Derek, Daryl, Jillian, Nia, and Joe left for Halestow.

They'd heard nothing.

Jennifer didn't say it aloud, but the silence had started to feel heavy — like a prelude to grief.

Then — the faint rumble of an engine.

Anne leaned forward. "You hear that?"

Jennifer was already scanning the road beyond the southern treeline. "I do."

They both stood still, listening as the low hum grew louder, closer.

A shape broke through the trees — a single truck, coated in dust, headlights dim against the falling light.

Jennifer's hands trembled slightly as she raised the binoculars.

For a moment, all she saw was movement and shadow. Then—

"Oh my god," she breathed. "It's Derek."

Anne grabbed the binoculars from her. "You sure?"

"Positive. It's his truck. Jillian's with him... Daryl's in the back."

Anne smiled. "They made it."

Jennifer didn't smile yet. She reached for the radio.

"South Gate — this is Watch One. Confirm visual. Incoming truck — looks like Derek's team. Prepare to open on my signal."

A beat later, Munroe's voice buzzed over the radio. "This is South Gate. Copy that — we see them. The gate will hold until the signal."

Jennifer finally exhaled, her body sagging with the weight of days of tension.

Anne placed a hand on her shoulder. "Told you they'd come back."

Jennifer gave a soft, tired smile. "I didn't doubt it. Not really. Just... it's good to see him."

As the truck neared the gate, the guards moved into position. The reinforced doors groaned open just enough to let the vehicle pass, then slammed shut again behind it. The truck rolled into the yard, dust kicking up around the tires.

Derek climbed out first. He looked tired — his beard more unkempt, eyes shadowed with exhaustion — but he was upright. Whole. Jillian followed, stretching her arms and wincing at a healing wound on her side. Daryl slid off the flatbed and gave a quiet nod to the nearest guard.

Jennifer was already halfway down the stairs when she saw him. Derek spotted her, and for a heartbeat neither of them moved. Then he walked toward her — and she broke into a run. They met halfway, arms wrapping tight around each other in a silence more powerful than words. Behind them, the New Haven gate sealed shut once more — but this time, it felt a little more like home.

As Derek and Jennifer finally pulled apart, breathless with the relief of being together again, a voice shouted from above.

"Gate watch to ground — we've got movement. Two more trucks. Fast."

It was Munroe, calling from the other tower. "It's ours!"

Jennifer spun toward the gate, eyes wide. "That'll be Maggie and Lee."

Derek blinked, still catching up. "What the hell's going on?"

"I'll explain inside," Jennifer said quickly. "While you were gone, we organised three teams. Food, ammo, fallback and transport. Everyone's been stretched thin."

Derek gave a single nod, glancing toward the gate as the first truck rumbled through. Maggie was behind the wheel, Michone and Reggie piled into the back, hauling down crates marked with faded grocery logos. They looked tired — but alive.

The second truck rolled in close behind. Lee jumped out before it had even stopped properly, followed by Bill and Felix, all three of them with dust-covered boots and bandoliers slung across their shoulders.

Munroe jogged down from the tower, nodding to Derek. "Hell of a day to come home, mate."

"No kidding," Derek muttered, eyes scanning the trucks.

Jennifer stepped forward, her voice firm. "Unload first — debrief after. Council room in thirty."

Everyone moved with purpose. Crates were carried, bags tossed into storage. Lee gave Derek a small nod in passing — not overly warm, but respectful. Derek returned it, feeling the quiet shift in the air. Leadership was hard-won here... and never permanent.

Once the gear was secured and the gates locked, the council room began to fill.

Derek sat at the table, Jennifer on his left, Callum already flipping through the logs from the teams. Anne slipped in quietly. Maggie, Lee, Munroe, and the others filed in, their expressions a mix of fatigue and urgency.

Even Lexi and Sam from Halestow had taken seats near the back, listening attentively.

Jennifer stood. "Let's get this going."

—-

Jennifer had already briefed Derek on everything while the teams were still unloading.

Once they were seated in the council room, it was Maggie who went first — detailing the food run, what they found, what they brought back, and the promising signs of more stockpiles in the area.

Next was Lee. He laid out the ammunition haul, a solid success, and then mentioned the unexpected discovery — the helicopter tucked away under tarpaulin inside the hangar. "Might be useless, might be gold," he said, "but it's worth checking out."

Then it was Derek's turn.

He stood, shoulders squared but tired eyes betraying the days behind him. He spoke about Halestow, the Smilers — or Grinners as the Halestow group called them — and the explosion that tore through the forest. He didn't sugarcoat it, especially when it came to Mason's sacrifice. The room was quiet when he finished.

Turning to Lexi and Sam, Derek softened his tone.

"You're both more than welcome to stay the night," he said. "Rest up. If you want to head home in the morning, we'll help get you there."

Both nodded — grateful, quiet.

—-

As the council sat in the room, still digesting the updates, the conversation had circled back to the helicopter. Dr. Hensley was asking about the condition of the rotors when Ortega's voice suddenly crackled through the radio left on the table.

"Eh... guys? You better get out here. There's a bus coming in hot."

Everyone froze. Derek snatched the radio. "What kind of bus?"

There was a beat.

"Shit… it's Bellamy. And he's flooring it." Ortega responded. Chairs scraped. Weapons were grabbed. The meeting was over.

Chapter 27

Ortega's voice rang out from the guard tower just as the council reached the gate. "I can't see anything chasing them—but there's a bus coming in hot!"

The council members stopped in their tracks, eyes locking onto the dust cloud rising behind the approaching vehicle.

The massive double-decker screeched to a halt just short of the main gate, its brakes groaning under the strain. It was too tall to fit through. The engine sputtered as it idled, the front doors hissing open.

Steph jumped down, his face pale and slick with sweat. He was supporting Roary, whose shirt was soaked in blood, one arm hanging uselessly by his side, the other clutching at the fresh bandages wrapping what remained of his upper arm.

Derek's stomach turned.

He and Daryl sprinted forward as Ortega and Munroe moved in to assist. Steph passed Roary into their arms without a word, his face carved with worry.

"I'll secure the bus near the cemetery exit then come in that way," Bellamy shouted from the driver's seat. "Go! I'll catch up!"

Derek gave a quick nod, then turned his attention to Roary, now fading in and out of consciousness. He and Daryl all but carried him toward the infirmary.

—-

Inside the infirmary, Erin had already cleared a bed. The room smelled of antiseptic and stale sweat. They eased Roary onto the cot as Abby rushed in to assist. Without a word, Erin clipped the restraints onto Roary's legs and good arm, cuffing him to the bed.

Derek frowned. "Is that really necessary?"

Erin met his gaze without flinching. "If he turns, we need to be sure he doesn't hurt anyone else. It's a precaution. Standard now."

Derek nodded grimly, running a hand down his face as he turned to Steph, who had just stepped in behind them. "What happened?"

Steph looked exhausted. Blood spattered his shirt, and his hands were still shaking. "We found a bus depot," he started. "Rows of them. Two double-deckers still had some fuel. Looked like they'd run. We were sweeping for keys... Roary turned a corner, walked right into two zombies. No time to shout. They grabbed him." He swallowed hard, the memory flashing behind his eyes. "We had no choice. Bellamy cut it clean—above the elbow. As fast as we could. Cauterised it, loaded him in. He didn't pass out right away, but he's fading now."

Erin was already working, checking Roary's vitals, whispering instructions to Abby as she prepped antibiotics and IV fluids.

Derek looked down at Roary, pale and sweating, lips moving in delirium. He didn't look good—but he was alive.

For now.

—-

A knock came at the infirmary door, then it pushed open without waiting for a reply. Bellamy stepped inside, brushing soot from his jacket and rolling his shoulders like they were made of rusted metal.

"The bus is secure," he said.

Derek turned. "Where?"

"I parked it in the fire station across the street. Reinforced doors, decent cover. Should be safe there, at least for now." He stepped closer, eyes briefly flicking to Roary on the bed. "How is he?"

Derek gave a slow shake of his head. "Holding on. Erin's doing what she can."

Bellamy nodded. He didn't ask about the bite, or the odds. He didn't need to. Everyone in the room knew how it usually ended.

"You did good," Derek said, voice lower now. "Getting him back. Getting that bus. It'll make a hell of a difference."

"Won't mean a thing if he dies," Bellamy muttered, rubbing a hand over his beard. "But we move forward, yeah?"

Derek nodded again, the weight of the past week bearing down across his shoulders.

"One fire station. One bus. One friend who might not make it," Bellamy added. "But it's something."

He turned to go, but paused at the door.

"You should see it," he said. "The bus. Thing looks like it could survive a bloody warzone. Armor, grills, even had a reinforced door rigged onto the back. Someone tried to make it safe. No idea if they made it out." Then he left, boots echoing down the corridor.

Derek lingered at Roary's side a few seconds longer, then gave Erin a nod and followed after Bellamy. He caught up with Bellamy just outside the admin block, the evening sun casting long shadows between the buildings. Bellamy was heading toward the gates, but slowed when he heard the footsteps behind him.

"Bellamy—hold up." He turned, folding his arms as Derek approached. "Thought you'd be with Roary."

"Erin said there's nothing more I can do right now. Just waiting."

Bellamy gave a quiet nod, then glanced toward the road leading to the fire station. "Bus is locked tight," he said. "Won't fit through the main gates, but it's safe where it is for now."

Derek walked beside him in silence for a beat, then said, "You mentioned the bus was built like it'd survive a warzone."

Bellamy gave a faint smirk. "Aye. Reinforced panels. Someone tried to turn it into a damn tank."

"Could we get another one like it?" Derek asked.

Bellamy's face tightened. "There were more at the depot. Rows of them. We swept as much as we could, but between Roary's injury and running low on supplies... We didn't have time to check every bus. I reckon one more would be enough to get everyone out of New Haven if it came to that."

Derek frowned, chewing on the thought. "Alright. We'll put together another crew, make sure it's done right."

Bellamy glanced around them, the faint sound of wind catching on razor wire in the distance.

"Everywhere we looked was full of rot, Derek," he said. "Old farms, stores, housing estates. Nothing left but bones and ruin. This place—" he gestured toward the walls of New Haven "—it's solid, for now. But if they come again, like Silverburn...?"

Derek looked at him, and for the first time since they returned, Bellamy seemed... uncertain.

"We talked while we were out," Bellamy continued. "Me, Steph and Roary. About fallback plans. Somewhere we could go where the dead won't just stumble up every week. Somewhere we could breathe."

"And?" Derek asked.

"An island," Bellamy said, simply. "It's the only thing that makes sense. A place with one way in and out. Somewhere defensible. Somewhere we can finally stop looking over our shoulders."

Derek's brow lifted slightly. "You got somewhere in mind?"

"Skye," Bellamy replied without hesitation. "It's big enough to hold us. Small enough to manage. And it's got a bridge — one road, easy to guard. We get across, blow that bridge if we have to, we're safe."

Derek folded his arms, eyes scanning the horizon as if he could see the island from where they stood. "It's a risk," he said.

"So is staying here," Bellamy countered. "But that place... if we could clear it, rebuild—? It could be everything we've been trying to make here. Without the constant fear."

Derek nodded slowly. "Alright. We'll talk to the council. After Roary's stable, after we secure that second bus... we'll start planning."

Bellamy gave him a firm nod, then turned and walked off toward the fire station. Derek stayed behind, gaze fixed on the fading skyline.

Skye.

It wasn't just survival anymore. It was hope.

—-

The council room was heavy with tension as Bellamy finished speaking. A silence hung in the air—uneasy, suffocating—as his final words settled in. "Mainland Scotland is lost," he repeated grimly. "We drove for hours. Towns, villages, farmlands—gone. Overrun. Nothing left but ruins and rot."

Jennifer folded her arms tightly, eyes flicking to Derek, then back to Bellamy.

"Are you sure it's that bad everywhere?"

Bellamy nodded slowly. "I wish I wasn't."

Anne let out a quiet breath, her hands resting protectively on her stomach under the table. Maggie leaned forward, her voice steady but low. "Derek, you said Halestow's holding. Barely. And we've lasted here... so far."

Derek gave a small nod.. "They were lucky. If those Smilers throw everything at us like they did at Silverburn or Halestow, we won't hold out forever. We all saw what happened when they lured us into a trap."

Munroe was the first to speak up after that. "So we're talking about moving?"

Callum leaned forward, arms on the table. "Not yet. But... we need a fallback plan. A serious one."

There were a few murmurs of agreement. Tension, fatigue, and concern etched every face.

That's when Lee stood. "What about the helicopter?" The room quieted again, all eyes turning to him. "The one we found at the base. If it works, and if someone can fly it—we could use it to scout Skye. See if it's overrun. See if the bridge is intact. Hell, see if there's anything at all left out there."

Felix raised an eyebrow. "You think it'll even start?"

Lee shrugged. "No clue. But we've got enough mechanical minds here to find out. And if it does work, it's the safest way to scope out the island without sending anyone into danger."

Daryl rubbed his jaw thoughtfully. "Could save us from walking into another Silverburn."

Jillian, quiet until now, added softly, "If there's even a chance it's safe... we have to at least look."

Dr. Hensley glanced around the room. "Assuming the fuel is good, and the rotors still functional, we might be able to power it using one of the solar rigs. But we'll need a pilot."

Everyone fell quiet again.

Bellamy eventually said, "I'll check the chopper. See what condition it's in. If we can make it fly, I'll go up myself—if someone shows me how."

Maggie gave him a dry look. "You've been a soldier, Bellamy. Not a damn pilot."

He gave a faint smirk. "Didn't say I'd land it. Just said I'd go up."

A ripple of laughter—thin, but welcome—moved through the room, lightening the mood for a moment.

Derek finally stood. His face was tired, pale under the weight of everything they'd faced.

"We move in phases. First, we test the chopper. If it works, we scout the island. If it looks viable, we plan a relocation. Not now—but soon." He looked around the table, each face watching him. "We owe the people here more than just survival. We owe them hope."

The council nodded slowly, the grim reality tempered now by a spark—an idea that maybe, just maybe, there was something better out there.

Somewhere safe.

Somewhere to finally start over.

—-

The next morning in the council room, the air was crisp, sunlight pouring in through the high slats of the old prison windows. Derek stood at the head of the long table in the council room, arms folded as he looked around at the familiar faces — and a few newer ones. Lexi, Sam, and Henry had joined them one last time before heading back to Halestow.

"Only two things to deal with today," Derek began, his voice calm but purposeful. "Lee — take a team to the helicopter site. See if you can get her running. Bellamy, I want you to go with them. You know the terrain, and I trust your eye on how salvageable it is."

Bellamy nodded. "You got it."

Derek continued. "I'll take Callum, Ortega, and Daryl back to the bus depot. Try and get a second one running. If we can secure it, that's enough wheels to move everyone if and when the time comes."

A few murmurs of agreement passed around the table. The stakes were clear now. Every trip out was no longer just a run — it was groundwork for survival.

Just as Derek was about to call time on the meeting, Henry shifted in his seat and stood awkwardly. "Um... Derek? Before we go..." All eyes turned to the boy. "I want to stay. Here, I mean. At New Haven," he said, glancing at Lexi, then back at Derek. "I've been helping Erin. I want to keep learning from her — help in the infirmary."

Lexi frowned, already shaking her head. "Henry, we talked about this—"

"It's his choice," Derek cut in gently, but firmly. He looked at Henry. "If you're serious about it, you're welcome to stay. Erin could use the help."

Lexi sighed but gave a reluctant nod. "Alright. But you better listen to her, you hear me?"

Henry smiled, relieved. "Yeah. I will."

Derek stepped back and clapped his hands once. "Okay. Let's roll out."

Chairs scraped back. Gear was gathered. Within the hour, the trucks would be loaded and two new missions would begin — one toward the skies, and one back into the shadows of the mainland.

—-

Everyone else had filtered out of the room — chairs left slightly askew, a few notes scattered across the table — but Derek stayed behind, hunched over his usual spot, scribbling updates into the worn ledger they used for council records.

Jennifer lingered near the doorway, watching him in silence.

"I can't believe you're going out there again so soon," she said finally, her voice tight, frustration bleeding into it.

Derek let out a heavy sigh, his pen pausing. "I know, Jen. I know." He stood, rubbing his face with both hands before walking toward her. "But if we can get this sorted... if Skye is safe... maybe we won't have to keep doing this. Maybe we can finally stop running. Settle. Breathe."

Before she could respond, he closed the distance and kissed her — gentle, but full of weight and worry and all the things they hadn't said.

When they parted, she looked him dead in the eyes. "I'm holding you to that."

A soft smile touched his lips. "You always do."

They kissed again, slower this time, and when they finally pulled apart, they walked out together, the door creaking closed behind them.

The next phase was beginning — and with it, the faint hope of something better.

Chapter 28

Lexi and Sam stood just beyond the main gates of New Haven, a packed car idling at their backs. It wasn't much — a beat-up estate car Derek had promised would get them home and back without trouble — but it was theirs for the journey.

"Tell Paul we'll be in touch," Derek said as they left. Lexi gave him a nod, Sam raised a hand in farewell, and they disappeared into the distance.

Not long after, Derek's team rolled out — himself, Daryl, Callum and Ortega. Their truck rumbled over the old roads, heading once again for the depot where they'd found the first bus. It was a long drive — a few hours at least — but uneventful. When they arrived, a light fog hung over the cracked concrete. A handful of zombies — maybe six or seven — wandered the outer edge of the depot.

"Too easy," Daryl muttered as he jumped out, pulling his knife free.

They made short work of the zombies, blades and suppressed pistols keeping the noise to a minimum. Once the area looked clear, Daryl and Ortega split off, circling the rear of the building to make sure nothing else was lurking.

Derek and Callum entered the lot. The buses still sat where they'd left them — old, faded double-deckers lined up like forgotten beasts. They started their search. Door after door creaked open. Most were empty, long-dead batteries and dry tanks. But then—

"Got something," Callum called out.

Derek climbed up behind him. The visor of one bus had a key tucked just behind it. When he turned it, the dashboard lights flickered. A quarter tank. Enough to get home. By the time Daryl and Ortega returned, the bus was running.

"Clear out back," Daryl said. "No zombies left."

"Good," Derek nodded. "We're going to need more than this if Halestow joins us. Probably three buses at least."

"You're right," Daryl said.

Derek turned to Callum and Ortega. "Take this one back, leave the truck just incase. Park it at the fire station by the cemetery. Radio ahead so they open the dunker door."

"You got it," Callum replied. He tossed Derek the walkie, then climbed into the driver's seat. As the engine coughed to life, Ortega jumped in beside him. A few seconds later, they rolled out. Derek and Daryl stood alone in the silence.

"Let's find one more," Derek said.

It didn't take long. A few rows over, another bus sat almost pristine — not a scratch on it. Daryl climbed up, checked the fuel.

"Jackpot," he grinned. "Full tank."

Derek exhaled, the tension easing slightly. The pieces were falling into place. Transport secured, the community protected — and if Skye proved viable... maybe, just maybe, this nightmare had a next chapter that didn't end in blood.

They started the engine and headed for home.

—-

The second vehicle out of New Haven that morning was a two-truck team bound for the old military outpost, the one where they'd found the helicopter.

Lee drove the lead vehicle, Bellamy beside him in the passenger seat. Behind them sat Steph, quiet and sharp-eyed as always, and Nina, New Haven's newest mechanic — a woman in her early thirties, with sun-worn hands, close-cropped dark hair, and a thick canvas tool bag tucked at her feet. Her expression was unreadable, but her eyes rarely stopped moving.

Bringing up the rear was a second truck driven by Corwin, with Reggie riding shotgun. Both had their crossbows resting on the dash, their rifles stowed within reach. Corwin hadn't said much since they'd left, but his presence was steady — dependable as ever. The road to the military base was strangely quiet. Not a single zombie had been seen. No birds. No wind. Just the low hum of engines and the occasional creak of shifting gear.

"Almost too quiet," Steph muttered, watching the treeline roll by.

Bellamy nodded. "Let's not jinx it."

It was early afternoon when they finally turned off the cracked tarmac and followed the winding access road to the old hangar. The gates were still closed, but Lee pulled the truck around the side and stopped outside the massive sliding door.

"This is it," Bellamy said, nodding to Nina. "Let's see if this bird can still fly."

They climbed out and moved fast. They pushed open the groaning hangar doors just enough to slip the trucks inside before dragging them shut again. Reggie and Corwin scaled the metal stairs inside to the upper observation walkway, rifles out, checking the broken windows for signs of movement.

Inside, dust swirled in the filtered sunlight. The helicopter sat like a sleeping beast in the centre of the concrete floor, its tail fin scratched and bent, but intact. Nina stepped forward slowly, reverently, before dropping to her knees with a small grunt and unzipping her tool bag.

"She's a beauty," she whispered, brushing the dirt off a panel. "If the rotor's good and the wiring hasn't been chewed through by rats, I might just be able to get her purring."

Bellamy walked the perimeter, checking the shadowed corners of the hangar. "Take your time," he said. "But not too much. The longer we're here, the more likely we'll draw attention."

"Corwin?" Lee called up.

"Clear so far," came the reply from above. "But if this turns into a trap, it's a big one."

Back below, Nina opened the rear engine panel and sucked air through her teeth. "Fuel lines are intact," she murmured. "That's something. Battery's dead, though. I'll need to borrow one from the truck and see if I can patch a startup." She paused, then glanced up at Lee. "Think we've got time?"

Lee looked to Bellamy, then back to her. "Make it quick."

—-

Nearly an hour had passed, and the patch job was complete.

Nina wiped a sheen of sweat from her forehead with the back of her hand and nodded to Lee. "Alright, let's see if this old girl still has a heartbeat."

Bellamy climbed into the cockpit, flicked the switches with care. A low hum vibrated through the frame as the lights flickered... then steadied. The fuel gauge shot up — nearly full. They all watched as the fuel system was primed. Nina gave a thumbs up.

Bellamy hit the starter.

The engine coughed once... then roared to life. Dust kicked up from the floor as the rotors spun, steady and clean.

"She's alive!" Nina shouted over the roar, grinning. "Everything's reading green!"

Bellamy let the rotors spin for a few more seconds before shutting her down. As the blades slowed and silence returned to the hangar, Bellamy climbed down, beaming.

"Let's get that door open," he said, "and roll this bird into the light."

Lee and Nina moved to unfasten the wheel blocks while Corwin jogged over to the large hanger doors. He braced himself, grunting as he slid one side open.

That's when it happened.

No one had noticed the danger outside. Not over the roar of the engine. Not with their eyes focused inward. The moment the door cracked open, they came. Two zombies pounced with terrifying speed, half-hidden in the morning shadow. Corwin barely had time to scream before teeth sank into his arm — then his neck. Blood sprayed against the steel doors as he collapsed, gurgling, twitching on the floor.

The two zombies stumbled back, jaws slick with fresh blood.

Bellamy reacted first.

BANG. BANG.

Two precise shots rang out. The undead crumpled. Corwin's body spasmed. Choking. Gasping. Bleeding out. Lee was beside him in seconds, kneeling by his side, one hand already reaching for his blade.

"No coming back from that," Bellamy said quietly, jaw clenched.

Corwin's eyes rolled back, breath rattling in his throat. Lee didn't hesitate. He whispered something none of the others caught, then drove the knife clean into Corwin's temple. The hangar fell still again. No one spoke.

They covered his body with a canvas tarp from one of the crates. It wasn't a grave, but it was the best they could give him. There was no time for more.

The helicopter was wheeled out. They checked it again. All systems held. With a final nod, Bellamy and Steph climbed aboard — Steph having insisted he stay with Bellamy and start learning how to fly it properly.

Lee and Nina loaded into one truck. Reggie took the other. As they pulled out from the base, engines rumbling beneath them and the helicopter lifting behind like a watchful eye, no one spoke of what had just happened.

They'd succeeded. The mission was a success.

But it hadn't come free. And New Haven would feel the loss of Corwin when they returned.

—-

Jennifer stood quietly at Roary's bedside, her arms folded tightly across her chest. The room was dim, save for the soft hum of the generator powering the overhead lights. The faint beeping of monitors echoed like a countdown.

Roary lay still, pale and sweating, his stump wrapped and elevated. A thin tube from the IV drip fed antibiotics into his system, but the colour hadn't returned to his cheeks. He was still shackled at wrist and ankle — standard procedure now.

Erin stood at the foot of the bed, clipboard in hand. Henry lingered nearby, eyes sunken, visibly rattled from the amputation. "We've done everything we can," Erin said quietly, not looking up. "The bleeding's stopped. Antibiotics are in. But it's out of our hands now."

Jennifer nodded, swallowing hard. "He's strong. Maybe—"

She didn't finish.

Roary's body suddenly jerked violently. His limbs convulsed against the restraints, eyes rolled back, mouth opening wide as his chest seized. The monitors flatlined.

"Shit!" Erin rushed forward, knocking the tray aside. She began CPR, hands pressing hard and fast against his chest. "Come on, come on—"

Jennifer pulled Henry back, shielding his view.

"Thirty compressions — no pulse," Erin muttered. She tried again. Still nothing. The room fell into a tense silence. After a minute, Erin stopped. Her shoulders slumped. "He's gone."

They waited.

Jennifer didn't move. She had seen this too many times not to know what was coming.

Then — the softest of growls.

Roary's glassy eyes opened. Milky. Vacant. Lips twitching. Jaw clenching.

Jennifer stepped forward. "I've got it." Without hesitation, she pulled the knife from her belt and slid it smoothly through his eye socket. Roary went limp, his body deflating like a punctured tent.

They all stood still.

The silence was thicker now.

"Well," Erin finally said, pulling off her gloves. "That confirms everything I thought."

Jennifer looked over sharply. "What do you mean?"

"I had a theory," Erin replied, voice flat. "That if you amputate quick enough... maybe the infection wouldn't take. That the virus needed time to spread."

Jennifer blinked. "And?"

Erin sighed. "Turns out it doesn't matter. Bite or scratch... you're fucked either way."

Henry sat down heavily in the corner chair, head in his hands.

Jennifer stared down at Roary's body — another name on the growing list of those they couldn't save.

—-

The sun hung low in the sky as the last of the teams returned. Dust settled in the wake of the convoys — the double-decker buses now tucked into the fire station, the newly revived helicopter resting quietly in the old west yard behind the outer fence.

Everyone had gathered near the south gate, fatigue lining their faces, but for the first time in days — all were accounted for.

Jennifer approached quietly.

Derek caught her expression before she said a word — and in that moment, he knew.

Roary hadn't made it.

He gave her a small nod, then turned to the others.

"Let's get everyone to the council room," he said quietly. "We'll go over everything there."

—-

The room filled with tired voices and quiet murmurs. Chairs scraped against the old tiled floor as the council and their support teams settled in. Some leaned against the walls. Others just stood, arms folded. Even Henry had joined now sitting quietly near the back.

Derek stood at the head of the room, eyes scanning the crowd.

"Alright," he began. "Let's start with the good. The buses are secured. We now have enough transport for everyone here and everyone at Halestow — should they choose to come."

A few nods. Some relief flickered across tired faces.

"We've parked them in the fire station across from the cemetery tunnel entrance. If the worst happens, we move fast. We move together."

He gave a moment's pause before nodding to Jennifer.

She stepped forward, voice steady but soft. "Roary didn't make it," she said. "Erin and Henry did everything they could. Amputation, antibiotics... we tried everything. But the infection spread too far, too fast."

The room fell silent.

Bellamy lowered his head, eyes closed for a long moment.

Jennifer continued, "He turned. Erin confirmed what we feared — it doesn't matter how fast you act. If you're bitten, it's already too late."

No one spoke for several heartbeats.

Then Bellamy stepped forward, jaw clenched.

"I won't dress it up. You've all seen the helicopter outside. Yes — it works. Nina got it running, Steph's learning to fly. But it came at a cost." He exhaled slowly, visibly holding back emotion. "Corwin... didn't make it. When we opened the hangar doors, two of those fuckers were waiting. They landed on him before we could react. Bit into him like dogs on raw meat." He shook his head. "He was gone before we could do anything."

The room was quiet again. A different kind of silence now — not just mourning, but acceptance. A deeper understanding of how close they all walked to death each day.

Derek spoke again, voice lower now. "We've lost two good people. Roary and Corwin." He let that settle. "But we've gained mobility. We've secured the buses. We've got eyes in the sky if we need them. And most importantly — we now have options. If Skye is viable, we might just be able to build something new... safer."

No cheers. No applause. Just nods. Quiet determination.

It was enough.

—-

As the council room emptied, the weight of loss lingered in the air like dust. Plans had been made, progress achieved — but at a cost none of them could ignore. Derek remained seated, hands resting on the table, eyes fixed on nothing. Outside, New Haven stood quiet behind its walls, the wind rustling through barbed wire and watchtowers. Tomorrow they would move forward — toward Skye, toward the unknown. But tonight, they mourned the price of survival.

Chapter 29

The sun rose over the walls of New Haven, casting long shadows across the courtyard — but not many inside had slept. The losses of Roary and Corwin hit harder than expected.

Derek had spent most of the night pacing the perimeter wall, his thoughts heavy, boots echoing softly against concrete. Down in the yard, Bellamy sat slouched in the helicopter's co-pilot seat, hands steepled against his forehead, replaying the moment Corwin opened the hangar doors. Again and again. Reggie hadn't spoken much since returning. Sometimes, when it was quiet, he swore he could still hear the screaming.

In the infirmary, Erin had done all she could — but guilt clung to her like a second skin. Henry tried to keep busy, but even he had begun to understand that some wounds didn't bleed on the outside.

New Haven was grieving.

By midday, the council gathered again. There was only one item on the agenda now.

"Skye," Derek said, voice flat from exhaustion. "It's time."

Bellamy straightened in his chair. "We scout it. Me and Steph will take the helicopter. We check the bridge — see if it's still intact. Look for a safe landing point. And if it looks good..."

"We start planning the move," Jennifer finished softly.

No one argued. No one smiled.

They were all just waiting for the next loss.

—-

The council meeting disbanded with little said. No debates. No back-and-forths. Just nods, tired glances, and the occasional murmur of agreement. The past few days had left them all stretched thin.

Outside, the mood wasn't much brighter. Even the kids had picked up on it — their usual laughter had quietened to whispers. No one asked about Roary. No one brought up Corwin.

Bellamy and Steph stood near the helicopter, already geared up. Steph adjusted the last of the straps on his vest while Bellamy ran a final check on the controls.

Derek approached them quietly, a folded map in hand. His face was grim but focused. "Remember," he said, handing the map to Bellamy. "Recon only. Head to Skye, check the bridge. If it's intact, see what's on the other side. We're looking for somewhere big — open, fortifiable. Something we can scale up fast if we need to."

Bellamy nodded. "Copy that. No heroics."

Derek looked up at them both. "If anything feels off — anything — don't push it. Just get eyes on, get the info, and come back, 24 hours guys then use head back "

"Understood," Bellamy said, already climbing into the cockpit.

Steph gave Derek a firm nod, then pulled the door shut behind him. The rotors began to spin, slow at first, then rising into that familiar thrum that filled the yard like thunder rolling in from the distance. Derek stepped back, watching as the helicopter lifted smoothly into the air, cutting across the blue sky toward Skye.

Others that were in the guard watched too. Lee, Jennifer, Callum, even Erin. A dozen faces turned skyward, all carrying the same hope.

That somewhere out there... a future still waited for them.

—-—

As the chopper faded into the distance, a quiet understanding settled over New Haven.

This was happening. Skye wasn't just a hope anymore — it was a plan. And plans needed action.

Within minutes, the yard was buzzing. Crates were hauled out from storerooms, dry food packed into boxes, fuel drums rolled out of the main supply sheds. Even the youngest residents were given tasks — carrying canned goods, fetching ropes, holding doors open.

No one stood idle.

The tunnel beneath the prison grounds — the one leading to the cemetery — became a thoroughfare of purpose. Supplies were stacked near the hidden exit. Bins of medical supplies, jerry cans of water and fuel, tightly wrapped bundles of spare clothing and blankets.

Everything they didn't need for day-to-day survival was being moved out. Just in case.

Reggie, Maggie, Sarah, and Ashley worked seamlessly loading the buses at the fire station. They moved in a rhythm that spoke of urgency but not panic. Every crate was secured, every compartment checked, fuel levels double-checked.

Callum, Daryl, Derek, and Ortega formed the outer ring — a silent, watchful guard. Rifles in hand, eyes constantly sweeping the treeline and distant roads. They hadn't forgotten the last time things seemed calm.

By mid-afternoon, the buses were packed. Supplies had been stowed in every available space — under seats, in roof racks, across luggage holds. Even water barrels had been strapped between wheel wells.

The fire station was locked up tight — all windows boarded, rear doors reinforced, perimeter cleared.

Once everything was secured, the group fell back in quiet formation toward New Haven, closing the cemetery doors behind them.

Back within the walls, there was a moment of stillness.

Not peace. But something close.

A shared breath.

A flicker of unity.

And above all —

Readiness.

—-

Late Afternoon – New Haven

The shadows stretched longer across the courtyard, golden light filtering through the makeshift barricades and prison gates. The heat of the day had mellowed, but the tension hadn't.

Inside the main building, Anne sat on a bench in the infirmary, her hand resting on the small swell of her stomach. Erin was finishing up reorganizing supplies — everything they'd decided not to send with the buses. Anne watched in silence, heart thudding with a mix of nerves and cautious hope.

"Do you really think we'll be safer there?" she asked quietly.

Erin didn't answer right away. She adjusted a row of syringes, wiped her hands on a cloth, and finally met Anne's eyes.

"If we're not… I don't know what else is left."

—-

Out by the wall, Munroe stood beside Bellamy's empty watch post. He lit a cigarette, shielding the flame with his hand. The cigarette had been in his coat pocket for weeks — he'd forgotten it was there. He didn't even want to smoke it.

Just… needed to hold something steady.

He looked out across the treeline.

He'd seen hell out there. And whatever was beyond Skye…

It had to be something different. Something better.

—-

In the far corner of the yard, Michone was perched on an old wooden crate, watching the kids play. They were using sticks and rocks to build their own "fort," oblivious to the weight pressing down on everyone else.

She smiled, but it faded quickly. She'd grown attached to this place. The routines, the noise, the silence. New Haven had become something resembling home — something solid.

And now they were talking about leaving it behind.

—-

Up in the council room, Jennifer was standing at the window, arms crossed tight against her chest. The courtyard below buzzed with quiet activity. She could see Derek down by the water barrels, giving orders, checking lists.

He looked tired. Worn thinner than ever.

She knew what he'd promised —

"One last run. Then Skye. Then we settle."

She just hoped he meant it. Because if he didn't…

She wasn't sure how much more either of them had to give.

And somewhere on the top level of the east wing, tucked into a quiet room away from the noise, Jillian sat on the edge of a bunk, turning a broken crossbow bolt over in her hands.

She hadn't spoken to Derek since he'd come back.

Not really. Not properly.

She told herself it didn't matter.

He had Jennifer. He had a community to lead.

But part of her wondered if they really did make it to Skye...

Would things finally change?

Would he see her again?

—-

The sun dipped lower, painting the concrete walls in fading gold.

New Haven — their home, their prison, their fortress — stood ready.

But for many, that night, sleep would be hard to find.

Because tomorrow might be the start of something new.

Or the end of everything they'd fought to hold onto.

Chapter 30

The early light bled over the treetops, soft gold turning the concrete walls to amber. The air was cool but still. Not even the crows stirred.

Derek was already in the yard, standing near the painted circle they'd cleared for the helicopter. His arms were folded, eyes fixed on the distant sky like he could will the thing to appear. It wasn't due back until midday — but that didn't stop him from watching.

Footsteps behind him broke the silence. Daryl approached, tugging on his jacket, his crossbow slung lazily over his shoulder. "You'll drive yourself crazy waiting for them," Daryl muttered, nodding to the empty sky. "Trust me, you won't miss them coming back. That thing's louder than Maggie's snoring."

Derek gave a short chuckle, rubbing his beard. "Yeah, maybe. Still..."

"I know," Daryl said, clapping a hand on his shoulder. "I get it."

A quiet moment passed between them. Familiar. Comfortable. Worn-in, like the battered boots they both wore.

"Anyway," Daryl continued, "I'm taking Ortega, Maggie, Reggie, and Lee out to the old ridge line to check the traps for rabbits. Set 'em late last night. If we're lucky, we'll have something fresher than tinned peaches for breakfast."

Derek gave a sideways look. "Five of you for rabbits?"

Daryl raised an eyebrow. "Don't trust Reggie with a snare. Plus, figured we'd sweep a bit wider. Make sure nothing's creeping close while everyone's focused on the big move."

Derek nodded. "Just don't bring back another bloody bear story."

Daryl smirked. "No promises."

They shared a final glance, something unspoken passing between them — a thread of old trust forged in fire and ruin — then Daryl turned and waved the others over.

As the team headed out through the side gate into the treeline, Derek remained, silent and still.

Eyes to the sky.

Waiting.

The trees closed in like old sentries as Daryl's group stepped through the narrow break in the fortified treeline. The path was overgrown, trampled only by wildlife and their own quiet movements over the past few weeks. It was calm this morning — almost too calm.

They walked in single file, boots soft on damp ground, sunlight filtering through the high canopy in pale golden beams.

"Just up here," Daryl said, nodding to a bend in the trail. "Left the snares around the old creekbed and the east tree cluster."

They split into pairs, checking traps and exchanging nods as they moved quietly and efficiently through the terrain. A few minutes later, Maggie held up a limp rabbit, its neck cleanly snapped in the wire.

"That's one," she said.

Lee whistled low, lifting two squirrels from his sack. "Call me the Squirrel King."

"Let's not," Ortega muttered, grinning as he inspected another snare nearby.

By the time they regrouped near the narrow creekbed, they had three rabbits and four squirrels in total. Not a feast, but enough to give New Haven a decent breakfast.

"See?" Daryl said with a smirk. "Told you. Long as the zombies don't learn how to hunt, we'll be alright."

Reggie, grinning, had wandered a little toward the slope just beyond the ridge, crouched beside a snare. As he reset it, there was a sudden flurry of feathers — a bird burst out of the underbrush, squawking wildly.

"Jesus!" Reggie yelped, flinching back.

His foot slipped.

The ground was damp, the slope sharper than it looked.

Reggie tumbled backward down the hill with a surprised yelp, arms flailing, landing in a tangle of limbs and leaves at the bottom.

For a beat, there was silence — then laughter erupted from the top.

Ortega leaned over the edge. "You alright down there, Bambi?"

"I think I landed on a root!" Reggie shouted up. "Or it landed on me, I dunno!"

"Hold on," Daryl said between chuckles. "We're coming."

He and Ortega started carefully down the hill while Lee and Maggie checked the edge for anything dangerous.

"You good?" Daryl asked as they reached him.

"Just bruised my pride," Reggie grunted, accepting Ortega's hand as they helped him to his feet, brushing leaves and dirt from his back as he grumbled, "Bloody bird near gave me a heart attack."

But Daryl wasn't listening. His eyes were fixed on something in the trees ahead — something barely visible, but wrong. Twisted shadows. Shapes that didn't belong.

He stepped forward slowly, crossed the shallow stream with one boot slipping on the slick rock beneath. He squinted into the gloom.

Ortega, meanwhile, had crouched down behind Reggie, frowning.

"Hey," he said, lifting a clump of sticky dark ooze from Reggie's jacket. "You've got something on you, man... this ain't mud."

A cracked shell fragment was stuck in the mess — thin, grey, and veined.

Daryl's voice cracked like a whip from the trees.

"Oh fuck—WE NEED TO LEAVE. NOW! EVERYONE RUN! FUCKING RUN NOW!"

—-

He was already crashing back across the stream, stumbling, wild-eyed.

The panic in his voice lit a fire in the others. Reggie spun, eyes wide. Maggie's hands trembled. Lee took a step forward, heart pounding.

"What the hell's wrong? What did you see!?"

Daryl barely looked back. "Reapers!"

That one word was enough.

They turned. All of them.

And then—

A low, wet growl rolled through the trees.

Another.

Then another.

From the shadows, they came — tall, grey-skinned horrors with long limbs and glistening claws. Teeth bared in lipless mouths. Dozens of them.

"Jesus Christ," Lee gasped, raising his rifle. "THERE'S FUCKING LOADS!" He fired.

The first reaper took the shot in the chest and barely flinched.

Maggie screamed as they ran, feet pounding through the underbrush.

Daryl shoved Ortega forward, then grabbed Reggie and hauled him by the arm. "MOVE!"

But behind them—A scream.

Lee turned just in time to see one of the Reapers grab Maggie from behind, claws tearing into her back. Blood sprayed.

She didn't even get to scream a second time.

"NO!" Lee shouted, raising his rifle, but Daryl grabbed him, yanking him backwards.

"We can't—SHE'S GONE—GO!"

The forest erupted into chaos.

Bullets and bolts tore through the trees, striking the Reapers — but they didn't slow. Grotesque figures moved with an unnatural speed, limbs jerking with terrifying precision.

"Nearly there!" Daryl shouted. "Aim for the gap — the two thick trees marked with red paint!"

Branches snapped behind them. The guttural howls were closer now.

Then—Another scream.

Reggie.

He'd slipped again, and one of the Reapers was on him, dragging him back into the underbrush. His screams turned to gurgles as the creature tore into him. Blood sprayed across the roots of a fallen tree.

"Keep moving!" Ortega bellowed, forcing Daryl forward.

The exit was ahead — they could see the jagged barrier of barbed wire and spikes.

Almost there.

Another scream — raw, guttural.

Lee.

He was firing wildly, backpedaling, until a second Reaper tackled him from the side. Daryl turned to help, but Ortega grabbed his arm and yanked him forward.

"He's gone!" Ortega shouted. "We can't help him!"

Daryl and Ortega burst through the treeline, their boots pounding into the soft earth just before the barbed wire perimeter. Behind them, the Reapers hit the traps — one impaled, another tumbling into the spikes.

The others skidded to a halt behind the barricade, snarling and pacing. Their dead eyes locked on the two men — but they didn't follow.

For now.

Breathing hard, Daryl sank to his knees, covered in sweat and blood. Ortega stood beside him, chest heaving, rifle still raised.

They'd made it out — barely.

But Reggie, Maggie and Lee were gone.

—-

As Daryl and Ortega caught their breath, slumped near the barricade, movement flickered behind them — boots on gravel, urgent voices.

From behind — Derek, flanked by a small group from New Haven, came running down the slope. Weapons in hand, eyes wide.

Ortega saw them first. He yanked Daryl to his feet, panic in his voice.

"Turn back! TURN BACK!"

Derek's pace slowed, confused — but then he saw it too.

Figures in the trees. Dozens. Pale, towering.

Reapers.

They were moving — some dropping from branches, others stepping from behind trunks, forming a grotesque line just beyond the barbed wire.

Derek's voice cut through the chaos. "Oh fuck. BACK TO New Haven. RUN — RUN!"

The two groups collided and turned as one, sprinting up the slope, hearts pounding, weapons clutched tight.

They crashed through the gates, slamming them shut just as the first Reapers reached the wire.

Locks clicked. Bars dropped.

"Where's the others?" Derek asked.

"They didn't make it!" Daryl replied.

They bolted up the stairs, taking position in the watchtower, every eye on the treeline.

Nearly forty Reapers.

Just standing.

Watching.

The forest was deathly still... until—A distant sound. Like thunder rolling in from beyond the hills.

It didn't stop.

It grew louder.

And then louder.

—-

Derek grabbed his rifle, dropped to one knee and peered through the scope.

"HOLY SHIT."

Daryl, already reaching for his binoculars, didn't ask — he raised them and scanned where Derek was looking. A second later, his breath caught in his throat.

Others around them — Felix, Callum, Munroe — lifted their rifles and tracked the line of Derek's stare.

There it was. Maybe half a mile out, just cresting the rise near the ruined railway line.

A horde. Not dozens. Not hundreds. Thousands. Shambling, dragging, clawing their way forward. A rolling tide of death. But that wasn't the worst of it.

At its front — the Smilers.

At least twenty.

Walking like shepherds with their cattle.

Arms raised, guiding the dead forward like puppeteers pulling on invisible strings.

"SOUND THE ALARM!" Derek bellowed, spinning on his heel.

The air split with the sharp clang of the old prison alarm bell.

It rang once.

Twice.

Then three times — the signal.

Red alert.

From every corner of New Haven, people dropped what they were doing and ran. Kids were scooped up, elderly and injured ushered into the shelter. Mothers grabbed bags already packed — go bags they'd rehearsed with too many times to count.

Within 20 minutes, New Haven's fighting force of 33 had formed along the outer walls and towers — rifles, bows, spears, even blades in hand.

Everyone else — over seventy souls — were now safely tucked in the reinforced shelter. Guards posted at the inner corridor.

Derek moved along the southern wall, adrenaline humming in his veins. He passed Jennifer, rifle in hand, posted at the eastern corner, Jillian beside her with her crossbow already loaded. Callum, Ortega, Bill, and Munroe were on the west wall.

New Haven was ready.

But so was the enemy.

—-

It didn't take long for the horde to reach New Haven.

Two hundred feet away. An ocean of rot and rage.

On one side — an army of the dead, standing, growling in mindless hunger, driven by the Smilers who stood in front of them, arms by their sides like conductors of chaos.

On the other — Reapers, crouched like beasts, snarling, pacing, waiting for the order to strike.

From the wall, the defenders of New Haven watched, weapons ready, breath held.

Then, it came.

Both sides let out an almighty growl.

The Smilers stood still — faces twisted in their eternal, lifeless grin. And then, in eerie synchronicity, they lifted their arms once more.

A massive, guttural roar erupted.

The Reapers charged.

The dead followed.

And from the walls of New Haven, Derek shouted:

"OPEN FIRE!"

To be continued...